Praise for *The Joshua Files*

"An exciting adventure and coming-of-age story
with plot twists and cliff-hanger chapter endings that will
keep you up all night to finish."
San Jose Mercury News

"It's the Mexican and Mayan flavorings that give
Harris's adventure yarn that bit of extra bite as she weaves a
satisfyingly twisty plot."
Financial Times

"Josh's race to decode clues, sort out the good guys
from the bad and his feats of derring-do make for an
absorbing read."
The Australian

"M.G. Harris proves she has a deft touch and a real
skill for writing heart-stopping adventure in her code-
cracking debut."
Glasgow Herald

Also by M. G. Harris

Invisible City

Ice Shock

Zero Moment

Dark Parallel

Apocalypse Moon

THE DESCENDANT

M.G.HARRIS

THE JOSHUA FILES

First published in 2012 by Darkwater Books
An imprint of Harris Oxford Limited.
41 Cornmarket Street, Oxford, OX1 3HA

ISBN 978-1-909072-13-8

A CIP catalogue record for this book is available from the British
Library.

Cover design by Gareth Stranks

www.themgharris.com

For David,

While I was writing this with my broken leg, you were taking care of all of us. Thank you so much for helping me begin an exciting new career.

Abu Shahrain, Iraq, January 2003

In the midst of the desert, the weapons inspectors found a well. There was little visible sign of it, only a vague discoloration of the sand between rocks. A young airman's foot found it and under the sun's scorching stare, it swallowed him.

Powerful flashlights beamed deep into the void, without sight of the bottom of the well. Light simply fell, apparently endlessly, towards the center of the earth.

Lieutenant Connor Bennett stumbled into the well. It was his first tour of duty outside the US – he'd hit the jackpot. He'd been escorting the team from the United Nations Monitoring, Verification and Inspection Commission. They'd crossed the desert near Abu Shahrain, about two hundred miles southeast of Baghdad. They'd pored over crumbled mounds; the ruins of the ancient city of Eridu.

Deep inside the darkness of the well, Lieutenant Bennett's voice was clearly audible. Perched on a ledge about twenty yards down, he'd managed the drop with only an injured wrist. Moments later he flashed his torch down to reveal a plunging void. The embarrassment of his tumble vanished, replaced by a rush of relief, the thrill of discovery.

The political pressure to find concealed W.M.D. – weapons of mass destruction – was increasing by the day. Each member of the team held their breath. This well appeared on none of the detailed maps of the region. It was long-forgotten, or perhaps a well-guarded secret.

The team made preparations to the background of an energized hum; quiet anticipation. Their Geiger counters had detected only a normal, background level of radiation. If the weapons of mass destruction were indeed hidden down this ancient hole, they were efficiently shielded.

The managed descent of their infrared video camera was an exercise in patience and control. The inspectors gathered around the video monitor which they had set up near the opening in the ground. Long minutes passed during which the camera sent nothing but images of wall, wall, yet more wall.

Then, collectively they blinked as an image burst onto the screen. The camera panned slowly, revealing the subterranean chamber. The lead inspector tapped the monitor, indicating an area of intriguing complexity. The camera zoomed in.

The team members shuffled slightly as the images appeared on the screen. "Hieroglyphics?" breathed one.

The sole female of the group, Dr. Harper Fletcher spoke. "Not hieroglyphs; cuneiform. Ancient Sumerian."

"Did the city of Eridu extend this far?" The team members turned to Fletcher. She said nothing.

The lead inspector frowned. Satellite scans had ruled out the existence of any underground structures this far from the main ruins of Eridu. Yet, there was no denying the images on the monitor. There were buildings down there. From what he could see on the monitor, these remains were remarkably well preserved.

"I need volunteers to go down."

Lieutenant Bennett watched as Dr. Fletcher's eyes came to rest on him. With a mere blink, Bennett acknowledged her silent instruction. He stepped forward.

"Let me go, sir."

The lead inspector peered from under his baseball cap at another of his team. "How about it, Adams, you want to make the discovery too?"

Bennett waited, wondering why Fletcher hadn't volunteered. That had been their agreement, quietly made at the airbase that morning when in front of his superior officer she'd shown Bennett her CIA identification card. "I'm representing the National Reconnaissance Office, airman. If I need assistance, you're my guy."

He could see Fletcher breathing lightly through open lips. She looked watchful, tense. He leaned back as one of the team attached a winch to the equipment which stood over the shaft, then clipped one end of the rope first to the weapons inspection team member called Adams, then to Bennett.

They began to lower Adams into the shaft. He vanished into the gloom. Bennett followed, no more than a minute behind. When Adams reached the bottom of the well, he called out. Bennett could see a flashlight dancing against the wall below. It disappeared down a tunnel as Adams began to walk. Bennett switched on his own headlamp, watched the light bounce back against the rock, less than one yard away.

"There's a bunch of inscriptions," came Adams voice. "Some kind of chamber. Looks like we got some of them there . . . what are they called? Sarcophagi. Yeah. We got some kind of burial thing going on here."

Bennett's boots hit the ground. He unclipped the rope, drew his weapon. He took six steps down the tunnel, following Adams. Then he heard it: air sucked in, a brief gasp of astonishment. Within seconds, the sound had transformed into a wail of abject terror. A scream of pain followed. For a moment fear gripped Bennett, held him breathless against the wall.

Adam's voice rang out, piteous, horrified. "Oh God, help me, please . . . help me!"

In another second, Bennett overcame his own reluctance to budge. He rounded the corner into a hollow in the midst of space, dark shadows which hid walls that Bennett could instantly see, were man-made.

In the middle of this blackness Adams had fallen to his knees, a helmet light beaming from his forehead, his voice a prolonged scream of agony. Caught in the beam of Bennett's own flashlight, dark fluid streamed from his eyes and mouth.

Bennett couldn't move. "What did you do?"

But Adams could only turn to Bennett, his features now gruesomely disfigured by the blood pouring from openings in his face. From Adams's hand an object fell, clattered to the ground and vanished into the shadows.

Bennett stared, struggling to regain the use of his own voice. In his earpiece he could hear the demands of the lead inspector above. Everything he saw was being transmitted to a monitor on the surface, where the team watched in silent, disbelieving horror.

"What's happening? Lieutenant, report, now!"

Bennett's voice was barely above a whisper.

"Sir . . . there's something in this room . . ."

The voice in his ear ordered, "Get out of there!"

"Don't leave me . . ." Adams begged. The words were barely audible as he began to choke on his own blood.

Bennett wanted to go. But his legs wouldn't obey him. Instead, he found himself reaching out, taking the hand of the dying man. The light from his headlamp kept catching fragments of the walls in its beam. Wherever the light fell, he saw inscriptions.

A moment later, it was over. Adams slumped to the floor, landed with his face on one side. Bennett couldn't take his eyes off him. So much blood. What was the explanation? A booby-trap? Poisonous gas?

"What the hell is going on down there?"

"Adams is dead."

Then he heard Fletcher's voice. "Airman, report."

Bennett began to back away from the body.

"Is it W.M.D.?" insisted the inspector. "Bennett, did you find weapons?"

Shaking his head, Bennett spoke into his microphone, "It's not W.M.D."

The lead inspector stifled a curse.

Bennett began properly to examine the chamber. If there was some kind of poisonous gas, why hadn't it affected him? His foot touched something on the floor – the object that had fallen from Adams fingers. Was that the source of the poison? He aimed his flashlight directly at the object. It was flat, roughly six inches long, appeared to be made of some pale, alabaster-type stone, its surface covered with inscriptions. Cautiously, Bennett turned around. In the center of the chamber was what looked like an altar.

The chamber had to be ancient. Maybe thousands of years old. Yet something within was still very much operational.

"There's a reason they don't want us down here," Bennett murmured into his microphone. "This is something worth hiding."

He wondered again about Fletcher, her last-minute reluctance to enter the chamber. He stared into the dead, blood-soaked eyes of Adams's corpse. Only an airborne toxin could have ravaged the inspector's body so swiftly. Bennett had never been more than two yards away – surely close enough to be affected.

Why wasn't Bennett dead?

Vial In Pocket

Thin brown air simmered over Mexico City. Jackson Bennett leaned against the airplane window, pressed his cheek against the cold glass, gazed down at the city below. A dull ache was in his guts, as though a cold stone had become lodged there.

The anxiety wouldn't go. He took a gulp of iced whiskey from his plastic tumbler. A burst of acidity rose from Jackson's stomach as the liquid hit. Within seconds though, the alcohol began its soothing effect. He drank again, eager for relief from unsettled thoughts. He plugged the earphones of his iPod back into his ears and ran his fingers over the screen. He selected an Eminem track; "Mockingbird". He hadn't planned to think of his brother Connor but he did so anyway; he remembered the Christmas three years ago when they were still talking, when Connor had given him the CD.

Connor was older by a matter of minutes, but he had a way of making Jackson feel at least ten years younger. Now they were both nearly thirty. How could it be that his twenties were going to run out soon when it seemed like yesterday that he'd turned eighteen?

The airplane juddered as the undercarriage was lowered. The captain's voice broke in over the in-flight entertainment system.

"We're just making our final approach to Benito Juarez, Mexico City Airport. Please adjust your watches to the local time of 10.45am. May I take this opportunity to thank you for joining us on this Mexicana flight from San Francisco."

In the right pocket of his jacket, Jackson's fingers located the tiny objects of his disquiet; two small plastic test-tubes. Each contained a mere droplet of liquid; droplets which could land him in jail if discovered. Or at the very least in serious proceedings with the customs authorities.

But danger was theoretical – Jackson had never faced any serious consequences. Maybe this was the blissful naiveté of the inexperienced. Or maybe there was something special about his instinct for survival. After all, he reflected, wasn't his twin brother a decorated US Air Force captain, a veteran of wars in Iraq and Afghanistan? His brother had been flying fighter jets since he'd left college, and always at war. If Connor Bennett had something special which helped to keep him safe, maybe Jackson had it too.

Technically, what he was doing was smuggling, no denying it. But he had more important things to do than to fill in some dumb, pointless form. He was three months overdue to submit his doctoral thesis and still had two chapters to write. His lab bench was a mess of partially completed experiments. He'd foolishly agreed to review the latest college textbook written by a good friend of his lab boss. Now this errand to Mexico City, quite out of the blue. There wasn't time for everything.

Jackson knew perfectly well that the micro-organisms that he carried in those tiny test-tubes were harmless if handled correctly. His lab boss knew it too, but probably hadn't realized that Jackson was planning to travel 'vial-in-pocket'. The guy wasn't a stickler for rules; he cared about nothing but the bottom line: results. Yet he'd stick Jackson with one hundred percent of the blame if he were caught.

It wasn't unusual for biological scientists to bend the rules this way. Even so, Jackson always felt apprehensive when the moment came to stroll past the customs officials at the 'Nothing to Declare' desk. Lying didn't come naturally and he didn't get much practice.

The samples were harmless. They might, however, turn out to be worth a small fortune to the biotech industry. But that was in the future. Until the experimental evidence was in and the patents filed, these samples had a nominal value.

Definitely not contraband. At least, not in Jackson's mind.

He knew that customs officials looked for signs of nervousness in the eyes and body language of travelers. Drug traffickers were their main prey, but he felt sure that they wouldn't pass up the chance to bust a *gringo* carrying strange vials of an unknown, potentially lethal micro-organism.

So before landing, when travelling 'vial-in-pocket', Jackson made sure to steel his nerves, to relax muscles with three small bottles of whiskey.

Moments later he was waiting in the disorderly crowd that had formed at the customs station, just yards away. Ahead of him in the makeshift line, his neighbor from the flight glanced around. "I'll say this for the system here: it's pretty fake-proof."

"Pardon me?"

"See those buttons?" explained the passenger. "You press the button. It's attached to a random circuit which chooses – red or green. If you get a green light; that's it, you're through. Even if you look like Bin Laden. A red light, that's different. Get a red light and you're searched down to unrolling your socks and underpants."

"You gotta be kidding." Jackson felt sheen of sweat appear on his forehead.

"*Narco-traficantes* – the Mexican drug gangs. They know all the tricks to fake out the customs officials. But there's no way to beat this system. Everyone takes the exact same chance."

The passenger was saying this as he stepped up to the line and pressed the large red button indicated by the Mexican official. He made a face of mock anxiety and then exaggerated relief when the light turned green.

Jackson took a couple of quick breaths, forced a grin at the waiting official. He took his place in front of the button. He hesitated for just a second, wondering if any last minute reprieve could possibly save him from the potential disaster of a red light.

"Just press the button please, sir," insisted the uniformed woman. There was the subtlest hint of force in her voice.

He blinked hard as he pressed the button. A second later he opened them to register the verdict.

8

It was green.

"You look just a little nervous there, sir, you got something to hide?" asked the customs official. It was impossible to tell whether or not she was joking.

"No, ma'am." Jackson had rarely worked so hard to seem relaxed. "I just got a bus to catch. Didn't wanna be late."

With a dismissive wave, the woman lifted his suitcase onto the conveyor belt for the X-ray machine. Seconds later he retrieved it. He itched for a reassuring touch of the plastic test-tubes, but didn't dare to reach into his jacket pocket until he'd cleared the crowded arrivals hall.

He glanced at his watch. Six hours since he had removed the samples from storage at minus 70°C. Jackson knew that the sooner he managed to get them onto ice, the better the chances of their viability. He looked around for any sign of Dr. Pedro Juan Beltran, a scientific collaborator based at the Institute of Biotechnology of Temixco, Mexico. Beltran had promised to arrive in good time, with a thermos of ice with which to rescue the vials.

Jackson soon spotted Beltran eating a cinnamon bun and cradling a paper coffee cup in a small café.

"PJ?"

Beltran stood, grinned and stuck out a hand that was still hot from holding the coffee. "Hey! Jackson! Well, well; the newly minted Doctor Bennett, correct?"

Jackson stuttered slightly. "Not exactly. I'm kind of behind schedule."

"Ah. I looked you up on the Web. Found your blog. *Doctor* Jackson Bennett."

Jackson could feel his cheeks burning with embarrassment. That stupid blog. There was nothing there except a photo of him snowboarding. He'd named it prematurely, a joke, because the name "jacksonbennett.com" had already been taken, but "drjacksonbennett.com" was still available. It seemed idiotic to explain all that right now, so he simply continued to blush.

To his relief, Beltran chuckled. He had the grave, worn face of someone who worked in a concentrated and urgent manner. The sudden smile was a surprise.

Beltran pulled a small Thermos flask from his inside pocket. He unscrewed the top to reveal a densely packed mound of tiny ice flakes. This was it, the moment to perform the simple task he'd been sent all the way to Mexico for – the handover of precious biological samples. Jackson glanced around for the briefest of seconds to check that he wasn't observed, then moved a swift hand to his pocket. He palmed the vials, passed his hand over the top of the flask to drop them in with the minimum of movement.

Beltran's features broke into a wide beam. "Hey that's very good, my friend! You take a magician seminar or something?"

"An old Vegas trick I learned when I was a professional croupier," Jackson replied with deadpan humor. Beltran's smile lingered, with a hint of puzzled curiosity. It was clear that he wasn't sure whether Jackson was joking.

Beltran gestured broadly. "Bennett, make yourself comfortable. Take off your jacket – you're sweating like a pig!"

It was true. The alcohol may have helped to relax his face, but the heat of the hall and tension of the customs line had proved too much. Reluctantly, Jackson removed his beloved brown suede jacket. He folded it carefully over the seat next to his so that the pockets were not exposed to passers-by.

To Jackson's astonishment, Beltran leaned forward, his face instantly serious. Close to Jackson's ear he whispered, "There's a reason he sent *you*. I couldn't tell you via email. Or over the phone."

Jackson leaned back to look into Beltran's eyes. There was no hint of humor. He waited for a few seconds but Beltran continued to stare at him with a penetrating gaze. Eventually he said, "Are we still talking about my work with the *phoenix* gene?"

"What else? The thing is, I've stumbled across something. It's strange, unexpected. I thought I was working on something interesting, maybe something I could sell to the biotech industry. There's something more here, Jackson. Something big. There are other people involved. To be honest, there are things I haven't yet talked about."

"Sounds like maybe you should be talking to my boss?"

"No. This relates directly to your work. You need to know *directly*."

Jackson was speechless. High-level discussions with a scientific collaborator almost never by-passed the head of the lab. Jackson could scarcely believe that his boss had permitted it.

"Before you ask, no, your boss doesn't have any clue about what I'm about to tell you."

All Jackson could do was to nod. "OK... I guess! Thanks."

"Don't rush the gratitude. The first thing I need to do is to make something of a confession. Throughout this collaboration, there are things I have kept from you and the rest of the team."

"What are you saying? You haven't told me and the guys at UCSF? Or do you mean your own guys too?"

"I haven't shared this particular detail with anyone at the University of California at San Francisco. Nor anyone from my own team in Mexico, either."

Jackson stared at Beltran. The situation was becoming more confusing by the second. Withholding information from a collaborator could be a serious business. Research funds were hotly competitive. Without a promise of mutual openness, two teams of researchers could scarcely risk so much as a conversation.

Maybe this was why Beltran had asked to deal directly with him. Unlike his boss, Jackson was no scientific big shot. He wasn't particularly volatile either. His boss would probably punch a collaborator for holding out on him, then proceed to shred the guy's career.

Beltran's eyes hinted at contrition. "You know how it can be when your research is funded privately. Legally, I'm completely silenced. Just lately, however, I'm starting to get more than a little bit ..."

The Mexican scientist stretched his arms across the back of the booth, knocking down Jackson's suede jacket. Jackson made to stand up but he was effusive with apologies. "Listen to me, I get so melodramatic. Let me get that for you." He picked the jacket off the floor, made a show of dusting the surface clean. He handed it back to Jackson as carefully as if it had been a kitten.

Jackson couldn't stop himself checking the jacket himself. The floor of the café was sure to be sticky with coffee spills. He'd managed to act easy-going about Beltran's clumsiness but he was actually pretty irritated. The suede jacket was his most expensive item of clothing; the only garment he could count on in which to look semi-decent.

When he looked back at Beltran, Jackson was bewildered to see that the scientist had become suddenly very still, staring right past his shoulder. He glanced around, following Beltran's gaze.

A man approached, dressed in pale grey, unremarkable, ill-fitting suit, white shirt and anthracite-colored tie. He didn't look like a businessman or a scientist. When he looked back at Beltran, who was now pale with tension, Jackson's pulse began to race.

Mexican Customs.

Had they somehow caught up to him?

Stiff with tension, Jackson gave the newcomer a coolly polite smile. "Hi."

Their new companion stopped level with Beltran. He took a seat next to him and flashed what a perfunctory smile. His hair was immaculately cropped, as though he was fresh from the barber. It was thick, but almost uniformly silver-grey. From his face, Jackson wouldn't have guessed the man's age any older than thirty-five. Perhaps he was prematurely grey?

His attention shifted to Beltran. An unmistakable frisson of fear crossed Beltran's face as their eyes met for less than a second. Yet all he said was "Doctor Bennett. This is an associate from the Institute. It seems I'm on an earlier flight to Monterrey. So I gotta get going, Doctor Bennett. I'll see you around, OK?"

Two "Doctor Bennetts" in quick succession. Beltran had already poked fun at him being overdue with the doctorate. He was on the point of asking Beltran what kind of point he was trying to make.

The grey-haired man nodded. Speaking English with the merest hint of a Mexican accent, he murmured, "A pity we didn't get time to talk, Doctor Bennett. Perhaps we'll catch up in at the Institute, in Temixco?"

"You're leaving . . . ?"

Beltran's face was curiously devoid of expression as he turned away. The newcomer picked up the Thermos containing the test-tubes, which stood, quite forgotten, on the table.

"Your flask," said the man to Beltran.

For several seconds after they'd left, Jackson remained half-seated, half-way to standing up, unable to decide whether he should follow Beltran or not.

The grey-haired guy couldn't be with Customs – or else it would have been Jackson who would have been asked to leave.

Yet something was wrong – very much so. Beltran had looked frightened, yet his words had been bizarrely at odds with such a swift change of mood. All he'd said to Jackson was *Doctor Bennett this* and *Doctor Bennett that*.

In fact, that in itself was strange.

Why did Beltran keep calling me "Doctor Bennett"?

The Grey-Haired Man

As he left the coffee shop, PJ Beltran had to force himself not to glance back at Bennett. His mind was racing, trying to fathom the motive of the man who was leading him away. The truth was, PJ had never met the grey-haired man before, had no idea who he could be.

Inside the man's jacket pocket, there was a gun – PJ had felt it when the man had taken a seat next to him, in the café. He'd felt the hard, blunt nose of it against his side. As they'd walked away, PJ had been given a glimpse of the weapon.

"Please, Doctor Beltran, be calm. Ten minutes of your time is all I need."

The grey-haired man hadn't introduced himself further. But PJ knew without a doubt that he'd be shot if he dared to disobey.

The next two minutes had passed as though in a dream. As the two men walked down the airport concourse he spoke in Spanish, asking, "What happens now?"

"I'm a government agent. We're onto you, my friend. We have cameras everywhere. We need to know what kind of material you are carrying in that flask. I have your flask, but also, there'll be some questions."

PJ wanted to believe him. Aspects of the story rang true. Clearly the man had been observing PJ and Bennett. He had some idea of what was happening. Maybe PJ's darkest fears were unfounded. But his fear wouldn't entirely abate.

'Government agent' sounded convincing. The clandestine gun shook PJ's confidence. Did Mexican government agents threaten people with guns, practically in public? Maybe the guy is going to ask for a bribe, PJ hoped. He found himself clinging to the idea. The Customs Department could make difficulties for PJ. It might be worth risking a bribe to avoid trouble.

The alternatives were far scarier – what if this was a prelude to a kidnap?

Yet a darker, more ponderous fear scratched at the edge of PJ's thoughts; the anxiety he'd been trying to indicate to Bennett. The research he'd been doing had taken a surprising turn. He may have wandered into dangerous territory. Was it possible that PJ had underestimated just how dangerous?

PJ's thoughts went to Jackson Bennett. Why hadn't this 'agent' gone for the American scientist? Or maybe someone else was taking care of Bennett.

PJ had only been able to think of one way to signal caution to the American graduate student – calling him 'Dr.' Bennett. After the joke he'd made, Bennett was bound to have found that odd. Scientists this close to their doctoral exam tended to be hypersensitive to the issue. Fervently, PJ hoped that he'd understood.

***

Jackson sipped his coffee slowly. What the hell just happened? He didn't have any illusions: scientists as eminent as PJ Beltran often didn't have time for new kids on the block, like him. The grey-haired man was clearly more important than Jackson but there was something weird about the whole thing.

Beltran had looked scared.

Leaving, Beltran and the stranger had stuck close together – he spotted that they had even paused when other travelers had tried to walk between them, forcing them instead to walk around.

"Almost as if they were handcuffed together..."

Then it hit him: the reason for Beltran's odd behavior, his making such a point of calling Jackson 'Dr.' Bennett when the two had already established that he was anything but a 'Dr' yet. The grey-haired man had followed Beltran's lead. He didn't know that Jackson wasn't yet Dr. Bennett.

Beltran was trying to send him a coded signal.
Could it have been a warning?

The anonymous grey suit wasn't a businessman or a scientist. Maybe a government man?

With a gulp, he swallowed the coffee.

Beltran had been arrested. The flask, the test-tubes – the whole game was up. Yet somehow, Beltran had kept Jackson out of it.

He reached for his cell phone. Someone at Beltran's lab had to be warned. If the government were involved then reprisals might be swift. The only number he had for Beltran was a mobile number. There was an address for the Institute in Temixco, but no phone number. Jackson hesitated. He had to do something.

He picked up his jacket, peered down the airport concourse one last time to see if there was still any sign of Beltran or the stranger. There wasn't. Jackson rapped the table with the edge of his phone, thinking. The Institute was a long way to go, something like a two hour drive. What else could he do? He couldn't leave things like this.

At the Alamo office, he hired a car. With as much haste as he could muster, he stashed his rolling suitcase in the trunk of the car and slid into the driver's seat. He turned on the satellite navigation and tapped in his destination: 'Temixco'.

He was more nervous by the minute. The government was onto the whole illegal exchange. Presumably they would interrogate Beltran. It was just a matter of time before they were after Jackson, too. Presumably Beltran's colleagues in Temixco could advise him. Did he need a lawyer? Or would he do better simply to leave the country, right away?

No – that would be pretty cowardly. Beltran's colleagues might need help to cover Beltran's tracks. It wasn't cool to let someone else take the hit for something that also involved him.

Sweat flushed from every pore of Jackson's body. What was he taking on?

The drivers in this city were every bit as bad as he'd been warned. They drove almost intimately close in eye-wateringly narrow lanes, with an informality that made the sweat patches under his arms grow larger by the second. Jackson held his breath. He probably needed eyes in the back of his head to get to his destination without at least a minor crash.

If he'd been less frazzled, Jackson might have noticed the black Ford Explorer drop neatly into the southbound traffic, just two cars behind him.

***

PJ began to wonder where the expressionless man at his side was leading him. Brisk steps took them further down the marble floors of the airport concourse. PJ had expected simply to be led into one of the many discreet, unmarked airport offices. They had already passed at least a dozen.

Things were happening faster than his ability to process. Finally it struck him that it was odd that they were heading for the far end of the airport. They'd passed all the check-in desks for the domestic departures. Now the number of people around thinned to just a handful.

"I need to use the bathroom," the grey-haired man said. He stopped and gripped PJ's shoulder. His weapon dug hard into PJ's ribs. There was something forced about the man's tone, as though he wasn't used to sounding quite this accommodating. "You should take the opportunity too, Dr. Beltran. For you, this is gonna be a long night."

PJ flinched. So, there was going to be an interrogation. Who was in charge?

Abruptly, PJ felt himself steered into the men's room. It was empty, apart from a uniformed attendant who sat slouched over on a low chair reading a dog-eared, semi-pornographic comic book. With a cursory glance around the room, the grey-haired man held out a fifty peso note to the attendant. Politely, he asked him to fetch some more hand towels. The attendant's eyes boggled for a second at the size of the tip. He snatched the fifty pesos, tucked the comic book into the waist of his uniform trousers and left.

PJ's heart began to pound so heavily that his chest shook. For the first time, he was alone with the man who had escorted him away from Bennett.

"OK, Dr. Beltran. You first. In this cubicle." The grey-haired man reached inside his suit jacket, pulled out an automatic pistol. Beltran froze. He opened his mouth but the sound that came from it was muted. In silent disbelief, he watched as the man's hand went to a trouser pocket and pulled out a thick metallic cylinder. PJ's mind struggled to comprehend what he was seeing. PJ felt his breath turn to ice. Very calmly, the grey-haired man twisted a silencer onto the muzzle of the pistol.

PJ's hesitation ended as rapidly as it had overtaken him. He flung himself forward, only to find himself knocked back hard, into the cubicle by a swipe of the semi-assembled weapon. Sticky blood poured into his left eye. A wave of concentrated terror flowed through him. In that instant, PJ Beltran understood that he was going to die.

His muscles seemed to have become locked. He heard the grey-haired man's order to sit on the toilet seat as though from a great distance. PJ watched, almost detached, unable to move as the revolver was raised. At that moment he sensed the crumbling of the foundations of his ordered universe; this was the abyss that people talked about, the final abyss of terror.

PJ Beltran was staring deep inside.

The bullet entered PJ's eye with almost no sound.

It blew his eyeball out of its socket with a slight pop, streaming easily through his head. Bone shattered as the bullet exited and sank with a faint thud into the soft plaster wall behind the toilet. Blood and brain tissue spilled freely from the open wounds. The assassin stepped into the cubicle and locked the door behind him. He pulled hard at the pale blue shirt that Beltran was wearing, yanked the garment over the dead man's head. He made a makeshift knot at the top to stem the flow of blood. The assassin spooled out bunches of toilet paper. With meticulous care he wiped away all drops of blood and flecks of brain which had spilled near the neighboring cubicle.

The man then picked up the Thermos flask which lay, discarded on the floor. He manipulated PJ's body so that it sat quite stably. Finally, he hoisted himself over the barrier to the right, leaving PJ's body locked inside. He flushed away the handfuls of blood-soaked toilet paper, and left the cubicle empty. For a couple of minutes he stood at the sink, calmly washing his hands.

A moment later, the attendant returned.

"My companion doesn't feel so good," the grey-haired man stated flatly. He didn't look up. "A touch of amoebas. I think he'll be a while"

The attendant muttered sympathetically, "Poor thing." It probably meant a big clean-up job for him when the guy was finished, but in his job it usually paid to be extra polite.

Without stopping to check himself in the mirror, the grey-haired man left. He strolled rapidly towards the nearest airport exit and into a waiting black Ford Explorer.

Jackson finally caught sight of the welcome signs; toll booths for the fast road south to Cuernavaca, a large city close to Temixco. As he drove his car slowly through the booth, Jackson decided to stop at the nearby roadside service station. He'd pick up some Diet Coke and some spicy chips. A change of shirt also seemed like a good idea. His green polo top was soaked in two rounds of nervous sweat. As the air warmed up, his body was beginning to give off a sharp, acrid stench.

Jackson opened the trunk of the car and selected a blue pique polo shirt from his suitcase. Inside the men's room, he hung his suede jacket on the back of a door. He peeled off his shirt, thoroughly wiping his torso, then changed into the blue shirt. He rinsed his face and hands with cool water and used the old shirt to dry his face. He slid the jacket over his shoulders and dug his hands into his jacket pockets. He looked critically at himself in the mirror. Not too bad – considering the stressful morning he'd had. Presentable enough, especially for a scientist. Better than he usually looked when he went to his own lab in San Francisco.

To Jackson's surprise, the fingers of his left hand touched something unfamiliar in his jacket pocket. He drew out a green Post-It note wrapped around a small plastic test-tube. It was similar to the test-tubes he'd brought over from San Francisco. This test-tube was unlabeled, apart from something written in black marker pen on the lid. It seemed to be empty. He held it up to the light and flicked it a couple of times. A small volume of liquid coalesced in the bottom of the tube. The lid was sealed with Parafilm – a stretchy, synthetic membrane. He peeled away the film so that he could examine the writing on the lid.

It was long number, divided up by the occasional dash. It didn't take a genius to work out that it was probably a telephone number. There was no name.

Jackson's bewilderment lasted only a couple of seconds. Then he saw something that made him freeze.

Reflected in the mirror, he could see a part of the window giving onto the car park. Two men in grey suits, from their tanned appearance probably Mexicans, were walking around his rented Honda Civic. They tried the door and peered inside.

Jackson's eyes went to the test-tube in his hand.

Beltran must have planted it. That little accident with his jacket had been no such thing – Beltran must have used it as an opportunity to slip something into the pocket.

Had Beltran betrayed him, planted evidence that would exonerate Beltran and throw all the blame on him? If so, why would he bother with a cryptic warning?

He glanced out of the window again. The two men in suits were walking away from his car. They were heading for the bathroom block.

Jackson moved fast. He dropped the test-tube back into his pocket, ducked out of view from the mirror and crawled to the far end of the bathroom. Scrambling around, he looked for another way out of the place. A high window gave onto the rear of the block. He launched himself at the window, managed to grab hold of the top of the frame with both hands. He squeezed himself between the open pane and the frame, then fell heavily on his side onto a plastic dumpster, just inches below the ledge. Jackson rolled off that and to his amazement, landed on his feet.

Heaving rapid, shallow breaths, he cast his gaze at the vehicles going through the toll booths. He couldn't return to the car park – it was way too open. Whoever those men were, Jackson guessed that they had been following him since the airport. Maybe they even knew where he was going. After all, it was no secret where PJ Beltran worked.

He felt faintly sick as he realized; it had been stupid to assume he'd escaped the attention of the official. A quick phone call had probably confirmed who 'Dr. Bennett' actually was.

Cuernavaca and Temixco were out of bounds. So where could he go? Jackson struggled to think of the name of even one place in Mexico. For the tenth time that day, he wondered at his boss's decision to send him on this errand. How had Beltran convinced him? Or had his boss had some inkling of the danger? It seemed paranoid even to suspect his boss. Jackson couldn't seem to stop himself racking up one paranoia after another.

He knew no-one in Mexico, his Spanish was only high school level and little practiced. Jackson belonged on the next flight out of the country, not stuck inside a roadside service station trying to think of somewhere to go.

Checking briefly that he hadn't been spotted, he ran behind the next building in the complex, a step closer to the toll booths. A small lorry approached. The words "Nieves de Tepoztlan" were painted on the side, intertwined around a wreath of lime-green leaves. He recognized the name of the town from having flipped through the Lonely Planet Guide to Mexico, before his flight. There weren't many tourist attractions close to Temixco, but Tepoztlan was one. From what Jackson could recall, the town was known for its exotically flavored *nieves* – water ices, as well as some spectacularly-situated Aztec ruins and a new-age, hippy scene. There'd be Americans there, and Canadians – lots of them. The ideal place to blend in and become lost.

He rushed to the driver's side, made urgent hand signals at the lorry driver until he opened his window.

"Please, sir, help me. Do you speak English?"

The driver's eyes narrowed. He shook his head.

Jackson groaned. "My car – stolen. Need go Tepoztlan," he said in broken Spanish. "Please. Fifty dollars, OK?"

"Toll roads?" the driver barked, in English. "Dollars *americanos*, tolls?"

Jackson nodded. He knew he was lucky to be given any help – Mexicans could be notoriously unhelpful to *gringos*. "I'll pay the tolls also," he agreed, grateful for the driver's limited grasp at least, of road terminology in English.

"*Horale, vamanos!*" shouted the driver. He slapped the passenger seat.

As they drove past the car park of the service station, Jackson bent low, fiddled with a shoelace. He couldn't risk being spotted, even though his curiosity was almost unbearable. The logical part of his personality had begun to reassert itself.

Now, Jackson wondered if he hadn't perhaps overreacted by running. He may have created more problems for himself. If those guys were indeed the authorities – maybe even the same people who had picked up Beltran – then failing to cooperate could be very risky in the long term. He might find himself refused further access to Mexico. The Institute of Biotechnology in Temixco – a government funded organization – could refuse future collaborations with him. That would just about ruin any chance Jackson had to continue the work he'd done during the past three years.

Yet, something else told Jackson that his quick reaction had probably saved him from a serious fate, maybe even worse than being arrested for trafficking in biological samples.

As incomprehensible as the idea was, Beltran must have planted the test-tube. Beltran's discreet warning, and his strange words, minutes before they'd been separated. *"There's something more here, Jackson. Something big."*

Jackson clutched the test-tube tightly in the palm of his left hand. The tube contained something important, something Beltran was desperate for him to have. Something he couldn't risk handing over in the open.

Beltran must have known he was being watched. A plan had been set in motion. The lorry rumbled over a pothole. Jackson gripped his seat-belt. He wondered, once again, about the telephone number on that test-tube.

Pyramid Sacrifice

The ice truck descended into the valley behind the Ajusco Mountains through which they'd just driven. As they approached Tepoztlan, the landscape changed; ridges in the rock rippled in a dramatic backdrop to the village. At the top of one of those ridges was the small 'Tepozteco'; a white stone pyramid dedicated to Ometochtli-Tepoxtécatl, a god of the fermented maguey drink known as *pulque*, of fertility and the harvest.

After squaring his deal with the driver, Jackson made his way to the market and found something to eat. He realized that he had little idea of how Mexican justice worked. For all he knew, people could be held with no charges and no reason, if they were suspected of bio-terrorist activity. This, Jackson knew in his darkest thoughts, was the most serious suspicion which he and Dr. Beltran might face.

Jackson couldn't risk a call to Beltran's lab from his cell phone. The officials were bound to ask for the phone records of the lab, and the moment that his cell phone number was revealed, that was the end of his freedom. He'd need to call directory enquiries for the number. He paid for a phone card and headed for a call booth, dialed the number of Beltran's lab. It was best to be open with Beltran's colleagues. They were the only people on whom Jackson could count for help.

"Jackson Bennett! Hey, man. How come you aren't here yet?" Simon Reyes answered the phone, Beltran's newest doctoral student. Simon had graduated top of his class at university before he'd started a PhD program in University of California, San Francisco. He'd rotated through a couple of labs there before Beltran had persuaded the young man to join him in Temixco. Jackson had never actually met Simon, but his own boss at the lab spoke highly of the young graduate student.

"Simon. Listen, I think that Doctor Beltran – PJ – and I are in trouble. This is the scariest shit that's ever happened to me."

Jackson could tell from the silence that Simon was totally taken aback.

"Simon, you know anything about what PJ was working on? His personal research project, I mean."

"You're talking about *phoenix*, yes? Not too much. PJ's been real secretive about it. The funding comes from a pharmaceutical company in Switzerland."

Jackson closed his eyes in frustration. Beltran hadn't mentioned that he was also collaborating with a pharmaceutical company. That was fair enough; there were many aspects to any research project. Some might be of particular interest to a 'pharma' and most labs wouldn't turn away that kind of money. And pharmaceutical confidential disclosure agreements were notoriously troublesome. They could make productive scientific conversations almost impossible. "Anything you know, Simon. This is real important."

There was a long silence. "PJ doesn't tell us much. But . . . come to think of it I'm pretty sure that recently, he's made some kind of breakthrough. He didn't tell you?"

"He started to tell me. And then. . ."

"I had the impression that PJ's meeting with you had something to do with what he'd found. I saw him prepare a sample for you to carry, 'vial-in-pocket'."

Simon's words confirmed what Jackson had begun to suspect; Beltran was aware of a threat. That the same fate might pass to Jackson. What could be in the test-tube? Something which would protect him? Or the very item which had placed Jackson in the path of the people who'd taken Beltran?

Jackson said, haltingly, "Some guy was onto us at the airport. He may have been there when I gave PJ the samples. Then some goons showed up sniffing 'round my car on the way to you. They could have been government. I guess the Mexican Customs department isn't cool with me bringing this stuff in, undocumented. So I got the hell out of there. I'm in Tepoztlan. You know it?"

"Sure." Simon hesitated. "You need me to come pick you up?"

"I think maybe I shouldn't go to the Institute. These customs guys probably know that I was heading there. Can you take me somewhere safe nearby, and then I can meet with the rest of the lab?" Jackson gnawed anxiously on his lip. "So. . .seriously, PJ hasn't been in touch with you at all?"

There was an empty crackle on the line, as though Simon's doubt and growing anxiety was audible. "No."

"OK, let's talk when we meet up Tepoztlan."

"You have somewhere in mind?"

"How about on the pyramid? I wanted to take a look at it properly anyway. That way we should be able to see anyone approaching us from a ways off."

Simon breathed noisily. He didn't seem to like the idea much. "You sure, Jackson? It's quite a climb."

"It's fine. Simon, listen; you need to know something." He then related, as calmly as possible, how Beltran had left him at Mexico City airport. The phone was silent for a long time. Jackson continued, "PJ was trying to keep me in the clear. I guess he wanted me to carry some sort of message. If only I knew what."

"OK, so you don't go with anyone but me; I'm wearing, like, this orange Hawaiian shirt with, ah, a kinda pineapple design. And black jeans. You got that?"

Jackson raised an eyebrow. "Sounds like you're dressed to impress."

Simon Reyes jumped up from the seat by his employer's lab phone. "I'm going to pick up Jackson Bennett, that guy from the lab in UCSF. He's in some kind of trouble," Simon told the rest of Beltran's research group. He didn't want to elaborate, didn't have the time. Jackson had sounded pretty shaken. Simon didn't even want to think about what could have happened to PJ Beltran. But Jackson seemed to assume that PJ had been led away by the officials from the government. Whereas Simon was aware of another, even darker scenario.

Sequestrantes – kidnappers – had been the word he had not dared bring himself to use in his conversation with Jackson. A word Simon couldn't keep out of his thoughts now. Everyone in Mexico knew what kidnappers were capable of. Recently the gangs were branching out beyond the simple fare of cash-for-victims, exploring the corporate possibilities of industrial espionage. If anyone had got wind of what Beltran and Jackson were exchanging at the airport, kidnapping was a genuine and chilling possibility.

In the parking lot of the Institute of Biotechnology, Simon Reyes hastily maneuvered his old, silver Nissan Tsuru out of its position and made straight for the highway to Tepoztlan.

A black Ford Explorer which was parked across the road from the Institute pulled into the traffic behind him. Simon's heart began to thud as he watched, in his rear view mirror, the Explorer take the same lane as did he towards Tepoztlan.

Today, there could be no coincidences.

Desperately, Simon began to hunt for a way off the road, back into the tiny town of Temixco. It was hopeless; as soon as there were no cars in the immediate vicinity, the Explorer drew so close behind him that slowing down or turning off the road was an impossibility.

As the two cars moved further into the winding road to Tepoztlan, Simon began to feel the keen edge of fear. "They torture people," he remembered, with barely controlled terror. "They slice off your fingers, your balls."

Then it happened; the moment he had dreaded. The Explorer drew level with Simon's car, taking the other lane. As the window of the Explorer drew down slowly, Simon could see a pistol in the hand of the man in the passenger seat. Waving the pistol, the man gestured to Simon to get off the road. For good measure, a warning shot rang across the bonnet of Simon's car.

Shaking, Simon parked. He began to pray silently as he watched two men get out of the Explorer and walk over.

"Get out." The door to his car was opened; the order was barked by the younger of the two men, who pointed a gun at Simon's head.

27

They motioned to Simon to move off the road, into the woods alongside.

"God have mercy on my soul. . ." Simon mumbled, his voice cracking.

"Don't worry Simon. We won't hurt you bad, I promise. It'll be easy, quick." The older of the two men, a grey-haired man in his late thirties, spoke with apparent sincerity.

Simon broke down.

"Come on, come on. We all have to die. Finish your prayers like a good boy. Think of it this way; we're saving you from a cancer. Or Alzheimer's. Who knows, in the future maybe something even worse. You scientists invent new diseases to kill us as fast as you find the cures."

Simon sobbed uncontrollably. He was twenty-two years old, the first person from his family to even dream of being 'Dr. Reyes'. Simon didn't even bother to beg. The men were completely serious, carrying out their jobs with consummate professionalism. The grey-haired man took his arm, gripping him firmly but not painfully.

"Simon. We'll make this quick. Trust me, you won't feel anything. But you have to do something for me. Take off your clothes. The shirt, the jeans. Nice and slow. It's nothing weird or sick, don't worry. Just don't want to get blood on them."

Then, with unbearable clarity, Simon understood everything. The older man saw the light of recognition in his eyes.

"Yes, that's right. I'm glad you understand. I'm sorry. Dr. Beltran's phone is tapped. It has been for a while. We know all about PJ's research, and about your meeting with Jackson Bennett. We really need his help, you see. But I don't think he'll want to speak to us. So now, we need your clothes. Come on, Simon. Finish your prayers."

Moments later, the two men lifted Simon's body, rolling it into a ditch, where the dense undergrowth partially obscured it.

As he began to remove his own clothes, Simon's assassin commented, "I like the merciful touch, boss. It's classy."

"You think so, Fernando?" replied the grey-haired man, holding out Simon's discarded clothes for him to change into. "You should see me with the ones who struggle, or fight back. Violence is a precision weapon. You don't waste too much of it on a good man like this. Save it for the dangerous bastards. Because it ages you; it destroys you inside. If you want to last in this profession, you've got to have a plan for psychological longevity."

Fernando buttoned the orange shirt, hooking the pistol into the back waistband of the jeans. He lifted his palms and grinned. "What do you think, boss? Do I pass for a genius?"

The grey-haired man gave him an encouraging slap. "Son, you're Nobel prize material already."

On The Tepozteco

Legend holds that the Tepozteco pyramid marks the birthplace of the Aztec God, *Quetzelcoatl*. Jackson blinked in the harsh early afternoon light. He tried to spot the white stones of the cliff-top pyramid from the far end of Tepoztlan. As well as a walk to the other side of town, past a collection of Mexican handicrafts stalls and people hawking the trappings of new age, alternative lifestyle, there would be a brief hike through the thick vegetation, to the top of the hill on which the Aztecs had, hundreds of years ago, built the pyramid.

Jackson glanced at his watch. Just under one hour to get to the top. He sauntered casually down a wide cobbled alley, flanked with white adobe cottages covered with bougainvillea flowers, birds' nests clinging limpet-like to the eaves. The alley offered a direct view of the pyramid, visible merely as a stone structure perched on top of a sharp cliff edge, on a hill known as *Ehecatepetl*, or 'hill of the wind'.

As he walked, he was besieged by small children, imploring, "*Señor, señor*, a massage? A fortune by your palm? Incense sticks to help you reach enlightenment?"

Passing by one of the empty seats of the massage stalls, Jackson relented. A neck massage would certainly help loosen him up for the steep climb ahead. He nodded and took a seat. The strong hands of a stern-looking middle-aged Mexican woman took hold of his shoulders and began kneading his muscles. As he began to allow himself to relax, a girl about fifteen years old, dressed in a tight-fitting white T shirt and worn blue jeans, stopped in front of him. She gazed at him intently with solemn, brown eyes.

"*Buenos días,*" Jackson said, politely.

"I tell your fortune, yes?" the girl asked him, in English. "Twenty *pesos*."

Jackson sighed. Why not? He was perfectly aware that people disliked tourists who refused to part with a few dollars in the name of getting value for money, especially if they were American. With a wan smile, he dropped the money into the girl's grubby, outstretched hand and held out his right palm. The girl gazed into his eyes for a second, then took his left hand. "We use this one." She studied it for a few minutes, and looked back into his eyes.

"You are a thinker. You like puzzles – no that's not what it says. You like *questions*. Your love line is strong, but there's disappointment."

"I still haven't found the right girl," he said.

"You've been disappointed in love, and you will be again. Your life line is strong, but you live a dangerous life; there are breaks. Sickness or accidents – I can't tell."

"Accidents, probably," agreed Jackson. Most winter sports enthusiasts broke some part of their body, sooner or later, and he was obsessed with snowboarding. He felt himself immortal, naturally. The statistics were against him in the long run.

"Your fate line is deep; your life is controlled not by you but by things that happen to you."

He eyed her with a touch of cynicism. "You got any advice? Something I can actually use?"

"Look; where it crosses the life line. You see this tiny break in the life line? This means a serious betrayal."

Jackson smiled uneasily. "Ooh. Sounds serious."

"A girlfriend, perhaps? Or maybe someone in your family."

His masseuse spoke for the first time. "You should listen to my daughter. She has the gift, the third eye. If she tells you there is danger, then there is danger."

With this, the masseuse slapped his shoulders, the blow stinging very slightly at first, the warmth then spreading to his neck. Amazingly, for five minutes' work, Jackson actually felt substantially more relaxed.

It was nothing but new-agey garbage, he told himself. Normally Jackson would have nothing to do with unscientific superstition. But Beltran's planting of the test-tube on him had obviously unbalanced him. He took it out of his pocket once more and looked at the liquid in the tube. It was crystal clear, didn't look anything like a bacterial suspension. The fact that Beltran didn't seem to mind the test-tube being at room temperature made Jackson suspect that it could only contain one thing: pure DNA.

Why would Beltran give him an unlabeled molecule of DNA? To answer that, he'd have to analyze the sequence of the DNA, track down its molecular significance within the vast repository of information within the world's genetic databanks.

He had to get to a lab.

A little further down the road, Jackson came across a young, bearded man with a reflector telescope. Beside the tripod was a sign: "See the pyramid without the climb! Ten *pesos*."

He asked in English, "How good is it? Can you see the people up there?"

"You know someone up there?"

"Maybe."

The bearded man stood aside, letting Jackson put his eye to the telescope's eyepiece. He stood back for a second, impressed. The view was clear enough to see individual people clambering over the staircase of the pyramid, and some of the people on the way up. Slowly, he panned the telescope around the entire area occupied by the pyramid, then down the path leading to it. Then he found what he was looking for; Simon was on his way. He couldn't see his face but the orange pineapple shirt and black jeans could clearly be seen. Simon drew a wrist across his face and there was a flash of a golden watch glinting in the sun.

Jackson swung the telescope back to its owner. "Thanks. That's all I need." Moments later, he reached the end of the town, and looked up into the forest where a rocky path wound higher. Here and there he could see a few groups of tourists making the ascent. It was easy for an experienced hiker like Jackson. The first group he passed comprised some Americans in their early sixties, dressed in walking boots and tropical print shirts.

After another twenty minutes, he was sweating profusely. The day was not particularly warm, but his suede jacket was no good for a hike. He caught up with another small group of German tourists. They carried a large water bottle and when Jackson politely asked for a sip, they equally politely offered to fill his empty Diet Coke bottle.

The light was beginning to dim as he neared the summit of the climb. He looked with some satisfaction at his hand stitched Italian walking loafers – they were barely scuffed. He could see Simon sitting on a small platform next to two carved stone columns. Jackson approached the younger man, wiping his hands on his jeans.

"Jackson Bennett?" The man in the orange shirt stood, smiling, his right hand outstretched. His left hand remained by his side, the gold watch gleaming on the wrist.

As Jackson reciprocated, the image of a watch glinting gold in the sun jumped into his mind. Where had he seen that before? The image resonated, and with it, a lurch of dread. He thought back to when he had first seen this man, observing him from afar with the telescope. That was it; that was when he had seen the watch. Despite this, the sense of danger associated with a flash of gold on a wrist remained disturbingly close.

He shook the young man's hand. "Simon. It's good to meet you."

"Same here. Doctor Beltran is always talking about you. We're all worried about him. So, let's get you to safety. Ready?"

"I just wanna take a couple of photos." He took out his cell phone, began recording images of the pyramid and the deservedly famous views.

33

The guy in the bright shirt watched him closely. When Jackson was finished, he asked again. "Ready to go down?"

Jackson glanced at the path. The Germans had reached the top now and were clearly enjoying the prospect of having the ruins almost to themselves. The group of American retirees was almost ten minutes behind. Why couldn't he stop thinking about that watch?

"OK Simon, I've seen all I want to see. Let's go."

They began the descent, passing the Germans.

"Did you pass many tourists on your way up?" asked the newcomer, his tone light, conversational.

Then Jackson remembered where he had first seen the glint of gold in the context of danger. As clearly as though he had seen it for a whole minute instead of a just a second, Jackson recalled the image of the two men who had been searching around his car as he changed shirts in the washroom at the service station. One of them had been young, lightly built, and wore a shiny gold watch. Sunglasses had obscured the man's face, but 'Simon's face looked familiar enough to be sure that his suspicions were correct.

"Quite a few," Jackson lied, trying to stay calm. "Some old dudes should be along any second."

For the second time that day, adrenaline surged through him. Only furious concentration concealed his anxiety. Jackson clamped his jaw shut and reviewed his options. This guy – almost definitely *not* Simon Reyes– was probably armed and planning to attack him as soon as they left all witnesses behind. The forest at the side of the path was thick, the drop treacherous. At this time of day, a body could be quickly disposed of with minimal disruption.

Just so long as you had the element of surprise.

Jackson on the other hand, had no weapon. He'd taken a few kick-boxing classes, years ago, but doubted that he could seriously disable a determined assassin. Escape, therefore, was his only chance. Other assailants might be waiting, but for certain, this one had settled on a target. He stopped to sip from his Diet Coke bottle before offering it to the other man.

"It's just water," he explained, managing a genial smile. When the guy accepted and raised the bottle to his lips, Jackson made his move.

He spun hard, raised his leg in the only kick-boxing move he had ever seriously practiced. As his body swung around, Jackson's foot connected satisfyingly with the imposter's ribs. The guy was already going for a weapon under the back of his shirt, but Jackson had taken him entirely by surprise. The would-be assassin was thrown off the path and into the forest at the side.

***

Jackson bolted down the rocks on the path. A shot exploded from a gun. The bullet whizzed past his ear, a sound as terrifying as any he'd heard in his life. He faltered, lost his footing and hurtled to the ground. He rolled a couple of times before he felt something sharp rake across his upper left thigh. He gasped loudly then immediately clenched his teeth together, to stop any further outburst. A fallen tree lay beside him, one broken end of a small branch now coated in his blood.

He was shocked by the sudden burst of searing pain. A survival instinct had him in its grip. He leapt off the path and into the forest. In the corner of his eye he could just see his assailant, about twenty yards above. The man was taking aim. Jackson lunged forward, and skidded on pile of rotting leaves. Another bullet thumped into a tree trunk, just ahead of him. The air erupted with splinters; one shot straight into his cheek, just below the eye. He didn't stop, or look around again. He kept running, zigzagging through the forest, hearing shots ring out and the heavy rustle of the imposter giving chase. Jackson continued until his heart was hammering, his lungs ready to explode.

The guy wasn't going to give up. Jackson couldn't see him any longer but he could hear him crashing through the dense forest. The pain in his left leg rose to a sharp crescendo. A splinter of wood was lodged deep in his cheek. It stung like crazy, made his eyes water. He hardly slowed enough to pluck it out. His trousers were sticking to his skin, damp and heavy with blood. If he didn't stop soon, he might pass out.

After what seemed like ages, but was barely ten minutes, he paused behind a large tree with exposed roots.

Underneath the roots was a hole just large enough to contain one person, doubled over. Jackson scanned the undergrowth, and then climbed under the roots, pulling a pile of loose twigs and leaves over the entrance.

Seconds later, the assassin thundered past his hiding place. Jackson stilled every muscle. Inside his head, blood flowed as loud as a waterfall. It didn't seem possible that no-else could hear it. Any minute now, he'd be found. The assassin would catch him, and this time there'd be no element of surprise. Only a slightly delayed, professional execution.

His entire body was concealed by the tree. Under cover of darkness, with any luck, he'd be impossible to find, without search equipment.

Jackson remained there, unmoving. Time passed, perhaps an hour. There was no more sign of the assassin. At least, not yet.

Night fell; Jackson stayed put. There was no sense in moving, not until he had a plan. The assassins must know he was still somewhere on the pyramid hill. They'd be watching the exit points. He had nowhere to go. The Institute was obviously being monitored. The airport was crawling with customs agents.

He made a mental checklist of all the items still in his possession. His cell phone was intact, but was almost out of power. Jackson knew his device well enough to realize that there could be no chance of risking the GPS location app. A couple of minutes of that would gobble whatever was left in the battery.

His passport and wallet were in his jeans back pockets. His house keys were in the pocket of his jacket. To Jackson, his data was everything; phone numbers, credit card numbers, PINs, he couldn't feel comfortable without any of these. So really, he figured with a certain amount of optimism, he was almost as good as new. Except for a raw, bloody, gash in his left thigh.

The wound would be a problem. Blood had soaked the lower part of his trouser leg. He examined the laceration by the light of his cell phone. The broken branch had inflicted damage deep enough that blood loss could become a serious concern. He pulled off his jacket, tore the left sleeve away from the shoulder of his shirt and used the fabric as a makeshift bandage. He grimaced and pulled it as tight as he could bear. In movies, tough guys stitched themselves up with their own needle and thread.

Jackson couldn't help wondering if he'd be capable of that. He doubted it. For one thing, he'd never learned to sew. The wound would have to be repaired, somehow. A hospital would ask for his insurance papers. It seemed too much to hope that the Mexican Customs officials wouldn't be tracking him through all the databases. Would an insurance claim trigger a response?

Then it struck him. His entire hypothesis had been wrong. Had he totally lost his mind?

The guy who'd tried to kill Jackson was obviously not Simon Reyes. Yet he'd had been dressed in the clothes Simon had described. This could only mean one thing: their conversation had been overheard. Jackson's guess was that Beltran's lab phone was bugged.

Bugging phone lines sounded like government behavior. Murdering an innocent graduate student and using his clothes as a disguise for a second assassination – that was surely going too far. Jackson liked to think he was suitably suspicious about the government, but even he balked at something like this.

Either the government had some real evidence to link Beltran with something like bio-terrorism and Jackson himself had been lied to by PJ – or else the guys that were after Beltran and Jackson had nothing to do with the government.

As for poor Simon Reyes, Jackson guessed that the outcome had been pretty bleak.

"Damn, PJ," he muttered. "What the hell have you gotten me into?"

There could no longer be any doubt; Beltran's cryptic message, his warning, the appearance of the test-tube in Jackson's pocket: Beltran was trying to lead him along a path of discovery. Now that he'd had time to get his bearings, the next step seemed inevitable; the telephone number taped to the test-tube.

Jackson typed the number into his cell phone and waited. The line rang three times.

"*Bueno*?" A woman answered; she sounded tired.

In faltering Spanish, he mumbled, "Uh. . . You don't know me. Sorry. Pedro Juan Beltran gave me this number and ah. . . " He stopped, already out of his depth in the language.

There was a brief silence, then, "You wanna try English?"

"English! You speak English, great! OK well, Miss, frankly I don't know why, or who you are, but I know that PJ Beltran wanted me to call you."

"Who's speaking?"

"My name is Jackson Bennett. I'm a molecular geneticist, I'm doing some research in collaboration with PJ Beltran. I'm here visiting from San Francisco; from UCSF. Earlier today, he gave me this number, in case I ran into trouble. Which is what happened. And I could sure use some help."

Her silence was lengthy. Was it his imagination, or was this woman seething?

"OK, Jackson Bennett, molecular geneticist: If Pedro Juan told you to ask for help, then I'll help. Just tell me this: where is he now?"

Jackson's heart sank; he had dreaded this question, because what he had observed and been told, he somehow knew, did not match up with what had actually happened.

"Honestly, right now, I don't know." He ventured another question, this time in Spanish. "May I ask, with whom do I have the pleasure?"

He heard the reluctant smile in her voice. "Very nicely put, Mister Bennett. Or is it Doctor?"

"Almost, ma'am, almost."

"You work with my cousin?"

"Ah. You're PJ's cousin."

"Yes I am. Marie-Carmen Valencia Beltran. Pedro Juan is like a brother to me. And you?"

"Well, I'm no-one. I mean no one important. Just a messenger from a lab in UCSF. PJ is one of our most important collaborators. My boss asked me to bring him some stuff."

"Stuff?"

"Genetic stuff. It's kinda technical."

"I'm an archaeologist. Not entirely unacquainted with the ways of you geneticists."

39

"Subcloned DNA samples," Jackson replied firmly. "Genes that Beltran and I were studying."

"OK, all very intriguing. But you know what? It's kind of late in the night for a girl like me to be talking genetics over the phone with a total stranger. So Jackson: long story short?"

"I'm going to owe you big time for this." He took a deep breath. "I'm near Tepoztlan. In the woods. I'm lost. Someone just tried to kill me."

"Sounds terrible," Marie-Carmen said, clearly unimpressed. "And you're calling me, why?"

"Could you come get me? Please? You're the only one I can trust. Please."

Marie-Carmen paused. There was a mirthless chuckle. "I'd say that's one hell of a debt to repay."

***

There was thick cloud cover, and almost no ambient light. Jackson checked the battery on his cell phone. The call to Marie-Carmen had all but depleted the power. If he used it as a torch now, that would probably finish it off. Anyway, a sudden burst of light in the woods could expose him to the assassin.

"There's a road next to the hill of the Tepozteco pyramid," Marie-Carmen had said. "Keep going downhill and I'll find you. My car is a silver VW Beetle, the old kind, like the taxis. Keep hidden until you see my car; I'll be driving by real slow. Put something at the side of the road, something I'll notice; a shoe. When I see it, I'll stop; then, so long as there's no other car around, you get in. If there's another car, Jackson, I won't stop; you got that? Wait. Maybe I'll come back for you later."

She was right, thought Jackson. Whoever had tried to kill him would not be likely to give up so easily. They might have abandoned the search for him in the forest, but if Marie-Carmen could work out where he was, then so could they. If they discovered Marie-Carmen, nowhere would be safe.

He made his way gingerly through the forest, concentrating hard. He focused on the slope of the ground. Always downhill; it made for a few slips and grazes, but basically, the strategy seemed to be working. After twenty minutes he could hear cars as they sped by on the road below. The forest was too dense to see the road yet, but he knew it was close. Just a few minutes later, he could see the lights.

The traffic was relatively sparse on this minor thoroughfare; only one car passed every five minutes or so. Jackson descended to the road's edge, crouching low. He pulled off his right shoe and with calculated effort, tossed it into the road. Then he sat down. The pain from his thigh made him wince, but he bit his lip, prepared to wait.

"What kind of loser gets himself followed all the way from the airport?" Jackson muttered. He could still scarcely believe that he'd allowed it to happen. But now he was thinking like a marked man. This morning, he had been just another innocent.

He began more carefully to observe the cars, mentally tallying the make and models.

After half an hour, there was no doubt in his mind which car represented the threat. A black Ford Explorer had driven by three times before he thought to look at the registration. The fourth time, there was no question.

Finally, Jackson saw the round headlamps of a VW Beetle approach, moving slowly. He glanced further down the road. According to his observations, the Ford Explorer was due any minute. He waited.

The VW Beetle slowed to a halt near his shoe. Still Jackson waited. He dare not risk it until the Explorer had completed its reconnaissance. The door of the Beetle swung open and he heard a voice hiss into the hum of the forest: "Jackson!" He did not move. Then there were two sounds; the click of heels on the tarmac and the rumble of an approaching car. Jackson retreated into the shadows of the forest. Marie-Carmen moved her head; she'd heard him.

The black Ford Explorer slowed to a stop in front of Marie-Carmen's VW. A man stepped out, walked over to Marie-Carmen. They were close enough that Jackson could hear every word. His Spanish was good enough to understand most of their conversation

"*Señorita*. Can I be of assistance?"

"I thought I saw an animal in the road. But look, do you see? It's just a shoe."

"Oh yes, you're right." The man's tone was courteous, yet unmoved.

"I would save an animal."

"No harm done."

"No, thank goodness. I would hate to have hurt a living creature."

"Sometimes it is unavoidable."

"Well, that's true."

"You shouldn't stay outside, alone, *señorita*, in a place like this."

"You're right. Thanks for stopping to help, you're a gentleman."

The man dipped a small bow, watching as Marie-Carmen stepped back into her car and under the watchful eye of the driver of the Explorer, drove away.

After she had left, the driver peered suspiciously into the scrub at the edge of the road. He took out a torch and shone the beam around. Jackson froze in his hiding place, behind a tree. If they bothered to venture into the woods to search, he knew he would be forced again to run. He breathed a sigh of relief when a minute later, he heard the door of the car slam shut and the squeal of the tires against the road.

Now alone, Jackson swore profusely. That was it; his one chance. Maybe if he'd been quicker or if Marie-Carmen had happened along just a little earlier. Now it was over.

How would he possibly get away? The Ford Explorer, patrolling the stretch of road as regularly as it was, would not be fooled a second time by Marie-Carmen's car.

He dared not move, however, nor stray from the plan. Jackson was amazed that they had actually failed to regard the shoe as a potential signal.

Or maybe they had, and were just waiting for him to show himself. Eventually, he knew it, he would have to emerge.

Marie-Carmen

In the next half hour four more cars passed and the Explorer made six more passes. Jackson began to feel helpless. A brown Nissan Tsuru screeched to a stop at the side of the road. The passenger door opened and Jackson bolted for the car. Just before he reached the car, he moved to pick up the shoe. The Tsuru jolted forward, almost knocking him down. He heard Marie-Carmen's voice: "Are you insane? Leave it! Now climb in the back and lie down. Do it now!"

As he jumped inside, Marie-Carmen's foot leaned hard on the accelerator. They were clear of the scene with still no sign of the Explorer.

"Would you like to leave them a sign: 'Been rescued, see you in Mexico City'?"

"I'm sorry, sorry, I wasn't thinking." Jackson groaned. So much for his casual, Italian loafer look.

"I don't think you can afford to slow down on the thinking, do you? I think maybe you need to keep your wits about you."

He changed the subject. "Where did you get the car? D'you steal it.?"

Marie-Carmen swore roundly. "No, *pendejo*, I swapped it for the Beetle. You think I'm safe in that thing now?"

He hesitated. "That was pretty good thinking. Can the new owners trace this car to you?"

"A beautifully restored, old-style VW Beetle, with all the papers in order, for this piece of junk? Ha – no. They thought it was Christmas. They didn't ask any questions."

"That was seriously good thinking," he repeated. "Really, I'm impressed."

"That's nice for you. As for me, I'm amazed you've survived this long. Also you owe me a new car."

Jackson lay back across the rear seats, exhausted.

"You realize I can't afford to pay you back."

"God, I am so not surprised."

Marie-Carmen drove in silence as they passed through Tepoztlan, took the toll road back to Mexico City. Jackson leaned against the door, a hand nursing the piercing pain in his thigh muscle. The relief he'd felt at being rescued had almost gone. His anxiety levels were escalating again. How was this irritable woman going to be able to help him? He was in trouble with some pretty terrifying people. Jackson just wanted to get fixed up and get back to the USA. PJ's mysterious test-tube might hold the answer to why he was a target, but right now he was too exhausted to care.

Marie-Carmen glanced over. "You're in bad shape?"

"I'll survive. Thanks to you." Another thought struck him. "Jesus. My rental car; I can't even pick that up. My credit card account's going to explode."

"Jackson, stay calm. Things like that are fixable."

He said nothing, surprised at how resentful he felt at being told to stay calm.

"Look, I can see you've been through something here." Marie-Carmen appeared to pick her words carefully. "Forget what I said before. I was scared, OK? Those guys looked pretty violent to me. I've never dealt with anything like this."

"Me either. I'm sorry that you got involved. Wish I knew what was going on."

"Well Jackson, you know *something*, that's for sure. We'll go to my home, dress that wound. Tomorrow, you and me are going to figure out what the hell this is all about."

He exhaled, slowly. He just wanted to rest and now he'd hooked up with an amateur detective.

"I'm guessing this is something to do with my cousin's research?"

"That does seem the logical answer."

"Hey, you know more than that. I lost my car because of you, Bennett! You owe me some answers."

"Maybe it's safer if you stay out of it."

She snorted. "Maybe, no. *Definitely*!"

"Why don't you just take me back to your place and let me worry about it?"

45

"I don't think so. The way things are going you're going to wind up dead."

Jackson smiled slightly to himself. There was urgency and passion in her voice. He had to admit, it was nice to feel she was worried about him.

"You're going to wind up dead and my cousin will never be found."

"PJ is missing . . . ?"

"Yes, missing." Marie-Carmen's tone had turned sardonic, angry. "Don't pretend you didn't know."

He dropped his head.

With an obvious effort to be calm she said, "When were you going to tell me?"

"I was going to tell you what happened to him. Didn't know if he'd checked in yet."

"No, he's missing, his wife is going crazy with worry. She's in hospital, my niece Gabi is home alone. Pedro Juan's wife is too scared to tell the girl what's going on. So, Jackson Bennett, if you have some answers then you'd better start talking."

Jackson was silent. Part of him welcomed the chance to talk things through with someone, especially someone as obviously intelligent as Marie-Carmen. It didn't hurt that she sounded sexier by the minute or that could see the outline of her figure in the shadows – it looked pretty terrific. Jackson was already looking forward to the inevitable tension of spending a night alone in a stranger woman's apartment, with all the possibilities it might bring. On the other hand, he was under no illusion. PJ had dragged him into a dangerous situation. He'd tangled with some well-connected people who weren't afraid to use extreme violence. Jackson had known Marie-Carmen for minutes but his basic urge to protect a desirable female was already kicking in.

Hesitantly, he began. "Marie-Carmen, did you ever call PJ at the lab?"

"Not usually. Why?"

"You ever visit him in Temixco? Have anything to do with his work?"

"No, why?"

"This is really important. Is there any way that you could be connected with his work in any way whatsoever?"

"I can't imagine how."

Jackson shook his head. "Someone was onto Pedro Juan. They knew about his work with the *phoenix* gene. They knew he was meeting someone from the San Francisco lab to receive samples. Maybe they even knew I'd be the one bringing them over. I just need to be sure that they can't know of a connection to you."

"Your work with Pedro Juan; that's why someone is trying to kill you?"

"I don't understand yet. Our work was potentially exciting to the biotech industry, but that's as far as it goes. Least, that's what I figured. But I think PJ was onto something new."

"Like what?"

"I need to get to a lab to figure that out. Until then, we need to avoid contact with anyone else at PJ's lab, the police, the hospitals. Anyone connected to the government. And especially those guys in the Ford Explorer."

"You want to disappear for a while?"

He managed a wan smile. "It couldn't hurt."

"Then we're going to the right place. Mexico City; twenty millions of us there; we should be able to get lost."

She turned on the radio. It was tuned to a classical music station. A pensive piano sonata was playing. "You like Beethoven?"

"That's Beethoven?"

"Sonata number twenty-five," she said, softly. "And you didn't answer my question."

"Do I like Beethoven?" He hesitated. Another woman, he might have tried to bluff. "Honestly, I prefer rap. You like Eminem? Or reggaeton, you got some of that?"

"Reggaeton?" She turned to him with a quizzical smile. "Sure, why not?" She pressed another preset button. The heavy bass drop of Latin rap began to pound through the car. Quietly, Marie-Carmen chuckled. "Interesting. . ."

Jackson glanced over at Marie-Carmen. She was dressed as though she had just left work, in heels, slacks and white blouse. As discreetly as he could, Jackson stared at her legs working under taut fabric. Her upper arms and thighs were those of a dancer or, perhaps, a yoga enthusiast. Curvaceous but well-toned.

Marie-Carmen turned to him, her lips tightly pursed, eyebrows raised with a hint of questioning in her expression.

He looked at her directly for the first time, almost having to catch his breath when he caught the look of knowing amusement in her eyes. His apparent transparency before her embarrassed him. He forced himself to stare back into the road ahead.

If Marie-Carmen had been thinking of saying anything then, she evidently decided to hold her peace. "That's a nice jacket," she ventured diplomatically, after a few moments.

"Thank you. Probably the only decent piece of clothing that I own."

"Don't like clothes?"

"Don't like to shop."

"You're all about the work, hey, Jackson?"

Wincing slightly at the steady pulse of pain in his thigh, Jackson shook his head. "You're really not seeing me at my best."

"It's not been a very good day for me either," she conceded.

"Oh, I'd say you're coming out of this a hell of a lot better than me. My hero," he said, with a sidelong glance.

"I'd do anything for my cousin," she murmured. "I just hope you're worth it."

In a darkened car, driving through the mountains with the hazy, neon lights of Mexico City just visible in the valley below, a comfortable silence enveloped them.

Ninety minutes later, they reached Marie-Carmen's home in Tlalpan, a southern suburb of Mexico City. Marie-Carmen's apartment building was in a gated complex and as they passed through, Jackson heard Marie-Carmen ask the security guard if there had been any visitors for her. "No, no, Doctor. No visitors, no calls. But where's your Beetle?"

"You're going to laugh: I lost it in a bet. But if you see it, don't let it pass, deal? I didn't part on good terms with the new owners."

The security gate opened and Marie-Carmen drove through.

Jackson regarded her with a mixture of respect and misgiving. "*Doctor* Marie-Carmen?"

"Oh that's right, you don't have yours yet."

He changed the subject. "'Lost it in a bet'. You know something? You're a pretty convincing liar."

Marie-Carmen flashed a smile. "Yes I am. Don't ever play me at poker."

"Can you lie like that to anyone, about anything?"

Marie-Carmen parked the car wordlessly. "You're asking me if I'm someone who can be trusted."

Jackson was aware of his own heartbeat. "Yes."

"Do you trust me?"

"You saved my life."

"Maybe I'm saving it for later."

"Marie-Carmen. I don't know what's going on. I don't know what happened to your cousin. But PJ is the reason why someone tried to kill me. I don't know why he gave me your number. I'm sorry if I seem a little paranoid."

"I have to know if you trust me."

Jackson looked into her eyes, transfixed. They were a light, almost honey-brown. Fear gripped his heart. In that moment he realized that trust didn't come into it; he wanted to do whatever this woman asked of him. He felt powerless against his own desire, even though he sensed where it might lead.

"I trust you. Do you trust me?"

Dismissively, Marie-Carmen shook her head. "Jackson, we just met. But I trust Pedro Juan; for now, that's enough."

***

In the dim light of the apartment, the leaves of trees in the gardens cast jagged shadows across the large windows. Marie-Carmen led Jackson into the kitchen, switched on the light and pulled out a chair by a round wooden table.

"Let's see that leg."

Jackson slowly removed his jacket. The sharp pain in his leg had reduced to a throbbing ache. Still, he was apprehensive about actually confronting the damage.

Marie-Carmen touched his arm. "Try to relax. I can go out and buy dressings from the pharmacy."

Jackson said nothing as he unbuttoned his jeans, dropping them below the knee before sitting on the chair.

Marie-Carmen knelt down, carefully unwrapped the blood-soaked cotton sleeve which had served as a bandage. She was quiet for a few seconds as she examined his wound.

"This really needs medical attention. It's too deep to heal quickly without stitching."

"No hospitals," insisted Jackson. "You don't have some buddy who's a doctor?"

"Not the kind that I can disturb at this hour. And you shouldn't wait; there could be infection. You were in the woods; God knows what you could have picked up in this wound."

"Can you do it?"

She raised her eyebrows doubtfully. "I can buy all the stuff, sure. But stitching?"

"How hard could it be?"

50

"Presumably there's some kind of knack to it. Or else, what's the point of medical school?"

"You wouldn't be grossed out?"

Laconically, she replied "You should see the condition of some of the human remains I come across."

***

Marie-Carmen left Jackson to enjoy slices of *manchego* cheese, pickled chilies and a bottle of tequila, closing the apartment door quietly as she left to fetch supplies.

Jackson hungrily ate the food and began on the tequila. Marie-Carmen had advised him to drink at least six shots to prepare for the minor ordeal of the stitching. By the time Marie-Carmen returned, Jackson was feeling almost mellow.

At her behest, he stretched out on her bed, wearing only his one-sleeved shirt and boxer shorts. She began with cotton wool pads which she soaked in surgical alcohol from a fresh bottle. Meticulously, she cleaned the wound. Jackson struggled not to flinch. Then she produced a metal tool in a disposable wrapper, which she removed from its sterile environment. She held it against his thigh.

"Staples," she said wryly, "so you don't have to make do with my crooked sewing."

"Great," he murmured. "Metal spikes being fired into my skin; that's what this whole experience was missing."

"Quit fussing," she whispered, "and hold still."

With the surgical stapler, Marie-Carmen fastened the three-inch tear in his leg with a rapid succession of four painful, tattoo-like movements.

Jackson looked down at her handiwork.

"There you go." Marie-Carmen gave a smile of relief.

"You just keep amazing me."

She tore open another wrapper and removed a large waterproof dressing, then pressed it over the stapled wound.

They looked at each other for a moment.

"How much do I owe you for all this medical stuff?"

"Since I'm just a beginner, I won't charge for the labor. The parts, well, that will be five hundred pesos."

Jackson sat up, leaning back on his elbows. Only inches separated them now. Watching him, Marie-Carmen's expression was surprisingly tender, concerned. Jackson badly wanted to kiss her.

"And how," he asked slowly, his words charged with meaning, "Can I possibly thank you?"

Marie-Carmen exhaled. "I haven't even begun to think about that."

They were staring into each other's eyes and Jackson found himself wishing that he weren't drunk. She might be receptive, but could well be beyond making an accurate judgment.

The moment was broken as the telephone rang. Marie-Carmen answered it, clearly perturbed to be receiving a call so late. Jackson watched the tension in her shoulders as she took the call, saying almost nothing to the caller, except, "*Ay por Dios, no!*"

Marie-Carmen replaced the receiver, her hand shaking.

"What is it?" inquired Jackson. He'd already guessed.

Still facing away from him, Marie-Carmen spoke in a low voice. She was barely audible. "That was my brother. The police found Pedro Juan. He was in the airport. In a bathroom. His eyes were shot out of him. He was dead. My aunt and uncle are completely devastated. They've just found out, from Pedro Juan's wife. My niece Gabi is still alone. My God, Jackson..." She looked up at him, accusation in her eyes.

Jackson held rigidly still, afraid to move a single muscle.

"Marie-Carmen. . . I didn't know. Believe me! PJ went off with some man I didn't know...I thought he was being arrested. I don't know why this is happening, I promise you. Remember what you said: you trust me because you trust PJ."

Marie-Carmen stared at him. Her eyes filled with tears. She moved away, wiped her cheeks with the back of one hand.

"Start talking, Jackson. I want the whole story of you and Pedro Juan. From the beginning."

"I met PJ three years ago, at a conference in Keystone, Colorado. Do you archaeologists ever get have meetings there, in the Rockies? That's how I found out I wanted to be a scientist. When I left high school all I wanted was to be a snowboard bum. Pretty soon I was working as an instructor in Aspen. A lot of it was teaching idiot rich kids with more money than skill. But also, I spent some time working at the Keystone Symposia. It's a series of real high-level biology meetings, always in mountain resorts. Sometimes I'd have a few beers with the scientist types. One of those scientists helped me to get accepted into a genetics program at UCLA, which is a real good school. About four years ago I started my doctorate, at UCSF. After a year, I got enough data together to present a paper at a Keystone Meeting. And there I was, finally, doing what I'd seen those scientists do back then."

"Which was?"

"Spend all morning talking science. All afternoon on the mountain. Then back to the hotel for three or four martinis."

"That's your idea of a good time?"

"Pretty close to it," Jackson smiled.

Marie-Carmen nodded, thoughtful. "I see."

"So what do you archaeologists like to do?" he asked. Marie-Carmen ignored the cue. "Let's get back to you and Pedro Juan."

"PJ was this real eminent Mexican scientist, right? I offered to give him some snowboard instruction – actually he was already quite good, so he didn't want to join in with all the beginners. I told PJ we could go right up to the top and I'd show him how to get down the black runs."

"You're very good then?"

"I know a few tricks."

"I'll remember that, if I ever want to take lessons."

"I'll offer you a lifetime of free lessons, right now." He tried to stare into her eyes but Marie-Carmen smiled and looked away. "Continue."

"Afterwards, in the martini bar, I guess we got a little carried away. We got talking and decided that our research projects were pretty compatible, and if things went well we could earn millions if not actually win a Nobel Prize."

"Ah, you said you don't like money."

"I said I don't like the kind of people with money who go to Aspen. I have no problem with money, per se. I just don't have any."

"What a relief, I thought you were a socialist."

"You've got something against workers having rights?"

"No, but I dated a very earnest communist once, very dreary. Always wanted to pay his respects at Trotsky's house, in Coyoacán. It got boring."

Marie-Carmen wore a look of casual diffidence. Combined with the traces of sadness, it was somehow irresistible. Jackson could only think of how he might impress her.

"PJ and I really clicked. I phoned my boss and he agreed that I could try some experiments with PJ's lab."

Scientific protocol dictated that after that, the two senior scientists had managed the collaboration. Jackson, although he'd initiated the project, was relegated to junior partner. Even so, Jackson had enjoyed a couple of trips with his boss, to PJ's lab in Temixco, which boasted a Biotechnology Research Institute of international fame, thanks largely to its co-founder, Mexico's most famous molecular biologist, Francisco Bolivar.

Marie-Carmen poured them both a cup of coffee. "The real hook," explained Jackson, "was that it turned out that Pedro Juan and I were working on something incredibly similar. Even though his gene was from a variety of maize, and mine was from a fruit fly. I saw his poster, where he'd predicted the structure of the protein which his gene would produce. I'd only just sequenced my own mysterious bit of DNA. Even so, I could tell that the way Pedro Juan's protein folded, the DNA sequence had to be really, really similar."

"How could you tell?"

"I sort of 'see' protein structures in my mind. I've read so many DNA sequences that I tend to know what sort of amino acid sequences they code for – and since amino acids sequences make up protein structures, well, I also tend to have a knack for knowing what kind of sequences fold in which way."

Marie-Carmen looked impressed. Jackson grinned. "It's more like a parlor trick, or like having a photographic memory."

"I can see that – it's the same way with the hieroglyphs; people like me who learned to read them the hard way can still do it without computers."

It was Jackson's turn to look impressed. "You're not old enough to have started reading hieroglyphs before most of the texts were computerized."

Marie-Carmen hid a modest grin behind her cup. "I didn't wait until I was a doctoral student; I've been reading Mayan scripts since I was a teenager."

"Ah, a child prodigy?"

"It isn't so unusual. There are some smart people out there. Pedro Juan really is – was – the brilliant one in the family."

Jackson gazed at her, warmly. "I'm not so sure."

The memory evoked in her a sudden shift in mood. Tears once more appeared in her eyes, spilled over, rolling silently down her cheeks. Marie-Carmen seemed unable to speak, for several minutes just holding her fingers to her temples as very slightly, she trembled. Jackson could say nothing, he too was moved to silence, his breath held in check. He reached out tentatively to touch her shoulder, but at the last stayed his palm just millimeters away. She seemed lost for those moments. Her lips whispered inaudibly, in her eyes he caught a glimpse of a light flickering.

Neither of them spoke for what seemed like a long time. Marie-Carmen drew heavy, ragged breaths. Jackson found his gaze drawn uncomfortably to her rising breast, the tremble in her hands and shoulders. He longed to hold her, to comfort her, but he couldn't quite get past the suspicion that his attention might be unwelcome.

"I'm sorry," he whispered.

"I just suddenly thought of him, when I was a little kid. He'd won some prize at college. And my aunty bought a special cake from Sanborns. The whole family was inspired by him. Growing up it was always, 'you can be like your cousin!' His parents, they worshipped him. They'll never get over this, never. And my poor niece, Gabi . . . now she's lost her father."

Then, almost as if emerging slowly from a dream, she looked at Jackson. She focused, as though she'd only just noticed him.

"You were telling me about how you and he started to work together."

"It can wait. You're tired, you're upset."

Marie-Carmen smiled almost grimly. "Yes I am, but I don't want to stop. Somewhere in what you know, there's the key to why he died."

"OK," Jackson continued reluctantly, "If you're sure. So, PJ and I began to collaborate, comparing our two genes; he called his maize gene *phoenix*, and suggested I call mine *joust*."

"Strange names."

"They're Atari video games from the eighties. Fruit fly geneticists are like that; once someone starts a fashion, people follow on. For example, there's a gene called *sevenless*, because when it doesn't work properly, segment number seven in the fly's body is missing. Then some guys discovered other bits of DNA, genes with similar sequences, and called them things like *son of sevenless*, *bride of sevenless*. There's a 'jumping gene' in fruit flies, called *frogger*. PJ and I were following that tradition."

"These pieces of DNA, are they the reason Pedro Juan is dead and why you're here with me after someone tried to kill you?"

Jackson was pensive. "I thought maybe bringing the samples had gotten me into trouble with customs. It's illegal to take genetically-modified organisms across a border without declaring them."

"You don't sound so sure."

"PJ's been killed and I've been shot at. Would the government do that, do you think?"

Marie-Carmen shrugged. "In Mexico you can never be sure who might be on the payroll of who. I agree, it seems strange. Did you have another explanation in mind?"

"There was a chance that the samples could be very valuable. PJ's protein, for example, seemed to help his maize resist a high salt content in soil. That could be worth a lot to the biotech industry." Jackson stopped for a minute, thinking. "But what I think they were *really* after, was something that PJ gave me, along with your telephone number."

"Which was?"

"A test-tube with something inside. I have a hunch what it might be, but we need to go to a lab to check it out properly."

"Then it can wait until tomorrow. You and I need to get to bed."

Jackson's eye's widened just a fraction, he felt the rush in his heart-rate, his mouth went dry. One second later, though, it all came crashing down as Marie-Carmen declared with a note of finality. "Well come on, help me to make up the sofa bed."

The Poborsky Lab

Early the next day, they ate breakfast in a small coffee house on La Plaza Constitución of Tlalpan – a little square which Jackson noted contentedly, had all the charm of colonial Mexico; narrow stone alleyways lined with trees, venerable old houses painted in bright ochre and blues, heavy wrought iron gratings. Gazing at the large menu of Mexican-grown coffees – Jackson tried to distract his thoughts from Marie-Carmen.

By daylight she was even more attractive – dressed in tight-fitting jeans, cowgirl boots and a tailored, white linen blouse which emphasized her incredible figure only too well. In the evening, her long brown hair had been tightly pulled back, but now she wore it loose, tumbling across her shoulders in a manner that Jackson found entirely disarming.

When Marie-Carmen turned to fetch sugar and napkins, Jackson enjoyed the momentary freedom to rest his gaze on her particularly curvy, round ass. When she turned around, Jackson realized that he'd been a little slow to move his eyes. There was distinct amusement in her expression as she approached.

Even better, he thought. She wasn't annoyed.

"This is really great coffee," she said with one eyebrow raised. "They roast the beans in the shop. All from Mexico. You better not let me catch you drinking at Starbucks while you're here."

Jackson held up a conciliatory hand. "'Made in Mexico'. That's my motto when I'm here." He gazed at her with warmth. "It's a relief to see you smile again."

"You did such a good job with me last night," she said, letting the full weight of her meaning sink into the conversation. Jackson did his best to keep his expression even, and they almost stared each other down in a competition of earnestness. "Well," he murmured. "It was mutual."

"Your leg? That was nothing. But talking to me about Pedro Juan," Marie-Carmen continued. "Telling me about his work, your friendship. In Mexico, that's how we mourn; we remember our dead right from the first minute. No time wasted, we get right on with honoring them."

"I'm glad I could help."

Marie-Carmen took a sip from her steaming coffee cup. "My brother called again. The funeral is in five days."

Jackson considered this. "You should go. You should try, as far as possible, to do everything that you would normally do. They'll be watching for anything out of the ordinary to do with PJ."

"You think they'll be watching me?"

"At this stage, why would they? But if some close cousin doesn't turn up at the funeral, it could be just the thing to put them onto us."

Wordlessly, they drank coffee and ate Mexican breakfast rolls smothered in fine, powdered sugar. Jackson looked around the square. It would be so easy to believe he was now safe. The tranquility of the setting, with the raised central gazebo, the little park crammed with shrubs and flowers, tall trees casting a cool shade as the morning sun began to warm the air.

How could anything bad happen to him, he wondered, in a place like this?

After breakfast, they drove directly to the campus of UNAM – the National Autonomous University of Mexico at Mexico City. It was an immense campus, with its own parks, museums, highways and even security force. Marie-Carmen navigated expertly through the confusing maze of turnings, to the Biomedical Faculty.

"OK," she said. "Let's hope that my friend Magda feels in the mood to let us use her lab."

Dr. Magda Poborsky was a Mexican-born child of Polish immigrants, in manner as Mexican a woman as Marie-Carmen knew, but in physique, a statuesque blonde woman with high, Slavic cheekbones and a no-nonsense attitude.

She looked doubtfully at Jackson, clad very casually in the cheap jeans, grey T-shirt and sneakers that he'd picked up at the supermarket that morning. To Marie-Carmen, she said nothing, but her eyes said it all: *Where did you pick up this gringo loser?*

"I need a spectrophotometer, an electrophoresis gel and maybe a bit of time on a DNA sequencer," Jackson said. He and Marie-Carmen had agreed not to discuss the project in detail; instead he was claiming to have mixed up some samples and wanted to clarify the situation before he walked into the labs at a biotech company and lost all his credibility.

Clearly, to Magda he had already lost that.

"You got it. You can use this bench; it should have all the equipment you need. I'll book you a slot on the DNA sequencing machine in an hour's time." She shot a pertinent look at Marie-Carmen. "Better be thankful you got friends in the right places."

Marie-Carmen and Magda embraced. In Spanish Marie-Carmen murmured, "Thanks, Blondie, I owe you one," as she kissed Magda goodbye.

Marie-Carmen watched Jackson remove the test-tube from his back pocket. He placed it carefully into an orange acrylic test-tube rack and began to prepare more test-tubes, labeling them with a black marker pen.

"You think it's DNA?" she asked.

"Pretty sure. It's in a water-based solution: I can see that from the viscosity. It's obviously stable at room temperature, or else PJ wouldn't have supplied it to me that way. Other biological molecules, like protein, or RNA, don't tend to handle that kind of abuse too well. They just fall apart. Even whole organisms, like bacteria, or fungus should be looked after a bit better; at least refrigerated. DNA, on the other hand, can be incredibly stable. That's why you archaeologists and the paleontologists can get useful information from DNA found in mummies. So, I'm betting that it's DNA. I'm going to take just a tiny bit of it. . . "

He dipped the tip of a small pipette into the sample, and removed an almost imperceptible amount.

". . . and see if it absorbs light at a wavelength of two-sixty nanometers; hence the spectrophotometer. If it does, it's probably DNA. Then I'll run a bit out on a gel, to see how long it is."

"How long?"

Jackson concentrated on his work.

"DNA molecules have an electrical charge, which is directly proportional to their length – how many bits of code they have. If you separate them electrically in a gel-based medium, you can compare how far they've travelled in that gel with some other DNA molecules."

"Of known length?" ventured Marie-Carmen.

Jackson grinned. "Exactly. Now, let's just hope that this one isn't too long, or your friend's gonna be mad at me for using up time on her sequencer!"

****

Three hours later, Jackson removed a CD from the DNA sequencer. Now to cross-reference the data against all known gene sequences in the world's most recently updated data banks. Outside the faculty, Marie-Carmen was waiting in her car. With an air of triumph, Jackson slapped the CD against the window.

"There's an open reading frame."

"A what, now?"

Jackson dropped into the passenger seat. "Open reading frame: it's what we call the part of the gene which the cell machinery would translate into a protein. The rest of the gene is a set of instructions which tell the cell when to make that protein, and how much. Think of it like the introduction and index of a book; it takes up space and has important information, but the real 'story' is in the open reading frame. What's weird," he continued, "is that I don't recognize the sequence at all."

"Is that so unusual?" she asked, diverting the car to a nearby store selling *tortas* – large rolls spread with refried bean paste, stuffed with ham, cheese, pickled chilies and salad.

"When you work with a particular sequence of DNA, or a family of those sequences, you get a feel for it. Like I told you last night: you get to recognize portions. The same stuff pops up again and again all over the genome you know. You'd be surprised. Well, I got nothing from this sequence. It's like nothing PJ or I work on. But I really need to look for it properly in a gene data bank. Those are updated all the time – if anyone else in the world has published a sequence like this, I'll find it."

"What if they haven't?"

"It's not just the human genome that has been entirely sequenced by now. Lots of other organisms, too. For this to be unpublished, even as a sequence of unknown function, would mean that it was from some bizarre organism. Or else that it was from a very rare gene. A really rare gene might not have been picked up by anyone yet. The human genome project only sequenced a few peoples' genes. It wasn't the most representative of samples."

"You mean there could be entire genes that only some people would have?" asked Marie-Carmen.

"It's unlikely, sure. Most species have the same genes, just different forms of the genes. That's part of what makes individuals different. So it wouldn't be entirely out of the question. For example, like I told you, *joust*, the gene I work on, and PJ's gene also, are 'jumping genes'. They didn't originate in the fruit fly. At some point during evolution, they just appeared in the fruit fly's DNA."

"From where?"

"Probably a virus. *Joust* and *phoenix* are retrotransposons – in their DNA structure they look a bit like some retroviruses, like the kind of virus that causes AIDS. The human genome is riddled with those kinds of mobile genetic elements. They wouldn't necessarily actually work as genes. And they wouldn't be in every person."

"What do you mean – they wouldn't 'work as genes'?"

Jackson thought for a moment.

"Imagine a gene as a freight train carriage. It can't produce a result – deliver its load – without an engine carriage, a driver, the train signals, a whole load of equipment and events which need to happen to make the delivery. If any of those are disrupted; like, for example, if the signal lights are worn out, or the engine isn't working, then the freight doesn't get delivered properly, or at all. The freight carriage, engine carriage, driver, can all be there. It's just that something crucial, one element is missing. That's how it can be with a gene. Most of what you need to be there could be there, but just the wrong bit missing or altered and . . ."

"No delivery."

Jackson nodded. "Right – the gene doesn't make a protein. *Joust* and *phoenix* look like a lot of 'jumping genes' – they *look* like they mightn't work. Yet, they do. They make really interesting proteins. Also, not all fruit flies have *joust*, or maize have *phoenix*."

Marie-Carmen pondered for a second. "Maybe Pedro Juan found a new 'jumping gene'?"

"Maybe he did."

They sat side-by-side in front of the large flat screen monitor of a computer in the university library. Jackson loaded the CD with the freshly-sequenced DNA, then cut and pasted a section of the DNA sequence code into another browser window.

"This website has 'BLAST'," he explained. "A computer program that will search for your sequence in a huge gene data bank and process the result. I'm only checking for things that match up with the open reading frame; the bit which codes for the amino acids, the protein-y part. In fact a protein this small," he paused to count up the letters in the sequence; "only fifteen amino acids, is known as a 'peptide'."

"You're going peptide-hunting?"

"BLAST will show us all the similar sequences, in all species."

They waited for two minutes, Jackson impatiently refreshing the browser window every few seconds.

After this time, the program returned the result.

No significant similarities found.

63

Jackson sat back, shocked. "Wow."

"That just means that no-one's published it, right? It doesn't mean they don't know about it. People could be working on it."

Jackson thought for a minute. "You're right. Maybe instead of publishing, they patented it. That would mean we should be able to find some reference to it in the patent databases."

He brought up another browser window, typing in the Web address of a patent search engine. He copied a section of the DNA code from PJ's molecule and entered it into the search box.

Again, the search returned no results.

Jackson was pensive. "You mind if I check my email?" he asked.

Marie-Carmen shrugged. "Go ahead."

Among twenty-five new messages was one dated that day, from PJ.

"That's weird," Jackson said. "This was sent after PJ met me. I don't think he could have sent it. Maybe his email account has been hacked?"

"Unless he set up some kind of automatic email," Marie-Carmen suggested. "You know, like when you use the vacation settings on your email? You can configure it to send an automatic email. Unless you change the settings back."

"Can you set it to send a specific email to a specific person?"

"It's not difficult."

Jackson clicked on the email. "If PJ figured out that someone was onto him, maybe he did set something up to send automatically. He sure-as-hell covered himself."

He sensed, suddenly, an intake of breath from Marie-Carmen. Then Jackson saw what had alarmed her.

A warning icon had appeared in the bottom right hand corner of the screen: "Warning. Someone is trying to trace your IP address."

"And now," murmured Marie-Carmen, "they'll be onto us. Those searches you did must have tripped someone's IP tracing system. Your IP address is the address of your machine as it appears on the Internet."

"I know what an IP address is," Jackson said. "But someone can actually trace your computer's address down from a Web search?"

"Sure. You performed those searches on the Web, openly. A Web search is a query, a string of characters that is sent out as a request across the Internet. Whatever you search for will form part of that query. That search bounces the Internet; a message, waiting for an answer from the search engine.

"If someone else put a program out in the Internet, sniffing out searches with specific characters in the search string, they could easily trace the origin of that search; the IP address of this computer. They could quite easily trace that search down to this library."

Thoughtfully she continued, "I'm guessing the same thing happened to Pedro Juan. It led them to him. Jackson, we have to go. If they're in Mexico City, it won't take them long to get here."

With that, Marie-Carmen picked up her bag, removed Jackson's CD and methodically deleted all references to the work they had done that day.

Jackson sat back, saying nothing. He was beginning to understand why PJ had given him just one phone number as an escape route.

On the way back to Marie-Carmen's apartment, they stopped at a shopping mall, where Jackson picked up a cheap laptop to replace the one he'd left in his suitcase in the rental car he'd been forced to abandon. Afterwards, Marie-Carmen insisted he buy some decent clothes. To her amusement, Jackson had taken less than eight minutes to pick out three polo shirts, jeans, chinos, black jeans and a pair of dark brown, leather brogues.

"What?" he said finally, unable to bear her obvious and barely contained mirth.

"It's just – you are so conservative! Look at you; I bet that's all you ever wear."

"For your information, it's a successful combination, and it doesn't take any planning. Low overhead, see?"

Marie-Carmen continued to smile, a hint of flirtation playing about her lips. "I didn't mean to offend your ego. You should let your girlfriend take you shopping sometime."

"If I had a girlfriend, I'd just let her pick up whatever she wanted to see me in."

"And you'd wear it?" she asked, in fascination.

"If it made her happy, sure. What do I care?"

"You'd never hear a Mexican guy talk that way."

"Why not?"

"Because clothes send a signal. They are a kind of code. Mexican men like to be in charge of those kind of signals."

Jackson stopped in his tracks. "You know what? Maybe you're onto something."

"Meaning what?"

"The DNA sequence, Marie-Carmen. What if it isn't meant to be a real, biological sequence, but a code we're meant to be able to *read*; a message?"

Beltran Sequence

Later in Marie-Carmen's apartment, they sat together at her computer. Earlier in the day their physical proximity might have been pleasantly distracting. Now however, Jackson was overtaken by the enthusiasm that always gripped him when discussing his work. It was strong enough to displace almost everything else that preoccupied him.

"DNA is a biological molecule made up of four types of building blocks. We assign each of these a letter: A, C, G, T. A DNA sequence reads as a long string of various combinations of ACGT."

"Difficult to convey much meaning with those four letters."

"Precisely. But that DNA code is 'read' by the machinery of the cell, and translated into a code for making proteins. It takes three letters in the DNA code to code for one amino acid. For example, the DNA triplet codon 'AAA' is translated by the cell into an amino acid named 'lysine'. Proteins are made from around twenty different building blocks; each represented by a single letter code. With *twenty* letters, you can make a lot of words in English."

"Or Spanish. After all, it is Pedro Juan's code."

"We'll check both."

They watched as Jackson opened a Web browser window to a Web site entitled "ExPASy". He stopped for a second.

"Wait up. Can the IP tracing whozit get to us here?"

Marie-Carmen smirked. "The 'IP tracing whozit'?"

"Don't make fun."

"Not make fun of you?" she mused. "Then how would I pass the time? But the answer to your question, by the way, is 'wait and see'. I have a level of control over my own computer that I don't have over the one at the University. And I'm even more paranoid. Mayan archaeology is pretty competitive."

67

Jackson nodded slowly. "OK then. Here goes."

He pasted the DNA sequence into the box under the words 'DNA Translate tool' and watched the website return the translation of the DNA into a protein sequence.

They scrutinized the resulting string of fifteen letters for a few seconds. Jackson clicked the 'Print' button. A nearby printer stirred to life.

"It doesn't look very promising. You see anything in Spanish?"

"Nope. Nor English. Maybe it's an anagram?"

"Good thinking." He opened another browser window to Google. "Let's throw this at an anagram decoder." Jackson pasted the amino acid letter sequence into the anagram tool's box. This time, after a few seconds, the screen began to fill with a long list of possible anagrams, in alphabetical order. The possibilities streamed past, seemingly interminable pages of them. Patiently, they scanned the entire list. Finally, Jackson leaned back, heavily.

"This is stupid. PJ wouldn't do this. It's too vague; there are too many permutations."

Sighing, he opened another browser at the email login page. He looked again at the email sitting in his Inbox, from PJ and tried to open it. The virus warning message came up. Just then, Jackson's cell phone, which had been charging since last night, began to buzz. A yellow flashing light indicated a call from his boss's lab. He hesitated, then let the call go to voicemail.

"Look at that," Marie-Carmen exclaimed, staring at the computer screen. "It's just one of those automatic virus emails. You're sure it's from Pedro Juan?"

Jackson pondered. "Could be. Or maybe the warning just came up because it's got an *exe* file attached. Viruses often have an attached *exe* file; that alone is enough to set off the antivirus warning. But maybe he meant to send me a program that would run by itself."

"You want to run something that could be a virus on my computer?"

Jackson gave Marie-Carmen a lopsided grin. "Would you mind very much? After all, I'm already in to you for a new VW Beetle."

"Don't forget it!"

"I'll admit it's weighing on my mind. Some of us are still just graduate students, you know."

Marie-Carmen leaned across Jackson, taking the mouse in her hand. Jackson caught his breath for a second as her fingers brushed his aside.

"Some of us didn't throw away our teenage years on a snowboard."

"Wait until I teach you, you're going to have such a different perspective."

"Fine, snow bum, we'll run Pedro Juan's program."

He double-clicked on the email's attachment. The entire screen suddenly went black; then, a small animation beginning as a colorful blob began to grow larger, magnifying to the size of the full screen.

Marie-Carmen whispered, "What is it?"

"A 3D animation of a protein structure. I wonder . . ." Jackson muttered, staring at the screen in fixed concentration. "I think that's a three-dimensional structural model of Pedro Juan's *phoenix* protein. He's got a lot further with this research than I'd imagined."

"How can you tell?"

Jackson pointed to the animation, under which a stream of text was beginning to appear. "This is a recording of an experiment; a computer modeling experiment. What we see represents just a fraction of the time the experiment actually took. PJ's been looking for amino acid sequences which bind to this protein. It's a really new technique. From the target protein – the *joust* or *phoenix*, for example – you calculate the most likely binding sites. Then you use ask the computer to create a virtual peptide – a short stretch of amino acids – which has the right shape to fit such a site. Finally, you ask the software to test each one in a virtual reality binding reaction. It takes hours. The computer suggests possible, three-dimensional matches; sequences which could, in theory, bind to the protein sequence you're looking at."

"Does the match have to be perfect?"

"In biology, you need a fairly good match. An analogy would be a computer program which matches an outfit to a really fussy dresser. It takes up so much computer power that you have to use a supercomputer to do it. Costs a fortune to get time on a program like this. And plenty of people don't think it works."

As they talked, from the string of texts which were streaming rapidly under the animated structure, one emerged, enlarged, transformed into a bright blue- and pink-colored three-dimensional model and aligned itself against a portion of the much larger model of PJ Beltran's protein.

"Look. It found a match." Looking around for the printer, Jackson pulled out the printout of the amino acid sequence. He examined it for a few seconds, before tapping the paper. "I'll bet you a new Beetle that PJ's DNA sample – let's call it the BELTRAN sequence – is actually the gene for *this* peptide." He touched a finger to the blue-and-pink colored animated structure that had just materialized on the screen. The two animations now rotated together slowly, as if locked in a tight embrace.

Marie-Carmen rose to her feet. "Would you like something to eat? Some *quesadillas*?"

Jackson continued to stare, transfixed, at the screen. "Please!"

She paused by the kitchen door. "You know I'm not taking that bet, right?"

"Why would you? You know I'm right."

He was still glued to the screen when Marie-Carmen returned. She picked up a lime-green iPod nano that was lying, headphones attached, on a sideboard made of rustic, antique pine, and pulled out the headphones. She docked the iPod, selecting a tune. The sound of melancholy piano music filled the room. It sounded vaguely familiar.

"Beethoven?"

Marie-Carmen grinned. "Sonata twenty-five, second movement. You didn't give it a chance in the car yesterday. It's better than Eminem."

"Are you kidding? Beethoven was an eighteenth-century Eminem."

Her grin broadened. On the table, next to his right hand, she placed a blue-and-white patterned plate containing six folded tortillas filled with melted cheese. Jackson took one of the *quesadillas*. They were made from maize tortillas, the stringy melted cheese inside spiced up with pickled carrots and *jalapeno* peppers drizzled with oil. He picked up a pen and jabbed at the screen.

"This blue-and-pink thing; that's the best match the computer program came up with. The most likely of all the millions of structures it tested, to bind to the *phoenix* protein. That's why PJ sent me this recording of the experiment. He's telling me that the DNA he's given me can be used to make this binding peptide."

"Look, I can see it's an interesting find for you and everything. Why all the cloak-and-dagger stuff? How can this be worth killing someone over?"

Shrugging, Jackson said, "The way I hear it, life can be very cheap in Mexico. You got these gangsters who'll kidnap people for a ten thousand peso ransom. Imagine what people would do for a valuable bit of biotechnology. PJ must have had some inkling about what this protein could do, in maize. Maybe it's the key to some incredibly salt-resistant strain of corn. Imagine what that could be worth to countries with soil salinity problems from salty river deposits?"

"Millions?"

"*Billions*," Jackson said. "Well, I'm guessing that I'm PJ's secret backup. PJ had reason to believe that he was in danger. For some reason he couldn't trust, or didn't want to endanger his own research team. So, he passed on the BELTRAN sequence and his key experimental results to me."

A note of disappointment entered Jackson's voice. "It's kind of upsetting to see how far PJ got on this, without saying a word to me about it. He's way ahead of me. I've only just worked out a 3D model for the *joust* protein. I think PJ would have been prepared to go all the way to publishing this. I always knew he was a competitive bastard! But something scared him off, Marie-Carmen."

An imperceptible shiver ran through both as they regarded, with wonder, the glowing images on the screen.

71

"Well, PJ, now you're dead," Jackson muttered. "Why didn't you trust me sooner?"

He picked up his cell phone and checked his voicemail. He listened with astonishment to the long message from his boss's personal assistant. "This is kind of unexpected," he told Marie-Carmen, who was opening two bottles of Dos Equis lager. He took a sip from the bottle she offered; the beer was ice-cold and salty. "I've just been invited to a meeting in Switzerland with a group of neuroscientists who are working on a *joust*-like protein in the human brain."

"And you sound so surprised because . . .?"

He shrugged. "I've never heard of anything like *joust* in the human genome. They must know that I'm working on the structure of the *joust* protein, because I keep talking about it in scientific conferences. But I've searched all the human gene banks and never found anything like *joust*. Also, get this; it's not just any group of neuroscientists; it's Melissa DiCanio's team."

"Is she famous?"

"She's one of those super-successful scientists; a Cambridge University professor, head of one of the best neuroscience research groups in the world, not to mention something pretty major at Chaldexx BioPharmaceuticals. The only thing she's missing is a Nobel Prize. And from the rumors, it's just a matter of time before she bags that too."

Marie-Carmen smiled slowly. "Sounds like you're keen to meet this famous DiCanio."

Jackson feigned disinterest. "I don't even think the meeting is with her. It's with one of her groups at Chaldexx. Anyway, I already met her, a few years back. Although I doubt she remembers. I was thinking of going to work with her, but in the end I stayed in San Francisco."

"She's British?"

"Actually, no. She's a good ol' gal from Texas."

"Beautiful?" asked Marie-Carmen , mischievously.

"Not bad-looking, for her age. I'd guess she's mid-forties."

"Some guys like older women."

"Some guys like *all* women," he countered. "DiCanio's attractive in a WASP-ish, Martha's Vineyard kind of way."

"I have no clue what you just said."

"You wouldn't think she's from the American South," he explained, taking another slug of beer. "She's like a typical East Coast intellectual. I'm not surprised she left Baylor, in Houston. I'd guess that Cambridge couldn't believe their luck when they recruited her. After Tripoxan, she could have taken her pick of positions at Harvard, Princeton, Stanford. It must have been quite some package to tempt her."

"You want to 'get into bed with her', don't you?" Marie-Carmen said with a sly smile.

"What?" Jackson seemed genuinely taken aback.

"Don't you use that phrase for scientific collaboration? Like in business?"

He laughed. "DiCanio's name on my papers could not hurt one bit."

"What's her big achievement?"

Jackson frowned slightly. "You must have heard of Tripoxan? The wonder-drug?"

"The anti-depressant?"

"It started out as an anti-depressant. But often-times a drug's secondary effects become more significant. Like Viagra – that was meant to be a drug for hypertension. With Tripoxan, it turned out that there was a significant effect on people with OCD – Obsessive Compulsive Disorder. You know, that thing where people have to do all these rituals or they go nuts with frustration?"

Marie-Carmen said, "The hand-washing thing?"

Jackson nodded, took a second to bite into his cheese taco. "It can be hand-washing, or counting elements of a pattern in a wall, or a carpet, or a floor; each patient chooses their own personal purgatory. Anyway, the existing treatments are all some kind of anti-depressant, like Prozac and stuff. So it wasn't too much of a surprise when Tripoxan had an effect on OCD. What was really lucky for DiCanio was that not only did Tripoxan have a good effect, but it worked at much lower doses. It had fewer side effects than the existing drugs. Even better, she managed to get a handle on how it works. Which, to be honest, was a big black box as far as it goes for all the other drugs."

He remembered hearing the news of DiCanio's discoveries, exactly six months after he'd turned down a chance to work with her. It had been hard to avoid the odd pang of 'what if?' Jackson was a victim of this torturous game, like most scientists he knew. He'd been more annoyed with himself that he was letting on, that he hadn't after all gone to work with DiCanio. This invitation felt like a second chance.

A Second Chance

Marie-Carmen dangled the green beer bottle by the neck, between her thumb and forefinger. She stared at the shiny red-and-silver label, momentarily lost in thought. "OK," she said, slowly. "Melissa DiCanio discovered Tripoxan, then what?"

"Tripoxan was a big deal, something which could begin to dissect the molecular basis of the brain-mind connection. That's kind of a holy grail for the neuroscience community."

"Did it make her rich? Famous? Both?"

"It made DiCanio's name at the university where she had her first lab. As I remember it, a few years ago she was headhunted to a biotech company in Switzerland; Chaldexx BioPharmaceuticals. Cambridge University offered her a chair, in return for which Chaldexx funded a whole new floor in the Department of Neuroscience and the Chair of Neuroscience.

"By then she was calling the shots. See, her name was on the patent for Tripoxan. DiCanio sold the patent to Chaldexx. She raised around $250 million for the clinical trials; not bad for a new biotech company. They wanted to do all the clinical trials themselves. Huge risk; if the drug hadn't worked, they'd have been in deep, deep shit. It's pretty common too, for a young company to blow that kind of cash on a drug candidate, only to have it tank. It was a long shot. For once, it paid off."

Marie-Carmen shook her head in wonder. "Wow. This kind of thing doesn't really happen in the world of archaeology."

"Are you kidding? You guys discover lost cities and ancient scrolls!"

"I was talking about the money side of things. No-one's getting rich out of archaeology. At least not legitimately. For that you have to get into the illegal antiquities trade."

"Oh, lucrative?"

Marie-Carmen shook her head, wrinkling her nose. "They make for scary company, the customers for that kind of business. Jackson, when's this meeting? And where, exactly?"

"Two days from now, in Interlaken, Switzerland. That's the headquarters of Chaldexx. Actually, they were supposed to be meeting PJ. PJ was also collaborating with Chaldexx, something to do with the three-dimensional structure of *phoenix*. DiCanio got word that PJ's been murdered. She called my boss to ask if he had someone who could take over the seminar slot."

"The show must go on," Marie-Carmen remarked, sadly.

"Hey, it's a listed company. Don't expect sentiment."

"I guess."

"So anyway, the meeting is two days from now."

Marie-Carmen looked askance. "Two days? How are you going to get out of here in time? You can't risk the airport; the Ford Explorer guys found you there in the first place; they're sure to be watching the flight departures."

Jackson hadn't even thought of that. "Jeez, you're right! And if they really are connected to Customs . . ." He stood, took a couple of paces around the room. "I'm gonna make a couple of calls, OK?"

He disappeared into the kitchen, where Marie-Carmen heard an occasional excited exchange as he discussed, first with his own lab, then someone from Chaldexx, the arrangements for his transport. Five minutes later he emerged, grinning with satisfaction.

"No problemo. It's all fixed; they have someone flying the private jet from Chetumal tomorrow; they'll swing over to in Mexico City, pick me up around 8am in the airport and take it from there."

Marie-Carmen frowned. "Chetumal? What is their private jet doing in Chetumal?"

"I don't know, is there something wrong with that?"

"It's kind of a nowhere town."

"*Where* is Chetumal?"

"Right at the south of Quintana Roo state. The same state as Cancun," she said, when Jackson merely looked at her blankly.

"Maybe someone went to the beach?"

"Not in Chetumal."

"You think it sounds weird?"

Marie-Carmen hesitated. "Not necessarily. I just can't think of a good reason for a biotech company to be dropping in."

"You want me to ask them?"

"Yes. Maybe. Oh, wait. It could be the Si'an Ka'an bioreserve, just north of Chetumal. Maybe they're doing some research there."

"I guess that's it. So, you think I should go?"

"It gets you away from the guys in the Ford Explorer. Also, the police."

"You mean the Customs guys?"

"No." Marie-Carmen lowered her eyes. "I didn't want to mention it. But the murder of my cousin is getting some coverage in the papers. The police are looking for you."

Jackson gaped. This was a total curve ball. When he recovered his breath he said, "Unreal."

"Do you think your friends at Chaldexx can get you out of the country on a false passport? Because that's probably what it's going to take."

"What the fuck! Am I a suspect?"

"I don't think so, not yet. But they've found out that you were meeting PJ. They know you're in the country."

"I guess they've spoken to PJ's lab." Jackson thought of Simon Reyes. The poor kid was almost certainly dead. When they found his body, things would turn very nasty indeed for Jackson. Chaldexx would probably want to wash their hands of him.

"Jackson . . . I think maybe you should leave right away." She stared at him with an intensity that made him catch his breath.

"I guess I have to." He hesitated. "Is it OK if I take a shower? I should probably leave, like around six tomorrow morning. If I'm gonna get to the airport."

"Make yourself at home." Marie-Carmen leaned back on her elbows and gave him a long, appraising look. Jackson held her gaze for a moment and then turned away, confused.

Was it possible that she was flirting with him, that he'd missed her cues all evening?

He thought back over their conversation as he made his way to the bathroom. He stared with hostility at his reflection in the mirror. Some things – like women and his family – should be more important than work. Intellectually, he knew that. Why did he keep remembering when it was already too late?

When he emerged from the shower dressed in jersey boxer shorts and a T-shirt, Marie-Carmen was sitting on the sofa. It was obvious that she wanted to talk.

"Doesn't it strike you as odd that this invitation should come out of the blue?"

"Yeah. I already said it was unexpected."

"I mean, with all that's going on here. In case you've forgotten, people are looking for you, with a view to ending your life. Now it seems likely that in a few hours if not already, you're going to be a suspect in a murder case."

Darkly he added, "Or two. Yes, I have been thinking about that. But what choice do I have?"

Marie-Carmen appeared unconvinced. "Something feels wrong about this. Believe me. Call it a woman's intuition, if you have to be macho about it."

He was both touched and disturbed by her unease. His own instincts were also sounding a quietly insistent note of caution; at this stage he was putting it down to paranoia.

Maybe she's as disappointed as me that I have to leave?

Marie-Carmen disappeared into her bedroom for a moment. When she returned, she presented him with a small, black-and-orange sports bag. "You should pack."

"It'll take me all of five minutes." He watched as she departed, into her bedroom, shutting the door. And although he desperately wanted to say something before the moment passed, he couldn't. "Bennett," he muttered, "you dumb fuck."

Jackson was packed and already making up the sofa bed when he heard Marie-Carmen's bedroom door open. He stood up straight as she entered the room. She stopped by the door. She was dressed for bed, in red, plaid shorts and a white camisole top.

"You arrived so unexpectedly; now it seems you have to leave just the same way."

There was no doubt. Her was voice tinged with regret. Jackson knew that this was his final chance. "If you asked me to stay, I'd stay."

To his relief, Marie-Carmen displayed no surprise, saying only "But I know you have to go to this meeting. This is your big opportunity. The private jets leave from a different part of the airport, if you're worried that those guys are still looking for you."

"Even so, Marie-Carmen; if you asked me . . ."

She interrupted, speaking very softly. "How about if I just asked you to spend the night . . . with me?"

Jackson swallowed, once. In that instant he felt the dull ache in his leg vanish. His eyes lowered slowly, from the secretive smile that touched Marie-Carmen's mouth, down to her shoulders, then to the clinging fabric of her camisole which revealed the shape of her breasts. Quite suddenly he forgot how to breathe.

Unsteadily, he walked over to the door, took her hands in his. "I was afraid you'd never ask."

Eventually, they moved to the bedroom. Marie-Carmen was the first to relax into sleep. Her fingers curled provocatively near his hip. Jackson pulled away, watching her.

He was dazed, bewildered by the unexpected release. A peculiar combination of feelings assailed him. It would be so easy to seriously fall for this woman. But the heady delirium of that sensation was almost swamped by a new fear.

What if, because of him, Marie-Carmen was now in danger? How could he protect her?

IP Traced

As the night wore on, Jackson lay restless. Until only hours ago his thoughts of Marie-Carmen were a barely coherent mixture of respect, gratitude, lust. But these had crystallized into a recognizable bombardment of feelings; feelings he hadn't felt for many months, hadn't thought he'd feel again since his last serious girlfriend had thrown him aside in favor of his more-successful, former best friend. It was a memory he tried very hard to suppress.

Although devastated, Jackson had tried to move on. He'd had hated what it had done to him, the time it had taken out of his personal and professional life. It was as though a shard of ice had become lodged inside him and instead of melting, was freezing him from within.

Marie-Carmen had done more in one hour to erase that memory than he'd managed in almost a year. He turned to look at her as she lay peacefully beside him and felt a pang of longing. For the briefest moment, a terrifying clarity overtook him: *he very badly didn't want it to be over with Marie-Carmen.*

Jackson made his decision quite suddenly. He checked his watch; it was early morning in England. There was still time to change his plans with Chaldexx. He would email them right now so that they received the message first thing.

Stealthily, he maneuvered out of the bed to avoid disturbing her and went directly to her computer. On top of the desktop, the browser was still open at Google.

He pasted some text into Google's search box, assuming it was still the text containing DiCanio's name which he'd used to investigate her before. But evidently, Marie-Carmen had been looking over the sequence code again, because what he pasted in was in fact the amino acid code for Pedro Juan's peptide – the BELTRAN sequence.

Although he had searched across all manner of databases, Jackson realized that he had not actually searched for the occurrence of the sequence openly available on the Web.

Google returned just one result: a website which encompassed the entire amino acid sequence – and nothing else – into the domain name:

www.agylihrppreikgr.com

With a sense of disbelief, Jackson clicked on the link. The browser window went instantly black and then a smooth transition as a Flash animation began to play. A low sound crackled through the speakers. The hairs on his neck prickled. A series of strange, flame-colored hieroglyphs began to appear. The sound grew louder and more ominous, until it was a steady humming buzz – almost white noise but with an unsettling quality; that of a crowd, whispering.

A box resembling a chat window appeared. A series of numbers flashed past, beneath the box. Jackson watched for a few seconds. The sequence was counting down. In the white space for text, a cursor flashed, invitingly.

He clicked the mouse. Tentatively, he typed: **hello?**

Astonished, he watched as words began to appear on the screen in reply.

Hello, Mr. Bennett. I see you are still in Mexico City.

Jackson was too stunned to move. More letters appeared:

You may as well talk to me. You've already made your mistake. Here you are. Just a matter of steady, number-crunching, time before I track you down.

Cold dread swept through Jackson. But he couldn't tear himself away. His fingers moved almost mechanically: *Who are you?*

My name is Hans Runig.

The name meant nothing to Jackson.

A symbol appeared on the bottom right hand of the computer, just as at the library: WARNING. SOMEONE IS TRYING TO TRACE YOUR IP ADDRESS.

You were at the university library today weren't you? Rude of you not to wait to say hello. My men have put a lot of effort into meeting you. Make no mistake, before long, they will.

Jackson pushed back the chair. He had to wake Marie-Carmen. But before he turned around, he noticed a yellow shield symbol flash momentarily on the screen, giving way to a grey dialogue box on which the words: "IP Masking Software in use. Advise you disconnect Internet connection within 5 minutes."

From behind him, he heard Marie-Carmen's sleepy voice.

"You see. I'm not just a pretty face; and I don't like people who snoop on me over the Internet."

The text box where Hans Runig's words appeared sprang to life once more.

What's this? IP masking software? Impressive. I think you've found someone to help you, Mr. Bennett. You're not that smart around computers, are you? At least that's what Dr. Beltran used to say about you. So, who's helping you? Is it that pretty girl from the Beetle? That silver Beetle?

They both froze. Marie-Carmen's fingers touched Jackson's. Then she leaned over the computer, pulled out the connection from the wall plug into the DSL modem, effectively removing her computer and modem from the Internet.

On the screen were the final words typed by their correspondent:

The channels of investigation may encounter arbitrary resistance, Mr. Bennett. But clarity will prevail. This is mere digression. Everywhere we go, we are observed. Someone, somewhere, will be willing to talk.

Jackson and Marie-Carmen stared at each other for a few seconds, before Jackson managed to ask, "What the hell just happened?"

Marie-Carmen was already gathering belongings into a pile, hunting in a closet for a suitcase.

"I pasted PJ's sequence into Google. There's a website with that address?"

She stopped moving. "But . . . why?"

"Some kind of trap. Anyone who searches for that sequence on the Web is going to wind up clicking on that link. Someone called 'Hans Runig' starts getting all chatty."

"You know him?"

Jackson shook his head. "Nope. You?"

"Never heard of the guy. Looks like you tripped his IP tracing software again, like at the university. The software I installed can mask our computer's IP address, for a while. Then it becomes like a battle of wits. Their software tries to crack our software. My money would be on theirs. I didn't pay for mine, just downloaded it for free on the Internet. It gives you a five minute warning to disconnect."

"So – we're safe?"

Marie-Carmen shrugged. "Seems this Hans Runig has put a couple of facts together since last night. I'd guess they've realized that my stopping the car right there was just too much of a coincidence. They must have tracked down the new owners, got the license plate and model of the car I took, that heap-of-junk Tsuru."

He began to dress. "Come to Switzerland with me."

Marie-Carmen sighed, irritated. "Don't you get it? We can't be seen together anymore. We need to go right now, take a taxi, then separate. You go to the airport and wait for your ride to Switzerland."

Jackson took hold of her hands, stopping her as she moved busily, nervously around the apartment.

"I'm supposed to leave you to be found?"

Marie-Carmen gave him a tender smile. "Don't worry. I'll take a bus out of state. I've saved up some money and technically, I'm still on sabbatical. I'll go to Acapulco and hide in a hotel. I'll always be around people. We'll stay in touch over the Internet."

83

"Alone? In Acapulco?"

"Sure, I'll read books by the beach by day and go salsa dancing by night."

Indignantly, he blurted, "Guys will hit on you!"

She gave him a little shove in the chest. "Listen to you! How long will it take you to forget me when you're with the famous scientist lady in Switzerland?"

"But what should I do," Jackson asked, his eyes wide, innocent, "if she wants me bad?"

Marie-Carmen raised a highly doubtful eyebrow. "You tell her she's too old for you, *maldito*!"

"See, using bad words like that with your 'gentleman callers' could be the reason you aren't married."

Marie-Carmen's eyes flashed with genuine anger, obviously hurt. She shoved him again, harder this time. "Hey, where's *your* wife? Or are you one of those who likes to play the field until he's over forty?"

"I'm trying to be serious, just for a second. Is there someone else I should know about? Because I'd kind of like to know."

"There was. I made a big mistake."

Jackson ventured, "Was he . . . ?"

"Married? Yes. I was stupid."

"There's no-one now?"

She replied, "I don't know, Jackson. Is there?"

In response he kissed her, easing her back down on the bed.

"Promise me you won't go with some stupid, fucking Italian whilst you're in Acapulco," he murmured, quoting broadly from his favorite Mexican movie, *Y Tu Mama También*.

She chuckled, kissed him back and whispered, "I won't 'go with any stupid, fucking Italians'. Or Brazilians, Frenchmen, Americans or Mexicans."

"Good." He tried to sound satisfied.

"Don't you go with the glamorous rich lady."

"I won't," he said as he kissed each corner of her mouth. "Even if she begs."

Parting

Less than one hour later they left the apartment, strolled into the cool dark of the condominium's gardens. The sky was an opaque, rusty orange, the reflection of the city lights a solid barrier to the night sky. As they walked past the security post, the guard stirred to life.

"You're leaving, *señorita*?"

"Taking the bus to Valle de Bravo. Stupid car can't be trusted to make the trip!"

Marie-Carmen observed the guard carefully. He asked, "Is there a contact number?"

"Thanks, that's OK. My family knows where I stay in Valle."

They walked into the street, in which shadows danced between the old wrought iron lamps and the tall trees which lined the road. "'Valle de Bravo', hey?" murmured Jackson. "That's quite some diversion from Acapulco. Are you suspicious of your security guard now?"

"When they work out where I live, which we have to assume they will, the first thing they'll do is to bribe the security guard." She paused briefly. "Jackson, you really don't know anything about Hans Runig?"

"No clue at all. I was going to search for his name on the Internet but . . ."

"You should be very careful about what you search for on the Internet. Until you buy some secure Web surfing software."

"What's that?"

"There are programs that you can use to surf the Web anonymously. That way, your searches and emails sent via the Web can't be traced back to you. I'll look out for something and email the link to you."

"When will I see you again?"

Marie-Carmen just stared at him, shaking her head. "I don't know yet, but we'd better think of a plan."

They walked to the nearest taxi rank – Marie-Carmen refused to risk picking up a passing taxi – and rode together to a large shopping mall near the *Universidad* metro station where they found a late night VIPS café. The place was relatively busy with a mixture of the excitable post night-club crowd and exhausted shift workers. They picked one of the red leather-seated booths and held hands, sharing coffee and frozen lemon cream pie.

Jackson picked up the fresh paper drink coaster. An idea hit him. He removed the DNA sample from his pocket; at the lab he had diluted it further, so there were now almost 250 micro liters – a volume roughly equivalent to two teardrops. He flicked the tube so that the sample landed, blotting onto the coaster. He asked for a clean, sharp knife. With immense precision, he sliced the coaster into two parts, placing each in a clean napkin. On each he had written a brief note of instructions, a name and address; two people in San Francisco.

He handed them to Marie-Carmen.

"Can you mail these for me? As soon as possible? It's really important that you don't touch them with your fingers, or anything which could be moist."

She received them into an open paperback book.

"Now, that's *my* secret backup."

At 5am the café closed. The clientele spilled out onto the steps next to Plaza Universidad. It was still dark when they emerged. To one side was the rare sight of Avenida Universidad relatively free of traffic; to the other the empty parking lot of the now sleepy shopping mall.

Jackson sensed a sudden awkwardness between himself and Marie-Carmen. He could hardly believe that the moment had finally arrived to take their leave from one another. It really felt as though he should take the initiative, set the tone for the farewell. But he balked. Words, phrases that had been forming in his head already sounded trite as he imagined himself mumbling them.

As Marie-Carmen stood next to him, waiting expectantly on the steps in front of VIPS, Jackson found himself speechless, reduced to an uncertain smile.

"What's wrong?" she asked him. "You don't want to kiss me goodbye?"

Marie-Carmen clasped her arms around his neck. He couldn't resist returning the embrace. Even through their clothing, he could feel the warmth of her body. With her fingers she traced the line of his jaw. He shivered at the memory of her skin flowing beneath his.

"I don't want to say goodbye either," she said, "But since I don't know when I'm going to see you again . . ."

She kissed him deeply and without reserve. Jackson clung to her for minutes, refusing to let go.

"Make me a nice farewell," she insisted.

He replied with a helpless shrug, "It's no good. Can't do it."

Marie-Carmen pulled away, brusquely. "You're going to have to do better than that," she said, walking away.

He gave her a conciliatory wave and called out, "I'll see you again real soon. In the meantime, I'll write."

"Sure; I can imagine. The last of the Great Romantics." Marie-Carmen turned on her heel as she approached the taxi rank. She rewarded him with an unexpected, adorable smile.

***

Marie-Carmen took a taxi to the southern bus terminal, Jackson to the city center. He walked the streets of the old colonial heart of the city, a few moments of quiet tourism before taking a Metro train to the airport.

Even at this hour the airport hummed with activity. Jackson bought a paperback and hid behind it at a coffee bar. He was well aware that he'd chosen the furthest one from where he'd met PJ Beltran, just two days ago. Jackson doubted that he'd ever again be able to eat anything; the thought of what had happened to PJ made him feel queasy. With just ten minutes to go before his rendezvous with the Chaldexx representatives, an impulse took hold of Jackson. He went to the Internet café and paid for the minimum five minutes.

Straight away, he logged onto Hans Runig's site.

In the crowded, noisy hall of the airport, the animated, flashing symbols and gloomy music had nothing of the impact of the night before. Jackson waited, watching the ticking of the counter for his Internet access. With just two minutes to go before his time ran out, text began to appear in the window.

Quite a surprise, Mr. Bennett.

Jackson typed: *What's your interest in all this?*

I'm someone whose business interests were being threatened by Dr. Beltran. That had to end.
What makes you think I'm Bennett?
Because the only other person who knows the code sequence is dead. Unless you told your friend, your helper.
You're on the wrong track there. The girl who gave me a lift dropped me at the university. You're wasting your time looking for her.
Now . . . why would you tell me that?

Jackson's heart almost stopped. His adversary was clearly no fool, why had he risked such an obvious lie?

I think you're lying. You're trying to protect her. She matters, doesn't she? Who is she? A friend of Dr. Beltran's? Whoever she is, Mr. Bennett, we'll find her. We'll find you both.

The Internet access timed out. A deep chill began to invade Jackson's chest, a sense of his own stupidity and the desperate consequences that might now follow.

The Princess

The lobby of the Fairmont Acapulco Princess Hotel bustled with the daily arrivals and departures; white-uniformed porters whisked about, their trolleys piled high with luggage, guests queued to check in and out.

Marie-Carmen stepped out of the taxi, enjoying the cool breeze which swept in directly from the Pacific Ocean through the hotel's marble lobby. It was a huge space; the hollow center of a pyramid-shaped hotel which had once been the most famous hotel in all Mexico.

As Marie-Carmen waited, she noticed a large poster board on which was written "Fairmont Acapulco Princess welcomes the 15th Annual Meeting of the American Society of Ancient History Teachers." A few nervous-looking pale, predominantly white, Anglo and female persons had begun to aggregate in the vicinity of the poster; it seemed that the conference was beginning that day. Just then they were joined by a tall, good-looking man in his mid-thirties. He sported a crisply-ironed *guayabera*, similar to those worn by the hotel staff, and an infectious grin. The group immediately perked up. His sandy-brown hair was short at the back but with a long, unruly fringe. Twice, while Marie-Carmen was looking, he ran a hand through his fringe as he stared into the middle distance, like a yachtsman in a sea breeze.

Behind a hand, Marie-Carmen smiled. In her experience, guys like that were perfectly aware of every ripple of attention they drew. Every gesture was calculated to reinforce the initial, usually favorable impression. She found herself thinking immediately of Jackson. There was a good chance that he didn't even realize how attractive he was. He certainly didn't seem to spend much time worrying about what impression he made.

The sandy-haired guy was surrounded by his apparently admiring, mainly female colleagues. Out of the corner of her eye, Marie-Carmen thought she sensed his eyes on her, just for the briefest minute.

She was well used to such glances, often covert, usually investigative. In this case, however, her response was modified by an additional factor; the uncomfortable sense of being hunted. Her eyes wandered around the lobby, watching for anyone whose gaze might seem to be fixed for anything more than a fraction of a second, on her. Some people returned her glances, but only for acceptably short stretches of time.

She forced herself to calm down. There was no way she could have been traced to this hotel, or even at this stage, to Acapulco. Marie-Carmen had thought carefully through the trail she'd left, concluded that it could lead no further than the security guard at her condo building. He'd been briefed to divert attention to the lakeside town of Valle De Bravo, a popular holiday destination from Mexico City.

Anxiety was useful only as far as it kept her alert. Rampant paranoia, she figured, was best avoided.

Within the hour Marie-Carmen had checked in and changed into a deep orange bikini and a green silk sarong shot with golden thread. Anywhere else it would have been an arresting outfit. At the Acapulco Princess, Marie-Carmen was fairly certain that it would help her to fit in. She looked out of the window of her 19th floor room, staring at the view over two 18-hole golf courses studded with palm trees and glittering blue water traps.

In its eighties heyday, the Princess had been a retreat for the rich and famous. The spectacle of a huge, modern architectural homage to an ancient Maya civic center in the midst of tropical gardens, lagoon style pools and waterfalls became one of the best known postcards of Mexico.

Although the splendor of the surroundings and service were still as impressive as ever, Acapulco itself had taken a blow as Mexico's premier beach resort. Other resort developments such as Cancun and Huatulco and lately, Cabo San Lucas, had siphoned off the cream of the tourists and seen to it that the Princess was now – just – within the reach of Marie-Carmen's salary as an archaeologist. One who liked to live extravagantly, at least.

Marie-Carmen reasoned that it would be one of the last places anyone would search for a modest academic. She opened her MacBook laptop computer on the glass table, in front of the open balcony.

First she searched for some cast-iron secure Web surfing software, which she quickly purchased and installed on her computer. Then she opened her webmail and emailed a quick message to Jackson, with a link to the software. Now, provided that they both surfed the Web from behind the protection of the software, there would be no way to track down the IP address of their computers; no way to link them to an obvious commercial, academic or geographical location.

With meticulous care, she typed in the sequence of Pedro Juan's DNA molecule, transcribing from a printout. Marie-Carmen was not yet satisfied that Jackson had searched thoroughly enough. Yes, he had searched in the databases of known DNA and protein sequences, and also in the patent databases. However, that still left plenty of places where they might find mention of the sequence.

Many authors were now publishing information straight onto the Web, not waiting for the slow process of print publication. Maybe some geneticists somewhere in the world were discussing something similar?

Marie-Carmen determined to search thoroughly, leaving no stone unturned. One hour later, she was satisfied that she had exhausted all possibilities.

The BELTRAN sequence – in its entirety as a DNA sequence or as its amino acid translation – appeared nowhere on the Web.

What about a sub-section? What if some scientists had discovered a smaller section but not the entire sequence?

Marie-Carmen's knowledge of molecular biology had reached a limit. For all she knew, a match with a smaller section would be irrelevant – a mere coincidence with no biological impact. Even so, the whole sequence of what Jackson had called the 'open-reading frame' – the part which made a product – was only 45 DNA bases long. That was short enough to try a few sections, just for fun.

Marie-Carmen took the first fifteen bases, and searched for them. Nothing. She took the middle section, then the last section; still nothing.

She glanced outside; the sky was beginning to darken. By now, however, she was gripped; she had to get a result, one way or another.

Opening a Visual Basic application, she wrote a short computer program which would submit the entire 45 letter sequence to the search engines, in a series of pieces, starting with nine letters and increasing by three letters at a time.

GCAGGUUAC
GCAGGUUACCUA
GCAGGUUACCUAAUC and so on.

Then the starting position would shift, starting at the second letter in the sequence:

CAGGUUACC
CAGGUUACCUAA
CAGGUUACCUAAUCC and so on, until the entire sequence of 45 letters had been sectioned.

Being on the cutting edge of her specialization – ancient Mayan writing – had required Marie-Carmen, years ago, to learn some simple programming. It had been a challenge, but one which had served her well. To Marie-Carmen, deciphering puzzles and codes was almost a compulsion – once she had begun, she simply had to make some progress before she would allow herself a break.

Satisfied that her scrappily-written program would at least cover a large number of the huge range of possible sequences, she coded into the evening. It was dark before the program was finished. The day's sun had been entirely wasted.

"If I get this done tonight," she promised herself, "I can go to the nightclub".

By the time her program was ready to run, she was exhausted and parched. She strolled to the cold drinks machine in the corridor, returned with sodas and a bucket of ice. The computer screen displayed a number of search results. She poured herself a tall, ice-filled glass of Mountain Dew, and began to examine the list.

This was exactly the distraction she needed, Marie-Carmen reflected. How easy it would be to fret over her cousin's murder and the insane stories that her brother had told her were now appearing in the press. It really was beginning to look as though Jackson was a suspect in PJ's murder. The injustice of it made Marie-Carmen seethe, but she reminded herself that the police didn't know what had happened to Jackson since he'd left the airport.

She and Jackson simply had to track down the identity of Hans Runig or any of his hired killers. Or at the very least, they had to find a witness to Jackson's story about being attacked in Tepoztlan.

Otherwise it would be Jackson's word against that of the police. In most justice systems, including Mexico's, that wouldn't count for much. Even though Jackson was out of Mexico for now, if the Mexican authorities put a case together, there was a good chance he'd be extradited right back.

Marie-Carmen decided to avoid thinking about this. She had to concentrate on cracking the puzzle that her cousin had left for Jackson to solve. Somewhere in that DNA, there was a message.

When she thought of Jackson, Marie-Carmen found herself experiencing an unexpected sensation of guilt. She'd allowed things to get pretty intense. Now she thought about it, she'd made all the running. It was possible that Jackson might read more into the development than she'd intended. But he'd been almost impossible to resist. Unusually vulnerable and kind of pathetic; obviously desperate to please her but without any clear strategy. Desire had oozed out of Jackson from the minute she'd picked him up in her car. The more he'd tried to conceal it, the more attractive he'd become.

Jackson couldn't have been more different from the men she usually dated, who were confident to the point of arrogance, typical machos. Not that Jackson wasn't manly; she'd sneaked a peek at some of his snow sports photos on the Web and decided that he looked pretty hot on skis. But when it came to dealing with women, he was either relatively inexperienced, just plain shy – or maybe scared. He wasn't too young to have had his heart broken, either. Maybe that was the problem? Marie-Carmen wasn't sure how she felt about that. Her own insecurities hadn't taken long to surface when he had teased her about why she wasn't married. What if there was a similar misery tucked away somewhere in Jackson's past?

Marie-Carmen forced herself to stop daydreaming about what would probably turn out to be just a one-night-stand. The more work she could do on the mysterious BELTRAN sequence, the more information she'd be able to send Jackson, in case he did wind up being arrested for PJ's murder.

After a while this turned to disappointment. She clicked on website after website only to find a partial match to the BELTRAN sequence appear in a totally irrelevant, non-biological context. Finally, one of these caught her eye; an article entitled: *Ancient Sumerian Biologists: Did the Sumerians know about the genetic code?*

The bad news was that the article was on a website whose domain name made Marie-Carmen's hopes slide:

www.archaeologyconspiracies.com

Chaldexx

Jackson studied his watch. He surveyed the myriad faces around him. Which one looked as though they might be meeting a stranded geneticist? He'd been at the meeting place for five minutes. With what he'd just experienced in his online communication with Hans Runig, five minutes had already stretched into an eternity.

He itched with a desire to leave, to vanish into the anonymity of the crowd, take a Metro train deep into the center of the city and once and for all place himself beyond the reach of Runig's people. Paranoia, he decided, is not a state of mind but rather, a physical sensation; a crawling of the flesh where the focused gaze of the object of fear fires sensors in the hairs of the arms, of the back of the neck.

"Jackson Bennett?".

He'd strayed into a reverie; the clipped tones of an African-American man in his late twenties awoke him with a snap.

"Alex Douglass – meeting you for Chaldexx Biopharmaceuticals? If you're ready to leave, we'd like to take off as soon as possible."

Jackson eyed Douglass with suspicion. Dressed in a dark blue suit and pale blue tie, Douglass looked every inch the corporate executive. Jackson didn't move.

"You got any I.D., 'Alex Douglass'?"

Douglass raised an eyebrow as he took a wallet from his jacket pocket, flipped it open to display his Chaldexx security I.D. card. The name and photo were a match. Jackson nodded.

Douglass regarded him with a bemused grin. "You seem a little jumpy."

Jackson decided to come clean. "I kind of might be in a bit of trouble with Mexican Customs. I brought some samples in VIP a couple of days ago."

"You went vial-in-pocket!" Douglass chuckled. "So what? Who hasn't?"

"Well, I have my reasons for thinking they might, on this occasion, be a little mad at me." Jackson decided that he wouldn't mention the news reports that the police were after him. A little Customs 'misunderstanding', however, was understandable. Indeed, Douglass seemed to think he was already too worried.

"Who gets caught doing vial-in-pocket? Look, just let me worry about this."

Jackson shrugged. "OK. Lead the way."

Douglass worked his way through the crowd, with Jackson following. They passed through to a part of the airport which Jackson hadn't noticed, through the quiet one-desk immigration control where his passport and Douglass's underwent a brief examination. He watched, his breath held as the immigration officer simply flicked through and then stamped both booklets.

Jackson's name didn't seem to have triggered any watch-list. Maybe Customs weren't bothered with the possibility of him leaving the country? Maybe it was because his passport wasn't yet the newer, digital kind. Or maybe the rules were different in this part of the airport? Looking around, Jackson noticed a tangible air of privilege. Just beyond the desk the departure lounge was populated with handful of urbane, sleekly-dressed men and women, awaiting their private jets. A few sipped sparkling wine from fluted glasses.

"See?" Douglass turned to Jackson with a broad grin. "No problem."

"OK so maybe I am a little paranoid. But seriously, how did you do that?"

Douglass took him down some stairs, before answering.

"Let's just say that in this part of the airport we pay a little extra for treatment that's fast and hassle-free."

Jackson followed Douglass out of the terminal and onto the tarmac where fifty yards distant, stood a ten-seater Gates Learjet. They climbed aboard. Minutes later, the jet began to taxi towards the runway.

The jet had been furnished to an appreciable level of comfort. Seats were thickly upholstered; there was a soft, brown leather-covered couch. After the take-off Douglass unbuckled and took a seat on the couch. He opened a small cupboard set into the table in front of the couch, removed two glass tumblers and an ice bucket.

"What are you drinking?"

Jackson clicked open his safety belt. "J&B with a little ginger ale. Isn't this plane kind of small to be going all the way to Switzerland?"

Douglass grinned. "We're going via Miami. You're booked on a Swiss Air flight which leaves in around four and a half hours, gets you into Geneva for tonight."

"Uh huh." Jackson paused briefly. "Seems like a lot of trouble to go to, maybe I should have taken a commercial flight from Mexico City?" It seemed only reasonable to acknowledge the extra effort being made by Chaldexx to help him.

"Melissa . . . Professor DiCanio, is keen to meet with you as early as possible. The flights from Mexico City were full until the day after tomorrow."

"We in a hurry, Alex?"

Douglass clinked his glass to Jackson's. "Oh yeah, Melissa's one driven lady; she's always in a hurry."

Jackson could imagine; he'd come across the type before, running from meeting to meeting, always too important to arrive on time, always taking 'urgent' calls on their cell phones. As much as he usually hated this behavior, in a woman he found it somehow appealing.

"How long have you worked at Chaldexx?"

"I helped set up the US office. We're based out of Boston. It's mostly business development, investor relations and such-like. All the research goes on in Switzerland."

"You flew in from Chetumal, right? So what's the interest there?"

Douglass hesitated. Jackson felt certain that he saw the executive's jaw tighten. "Oh, we have some interests in biodiversity. There's a nature reserve in Quintana Roo state."

"You have a base there, or what?"

Douglass's smile couldn't have been more glacial. "Something like that. So tell me, Jackson, how'd a guy like you get the attention of Melissa DiCanio?"

Jackson considered. "I met her a few years ago, visited some labs in Baylor. I was looking to take up a PhD position there, but it didn't pan out. Didn't really want to move away from San Francisco."

Douglass nodded. "SF is a cool city. Anyway, Melissa moved to England around then."

"Yeah. All the same, you know what? Melissa had some influence on my work, even if I didn't end up going to her lab."

"How so?"

"I'd almost forgotten," Jackson mused. "But actually, a conversation with Melissa led me to start working on *joust*. We were talking about the role of transposons in evolution, wondering whether or not there could be transposons from two completely different species; say, a fly and a human, but which would have significantly the same DNA sequence, and even a similar function. Just dreaming, really, the way you get to doing sometimes. Melissa said that it would be a really interesting project, and I guess I agreed, was intrigued, and I followed it up."

Douglass smirked. "You must have made an impression."

Jackson burst out laughing. "Hey man, don't hold back. I may not have quite put the finishing touches on my thesis, but that's only because I've been kind of busy with *joust*."

"You don't want to stop to write up, I get that. You'll never find a job if you don't get the doctorate."

Jackson swallowed the last of his whiskey. His boss often made the same point. Yet still he couldn't bring himself to stop the experiments and get on with writing.

Douglass leaned over with the bottle of J&B and refilled his glass. "Jackson, why not relax, make yourself at home? You're booked first class on the Swiss Air flight, so pal, you've got some sixteen hours of luxury coming to you."

Jackson sipped his whisky. He sank deep into the couch and closed his eyes. For the first time in three days, he felt safe.

The following morning a driver met him in the lobby of Interlaken's Hotel Victoria-Jungfrau. Jackson had risen early to enjoy a sauna and then dressed in the new shirt and trousers that Marie-Carmen had picked out for him, as well as his suede jacket. He felt nervous and curiously eager to make a good impression in this second meeting with DiCanio. With PJ out of the picture, Jackson was now pretty much the world expert on the biology of jumping-genes like *joust* and *phoenix*. It was a fairly arcane area of biology. He couldn't help but wonder why a drug company like Chaldexx would be remotely interested in their work.

The car drove through crisp, mountain air towards the lakeside headquarters of Chaldexx BioPharmaceuticals. The five-story building was starkly presented glass and smooth concrete, the water-facing side clad in pristine, blond pinewood. The main staircase was on the outside, floor-to-ceiling glass providing spectacular views of the deep blue-green Lake Brienz.

The driver stopped the car, then ran over to open Jackson's door. He escorted Jackson to the entrance, where Jackson was met by a man in his twenties dressed in jeans and a sports jacket.

"Hi, you must be Jackson Bennett! I'm Andrew Browning. It's really good to meet you."

The British man shook his hand with enthusiasm.

"Melissa's just finishing off a presentation to some guys from the Frankfurt Stock Exchange."

The young man continued energetically, leading Jackson through the marble-floored lobby, grabbing a visitor badge at the reception desk, and then on into a wide corridor.

"She asked me to get you anything you want from the staff restaurant, and then to give you the tour. She told me to be sure to tell you that she's *really* sorry that she couldn't do the tour herself, but, you know how it is."

Jackson was acutely aware already that he had absolutely *no* idea how it was to be a top biotechnology executive, with a private jet at his beck and call, a crowd of highly educated young people eager to do your bidding and a diary crammed with dates with the commercial world's most influential 'movers and shakers'. He didn't buy that Melissa was 'really sorry' at all – people in her position didn't give 'the tour' to people like him. In fact, he was faintly surprised that Browning had been told to say that she was. Yet, the vigorous young British man seemed absolutely sincere.

"Melissa wants us to make you as comfortable as possible. Frankly, we were completely taken aback by the news about Pedro Juan Beltran. It's unthinkable. Do you know if the police have any leads yet, on who killed him? Or why?"

"You knew PJ?" asked Jackson.

"I met him a couple of times here over the past few months. He'd been involved in collaboration with us. Melissa goes way back with PJ's boss. They were all hoping to get a thing going between Chaldexx and Temixco. Melissa loves Mexico; I think she misses being in Texas and being able to nip across there whenever she likes. Her mum lives in Mexico – San Miguel de Allende, you know. Retired. An artist. Got a fabulous house, by all accounts. Melissa's seen her right since things started to take off for us here."

Andrew continued, merrily chattering on about DiCanio and her achievements at Chaldexx. Jackson was simply flabbergasted. It wasn't so much unusual for a highly-placed executive to inspire such apparent devotion in an underling, as unheard of. He remembered DiCanio as a somewhat attractive if awkward and rather formal woman. She hadn't exactly exuded charm. Could it be that the trappings of power and success had changed all that? Or maybe she'd been sent on some particularly effective leadership training? He found it hard to imagine DiCanio worshipping at the feet of one of the world's more eclectic management gurus, but you never could tell. Money and influence changed people; that much he'd seen at first hand.

But was that all? Listening to the Chaldexx man, Jackson felt a vague sense of displacement, as though a gear was being turned inside his brain. Whatever he'd expected from the meeting, it wasn't this. He sensed he was being drawn into territory that was both foreign and entirely irresistible.

Marie-Carmen picked up the phone and ordered a salad *niçoise* from room service. Waiting for the delivery, she plugged her iPod nano into the room's stereo system, selected a playlist of tropical dance music. She smiled at the memory of Jackson trying to ingratiate himself with her by claiming to enjoy reggaeton. It was always possible that he actually did, she told herself, but that would be unusual, for a white, Anglo, North-American guy like Jackson. Much more likely that he was trying to impress her. And quite cool, if so, that he hadn't gone for something more typically Mexican, like *norteños* or Luis Miguel.

After allowing the music to loosen her limbs a little, Marie-Carmen answered the door to the room service delivery and took her salad over to the glass table where she'd left her MacBook. The web browser was open at Archaeologyconspiracies.com

She'd had a run-in with this website before. The authors had reprinted an article she'd co-authored with Professor Andres Garcia of the University of Oxford, about the possible discovery of a fifth codex of the ancient Maya. The article had got Marie-Carmen into no end of trouble with her peers. A fellow Mayanist and former tutor of hers had even cancelled Marie-Carmen's appearance at a conference. He'd telephoned to explain her rejection, a conversation that still made Marie-Carmen's cheeks sting at the memory of the sheer disdain in his tone.

The idea that there might be an undiscovered, fifth codex of the ancient Maya, was not itself so controversial. It was the fact that the codex of which Marie-Carmen and Andres Garcia had written – the fabled 'Ix' Codex – was said to have the so-called Mayan 'doomsday' prophecy of 2012 as its theme.

Like all archaeologists, Marie-Carmen knew the 2012 'prophecy' was likely nothing more than a highly imaginative misreading of the Mayan calendar. As in all scientific pursuits, a tiny area of doubt remained; a doubt that required a continued search for new evidence. When Andres Garcia had asked for her a second opinion about the decipherment of some inscriptions he'd found, Marie-Carmen had agreed with him. The article they'd produced hadn't completely changed her mind, but she was now more open to the idea that a fifth codex might indeed exist.

But whether it could really have anything to do with '2012'? Such 'conspiracy theories', it seemed to Marie-Carmen, rarely advanced the knowledge of archaeology in any meaningful way. Yet she couldn't deny it – they raised the profile and glamour of her profession. Marie-Carmen knew only too well. The reality consisted of something far less exotic: painstaking, detailed research and endless verification of available evidence. Bizarre mythologies and dreams of buried gold had turned archaeology into a rather sexy undergraduate subject at university. As a tenured faculty member with a 'job for life', Marie-Carmen could only be grateful for that.

Nevertheless, she examined the article in more detail. The author was an amateur archaeologist. He described how he had acquired an ancient Mesopotamian pot several years ago in an auction, the original owner a German collector who had found the pot on an excavation of Tell 'Uqair about eighty miles south of Baghdad, back in the 1920s.

The pot contained five clay tablets, immaculately preserved, each inscribed with clearly visible cuneiform. The pot had probably been found originally in the ruins of a settlement. The place had been sacked and burned to the ground. This had the effect of firing the clay tablets, rendering indelible any writing.

Teaching himself from textbooks to read the Sumerian cuneiform script, the author claimed that one of the tablets was of particular interest because it used twenty symbols or 'logograms', whose meanings were known, but in an entirely novel context.

Marie-Carmen knew enough about Sumerian cuneiform writing to be aware that like some modern languages such as Hungarian (but unlike ancient Mayan, her own specialty), the language was 'agglutinative', a type of language in which words are built up by stringing forms together. Therefore, a basic word, symbolized by a collection of markings known as a 'logogram', could be made more complex by the serial addition of different vowels and consonants. These would be built up as additional markings on the original logogram. Together, the additional markings and the original 'root' logogram, would now convey a new meaning. Sometimes, two different logograms would be combined to create a composite logogram, with a new meaning.

The author had discovered that all five clay tablets appeared to deal with matters of medicine and the treatment of various ailments. Of these five, one tablet contained twenty logograms with 'supplementary signs' to help clarify any 'polyphony'.

Yet these supplementary signs were entirely mystifying. This made it impossible to understand the meaning of a single logogram.

The problem was polyphony – one word with multiple meanings. When teaching undergraduates this concept, Marie-Carmen would use as an example, the English word 'fleet' which can mean 'speedy' or alternatively, a collection of 'naval vessels'.

In Sumerian writing, polyphony was widely used. Supplementary signs appeared as modifications to certain logograms where more than one meaning was possible. These modifications would help place the logogram into the correct context. In the article, the author had used the example of the logogram for the word 'naga', which when modified in a certain manner could signify 'raven', instead of 'soap'.

The supplementary signs which appeared on this particular tablet with twenty logograms were totally unknown. They were unlike any which had already been observed on this set of logograms. The meaning of these logograms was logically, therefore, something other than it would be in any another context. But what?

The logograms were grouped into seven groups. The numbers of logograms in each group were one of six, two of three and four of two. Alongside each logogram on the tablet was a brief description, which the author translated as consisting of phrases such as:

entukumše igi – 'As long as the first'.

In addition, on the reverse side of the tablet the entire list of logograms appeared again, this time not grouped but simply ordered according to a single property, translated by the author as 'solubility'. The author had in fact interpreted the phrase *'ul eš'* as 'love of water' or more precisely, solubility.

The author's conclusion was astonishing. It would be thought radical by any respectable archaeologist, whether a Sumerologist or not. That included Marie-Carmen.

The fact that there were twenty of these strangely modified logograms and their groupings, had inspired something described by the author (perhaps in a moment of hubris?) as 'a remarkable flash of insight'. The revelation had been this: a stunning reminder of his biology classes at college. He'd remembered that just twenty amino acids were the basic building blocks of proteins, which performed most biological functions.

The twenty amino acids were grouped into one group of six (known by modern biologists as 'aliphatic'), two of three amino acids ('basic' and 'aromatic') and four of two ('acidic', 'hydroxlyic', 'amidic', 'sulphur-containing')?

The exact same number and sizes of groups as that of the twenty logograms.

Marie-Carmen realized now why the author was being featured in what was effectively a crackpot website. Ancient Sumerian understanding of amino acids? It seemed ridiculous. Knowledge of biochemistry, which had only come to light in the 20th century could not have been lost for thousands of years. Could it?

The author argued that these unusually modified logograms actually represented twenty amino acids.

Moreover, continued the article, the descriptions appended to each logogram seemed to compare each of the logograms to the others in the group, comparing properties such as their length and alkalinity. Finally, the entire list as it appeared on the reverse of the clay tablet could be used to place the logograms in order of inherent solubility.

This, claimed the author, was analogous to comparing the molecular lengths, alkalinity and solubility of the carbon-based amino acids. Using this rudimentary guide to the relative properties of each amino acid, reasoned the author, it should be possible to work out which logogram represented which amino acid.

Marie-Carmen read on in disbelieving fascination as the author continued, ending up with a table in which he claimed to have translated the logograms into their alternative, or secondary meaning as amino acids.

He concluded with a direct quotation from the clay tablet, which he claimed represented a sequence of amino acids. He translated the logogram sequence into the single letter amino acid code, and then into a DNA sequence.

This, Marie-Carmen realized, was how the Web search engine had picked out the article.

A sequence of fifteen letters from Pedro Juan's DNA code exactly matched a sequence in the DNA translation of the Sumerian clay tablet. For good measure, the author had added the Sumerian words and translation of each logogram in its unmodified, original meaning.

GYLIH = **GGUUACCUAAUCCAU** = lugal an un na ki = Master people of heaven and earth

Even without the requisite knowledge to pass judgment on the author's biochemical theories, she couldn't ignore the biggest problem with his thesis. It flew in the face of all that was known of the scientific knowledge of the Ancient Sumerian culture. The Sumerians were generally credited with having invented writing, but advanced knowledge of biochemistry? It was unheard of. Marie-Carmen doubted that any respectable epigraphy, philology or archaeology journal would have given the article the time of day.

Her own opinion was that the logograms were probably modified by a child, playing with the clay after the writer had finished his work: the ancient world's equivalent of drawing little hearts and flowers on the dots of the letter 'i'. The little act of vandalism may well have earned the child a beating – which, as far as Marie-Carmen was concerned, he deserved for the hours of wasted time he had cost the article's author!

Tired and listless from the apparently fruitless nature of her days' work, she stood, stretching from hours of sitting at the laptop. She'd had enough. The hotel's nightclub beckoned. She took a shower, was preparing to dress when she was overcome with a sense of just how tired she was. Suddenly the thought of being alone in a nightclub while on the other side of the world, Jackson slept, seemed impossibly, unbearably sad. Still in her towel, Marie-Carmen lay on top of the sheets.

Sleep invaded her senses, dragging her in like a swamp. Just before she was sucked under, her thoughts returned to Pedro Juan. There'd been so little time to think, she'd barely had a moment in which to mourn him. She hadn't seen him in several months, but could imagine the scenes of grief among her family – scenes which ought to have included her. What would her family make of her absence? Her presence at the funeral looked unlikely at this point. Marie-Carmen's sudden, unexpected disappearance would now add to her family's anguish over Pedro Juan's murder.

Pedro Juan had discovered something worth being killed for. The secret had to lie in the biochemical properties of the DNA samples that he'd planted on Jackson Bennett. Or else it was hidden in a message encoded by the molecule. Perhaps an anagram of the letters?

Was it possible that such a seemingly preposterous article could shed some light on the puzzle of the 'BELTRAN' sequence'? Her professional opinion of the article was low. Still, Marie-Carmen decided that it might be prudent to share her discovery with Jackson. And to call her family, let them know that she was safe. It was the last thought she had before drifting into a deep, exhausted slumber.

As they passed the boardroom, Andrew stopped in front of the door.

"She asked me to just pop in and give her the nod when we were halfway through the tour. Let's just give the old girl a wave, shall we?"

He then opened the door, in which four sharp-suited executives from the Frankfurt Stock Exchange were intently listening to the concluding comments of Melissa DiCanio. They seemed astonished at the intrusion. DiCanio herself just beamed and waved at Andrew and Jackson.

"Hey Jackson! Great to see you! I'll be with you in just a second, darlin'! Andrew's gonna take care of you real nice."

Jackson was beside himself with amazement. Last time he'd met DiCanio she had been coolly professional, distant. From the impression he thought he'd made, he would easily have believed her if she'd acted as though she had never met him before.

Finally, he said to Andrew, with a puzzled grin, "I don't get it. She's being so friendly. Yet, really, she hardly knows me. She's completely different to how she was four years ago."

Andrew was only vaguely interested. "It's probably because you're a Yank. She gets all freaked out about so many of us being Brits. Thinks we talk oddly and don't have good manners around ladies."

Jackson imagined what it would be like to be one of the only American fellows of a Cambridge college and on the board of a mostly European-staffed biotechnology company. Could it possibly be so isolating that one would begin to yearn for the company of a compatriot? Jackson found it unlikely. He'd have expected an Anglophile like DiCanio to be in her element.

Andrew escorted Jackson to the staff restaurant. They picked out apple-cinnamon muffins and white-glazed doughnuts from the morning tea selection.

"So, Andrew, let me ask you this," said Jackson. "What's your role in the organization?"

"I'm officially Head of Strategic Planning. Unofficially that means that I run around looking after Melissa and bouncing ideas with her, coming up with proposals, writing presentations for the Frankfurt Stock Exchange, you know, that sort of thing."

"Did you prepare an agenda for my time here?"

"Not exactly. Melissa wants to wing it a bit. She's cleared the rest of the morning to spend with you. Really, your guess is as good as mine."

"She's 'cleared the rest of the morning'? Aren't I going to meet with some of the scientists? Do you want me to give a presentation? Can you at least give me a clue?"

Andrew chuckled. "No idea, mate. Just relax. She wants to have a bit of a pow-wow is my guess."

Jackson had to ask the question that now inflamed his curiosity.

"Is this kind of treatment normal? By her standards, I mean."

Andrew appeared to consider this. "Well, she's got that whole southern United States courtesy thing obviously, so that's pretty normal. Melissa often does prepare agendas. Then again, she does have quite a few of these lock-in type sessions now and again. I don't get involved with all of them. Lots of what we do here is pretty hush-hush. I don't get nosy when I'm not invited. Your thing, though, is right up my alley. So I reckon I'll be joining you for part of the day at least."

Jackson was just polishing off the last of his muffin when DiCanio appeared. With a wide grin she walked over to greet him, hand outstretched.

"Jackson, goodness, it's so great to see you again after all these years! How the heck are you?"

Jackson stood up, shaking her hand. He took her in with his eyes. DiCanio's clothes and coiffure were much improved from what he remembered, as one might expect of a woman who now had the means to fund the best couture and grooming that money could buy.

Her hair, which had once been an unremarkable light brown color and style, was elegantly cropped and colored in subtle variations of blonde. She wore predominantly grey and cream, not a business suit as such but obviously carefully selected, expensive-yet-understated garments, cut and fitted with a practiced eye.

It was not a look that Jackson was accustomed to in the professional women he knew. Most of them were fellow lab scientists and shared his love for the shabby/casual. Others, in the professions or business would force themselves to wear business suits when necessary. He reflected on how loftily inaccessible DiCanio's clothes made her look, by comparison with Marie-Carmen's more naturalistic and frankly sensual mode of dress.

There was little doubt in his mind which type of woman he preferred. He almost smiled when he remembered his joking promise to Marie-Carmen, making a mental note to tell her by email that he was safe from DiCanio's charms.

The pleasantries aside, DiCanio's tone turned grave.

"We were so devastated to hear about Pedro Juan, I can't tell you."

"Yeah, it was awful. How did you hear?"

"When we didn't get a response to the email inviting him out here, well, we just called in to check things out. Then we hear this just *terrible* news about Pedro Juan and Simon Reyes, can you imagine?"

Jackson felt his heart sink; his worst fears were confirmed.

"Simon Reyes?"

"Yes. Didn't you know? I thought you'd know. Simon disappeared. Apparently on the way to meet you!"

Jackson's tone became urgent as the full implications of her phone call to the Temixco lab began to sink in.

"Professor DiCanio. . . did you mention, to PJ's people in the lab, that you would be meeting me here in Switzerland?"

DiCanio reacted with obvious puzzlement.

"Why, yes. What's wrong, Jackson? Do you have any idea what happened to Pedro Juan and Simon?" Concern and anxiety were inherent in her voice and eyes.

Jackson glanced at Andrew Browning. "Professor DiCanio, can we talk alone for a few minutes? I'm sorry, Andrew, but I've been through some stuff and at least one colleague is dead. I have to be real careful who I speak to now."

DiCanio dismissed Andrew with a sympathetic yet firm glance. He departed without a word, just a polite, friendly smile.

"By all means, Jackson. Also, please call me 'Melissa', everyone else does."

The restaurant was mostly empty now and no other staff were seated within earshot. Even so, Jackson lowered his voice.

"PJ's lab phone is bugged. Simon disappeared on the way to pick me up. I'm afraid he must be dead because we'd agreed on a meeting place, and he told me what he'd be wearing. Someone turned up for that meeting, and tried to kill me. I don't know Simon, but I'm guessing that it wasn't him."

DiCanio's eyes widened. "Oh my goodness! Now you're worried that. . . "

Jackson continued, his voice dropping almost to a whisper. "Exactly. If you told them on that phone that I'd be meeting you here, then the people who were looking for me in Mexico, who killed Pedro Juan and probably Simon too . . ., then they know just where to find me!"

"This is just too bad! Do you have any idea who's behind it?"

"That was going to be my question to you. PJ was working on something, something I think you know more about than me."

DiCanio's eyes betrayed just a hint of astonishment, then, "You mean the peptide-binding experiments? With *phoenix*?"

"Yes. How much do you know about it?"

"Chaldexx paid for the supercomputer time. Pedro Juan wanted to see if he could find a small peptide sequence which would bind to his *phoenix* structure. That was just one approach."

"OK, I think PJ had some kind of breakthrough. He tried to tell me about it."

"Tell you how?"

"At the airport, we met to exchange some bacterial expression clones that I'd been working on for him. I'd travelled with the samples VIP, so I guess I was a little nervous. So we're there in this airport coffee shop, and PJ tried to tell me something, when this guy in a suit appears, leads him away. I was worried that it was customs, something to do with the bacterial samples. Well, I just got out of there. Some people followed me out of the airport, but I managed to shake them off. I think that PJ was trying to tell me something about the *phoenix* interaction."

DiCanio frowned. "Did he say that he'd found a good target molecule?"

"He didn't get that far. But he was obviously excited about something."

DiCanio was quiet, lost in thought.

Jackson asked, "What do you know about a guy named Hans Runig?"

At the mention of this name, DiCanio paled. "Jackson, please, tell me you aren't involved with Hans Runig."

"I think he's trying to get involved with me. I've received messages – he's talked to me over the Internet. He claimed to be the one who killed PJ. He . . . he says he's going to kill me."

Once again, he carefully avoided any mention of the website with the amino acid sequence in its Web address, or of Marie-Carmen. He wasn't sure how much of PJ's work had been shared with Chaldexx and he wasn't about to break a confidence. For some reason PJ had chosen to trust Jackson with his secret results; until Jackson better understood why, he wasn't about to share them.

"You think Hans Runig bugged Pedro Juan's phone?

"I'm sure of it. It's the only explanation for how Runig could still have gotten information from the lab after PJ was gone."

She frowned. "That sounds rather ominous. Almost as though you suspected, at one time, that PJ might have been feeding information to Runig."

Despite himself, Jackson turned red with anger. "Given the way PJ died, I'd have to say that I didn't suspect him at all, not at any stage."

She shrugged. "Pedro Juan may not have realized the significance of the information he was passing."

"You mean he may have known about Runig and believed he was friendly?"

"It's possible."

"I don't think so. I trust PJ." He couldn't very well tell DiCanio that the main reason he trusted PJ was because of the way PJ had appealed to Jackson, sent him a carefully coded message and entrusted him with the contact details of his favorite cousin. Yet he could see that from DiCanio's position of limited information, it might look as though Runig and PJ had once cooperated.

DiCanio rose to her feet.

"Very well, let's continue this in my office. There is something I want to show you. And I'll tell you about Runig. First, I'll make some calls. You should change hotels, in case you were followed."

"Change hotels? You're kidding."

"No. Trust me on this – Runig is extremely resourceful. If he knew you were coming to Interlaken, then it's safest to assume you've been followed."

It was only many hours later that Jackson began to wonder why, at that point, DiCanio had not suggested the most obvious and sensible move – to involve the police.

DiCanio closed the door behind them as Jackson and she stepped into her office. The minimalism of her outfit extended into her environment; grey, frosted glass-topped tables, sleek lines of cherry wood, the only splashes of color present in cobalt blue chunky glass vases containing plump bunches of blue hyacinths. Two pieces of abstract art adorned the walls.

They faced each other over the meeting table. DiCanio seemed to consider her words carefully.

"I think, from what you've told me so far, that you won't be surprised when I tell you that we asked you here to talk about a lot more than the structure of *joust*-like proteins in the brain."

Her words struck a chord, a nagging query which had gnawed at him since he'd first learned of PJ's collaboration with Chaldexx and the scheduled meeting with DiCanio. Why had Jackson, who was known for his work on *joust*, not been included in Chaldexx's work?

He gave her a level gaze. "I kind of guessed that, from the private jet and all the fuss you're making over me."

"Why don't you let me tell you from the beginning?"

DiCanio clicked a slim tablet computer which lay on the table before her. Touching a finger lightly to the screen, she continued, "Some years ago, we found *joust*-like gene sequences in some brain tissue DNA. You won't have read about any of this, of course. We haven't published anything around this work. The brain tissue was found in individuals who had experienced visions, headaches and other neurological symptoms, before experiencing what you could only describe as a major psychotic episode, followed by death by suicide. The pathology was unlike any known disease."

Jackson had been intrigued from the moment he'd learned, back in Mexico, that Chaldexx had found *joust*-like sequences in humans. For investigators working in the 'lower' order creatures such as bacteria, yeast or even the fruit fly, there was a trade-off between the flexibility of the experimental system and the importance of the discovery. You could perform incredibly powerful manipulations in non-human biological systems, but then the mere discovery of a human version of the same gene, especially if it were found in an interesting context, could blow a non-human gene discovery out of the water.

In fact this was precisely why he felt slightly irked, as well as excited, to hear that *joust* – or something similar – had been found in humans. In six months of searching for precisely the same thing, he'd drawn nothing but blanks.

DiCanio was saying, "We decided to take it seriously, unlike most of the patients' physicians. We were interested in the fact that each of the patients claimed to be able, under some circumstances, to hypnotize people, an ability which none of them had previously had."

Jackson interrupted. "Hypnosis? You're taking that seriously?"

DiCanio looked him straight in the eye.

"Absolutely. Much of what people practice is pure PT Barnum, it's true. Only a few cases hold up under scrutiny. In a few cases we looked at there's no doubt that you can measure unusual brain activity during hypnosis – in both the hypnotist and the subject.

"These patients who killed themselves all claimed to be able to hypnotize people. The psychosis usually followed within a few days. We thought their brain tissue was worth looking at, so we got on it. We looked for expressed sequences, and found that in all of them, a *joust*-like protein, also coded for by a transposable element similar to *joust*, was being produced at quite high levels."

"How did you get access to the samples? Patients aren't usually all that happy to hand over brain tissue."

"That's the main advantage of having kept a pure-research lab going in Cambridge. That's where we did most of this work, at first. It grew out of the work we did on the activity of Tripoxan."

He sat back, quite amazed. He wasn't surprised that PJ had kept him in the dark about his own research results: PJ himself would doubtless have been bound by a secrecy agreement.

DiCanio turned the tablet so that Jackson could also see the screen. A three-dimensional animated model of a protein rotated slowly before his eyes. Jackson could see a similarity to the structures of both *joust* and *phoenix*.

DiCanio continued, "You can imagine the experiments that followed. We looked for the sequence in mice. Well, that went nowhere. We looked for the gene in the general human population. It's rare, Jackson, really rare.

"With no naturally-occurring mice with the gene, we had to make a transgenic mouse for the first brain experiments. That way, we'd have a line of mice which possessed the *joust*-like gene. By now, we were calling this Joust-Like-Factor, or *jlf*."

DiCanio pronounced the name *jlf* as 'jelf'. A touch sardonically, he asked, "How do you test to see if one mouse can 'hypnotize' another?"

"Well, you might ask," smiled DiCanio. "We put several mice in a cage with only enough food and water for one mouse. Occasionally, the transgenic mouse would be the one to survive the first starvation. When we did the same thing again, the transgenic mouse always survived. The other mice rarely even approached the food or water. Even though they were dying. The mouse with the *jlf* gene always won, Jackson.

"But the really interesting thing was this. The transgenic mouse, with the *jlf* gene, would almost starve to death before it started to do whatever it was doing to stop the others getting the food."

"So, the gene was only activated under conditions of extreme stress?"

DiCanio nodded vigorously. "Stress or starvation, we didn't get around to finding out which. Because in the meantime, we'd been looking for peptides – short sequences of proteins – which could bind to the *jlf* protein; stick to it really tight. We had a few candidates. We injected some of this into the brain of the transgenic mouse before it went into the second starvation cage.

"This time, the mouse didn't wait to starve. Those other mice didn't get a look in. They stayed away from the food. The males kept their distance from the transgenic. The females didn't approach. But they were receptive to any attempt at all by the transgenic to mate with them! Yes sir, once we injected him with our peptide, that little *jlf* mouse seemed to rule the roost."

Jackson thought with distaste about the experiments which the Chaldexx team had done, and all the starving mice. He hated animal experimentation. His limit was the fruit fly.

DiCanio took a deep breath. "Then we moved the trials into humans." She watched his stunned reaction with evident enjoyment. "All volunteers, Jackson; a few rare people we dug up who have this gene. Injected with the peptide, they asked volunteers to do simple acts, like recite nursery rhymes, make them cups of coffee, give a dance lesson: all very benign stuff. Well, it was like being at a hypnotism show. Except it was real: we'd created it!"

This far exceeded any of the wildest theories that Jackson had come up with to explain the invitation to collaborate with Chaldexx.

"You got a name for your peptide?" he asked, "Cos I could suggest something."

DiCanio gave a wan smile. "We like to call it 'hypnoticin'. But that's only between the closest members of the team. Officially we refer to it as 'hip33'."

"Hypnoticin," Jackson repeated, trying out the word. "That's not bad."

"Imagine, for a second, the possibilities of a drug like this, in the hands of the wrong people. To someone with political ambitions, for example."

Jackson had a sudden insight; "Hans Runig?"

"Right. So far as we've been able to work out, he's a Swiss businessman with interests in biotech, nanotech, semiconductors . . ."

"All the cool stuff."

"He started as a business angel, helping companies to start-up. Now he controls a number of small, promising companies."

"I couldn't find much about him on the Internet. Isn't that kind of weird?"

"People like Runig pay a lot of money to public relations firms to achieve precisely that, Jackson – relative anonymity. The one thing I know about Runig is that he always approaches the scientists directly when he wants to invest. He never waits for companies to go to him."

"I guess the early bird catches the worm."

She nodded, thoughtfully. "I'd say that's an extremely astute way to put it. He's always early to the worm. God knows how he does it. He approached us some months ago, offering to buy the patent for the *joust*-like factor gene. We don't know how he got his information, because on its own that wouldn't do much. Somehow, he seemed to know it was worth something. Of course, we refused."

Jackson was beginning to see everything clearly now. Runig had failed to acquire the *joust*-like factor gene by legal means. There was a good chance he'd resorted to industrial espionage. It had worked. He was willing to bet that Runig already knew the amino acid sequence of 'hypnoticin'.

It had to be the same as the sequence which PJ had passed onto him: AGYLIHRPPREIKGR

Runig had created a website to trap anyone else who knew about the sequence. Jackson had given himself away when he'd logged on. Whatever Runig wanted with Jackson, he couldn't imagine it would be very friendly.

"You know what I think, Melissa? I think you got yourself a mole. Right here in Chaldexx."

Her features were at once cold, hostile. A second or so later she seemed to regain control and forced a smile. "That had occurred to me."

Chaldexx already had found the *joust*-like factor. They also had a peptide – hypnoticin – which appeared to activate *jlf*. They had proof of a pretty spectacular biological function – the power to hypnotize.

The question was – what could Chaldexx possibly want with him?

"What's on your mind, Jackson?"

"I was just wondering. Have you been able to find hypnoticin in any natural context? Like, a hypnoticin gene?"

This was the crux of the matter. PJ had evidently managed to isolate a naturally-occurring gene for hypnoticin. Had Chaldexx done the same? Were they even aware of PJ's discovery?

DiCanio answered by peering at him curiously, as though she were considering him rather than his question. Finally she admitted, "No. No, we've searched hundreds of gene libraries, but so far nothing. We don't have any evidence that it occurs naturally, at all."

"That doesn't strike you as unlikely? I mean, why have a gene which unlocks this kind of incredible functionality, unless you have a way to use it, a way for natural selection to preserve it throughout evolution?"

"We don't know the answer to that. But you're right, it is strange."

DiCanio went over to her desk and picked up the phone.

"Shall we get some tea, or coffee?"

"Oh, coffee, yeah, coffee is good," Jackson mumbled, distracted.

How odd that PJ hadn't shared with DiCanio his discovery of the gene. It seemed that what Chaldexx had failed to discover, PJ had found. Jackson blazed with curiosity. Where had PJ had found this naturally occurring version of hypnoticin? Somehow, it had been PJ, not the rich, powerful Chaldexx, who had finally cracked the problem.

Even more curiously, until PJ had transferred that test-tube into Jackson's pocket at the airport, he'd kept that information from both Chaldexx and Jackson. He could understand if PJ had wanted to be first to publish or patent the finding. It was still a fairly shady way to treat a collaborator.

A drug which conferred the power to hypnotize. Something like that would be difficult to get past the strict drug regulatory authorities. Who would it benefit? Surely it would infringe the rights of the innocent subjects?

Why would Chaldexx spend so much investigating a drug which would almost certainly never be approved?

DiCanio was right to fear the drug falling into the wrong hands. What was Hans Runig's motive? For that matter, what was Chaldexx's?

DiCanio had the air of one who was still withholding something crucial. Jackson felt sure that she was getting ready to deliver the real bombshell. He was itching to find out what it could be.

Just then, a pert, very fair-haired young woman entered carrying a tray with a silver coffee pot and china cups and saucers. DiCanio busied herself with serving them both. She mused, "One thing you can say for the Swiss, they know really how to make coffee."

Jackson focused his attention back on the computer screen.

"So what you're onto, basically, could be a molecular basis for hypnosis, or something that looks a hell of a lot like it. It's an amazing bit of science, Melissa. Presumably from this you can start to investigate the factors around it, maybe even get deeper into the biology of the brain-mind connection?" He rubbed his chin, thoughtfully. Maybe there was something in this for Chaldexx after all. For DiCanio, it could lead to that elusive Nobel Prize.

DiCanio seemed delighted. Her enthusiasm was infectious. "The really interesting thing is when you start to look at the occurrence of the gene for *jlf*, in the human population."

"You said it was rare."

"Pretty rare. It only occurs less than 0.001 per cent of the human population. So we started looking at older sample from ancient human remains. We wanted to see how old this gene was. Because it came from a transposon, it could theoretically have entered the human genome at any time in the past. The question was when."

"You think it was a retrovirus infection or something?"

"Maybe. We wanted to trace the approximate date of the introduction of the gene; the date when we could calculate that there would be only around one person with the gene. We felt that the best approach would be to actually look for the presence of the gene in DNA from ancient bones.

"We got samples going back to twenty-thousand BC. You simply cannot imagine what a piece of work it was just to persuade all those museum curators to give us a few scrapings from their exhibits! And the evidence is absolutely clear; there's no sign of the gene whatsoever before around three thousand BC. After three thousand BC, you can find it in people right through to the present day. But before three thousand BC, nothing."

Jackson was beginning to feel distinctly uneasy. The work she was describing would have taken years. Chaldexx might well have the resources – he even believed that they had the inclination – to fund the brain research. She wasn't being straight with him.

Yet, researching ancient molecular biology? Where was the potential commercial gain?

"Chaldexx did all this work?"

"Indirectly, yes." DiCanio's admitted eventually, her face somber. "Although there are other parties interested. This has been a project of mine for years. You see, Jackson, I've been a member of a society which is dedicated to the future health of the planet. Not just its citizens, although obviously that's my main reason for being with Chaldexx. But also, the planet and the survival of every creature living here."

Jackson was so astonished by this latest revelation, that he couldn't prevent a gasp of disbelief. He turned it quickly into a cough. "That's ah, very laudable."

"Don't be patronizing," DiCanio said. Her voice was tinged with a quality which made Jackson feel, quite suddenly, somewhat uncomfortable.

"The society was formed years ago, when I first found the *jlf* gene. Because not long afterwards, I discovered that I am a carrier, by no means the only one. Chaldexx purchased rights to dozens of DNA banks. It's mainly men, obviously, given the source of most available genetic material; sperm banks, college student clinical trials volunteers. Over the years, we've contacted many of the other carriers we've identified from our genetic screening program."

"I guess it's all making sense now. *You* can use hypnoticin?"

DiCanio stood, began to pace the room, two steps along the desk and then towards the flat grey sky and dense cloud-cover that dominated the view from the window. "The society consists of other carriers of the gene. Do you understand what that means? What the potential of an organized group of such individuals could achieve? Each member of the society has recognized their duty and their potential role." She turned to face him, with a dramatic flourish. "Joining us, they come to understand the true purpose of their life: to protect the planet."

Jackson phrased his next sentence carefully. "When you say 'the health of the planet', what are we talking about, specifically?"

"What would you say are the top three threats to the future existence of human civilization?"

He considered briefly. "Asteroid impact, climate change, pandemic of some appropriately lethal virus."

"Agreed. Which of those can we do anything about?"

"I'm guessing you're not a believer in the Missile Defense System's ability to blow the asteroid out of the sky?"

DiCanio allowed herself a smile. "You got that right. I do think that we have a duty to do what we can, as citizens of the planet, to prevent anthropomorphic climate change and pandemic."

"It's hard to argue with that."

"Some would. Some think we should just leave problems like that to the governments of the world, and use our ability to enrich ourselves personally. Or to infiltrate the established power structures. Hans Runig, for example, has an entirely different agenda. Hans Runig has the gene, but we've never asked him to join. We don't see his type as an asset. He has ambitions, Jackson, in the political sphere. As I've already said, that would be ill-advised."

Jackson was silent for a several seconds. He still couldn't figure out why DiCanio had brought him over to Switzerland. The appearance of Hans Runig at the periphery of her world troubled him. He was beginning to lose track of who knew what.

DiCanio seemed to sense his disquiet. Her gaze was suddenly as tender as a mother with her son. "You must be asking yourself why I brought you here, to Chaldexx?"

Their eyes met.

"Yes." From the moment she'd mentioned college students enrolled in clinical trials, he'd wondered if this was where she was heading. To supplement his income during his snowboarding years, Jackson had once taken part in a two-week trial of a new 'flu treatment. Somewhere in Boston, his blood and DNA were in a freezer.

"You're one of us, Jackson," she told him with a gentle smile, tinged with sadness. "You're a carrier. You have the *jlf* gene. You will respond to, and can use, 'hypnoticin'."

Schwendi Bei Grindelwald

DiCanio's driver dropped Jackson at the rail station. A train was standing at the platform. The station master stood beside the train, one arm raised, staring up at the digital clock that hung over the platform. As the time changed to seventeen minutes past three, his arm dropped. The train began to move. One second later, Jackson leapt. Exactly as instructed by DiCanio, he was the last man aboard.

"I'll text you instructions about where to get off," she'd told him. "Runig's men are probably watching the Chaldexx offices. They'll probably see you get on the train and try to follow to see where you get out. It's not easy to outrun this train. One farm truck is enough to hold up the whole road."

"Are there a lot of farm trucks?"

She'd smiled blandly. "The Swiss like to burn wood. You can't go twenty miles without getting stuck behind a logging truck."

Too tense to sit, Jackson stood in the connecting section of two carriages with his suitcase, which Chaldexx officials had retrieved from the Hotel Victoria-Jungfrau. He gazed out of the window, watching the surroundings change from the elegant, urban city of Interlaken to a rural idyll of wooden chalets, snow-encrusted slopes and stark, tall pines. The train headed straight at the wall of rock which began the Alps. Rising behind the foothills above a faint ribbon of cloud, he could clearly see the craggy, bleached white peaks of the Jungfrau valley.

Jackson leaned into the side of the carriage, his eyes closed, his muscles already weary. The stapled tear on his leg was pounding, waves of extreme discomfort beginning to break through the pain-killers he'd taken that morning.

The past three days had been pure disorientation. Pursued by killers, then experiencing the most unexpectedly stirring sexual encounter of his life. Now he seemed to have stumbled into a riveting mystery.

Jackson's only regret was that he'd missed out on the actual scientific discovery. It made PJ's death even more tragic; a tragedy and a waste. What PJ's life must have been like this past year. First, the excitement of PJ's own discovery of the amino acid sequence which bound to *phoenix*. Then the realization that it might have similar properties to the hypnosis-inducing factor they'd discovered and synthesized at Chaldexx.

Yet it couldn't all have been plain sailing. At some stage, PJ had become spooked, aware that his life was in danger. Jackson wouldn't easily forget the helpless, resigned expression in PJ's eyes during those last moments at the airport. Did he know he was going to die? He doubted that anyone could quickly accept such knowledge.

Jackson wondered if PJ had ever really understood the extent of the danger; the lengths to which Hans Runig was prepared to go to protect what he thought only he and Chaldexx knew.

His cell phone buzzed into activity: a text from DiCanio.

Schwendi.

The train slowed. The announcer spoke first in German, then French and finally English.

"Next station is Schwendi bei Grindelwald."

Jackson gripped the handle of his suitcase, ready to be first off the train.

Two minutes later he was walking along an isolated station platform. A lone wooden chalet was the ticket office. Jackson hurried through it, wondering where to go next. Outside, a taxi was parked, the driver standing outside. He carried a sign that read "Eiger Tours".

He was walking past when his cell phone buzzed once again.

Eiger Tours.

He stopped, walked back to the taxi.

"Eiger Tours?"

"Mr. Bennett?"

Jackson nodded. DiCanio's organization was like a well-oiled machine. He took a seat in the rear of the taxi and placed one hand on his suitcase. He longed to call Marie-Carmen but he didn't want to risk missing another instruction from DiCanio.

The taxi dropped him at an inn called 'Die Bären' a rustic bed-and-breakfast. A clutch of round tables made from sliced logs were dotted around the garden. The sun was still bright. Three men in their sixties sat around one of the tables, smoking. They peered up at Jackson, briefly, as he shuffled towards the entrance. A second later they were back to dragging on their cigarettes.

The chalet's walls and ceilings were constructed from dark-stained pine. At the reception counter a gruff, grizzled man with a white, handlebar moustache greeted Jackson in English. "Mr. Bennett, yes? We have your room ready for you, sir. All paid for by Mr. Andrew Browning. You stay one night, yes? Breakfast is from seven until nine."

Moments later Jackson dropped his keys, wallet and jacket on the bed. He unzipped his suitcase, removed his laptop computer and logged into the hotel's wifi. He checked his email. There was a message from Marie-Carmen. Jackson's spirits dipped slightly when he read it. The message consisted solely of a link to the secure-surfing software.

His mouth formed the words. "IP masking software."

Marie-Carmen had thought of everything.

Jackson's heart was thudding as he logged into his Facebook account. He checked his watch. It would be late morning in Acapulco. When he saw Marie-Carmen's name on his list of chat contacts, he felt a surge of delight.

***

Jackson: It's so great to talk to you again. Even like this.

Marie-Carmen: I wish you were here with me. In the morning the ocean is beautiful. Surf's up at 8am. I take a walk, watch the surfers before breakfast.

Jackson: Surfing's not my thing so much. I'm pretty much a winter-sports guy.

Marie-Carmen: That's a shame – Mexico's great for water sports.

Jackson: I already have a very good reason to be in Mexico.

They both paused for several seconds. Jackson desperately wanted to sense a connection with Marie-Carmen that went beyond a few strings of letters on a flickering plasma screen.

Jackson: There's a lot going on over here. But I can't stop thinking about you.

Marie-Carmen: Well, I got a lot less going on, so imagine my situation.

Jackson: To be honest...I can't stop thinking about the . . . you know . . .

Marie-Carmen: The sex?

Jackson: :)

Marie-Carmen: The memory has been keeping me going here, all alone, without you.

Jackson: You can't imagine how frustrating it is to hear that. If I was there I know what I'd do.

Marie-Carmen: Change the subject.

Jackson: I'd rather not.

Marie-Carmen: Seriously. I want you to say these things to my face.

Jackson: Me too, hopefully soon. But for now?

Marie-Carmen: Well, how about this? When we see each other again, I promise to tell you, directly and in detail, the impression you made on me that night.

Jackson: OK! Can't wait.

Marie-Carmen: And you have to do the same. Deal?

Marie-Carmen's reticence was a little disappointing. Still, her promise filled him with hope. It was evidence that he was still on her mind. Clearly, she wouldn't be drawn further on this topic, so he changed it.

Jackson began to relate part of the afternoon's experience at Chaldexx. He finished by telling her about his suspicion that Chaldexx had been searching for a naturally-occurring version of their mysterious peptide, hypnoticin.

Marie-Carmen: Did you tell the Chaldexx woman that PJ found a naturally-occurring version?

Jackson: No. Figure PJ had his reasons for not telling his own collaborators something that important. No clue what those reasons are. Until I understand more about what's going on, that's between you, me and PJ.

Marie-Carmen: Ah. Now you're keeping secrets, too.

Jackson: DiCanio has been screening DNA banks, finding people with the gene. She's actually created a society consisting of members who have it.

Marie-Carmen: A society of hypnotists?

Jackson: That's not how she sees it. She says it's about creating a society of people who'll use their ability to influence the world to change its attitude over issues like climate change, poverty, war, that kind of thing.

Marie-Carmen: What's DiCanio's role in this society? Does it have a name?

Jackson: Didn't really talk about that. It's been more about the science. I watched videos of the human subject experiments. Completely incredible. Also – major news – turns out that I have the *jlf* gene! This hypnoticin drug should work on me; turn me into this master hypnotist. Tomorrow, she's going to let me try it out.

Marie-Carmen: You've got to be kidding me.

Jackson: No, totally serious. DiCanio – she's cool.

Marie-Carmen: OK – here it comes. She's like twenty-years older than you! Hey. What did I tell you?!

Jackson: It's not like that. Like I told you, I have this gene. She wants me to join her society.

Marie-Carmen: Still worried.

Jackson: I can't tell if you're joking.

Marie-Carmen: Listen, I've been doing some research on that DNA sequence.

It was Marie-Carmen's turn to relate the outcome of her own investigation. The final outcome had been pretty lean on decent results. However you looked at her conclusion, it was bizarre. Even so, she was proud of the thoroughness with which she had conducted her research.

Jackson: So according to this article, the clay tablet had the exact same DNA sequence AND amino acid sequence as PJ's DNA molecule?

Marie-Carmen: Yes. Is that important?

Jackson: It's quite a coincidence. Those same five amino acids could be made by many different combinations of DNA. Genetic code has some inbuilt redundancy. All but two of the 20 amino acids can be coded for by more than one set of three DNA letters. Some can be coded for by six different combinations of three letters. For both the DNA and amino acid sequences to match exactly is quite a coincidence.

Marie-Carmen: OK, want to hear something else crazy?

Jackson: Go ahead.

Marie-Carmen: Those 'five amino acids' . . . when he translates the symbols into Sumerian words he gets this: 'before Master people of Heaven and Earth'.

Jackson: Does 'Master people of Heaven and Earth' mean anything to you?

Marie-Carmen: It's not my field, so not much.

Jackson: Wait – there's a call on my cell phone.

Marie-Carmen: Do you have to go? It's so beautiful here; it seems a shame to be wasting my money being here alone. I know how much guys hate to 'talk about the relationship', but don't you think we need to get a handle on what's happening here?

He stared at the screen. He wasn't imagining it. Whatever was developing between them, she felt it too. He desperately wanted to touch her: it was almost a perceptible ache. It was a struggle to pay attention to DiCanio's personal assistant on his cell phone.

"Professor DiCanio would like to invite you to dinner. A car will arrive to pick you up at seven."

Jackson: I have to go. I'm really sorry. I need to go shower and find something respectable to wear. DiCanio wants me to go out for dinner.

Marie-Carmen: Aha, you see? Now it begins!

Jackson: I won't forget my promise. I'll look for you later?

Marie-Carmen: Get out of here!

Jackson grinned. He felt a wave of warmth towards Marie-Carmen that he wished he had time – or the skill – to communicate to her in writing. The only things he could think of to say sounded either hopelessly clichéd or slightly vulgar. Maybe she'd be into it but on the other hand, maybe not. It was a risk. He might come across as a dunderhead and an idiot. He very badly wanted to avoid that.

In The Shadow Of The Eiger

By the time the car arrived, Jackson was beginning to realize just how inadequate his clothes shopping had been, given his abrupt change of plans. His outfits suited the light cool of Mexico City in December; jeans, polo shirts and his suede jacket. Not even close to enough for the alpine winter. He peeked through the small window. A fresh tract of snow glittered in the beam of the taxi's headlamps. He buttoned up his jacket, pulled open the door and steeled himself for the blast of icy cold.

A light snowfall persisted as the taxi drove Jackson to the mountain town of Grindelwald. Apparently the town lay nestled in the shadow of the Eiger Mountain – the great 'ogre'. Its notoriously sheer north face dominated a landscape that, the driver assured him in excellent English, was one of Switzerland's finest.

When the taxi left him in front of yet another snow-drenched chalet that looked almost exactly like the gingerbread cottages sold at Christmas, Jackson eyed the pure white snow of the slopes. He longed to be heading up towards the ski resort of Kleine Scheidegg with a snowboard under one arm. The chill outside was tolerable for less than two minutes. Soon enough he was tucked back into the woody gloom of another chalet. The air inside was thick and warm. It smelt of burning wood, cigarette smoke and cheese. A waitress led him downstairs to the private dining room. At one end of the long room, logs sizzled in orange flames. Half of a huge round of Swiss cheese was impaled on a hook and hung in front of the fire, dripping onto a wide plate below. The waitress snatched the plate of fire-melted cheese and with a practiced motion, replaced it with an empty one. She carried the plate to the other end of the room, about three yards away, where Melissa DiCanio and her fellow diners stood gathered around a table.

"*Raclette*," said the waitress. She placed the plate of melted cheese on the table. Eager hands reached with forks into a basket of boiled new potatoes, then dipped the potatoes into the pale yellow cheese. Contented sighs followed as they ate.

"I'm sorry we began without you, Jackson, but they already had a big hunk of *raclette* on the go. You gotta try some," DiCanio told him with a smile. He accepted the glass of white wine that she held out to him. He sipped. Jackson's right hand went to his jacket pocket and, for a few seconds, searched in vain.

DiCanio watched him for a moment and then asked. "Everything OK?"

Jackson grimaced. "I must have left my cell phone in my room."

"Expecting a call?"

He shook his head, tried to disguise his irritation with himself. "I guess not."

DiCanio had changed into a charcoal-grey and white silk dress. The fabric dipped just below the knee and clung at every curve. Jackson tried not to glance at her cleavage, which was set off by a single pendant of polished jade. He found himself wondering whether, if not for Marie-Carmen, he'd consider having a fling with a woman twenty years his senior. The way DiCanio held his eyes for just a fraction of a second too long made Jackson wonder if maybe she was having the same thought. Within a minute, however, his attention was distracted by a stunning Asian beauty that appeared at DiCanio's side. In her early twenties, the woman was dressed in a silk sari, coral pink with a border of silver brocade. Her eyes were subtly made up in tones that just offset the cinnamon color of her skin. The overall effect implied softness, understated elegance.

"Jackson Bennett, meet Priyanka Desai. She's just won a prestigious Junior Research Fellowship to Aquinas College in The Other Place, as we like to call it in Cambridge." DiCanio's smile was like a warm beam of sunshine in which the Junior Research Fellow basked.

Jackson shook Priyanka's hand. "Congratulations! What's your field, Doctor Desai?"

The woman's voice was rich and sensual; her pronunciation was cut-glass British with an Indian twang. "Call me Priya – please. I'm not a fully-fledged 'doctor' yet."

"Jackson Bennett. And – I'm not a 'doctor' yet, either."

"Why don't agree not to hold it against each other?" Priya said with a steady gaze, her tone entirely suggestive. Jackson blinked in disbelief. Her meaning couldn't have been plainer. He glanced back at DiCanio for a second, slightly thrown.

Was he being set up with Priya?

"I'm a chemist originally, but my doctoral research is in climatology."

Jackson's gaze went straight to DiCanio, then back to Priya. "Anthropomorphic global warming?"

Priya smiled. There was a trace of something concealed about her expression. "Don't tell me you're one of those climate change deniers."

"Denial?" He shook his head and grinned. "Heck, no. I guess you guys know what you're talking about – it's really not my area."

Priya smiled again, this time carefully. Delicately she said, "Well, I'm glad to hear that you're not one of those who won't give scientists credit for being experts in their own areas."

DiCanio turned to Jackson. "Whatever banal reports you read about from so-called climate change summits in luxurious resorts like Bali, nothing much really changes. The world's economy is still addicted to burning fossil fuels. We fight wars to protect US oil interests."

"You don't think the politicians are serious about climate change?"

DiCanio shrugged. "I'm from Texas, honey; I know how the oil fellas think. They're not going to sit back and watch their livelihood disappear. And these new guys in China and Russia? They make the good ol' boys from my neighborhood look like a bunch of boy scouts."

DiCanio's liberal views were well-known. It didn't seem to square with her role as a successful business-woman, but that was increasingly common. San Francisco was rife with left-leaning millionaires. Even saving the environment was big business now.

Jackson felt himself tuning out as Priya's and DiCanio's conversation become even more enthusiastic and political. He tipped more wine into his mouth. The two women were really getting going now. They didn't seem to have noticed that they'd lost his interest.

As he pretended to be surveying the room, he became aware of the claustrophobic, even conspiratorial ambience of the setting. He didn't really follow politics, something else that infuriated his brother Connor. Maybe it was because with a dead war hero for a father and an ace pilot for a brother, any views to the left of Ronald Reagan's would make for vigorous argument.

He simply wasn't interested in arguing about anything outside of his own field of research. It was too much distraction from his experiments. When Connor had once asked, "Do you actually care about anything apart from that goddamn genetics lab, or snowboarding or getting laid?" Jackson hadn't replied.

The raging log fire in one corner of the room provided the only significant source of light. The faces of DiCanio and her associates were animated, lit in flickering orange, from one side only. Everything else was in shadow. Something stirred within Jackson, an ominous knock at the edge of his consciousness.

Still their conversation continued. The conversation had broadened to include a man seated opposite DiCanio, diagonally opposite from him. This rather saturnine man in his late forties was dressed in a midnight blue jacket over a white shirt, no tie. He seemed to enjoy the sound of his voice too. He didn't once as much as glance in Jackson's direction, but held forth to the apparently rapt attention of DiCanio and Priya.

Jackson speared a perfectly round new potato on a fork. He dipped it into the plate of cheese. As a mixture of dairy fat and tang of flavor flooded his mouth, he reflected that maybe Connor was right. Maybe he didn't think enough about things like politics. It certainly put him at a disadvantage for these types of gatherings of 'high-powered' intellects.

Science was like that; all-consuming. It wasn't like fighting battles or even war. Sooner or later, the fighting ended and Connor would be home. He was on his third sortie in Iraq now, yet they always ended. But science didn't end. The immediate answer to every question you asked was just another question. And the appetite for answers could be insatiable.

So Apocalyptic

"You're very quiet," Priya observed. "Do we take it that you're not worried about climate change?"

Jackson smirked. "Hey, now. That's like a 'when did you stop beating your wife' question."

"Priya's kind of a firebrand on the topic," DiCanio said. She nodded at a young, fair-haired waiter who was standing by silently. "Maybe Jackson would prefer to concentrate on the *raclette* – and the wine."

"It's not that I'm not interested," he told Priya. Her disappointed pout was all the more attractive for the fact that she obviously struggled to conceal it. "But I'm just a molecular geneticist. Like you – but unlike Melissa here – I don't have my doctorate yet. Kind of need to focus, you know what I'm saying?"

"Oh, and I admire focus," DiCanio said as the waiter filled her glass. "Most especially in a man." She gave Priya a benevolent smile.

DiCanio turned to the man opposite her, who seemed finally to have decided to eat rather than talk. His close-cropped dark hair was flecked with silver, which gave him a slightly less bullish appearance than the extreme haircut might suggest. Jackson noticed how the man's jacket bunched around his shoulders. He guessed that the guy probably worked out, pretty hard too.

"This is Jonas Kitrick. He's also based in Oxford."

"For a Cambridge professor, you have a lot of contacts in Oxford," Jackson observed.

"Sugar, I've been around. Oxford didn't last very long though. Cambridge made me an offer I couldn't refuse."

Jackson closed his eyes as if enraptured. "Man, I've always wanted to hear someone say that to me!"

DiCanio laughed. It was a slightly disorienting sound, smaller and higher than he'd have expected from her rather strident, Texan- inflected voice. It sounded like the peal of bells.

Jackson asked, "So, Doctor Kitrick, what's your field?"

Kitrick blinked slowly and without expression. He eyed Jackson with a faintly imperious air. "I'm an astrophysicist. My group works on dark matter, galaxy clusters, dark energy. . . " His voice trailed off, almost as though he were too bored to answer.

"Jonas is putting together a really exciting project," said DiCanio. "I like to think we'll talk about it in more detail, when you've had a chance to know us all a little better."

Again, Kitrick blinked. Jackson sensed it was deliberate, rather than a reflex. Kitrick lifted his glass and paused before drinking. "And we, you," he intoned.

In total, Jackson counted five diners, apart from himself. A man in his late thirties with a Hispanic appearance sat to DiCanio's right. He hadn't joined the conversation that had so engaged Priya, DiCanio and Kitrick. DiCanio introduced him as Dr. Antonio Vargas, a geophysicist from the University of Utah.

"I work on calderas...they're massive, volcanic pools of magma which lie under the Earth's crust."

"Like the one at Yellowstone National Park? The 'supervolcano'? I've been hiking around there. A couple of times."

Antonio Vargas grinned broadly, showing a set of even, polished white teeth. He smelt of cologne. He wore a silk tie with a textured weave of six, tightly intertwined colors. Compared to other geophysicists that Jackson had met, Vargas seemed pretty well-groomed. In fact, as Jackson glanced around the table he had to acknowledge that the gathered company, who all seemed to be scientists of some type, had made a far greater effort with their appearance than him. Even if he hadn't lost his suitcase in Mexico, he wouldn't have been much better attired. Jackson couldn't ever remember sitting down with such smartly dressed scientists.

Vargas poured wine into his own glass and then Jackson's. Then he answered Jackson's question.

140

"Actually, the Yellowstone caldera is a specialty of my university." Vargas spoke with a cultivated tone and strong, Spanish inflections, which sounded quite different to the lilting, Mexican-accented English of Marie-Carmen and PJ.

"When's the next super-volcano explosion due?" said Jackson.

Vargas seemed slightly embarrassed by Jackson's use of humor. He paused very slightly before replying, "Do you know what would happen if the Yellowstone caldera were to explode?"

Jackson glanced at DiCanio. She seemed again to be sitting back, like someone watching a performance for her benefit.

Eventually, Jackson replied, "I'm guessing it wouldn't be good."

"Imagine an explosion two-and-a-half thousand times bigger than the one which blew up Mount St Helen's. You'd be able to hear it over much of the planet. The eruption would destroy everything within a thousand miles. Almost a thousand cubic kilometers of ash would be spewed into the atmosphere. Darkness and acid rain would fall over much of the United States, wiping out the harvest for that year, and for several years afterwards. It would be like a nuclear winter. The economy of the USA would most likely collapse, bringing down much of the rest of the world with it. The destruction and the knock-on effects would be devastating beyond our wildest imaginings." Vargas paused as he surveyed the audience of Priya, DiCanio and Jackson. He ran the tip of a finger under his lower lip. "It might even be the end of civilization as we know it."

The waiter arrived and took their orders. After he'd chosen the grilled trout with almond rice, Jackson turned to Vargas. "The caldera is dead, right? It's an extinct volcano."

"That's what everyone thought. Until a few years ago. Lately it looks as though there's activity. To be honest, there could be another explosion, any time in the next thousand years."

DiCanio spoke. "It wouldn't be the first time something like this has almost brought the human race to extinction, either. I take it you're aware, Jackson, of work on mitochondrial DNA in the human fossil record, which shows the changing rate of genetic diversity in human populations?"

Inwardly, Jackson groaned. His scientific reading was way too specialized. He'd been lost for the past three years in the world of *joust* and transposable elements. But it didn't look good to appear ignorant. He ventured an educated guess.

"Yeah, I've seen that. They were trying to work out whether the human population today descends from a single point of origin, or several. The genetic diversity in human DNA is absolutely tiny; genetically we are all almost identical."

His gamble paid off. DiCanio interjected, "Yes, it's been calculated that the people alive today must have descended from a population of ten thousand or less, who were alive around seventy to eighty thousand years ago."

Jackson frowned. "Right, but *homo sapiens* is, like, one hundred thousand years older."

"Exactly! So the question is," DiCanio smiled, "what happened to all the people?"

Jackson was fascinated. "You think it was a caldera explosion?"

Vargas nodded. "There was an event, a cataclysmic explosion, in Sumatra, around seventy-four thousand years ago. The crater from the explosion is now known as Lake Toba."

"The timing for the Toba caldera explosion fits the model for near-extinction of humanity sometime around then," DiCanio said gravely. "Imagine it. The sun blotted out for years. A sudden drop in temperature. The failure of agriculture; death of the wild game. Most people would have starved to death – or killed each other for food."

The food arrived. Jackson picked up his knife and sliced into the pinkish flesh of his trout. DiCanio seemed oblivious to the fact that he was eager to eat. She didn't give her own food so much as a glance.

"Think about those survivors, Jackson. There may have been fewer than ten thousand. All over the world, small pockets of people who somehow clawed their way through it. We are all their descendants."

"Well, Melissa, so far, so apocalyptic."

A note of formality entered her voice. "Maybe so, but get ready for the serious stuff."

Jackson could remember few days in which he'd had to listen to so much 'serious stuff', but he prepared himself for an even bigger revelation.

"Earlier today I spoke of a society I've been involved with, Jackson. You've probably guessed that the people here today are some of the other members."

"Actually, I didn't."

"Everyone here tonight was recruited to the society by me."

Jackson nodded, unsure of what to say.

"The society has an interest in an object which is currently under the control of the US military, in Iraq."

He swallowed a forkful of rice drenched in almond sauce. "Iraq?"

DiCanio leaned forward, speaking so that only he would hear. "Doesn't the date three thousand BC mean anything to you, Jackson?"

He shrugged. The narrow span of his knowledge could sometimes be a little embarrassing.

"The oldest civilization on earth, the Sumerians of Ancient Mesopotamia, invented cuneiform writing around that time. They weren't the only ones. All over the world, in cultures as disparate as the Maya in the Americas and the Ancient Egyptians, an explosion of culture began. Writing, the recording of history, collective efforts to divert rivers, farm inhospitable land, the construction of the first pyramids of Egypt, the cities of the Indus Valley, the ziggurats of Ancient Iraq, all had their roots around three thousand BC."

"And the Mayan Long Count starts in three thousand one hundred and fourteen BC," Jackson said brightly, as one useful factoid came to him.

DiCanio's face was alight with fervor; she seemed to glow with conviction. "Exactly. Well, that's when our gene appears, Jackson. That's when it all begins."

"Not a coincidence, then?"

Once again, DiCanio ignored his attempt to be glib.

"As well as many extremely talented scientists, present company included, our society includes individuals placed highly within the United Nations. Their information is that back in 2003, the UN weapons inspection team did actually find something in Iraq." She hesitated. "Something that might even have been worth going to war to capture. It wasn't a weapon."

From the moment she'd mentioned Iraq, he'd begun to have a sense of where this conversation might lead.

Was this why she'd brought him to Switzerland?

"You know, my brother worked with some of those inspection team guys."

DiCanio smiled, rather enigmatically. He couldn't be sure if she was trying to close him down or to convey that she already knew.

"What they found, Jackson, was not a weapon. Yet the inspectors recognized, pretty quickly actually, that they'd stumbled across something of tremendous historical value. Now that we understand more about the finding, it's pretty clear that they've found the secret to the origin of our society. The gene we carry, Jackson. We know where it comes from."

He gave a nervous laugh. "I'm almost afraid to ask."

"The weapons inspectors and your brother's Air Force unit: they discovered an ancient burial chamber. Perfectly intact. A burial chamber older than any construction on the planet."

A Proposal

The dessert course arrived: crisp meringues with soft, marshmallow centers under clouds of whipped cream. DiCanio seemed reluctant to say more on the subject of the mysterious burial chamber. In the meantime Priya was being drawn into a teasing conversation with the geophysicist, Vargas. Jackson couldn't fail to notice the exchange of flirtatious gestures and words. It gave him an oddly voyeuristic sensation. Yet at the same time, he couldn't shake the feeling that Vargas and Priya were actually performing for him.

As he scraped the last traces of cream from his plate, DiCanio leaned towards him. She gestured that he should come in closer. "I'd like to leave now. Priya, also. I think it's best if we take you back to your hotel. I don't want to leave you alone with my associates."

Jackson stared, bemused. He wondered how DiCanio might react if he refused, yet found himself standing up, pulling on his jacket. The sight of Priya straining against the tight wrappings her sari proved too distracting. Vargas glanced at him. One corner of his mouth rose in a wry grin. "Sleep well, Mr. Bennett."

The car which picked them up was an E-Class Mercedes. The driver wore a dark grey suit with a plain tie and addressed DiCanio by name. By the time he dropped them at Jackson's hotel, fresh snow lay almost two inches deep. To Jackson's surprise, both Priya and DiCanio followed him into the chalet, whose sloping roof was now highlighted with a smooth coating of crisp white powder. He stamped his feet on the mat at the threshold and held the door open for the two women.

"You're staying here too?" Jackson was somewhat confused. He'd seen no sign of DiCanio or Priya at the hotel earlier that evening. Surely DiCanio would have a home nearby?

DiCanio didn't reply. Instead she guided Jackson to a cozy nook opposite the bar. A leather sofa stood next to a low table, opposite two heavy chairs of smooth, worn pine. DiCanio slid into the sofa and nodded at Jackson. "Jackson. C'mon, darlin'. Let's talk."

In silence, Priya took a seat next to Jackson. DiCanio ignored her completely. Jackson watched the young woman for a minute. He signaled to the bartender. Apart from the same trio of elderly smokers who had now moved inside to the bar, the place was deserted. Jackson ordered a bottle of San Pellegrino for himself and chamomile tea for Priya. DiCanio seemed amused by Jackson's gesture. She added a large French brandy to the order.

DiCanio sank contentedly into the deep sofa chair. She turned to him with a smile. Jackson watched, wincing slightly as the staples in his leg pulled against the flesh.

"Something wrong?" DiCanio asked, politely concerned.

"I took a bit of an injury, in Mexico. Running away from Runig's people."

Her face fell. The transformation was rapid and rather astonishing. It was the second time he'd seen mention of Hans Runig turn DiCanio almost white. "Runig actually *found* you?"

Jackson was surprised; he thought he'd already told DiCanio about this.

"Well sure, one of his people did. They sent a guy to meet me, dressed as Simon Reyes, from PJ's lab."

"How did you get away?"

A sardonic laugh escaped his lips. "I ran!"

"You got back to Mexico City? How?"

There didn't seem to be any harm in telling DiCanio at least part of the story.

"I managed to get down to the road. I hitched a ride back to Mexico."

DiCanio was appreciative. "Some luck!"

Jackson remained silent. Marie-Carmen's identity would be his secret, he'd decided, from everyone. That and PJ's DNA sample, which he'd mailed to friends in San Francisco, would hopefully prove to be a shrewd insurance policy.

"So far, this whole thing feels more like *bad* luck."

"You think maybe PJ told them something which led them to you?"

"Yes. I still don't know what."

"My guess is that Runig thinks you have Pedro Juan's *joust*-like sequence."

He concentrated hard on keeping his expression bland, his voice mild as he appeared to take this on board for deep consideration. "Could be."

"Have you, Jackson?"

"No." Jackson could not quite meet her eye as he said this. Instead, he glanced at Priya. DiCanio didn't seem to care that she was entirely excluding her from this discussion, just as she had earlier ignored him.

"Maybe you do, but you don't know it yet?"

Jackson only nodded. DiCanio seemed keen to know exactly what PJ had told him. It made him wonder – what was really going on between DiCanio and Runig? Ever since her enigmatic statement at the dinner table, DiCanio's business dealings were now of rather less interest.

"This ancient chamber in Iraq – is there more to tell?"

DiCanio smiled. "Ah. That. It's in southern Iraq, near the ruined city of Eridu. Not far from the site of the ancient biblical city, Ur of the Chaldees."

"That was the inspiration for your company's name, Chaldexx?"

"We've always suspected that the hypnoticin-response gene may have originated in the region. There's a cluster of people with the gene, who originate in the Mid-East."

"Really? I didn't see too many mid-eastern types at dinner tonight."

"Jackson, my mother is Lebanese," DiCanio said with just the hint of a chastising tone. "It's not always obvious. Now, the discovery of this chamber, which I'm told dates back at least to three thousand BC. We're learning a lot about ourselves; who and where we are, just what we can do under the influence of hypnoticin. There are so many more questions, mysteries which remain a puzzle. Where did all this begin? Why would such an ability develop at all? How would it be used? Without an injection of hypnoticin, we're just like anyone else. Did hypnoticin occur naturally in something our ancestors consumed . . . is that how the ability was originally discovered and used?"

"Melissa," he interrupted, "what the hell is in this for Chaldexx? I'm assuming that your shareholders aren't all carriers of the gene. How does this make you any money?"

"What it gives us," she told him, "is a model system for looking into drugs which can suppress behavior. I can't go into details; it's all under confidential disclosure. What I can say is this: we've been able to come up with several promising drug candidates. They can modify behaviors linked with obsessive compulsive disorders, Tourette syndrome and other disorders thought to be associated with 'free will'."

Jackson thought this over. No wonder Chaldexx were doing so well. With secret tools like hypnoticin and its genetically-rare response protein, they would be well ahead of the competition.

"The ancient chamber in Iraq," DiCanio repeated, determined to finish her soliloquy, "could be a significant part of the puzzle. As I said, we have someone inside the UN, Jackson, someone feeding us information."

Only now did Jackson begin to see how powerful DiCanio's network of gene-carrying associates might actually be. If they could get someone with the highest level of security clearance required to give them this kind of information, the must have not only money but also, some highly-motivated operators.

"This society of yours: how many are you?"

"Almost two hundred. I can't tell you any more, Jackson. Our rules are very strict. To join, one must not only have the gene, but be of the right background, education and inclination. Then, a candidate must demonstrate loyalty and potential usefulness, by accepting a mission. It might be a small thing, like giving someone help with their professional life. Or something bigger, like feeding us classified information."

Priya sat in absorbed silence, listening. She seemed very young to be part of an influential society. Was DiCanio in the business of recruiting members on the way up in their careers, maybe helping them along the way? It wouldn't be a bad strategy.

Except that DiCanio's society had the potential for an advantage even greater than money and connections than the exclusive university societies which boasted prime ministers and presidents amongst their former members. The more Jackson thought about it, the more he realized: a society like hers might actually acquire enough power and influence to change the world.

"Pardon me for saying this, Melissa, but your society is beginning to sound kind of ominous. Genetic exclusivity, nepotism, tests of loyalty?"

DiCanio seemed momentarily thrown. Within seconds the expression of irritation that flashed across her face was replaced by a resigned chuckle. "I can see how you'd think that. The genetic exclusivity is by necessity; without that there's no advantage to using hypnoticin. Pure motivations; well frankly, Jackson, that's why we don't take people like Hans Runig. Only people who are prepared to demonstrate their commitment to the well-being of the planet. For example, each and every one of us has seen the evidence of the global warming threat, and is determined to take what steps we can to reverse the trend. We are not a military organization. We do not use violence, only subterfuge."

"So, you want me to join?"

"I knew you'd see it."

He could see the next move too; suddenly the pieces were beginning to fit.

"Because of my twin brother, Connor."

DiCanio produced a slow smile. "Because of Captain Connor Bennett, yes."

"Why didn't you just ask him?"

DiCanio's candor was almost disconcerting: "Oh, we did."

"But he's loyal to the US Air Force?"

She nodded, gave a sad little shrug. "Even approaching him was a risk. It required a great deal of exposure of ourselves, as with you."

"You expect me to help you, when my own twin brother wouldn't?"

"You aren't like him, Jackson, though, are you? You're not a creature of the US military. Perhaps more importantly, you're not – yet – part of Hans Runig's organization."

"And Connor is?"

"He won't even be aware of it, but yes. Runig's companies have huge contracts with the US Department of Defense. Like most of the US military in Iraq, Connor himself probably has no idea what the US was really doing there.

"Apart from 'protecting US oil interests'?" Jackson challenged, quoting DiCanio's claim earlier that evening.

"That isn't all. When those UN weapons inspectors found something in Eridu, the order to begin the bombing of Iraq was given the very next day."

DiCanio stood. Her face was slightly flushed from the brandy.

"That's enough for tonight. There's something you can do for us. It is risky, but only you can do it. You'll have the advantage of using hypnoticin. You won't have to kill anyone. If you do this, it will be a major favor for the society and will be taken as your acceptance of our offer to join us. Once you join us, I promise you, your life will change. We will keep you safe from Hans Runig. Opportunities you may not have dreamt of will open to you. I'm prepared to be specific and promise you this: two million dollars for your own research. You'll be totally set up to start your own group."

Jackson's mouth fell open. DiCanio had fallen silent.

"OK, Melissa. You got my attention, definitely."

"We need you to impersonate your brother. Connor has access to the burial chamber at Abu Shahrain. We need you to retrieve an ancient artifact from the chamber. You walk in as Captain Connor Bennett, walk out and bring us the artifact. That's it."

They faced each other in silence. Jackson steadied himself for a moment. He glanced with longing at DiCanio's glass of brandy.

Treason. That was what DiCanio was asking of him.

He breathed out slowly and forced a smile. "I'm gonna need to sleep on it."

The Bodyguard

DiCanio left him with Priya, making an excuse about a call to one of her associates in Oxford. Jackson hesitated for a second, then offered to see Priya to her room. It really was looking as if she'd been sent to sweeten the deal. But even if not for Marie-Carmen, he would have had his doubts. The girl was beautiful, but she'd scarcely said two dozen words to him all evening. He suspected she'd drunk a little too much – it would certainly explain her recent silence. He wondered how much pressure DiCanio had exerted. Was this to be Priya's favor, the price of her admission to DiCanio's exclusive society?

"No," she corrected him, with a sultry giggle. "I'll see you to your room, dearest Jackson Bennett, new favorite of the queen."

He edged backwards in his seat. Priya rose to her feet and held out a hand to him. "Come on. I'll see that no-one harms you."

"You'll what?"

Priya blinked, slowly and with beguiling innocence. "I'll protect you. That's what Melissa wants. Runig's people could be anywhere. I'll sleep in your room tonight, be your bodyguard."

He could scarcely get the words out. "My bodyguard?"

"You needn't look so shocked, yah? I'm a sixth *dan* in *taekwon-do*." She leaned over Jackson, her cleavage inches from his face. "That's just in case things get personal. As well as that, I have a gun."

He found it hard to suppress a grin. "Hey, I've done a little kick-boxing in my time too, but seriously? You're my bodyguard?"

She stretched to her full height. "You doubt it?"

He stood up, nodding. "A little bit, yeah."

Priya replied with just one word. "Upstairs."

Jackson had to take the steps two at a time to keep up with her. Outside the door to his bedroom, she eyed him hungrily. The second he was inside she gave one rapid-fire warning, "Protect yourself!" before launching herself at him, a flying tangle of rock-hard, spinning kicks. He managed to dodge the first, parry the second, but was swiftly overwhelmed with her speed. In less than five seconds he was on his back on the rug, breathless, with Priya's foot lodged against his neck.

Smiling, she stepped back and watched Jackson stumble to his feet. He rubbed his neck, thoughtfully. Amazing how even the residual desire he'd felt for the girl had absolutely vanished. Brilliant and deadly was supposed to be irresistible. Now he knew that it wasn't. He suppressed the impulse to tell her to get out, there and then.

"All right, I believe you."

"Are you hurt?"

Jackson fingered his ribs. She'd delivered a couple of blows there but he felt sure there was only minor bruising. "I'm OK. Did Melissa tell you to do that?"

"No; Melissa told me to protect you."

"Good start."

"It's amazing how patronizing some men can be."

"Well, you sure showed me."

Priya rearranged her sari, which had come loose around one shoulder. "Don't be bitter, Jackson. It's not an attractive quality in a man. Nor is self-pity."

He thought about Marie-Carmen, what she'd say, angry with Priya for the unnecessary humiliation. To think he'd wasted a single chivalrous thought on her. "I'd like to go to sleep now. Is there any chance you can actually leave me alone?"

"There's an inflatable mattress in my room. I'll bring it in here."

When she'd left, Jackson bent low and straightened out the rug next to the double bed. If that was what Priya was capable of when she was slightly tipsy, he guessed she'd be formidable at the height of her powers.

That's when he noticed that his cell phone was on his pillow. It wasn't where he remembered leaving the device. Electricity surged through him; he rushed to examine the sports bag he'd brought from Mexico. The contents had been moved, discreetly. While he'd been out at dinner with DiCanio and her associates from the society, his room had been discreetly searched.

Runig's people were still hunting for the vial. Jackson's skin crawled as he flicked through the record of telephone numbers. Marie-Carmen's cell phone number was the last number he had dialed.

Jackson locked the door and grabbed his laptop. The screen was password-protected, unlike his stupid cell phone, so there was a chance that whoever had searched the room hadn't been able to get in. He checked his browser history, groaning. Hans Runig's website was there, as well as Facebook.

There was a knock at the door. After three more knocks, Jackson called out; "Priya, I don't need you in the room. If you want to protect me, fine. But you're gonna have to stay outside."

He could hear her hesitation. "Don't be unreasonable."

"Please – go away. I'm fine. I'll keep the door locked. See you at breakfast."

He waited for several minutes until he heard her leave. Then he checked his email. There were two messages in his inbox. One was from Marie-Carmen. The other had the subject line: I Know Her Name.

The sender had routed the email via an anonymous email address. Jackson opened the email. Dread swept through him, once again.

Dr. Marie-Carmen Valencia. I'm right, aren't I? I know her name, I know her telephone number, and I know that she's not at home. I'll find her soon. If you'd like to make a deal, let's meet tomorrow, 8.30am, Restaurant Bahnhof, Kleine Scheidegg.

The second message was from Marie-Carmen.

Jackson,

I've spent the day walking along the beach. Guess what?
I find that you're in my thoughts as I stroll past the couples
sitting together at the bars, the restaurants; at night as I look out
from the balcony into the night lights glowing on the paths
around the golf course; at sunrise as I watch the mist roll back,
distant velvet mountains revealed by unfurling layers of cloud.

It's late and I haven't heard from you; I guess your
dinner with DiCanio went on too late? Maybe you've gone to bed
already and I won't hear until tomorrow morning. Which brings
another melancholy. I wanted that morning of ours, wanted to
waken exhausted by you, still craving you.

Forgive me for making us leave so quickly? Even another
hour would have been worth the risk.

Write back – I know you'll be tired, but send something
short, so I'll know you've read this.

Your Marie-Carmen

Jackson felt a rush of tenderness towards Marie-
Carmen. He'd never written or received a letter like it in his
life. Somehow, he had to find the words to respond in a
similar vein. He pressed the reply button and wrote:

Marie-Carmen,

Being with you was like jumping out of a plane without
a parachute and discovering you can fly. So no, I'm not too tired
to reply, if you were here now I'd spend the whole night making
you feel as good as you make me feel.

I'm not used to things happening this fast; I've gone to
some effort to guard against it. I love to think that your thoughts
are of me. I can only dream of the luxury of mental space to do
the same about you. DiCanio is keeping me occupied every minute
I have. She invited me to join the society, to go on a mission for
them to Abu Shahrain in Iraq. I don't know if I can bring myself
to accept. Meanwhile, Hans Runig sent me a message: you were
right about him being onto you, they got hold of your name and
cell phone number.

Turn off your cell, in case there's a way they can trace
you. It's time you got out of there. Find someplace else that is safe.
Keep me posted. I NEED to know you're OK.

J x

He re-read the message, pausing a second before sending it. He couldn't think of an appropriate way of finishing the letter, so left it simple yet obvious.

His palms were damp as he then entered the address of Hans Runig's website. A small text box appeared, rotating until it settled in the middle of the animated hieroglyphic symbols.

Mr. Bennett! Hello.

Rapidly, Jackson began to type.

What do you want? I'm not accepting any new Facebook friends.

That was funny, Jackson. I'm glad you can be funny with me. I feel like we're growing closer. This would all be so much easier if you'd agree to work with us. That's all I want.

What would I have to do?

Can't you guess?

Hand over PJ's DNA molecule?

You see, it's not so hard to write. Now you just need to do it.

Why? You already have the amino acid sequence.

Indeed. But not the whole gene, with all the control sequences. Chaldexx are so far ahead of me. I have much to catch up with. I think you already know that.

I don't have the DNA anymore. I grew kinda tired of being chased for it, so I've put it somewhere safe.

With the young lady from the silver Beetle, no doubt.

If you harm Marie-Carmen I won't help you.

Understood. You know, we're very surprised about your connection with her. You didn't mention it in any of your conversations with Pedro Juan.

Jackson did not reply, instead concentrating furiously, trying to recall every telephone conversation with PJ over the past few months. He didn't dare take Runig at his word, was acutely aware of the danger of implicating himself or Marie-Carmen further.

156

So what's in this for me? Apart from not being killed?

I regret so much that you think we're trying to destroy you. Fernando was not going to kill you.

I'm gonna have to take issue with that.

Become part of my organization. Why waste your talent helping DiCanio and her environmentalists? With my help you can be rich and powerful; there will be nothing you cannot be. You and Marie-Carmen.

Let's say I'm interested. How would this work?

I was hoping we might discuss that tomorrow, at Kleine Scheidegg.

Explain more NOW. Or this discussion is over.

We want you to retrieve an artifact from Iraq.

Why?

We're aware of what DiCanio has asked you. Now I'm asking you, Jackson. Bring the artifact to us and all threats to your life, and to Marie-Carmen and her family.

You're bringing them into this?

I'm not a violent person by nature, Mr. Bennett. Curiosity is charming, to a point. And then it's dangerous.

Why do you want the artifact?

Simply put; to stop Melissa DiCanio. You don't know what you're tangling with there, Mr. Bennett. Did she tell you about her secret society?

Jackson stalled. He watched the cursor blink, relentlessly waiting for his response. When he did nothing, after two minutes Runig began to type once again.

You can imagine how little I can afford to leave an asset like you in DiCanio's hands. I like you, Dr. Bennett. You seem like a resourceful and intelligent young man. I won't allow sentimentality to interfere with my greater aims. The first step is to stop Melissa DiCanio. Get some sleep, Mr. Bennett. It's high time we met face-to-face. Be sure to come alone. The mountain waits.

With this, the text box disappeared, leaving Jackson staring at the screen.

Hans Runig was totally ruthless; Jackson could no longer doubt it. He was not safe from him, would never be safe until he gave Runig what he wanted.

The waves of the Pacific Ocean churned sandy brown as they broke on the Revolcadero beach, directly in front of the Acapulco Princess hotel. In the sky, the peaches and deep magentas of a perfect sunset were already casting flame-tongued reflections on the water. Tired but exhilarated, Marie-Carmen rode the boogie board out of the highest point of the surf and floated, paddling gently with both hands.

She checked her watch: 7.45pm. There was no point expecting Jackson to be available to talk at this hour. She had spent hours in her room that afternoon, waiting for him to return from dining with DiCanio. Eventually, anger and frustration had set in. Throwing the cordless mouse across the room, Marie-Carmen had made for the beach.

She had admittedly played on the jealousy angle for the sake of flirting with Jackson. Yet now she was experiencing genuine qualms. Marie-Carmen hadn't expected to feel as much as she had after their brief liaison. Yet what she'd assumed was a simple physical attraction seemed to have morphed into something more.

Unruly rip tides and waves afforded some distraction. Eventually though, Marie-Carmen's thoughts had inevitably returned to Jackson. There were any number of ways to analyze her feelings – and she had tried a few – but had to admit that there was nothing she could pinpoint; no intimate touch or gesture had accomplished the change between them. It was as though something in the balance of the physical universe had shifted, quite subtly. As if two separate and inanimate objects had suddenly acquired the ability to superimpose the properties of their molecules on the other.

One moment she and Jackson had been laughing, joking, the next, she'd realized with a degree of alarm, it was serious. Too serious. From Jackson's somewhat pained reticence the next day, she guessed he felt that too.

Even a day later, she could scarcely believe that it had actually happened. The memory of him refused to be diminished, a heavy sensation below her waist, almost a persistent ache, reminded her of the violent desire she'd experienced for Jackson's body. Now he was with another woman. It didn't matter that they were probably only talking science.

Girl, get over it.

She pointed her boogie board towards the beach and rode a wave in, then strolled slowly along the sands, back towards the hotel.

Marie-Carmen hadn't planned to stay in Acapulco more than a few days. At this level of luxury, she'd soon run out of spare cash. Luckily she was on a three-month sabbatical from teaching, or else she'd have a timetable full of classes. But the temporary reprieve was only because she'd won an academic prize. The faculty head would expect a quality research paper out of her this year. She didn't really have time to spare from her research.

What she had not foreseen, were the possibly longer term consequences of her sudden involvement with Jackson. If she couldn't get back to Mexico City soon, her job, her family relationships, would it all be compromised? What sort of future could she hope for with a Northern Californian scientist? It was unlikely that a guy like him would move to Mexico. Marie-Carmen was almost ashamed to be speculating so far ahead. Yet her instincts told her that Jackson's fate and her own were intertwined.

As Marie-Carmen started up her MacBook, her fears were confirmed. Jackson wasn't available to chat. There were, however, two new emails from him. The earliest one began with an outpouring of sentiment. Despite her anxiety, Marie-Carmen couldn't read it without a smile. The second email was blunter, more what she expected, from the little she knew of him.

Marie-Carmen,

Runig has your cell phone number. Switch it off and don't use it again; we have to assume he can trace the signal. Tried to find a single photo of Runig on the Internet – nothing. For a tech-savvy business guy he's pretty invisible. I'm supposed to be meeting with him tomorrow morning – he's prepared to drop the threats and negotiate. Mainly, he wants to block DiCanio. Not quite sure what he has against her, or Chaldexx. Runig wants my help but I don't trust him. I'm pretty certain that when he's got what he needs he'll dispose of me. I might still go to the meeting, though. It's up on a ski resort, so I figure it's out in the open. I'll try to get a photo of Runig, before he sees me. I don't know when I can write to you again; I'll try tomorrow. If you've used your cell phone in the last five minutes (check this email's timestamp), then GET OUT OF THERE.

And one more thing: I think I'm falling in love with you.
J x

Marie-Carmen couldn't know it, but Jackson had spent twenty whole minutes deliberating how to declare himself. In the end he'd gone for something simple, direct.

She had to read the email several times before she could tear herself away from the screen. Heightened awareness of the danger he thought she faced was probably a factor in Jackson's declaration. As soon as she read his words, Marie-Carmen found herself hoping that they were true.

She showered and washed her hair, then applied a few drops of argan oil before she used the hairdryer. Her makeup took very little time to apply, just enough to highlight her cheekbones and eyes. She finished off with a tiny amount of reddish-brown lip gloss, a spray of Thierry Mugler's Angel, then dressed in a simple dress of indigo rayon with narrow shoulder straps. Marie-Carmen grabbed her purse before stepping into the corridor.

There was no immediate pressure to take action – her cell phone had been switched off all afternoon. While it was off, there was no way for Runig to trace her. It was frightening to realize that Runig knew her name, had her cell phone number. Marie-Carmen forced herself to examine any possible trail. Unless she had been expertly followed since she left her apartment the previous morning, it was ludicrously unlikely that anyone could know where she was. She hadn't even specified a hotel to Jackson.

For now, she was probably safe.

The corridors were filling with people dressed for dinner. Five excited-looking, very pale American women in their late thirties and early forties joined Marie-Carmen in the elevator. They chatted quietly. As the door was about to shut, the tall, sandy-haired man she'd seen earlier in the lobby, thrust his arm through the door.

"Wait for me, ladies!"

He stepped into the elevator, pushing his long fringe out of his eyes with the gesture that Marie-Carmen felt sure was affected. She watched in silent amusement as her female companions in the elevator fussed over him. From their conversation she determined that as she'd guessed, all were attending one of the conferences being run in the hotel, the meeting of the American Society for Ancient History Teachers. He was clearly one of their party and a rare commodity: a good-looking, single male professor whose specialty was dominated by women. Dressed in a garish, tropical print shirt, he lapped up the attention.

Nevertheless, it was to Marie-Carmen that his eyes strayed. He looked directly at her in the mirrored walls of the elevator. With a slight shake of her head, she turned away. She thought back fondly to Jackson and his obvious discomfort when she'd caught him looking at her in the car. The handsome history professor wasn't put off, not at all. Marie-Carmen could feel his eyes on her even as he and his colleagues walked away.

162

At dinner, he continued to glance in her direction. Turning to the enthusiastic woman to his left, he whispered something in her ear. The woman responded by nodding, looking over at Marie-Carmen, then rose to his feet and joined Marie-Carmen at her table.

"Miss, excuse me, I'm really sorry to bother you but would you care to join us? It's just that we've noticed you seem to be alone. We'd be real happy for you to come over."

She looked over at the table. He merely smiled a lazy, knowing smile. There was something undeniably appealing about a guy this confident. Tonight though, Marie-Carmen was immune.

His messenger continued to insist, with endearing graciousness. She let just enough time pass so that she appeared reluctant, then strode over to their table. He moved along, sitting next to her, and introduced himself as Daniel O'Shea.

The other women began to ask her where she was from, why she was alone (if that wasn't a rude question), what did she do for a living (again, if not an imposition), was she having a nice time?

Marie-Carmen answered as briefly and charmingly as possible, and quickly turned the questions around to them. They were delighted to tell her about themselves. There was an almost collective swoon when she told them that she was a Mayan archaeologist.

"Oh my God, the Maya, that is just so fascinatin'!"

"You must have some of the most fabulous stories to tell!"

When the female professors went to fetch the dessert course, Daniel O'Shea hung back, smiling suggestively at her, but saying nothing.

Marie-Carmen smiled back, with a slight shake of her head. "You know you're pretty selfish."

Daniel's smile broadened. "Why's that now?"

She gestured towards his colleagues at the dessert trolley. "There are quite a few potentially disappointed ladies over there. You should concentrate on what's available to you and not get distracted by something you can't have."

He said nothing for a second, but lowered his eyes.

163

"They're not quite in your league, are they? You can't blame a guy for trying. Where beautiful women are concerned, it always pays to try."

Marie-Carmen laughed. "I guess that's one strategy."

Daniel laughed too. "It is. I promise you it works better than you'd think. It could have worked with you, but you look like you might be taken."

She nodded.

"Lucky guy."

"Thanks."

"Can we at least be friends?"

Her eyes widened. "I see. You want the waiting list application form."

Daniel gave a conspiratorial grin. "Plan B. But don't worry, I know the Waiting List Rules."

"Just so long as you do."

They smiled, both relaxed. Marie-Carmen asked, "You're here to talk about ancient history?"

He took a long drink from his frozen margarita before answering. "You mean, in my work?"

Marie-Carmen ignored the suggestive nudge. "Right."

"That's right. Mainly ancient Mesopotamia."

She struggled to appear unfazed. "Sumeria, Akkadia, Assyria? Anything in particular?"

"The whole bit. I work in a teaching college, so I don't have much time for research. I have to cover the history of most of the area, from the earliest settlements like Eridu, the archaeology, cultural history, religion, writing, everything."

"Has there been much upsurge of interest since the end of the Iraq war? Presumably the access to ruins has improved?"

Daniel nodded. "Got myself interviewed once on TV, as an expert. Kinda fun!"

"So, where do you stand on the age of Eridu?"

"Well, the earliest parts of the city date back to around five thousand BC. They began to build raised layers of the city when the filth in the streets started to run into their homes. Because they built everything in clay, when the cities were abandoned – usually because of flood, famine, fire. After time, erosion destroys much of the city. Sand blows in, fills in the gaps. Eventually you're left with a raised mound, known as a 'tell'. The oldest part of the city would be deepest inside. In Eridu, you've got everything from four thousand five hundred BC to six hundred BC."

"So," she said, leaning closer, almost flirting with him. "If I tell you something in Sumerian, would you be able to translate it?"

Daniel looked up suddenly, intrigued at the tone in her voice. "Well now. You've been using the Internet to look up how to say 'Daniel, I want you' in Sumerian, haven't you?"

Marie-Carmen grinned and tossed a bread roll in his direction, which Daniel just caught with a delighted laugh.

"Not quite, but you could help me out."

"I could live to help you out."

"What does *lugal an un na ki* mean to you?"

Daniel frowned, pondering. "Hey no fair! I thought you were just kidding around, now you want to consult my professional opinion? Gee, I dunno, I usually charge for this sort of thing."

Marie-Carmen tapped the table in mock irritation. "OK, what's it gonna take?"

"You have to agree to dance with me at least three times tonight in the nightclub."

"You know how to dance salsa?"

"That would be a no. But three's my price, take it or leave it."

After a moment's consideration, she shook Daniel's hand. "You got a deal."

"OK. Now it so happens that I think I can help you. *lugal* is easy; it means 'master', 'lord' or possibly 'owner'. Now by *an un na ki* I presume you mean *Anunnaki*."

"I do?"

"It doesn't make much sense otherwise; it broadly translates as 'the people who came from Heaven and Earth'. *Anunnaki* form an important part of the mythology."

"And who exactly were the *Anunnaki*?"

He took another sip from his margarita.

"They're from the mythology. Gods and minor deities who carried out their wishes. They're first mentioned in the *Atrahasis*; a clay tablet on which the earliest written version of the Sumerian creation and flood myths was carved. *Atrahasis*, he's like a Sumerian 'Noah' – the one person chosen by God to survive the flood.

"Eridu was allegedly established by the four main Gods, the original *Anunnaki*. I think the original text goes something like: 'After the kingship descended from heaven, the kingship was in Eridu'.

"The city of Ur was much more well-known and influential. I guess you'll know it from the Bible. It's about fifteen miles away from Eridu, or Abu Shahrain as it's now known. You remember hearing about Nasiriya, in reports on the Iraq war? It's around there."

Marie-Carmen didn't hear his last sentence. All she could hear now was the connection, realized far too late, between the *Anunnaki* and Eridu. She stood, trembling. She wasn't sure how or why, but she was certain that Jackson was walking into terrible danger.

Daniel regarded her with astonishment. "Is something wrong?"

"No, no, I just remembered I'm supposed to be waiting for a call."

"Oh," remarked Daniel with a touch of disdain, "no doubt from the dude! I'm gonna need a rain check for those dances, you know." As she stood to leave, he added indignantly, "Hey, don't let me keep you! It's been real nice talking. Hope to see you again?"

But Marie-Carmen was already running towards the elevator. She had to warn to Jackson.

Kleine Scheidegg

The train to Grindelwald arrived two-and-a-half minutes before it was scheduled to leave. Jackson stepped aboard. He checked back towards the platform. He had managed to slip away from Priyanka Desai while she showered, but she couldn't be more than a few minutes behind him. The next train wasn't for another half hour. By then he'd be aboard the train and ascending the slopes to the ski resort of Kleine Scheidegg.

Jackson was already freezing cold. His hands and face were getting the worst of it, but his feet weren't doing much better. Ten inches of snow had fallen overnight. For all their efficiency, even the Swiss took a few hours to clear pavements and roads. Jackson had almost slipped, just walking to the taxi. He'd waded through thick snow on the train platform. Inside his new brogues, his feet were turning to ice.

By day, Grindelwald's situation appeared even more spectacular. The north face of the Eiger towered over the village, blanking out a huge portion of the skyline, an impossibly sheer wall of pink-grey granite and glacial folds of blue ice. The village was blanketed in the fuzzy edges of white powder. As Jackson boarded he cast an envious glance at the early morning snow-seekers. They clambered aboard, heavy boots clattering against metal, skis and snowboards racked up in neat containers by the doors. Tourists grabbed the window seats where they'd get the best views, all the way to the end of the track, inside the Eiger itself and to the Jungfraujoch research station on top of one of the peaks.

The train pulled away, rose along a track which bordered a *piste* lined with white-capped fir trees and alpine cottages. Some trees were so deeply buried that you could only see the tips poking out through the snow. A toboggan track was being prepared by a grooming machine. The Eiger loomed to the left, its peak giving way to the neighboring, craggy peaks of the Mönch and Jungfrau. To the left were views of rolling slopes, distant mountains and cable cars that swooped across the valley. Jackson had spent many winters in the Rocky Mountains. He loved them, but he had to admit that this was a winter wonderland on a different scale.

Kleine Scheidegg came into view. Skiers were stepping off the train and directly onto a ski run. Guest houses and hotels nestled next to the mountain rides which climbed even higher. Beside the train track, skiers and snowboarders were already carving their way down to Grindelwald, about five miles away.

Deep inside the pockets of his suede jacket, Jackson clenched a fist around his cell phone. He checked, but there were no missed calls. Next to the train station, tables at Restaurant Bahnhof were already filling with people enjoying coffee, croissants, cigarettes. Jackson circled the periphery a couple of times, searching for anyone who was sitting alone.

For some reason he imagined Hans Runig as a large man. When he examined the kind of men that were seated there, he realized that Swiss guys, at least those who took to the mountains before nine in the morning, were more likely to be lean, weather-beaten and athletic.

Why had Hans Runig asked to meet up here?

Not knowing what Runig looked like gave Jackson an eerie sense of dislocation. The man could be watching Jackson this very minute and he wouldn't know it. The mental image he'd built up was something like a Sydney Greenstreet character, a human, Swiss version of Jabba the Hut. Yet now, as Jackson forced his mind to blank out the ridiculous images he'd conjured, he could only think of a spider; a fat garden spider sitting in the middle of a web, sensing the tremors from every thread that connected him to his prey. And then, pouncing.

He shuddered slightly and concentrated on imagining a new persona for Hans Runig. Slim and tall, face tanned and weathered from the slopes in winter, from cycling in the summer. A modern executive who might be as comfortable in lycra racing gear as in a Zegna suit and Patek Philippe time-piece. Jackson scanned the restaurant and neighboring *piste* for anyone of that description. There were several, but none returned his gaze.

Not a single table was occupied by a lone diner. Jackson waited a few more minutes, checked his watch. Eight thirty-eight. Surely the Swiss were punctual? He wandered over to the counter and ordered a double espresso. Priya would certainly be on the next train, if she'd guessed his movements from Grindelwald. He could only hope that she wouldn't work out his final destination. Jackson didn't sit down, but continued to hover around the tables, watching. At eight forty-five he checked his cell phone for messages. There was a long, very strange email from Marie-Carmen, sent some time last night while he'd been asleep. The title, provocatively, was 'Worried About Iraq'. He scrolled through it quickly, then back to the first paragraph.

Jackson, this idea of going to Iraq worries me. You receive secrets, messages over the Internet, telephone calls, a jet to Switzerland, now it's Iraq. It's like you're a chess piece, being moved around the board.

The phone began to vibrate in his hand. When he answered it a male voice spoke; youthful, urgent, aggressive, with a hint of an accent that Jackson couldn't place. "Mr. Bennett? You were told to come alone."

"Is this Hans Runig?"

The speaker ignored Jackson's question. "You've brought one of DiCanio's people. Get rid of her or we will."

The caller disconnected. Jackson turned around slowly, trying to catch sight of anyone who might be making the call. Through the windows of the café he glimpsed Priya stepping off the train. She was dressed in a one-piece, black-and-silver ski outfit and carried a pair of parabolic skis. He just about had the presence of mind to duck behind a pillar as she peered into Restaurant Bahnhof.

The caller was right. He'd been followed. If they'd also seen Priya, chances were that Runig – or his employee – were visible from Jackson's own position. He secured his cell phone in an inside, zip pocket and strode across the café, shielding himself from Priya's view.

When he caught up with her, she didn't seem remotely surprised to see him.

"How can I guard you if you run away?" she began, a little smugly. He grabbed her by the elbow. She froze, stared at him with flat, black eyes. "Get your hand off me. I mean it."

He withdrew his hand. "You need to leave."

"Melissa told me . . ."

"You've been seen! OK? Now get out of here."

Priya hesitated, watching Jackson glance anxiously over her shoulder.

"All right, yah? I'll go. But you have to come with me."

He shook his head.

"I'm serious, Jackson. You can't meet with these people. You don't have any idea who you're dealing with."

He leaned forward. "They'll kill you."

Priya's eyes widened, very slightly, but she didn't seem afraid.

"We need to go."

There was a distinct, but soft, popping sound. Priya groaned slightly. He looked down to see one silver patch on her shoulder beginning to stain with blood. This time he grabbed her, almost violently, dragged her across the platform until they were partly sheltered by a rack of skis and snowboards.

She was breathing in sharp, halting breaths. Jackson unzipped the top of her outfit. He pulled back enough to reveal the wound. She'd been shot in the shoulder. The bullet had gone right through and a ragged exit wound was now bleeding profusely.

Jackson gasped, speechless with shock.

"It's OK, it hurts but I'm all right . . ."

He could do nothing but stare at the blooming red stain.

"In my jacket pocket. There's a first aid kit, some bandages there." She collected her breath for a moment. "I'll ski back down to Grindelwald. They won't be able to catch me, not if I'm on the move."

He nodded. Tentatively, he put his hand inside her jacket. His fingers first came up against the pistol in a shoulder holster. Then he located the first aid kit, in a tin slightly larger than a cigarette packet.

"Can you do it here?"

He surveyed the area. They were tucked well into a nook at the end of the rail station, shielded on one side by ski equipment that had been left by the top of the nearest ski run by skiers at the restaurant; on the other by one of the platform's pillars. He unrolled the bandage. With Priya's help, he tucked it under her damaged shoulder, then wrapped it round and round until the fabric ran out. He tied a tight knot at the front. The blood was already starting to spot the top layers of the dressing.

"You really think you can ski back?"

"Yes. But you need to come too."

"You're in no shape to be my bodyguard now."

"Jackson. I can't leave you here with those people."

"I don't have any skis."

She nodded at the abandoned ski equipment. "Take something. Look inside the café for boots – sometimes people take them off."

He watched her for a moment, torn. Could he trust Runig not to harm either of them, now? The bullet had made so little noise. He had to assume that somewhere in the blinding white slopes that overlooked the station, a sniper was positioned, probably using a high-powered rifle equipped with a silencer. Nothing else could have hit Priya without alerting a single other person on the platform to the gunfire.

The opposite side of the platform, where the ski run began, had to be a safer option than where they were now. Jackson eyed the two snowboards that had been left in the nearby rack. One of them looked about the right size and had strap bindings. He was more confident on a board, and he'd have his hands free to use Priya's weapon. He stared into Priya's eyes one more time. Was she strong enough for the five mile ride down to Grindelwald? The next train would be safer, although it would mean going back onto the platform. Right now, there wasn't a train in sight.

"You really want to do this?"

"We don't know how many of them there are. We don't know where they are. The safest thing is to get out of here, fast."

He nodded, stood up. "Wait. I'm going to find some boots."

It didn't take long. The restaurant restrooms had a dripping tray for boots outside and a 'No Boots' rule. Jackson found a pair of size 11 boots. With a cautious glance at the door of the men's room, he lifted them. It took him a few seconds to swap them for his brogues, which he tucked under his jacket with the toe-ends pushed into the back pockets of his jeans.

Outside, Priya was still cowering in the sheltered spot they'd found. Jackson seized the snowboard and then stood before her, shielding Priya's body with his as they moved the five yards along to where the snow began. She dropped both skis to the ground, snapped her boots into the bindings and was away within seconds. Jackson followed her, pushing off with his trailing foot. They slid past the T-bar drag-lift and began on the first slope. He leaned over and fastened his second binding, mid slide. Priya was about twenty yards below, carving gracefully down the slope.

Jackson felt the buzz of the cell phone against his chest. His hips swayed, his balance shifted, adjusting to the stolen board. He stared directly ahead. A familiar surge of vertiginous pleasure hit him as he gazed down the mountain. Curving edges of snow glittered in the blue light of the morning. The ground beneath him fell away for hundreds of yards. In the distance, the next train from Grindelwald was chugging upwards. The village itself nestled in the valley, wood smoke curling from the roofs of a cluster of chalets.

Still ahead, Priya now held one pole under her good shoulder. In her right hand was a gun. She skied with confidence; rapid, elegant movements that disguised her speed. Jackson sliced across the freshly prepared ski run. He switched stance, from regular to goofy and then back, taking the opportunity to look behind him. Priya and he seemed to have cleared any danger. He saw nothing but casual skiers and boarders on the snow.

Then he heard it. The low growl of an engine; the shift to a higher gear. Jackson switched to a goofy stance, glanced up the mountain just in time to see a snowmobile break into view. It broke across from another ski run, sprayed an arc of fresh powder as it cut through. His heart pounded inside his chest, he forgot about the cold wind that was biting into his fingers. He pointed the board nose-first, directly down the slope. An icy blast of wind stung his face as his speed rocketed. In the next second he was screaming past Priya: "Faster!"

The snowmobile rider pulled on the throttle. The engine roared, accelerating towards Jackson and Priya. The ski run narrowed, the edges curved upwards into a pipe. He rode up the edge and flipped onto the ledge. He stopped short, just in time to see Priya hop into the air and switch to skiing backwards. He watched her shooting at the snowmobile rider. The rider braked hard, then ducked behind his steering wheel. Jackson noticed the rider had a rifle strapped across his back. But at this speed the weapon was unusable. Priya had rattled three or four shots off in the handful of seconds during which she'd skied backwards. Wide-eyed, he watched as she sped towards the hard, frozen edge of the piste. Just in time, Priya swayed away, flipped forwards and then schussed straight down the mountain.

Jackson doubted that she'd managed to inflict any damage. The rider was fairly well protected anyway, with that full motorcycle helmet. Then the snowmobile spun around.

Less than fifty yards away from Jackson, the engine screamed as it began to claw its way up the slope. He stared, gasping. He could never outrun the snowmobile. All he could hope was to go where the rider couldn't. He stepped hard on his leading edge, straight at the wooded border of the ski run. The trees grew close together, close enough to require intense concentration and skill. He could hear the snowmobile crashing about somewhere behind. With speedy, nimble movements Jackson managed to stay ahead. The trees thinned; ahead he glimpsed another piste. As he exited the woods, Jackson bent low, grabbed the leading edge of his board and lifted it just as the ground ran out. He soared through the air for a full two seconds, skimmed past two skiers and slammed onto the narrow ski run. The momentum carried him straight to the edge of the run and up a steep slope. Jackson took the slope with a drop down his back-side wall, steadied his tempo with a lengthy float, gripping the board between the bindings. When he landed he caught sight of the snowmobile, stalled at the lip of the piste. Faced with an impossibly tight perpendicular turn, the rider had simply stopped. Jackson faced straight down the mountain again. He rode hard, all the way to the base.

As he reached Grindelwald, Jackson cast about in search of Priya. His pulse began to slow. Jackson noticed that once again, the cell phone was vibrating.

Melissa DiCanio's number.

"Jackson . . . ?" The word hung in the air, tense with anxiety.

"I'm OK."

There was an audible gasp of relief. "We're right outside the ticket office. Priya's already here. Be quick!"

Isn't The World Going To End In 2012?

Jackson stepped into his brogues and leaned the 'borrowed' snowboard and boots against the wall of the refreshment chalet. Hopefully they'd be returned. If not, Jackson reflected that their owner could probably easily afford to replace them. This resort was on the pricey side – even the train ticket up to the ski lifts.

Inside the car, Priya had crumpled, lay huddled in one corner of the rear. Jackson was sure he could detect a faint but steady tremble throughout her body. DiCanio was in the front passenger seat, talking into her iPhone. Her driver was the same as last night's.

He drove away, smooth and efficient. When DiCanio interrupted her phone call to bark, "Faster!" at him, he didn't flinch.

He touched Priya's arm with a finger. She turned slightly, just enough to face him. Her face was drained, white with exhaustion. He remembered the last he'd seen of the young woman, pelting headlong down the steep, narrow run. It had to have taken sheer guts and resolve to keep going like that, with a bullet hole torn through her shoulder.

He tuned in to DiCanio's conversation. "Get the jet ready," she was saying. "We'll be there in about forty-five minutes."

Jackson was suddenly nervous. He hadn't expected action so rapidly to follow a decision.

"A jet . . . right now?"

She put the iPhone down. "We have to get you out of here."

Jackson opened his mouth to speak but inside his jacket his cell phone began to vibrate.

DiCanio said, "Take the call."

He put the cell phone to his ear.

It was the same, youthful voice. "Mr. Bennett. You're making a mistake."

"Look, Runig, if this is really you, don't you think that chasing me down a mountain is getting a little tired?"

The voice interrupted, sharply. "Don't be a fool! You cannot trust Professor DiCanio. Do you even know what their drug does?"

He hesitated. "Tripoxan?"

"Don't waste time, Bennett! I'm talking about hypnoticin. It's a *mind-altering* substance. DiCanio has been using it on you. You *cannot* trust yourself around that woman."

The caller rang off. In silence, Jackson put his cell phone away.

DiCanio was regarding him with a humorless, knowing grin. "Hans Runig?"

"Seems younger than I thought."

"Probably wasn't him at all."

"How old is he?"

She seemed to hold her breath, for about a second. Her eyes closed as she did so; controlled exasperation. "I don't know, Jackson. I've never met him. He refuses to meet me directly. He'll be in the audience at a seminar I give, then he'll call me afterwards."

"He has your phone number?"

DiCanio didn't answer but her eyes glazed for a moment, flat and dangerous. Jackson thought about what he'd just heard from Runig or his spokesman. They knew about hypnoticin. Did DiCanio realize how much her organization was leaking? He wondered if maybe her work with her secret, supposedly altruistic society, was absorbing too much of her time. It looked as though things weren't going so well at Chaldexx. Maybe she should be using the hypnoticin to better control her staff's loose tongues. Then again, the drug's effect was possibly too short-lived.

As the car wound its way through the fields and forests, through the valley and towards the nexus of lakes at Interlaken, Jackson found himself reflecting on the possibility that his thoughts and motives were being controlled.

Was Melissa DiCanio hypnotizing him into going to Iraq?

"This is how it's going to go, Jackson. We're going to fly into Basra. I've arranged some meetings with some senior Red Cross officials in Iraq. We'll be discussing some clinical trials. The airport security is unlikely to ask details about you; but if they do, you have to persuade them that you're a physician, not a research scientist.

"Once we arrive in Iraq, we'll check into a hotel and work on your appearance. I'm going to go over the plan with you in the airplane. You can meet yet another of our society members: Hafez Kazmi, who'll be flying the jet. He's a former fighter pilot, from Iran."

Jackson shook his head. He tried to smile. "Melissa," he began softly, "I haven't said that I'll go."

She hesitated, shot him a look that made him instantly regret what he'd said. It was genuine surprise, disappointment, confusion. As though he'd upset, with one word, some dearly held belief. Despite himself, Jackson couldn't help feeling as if he'd let a parent down.

It took her several moments to recover. When she spoke again her voice sounded controlled, yet hurt.

"I . . . I don't know what to say to convince you. Please, Jackson. If you can't do it for the money, do it for the idea that you'll be helping the world survive the cataclysms and horror that global warming and overpopulation will bring."

"I'm not sure that I believe that those things are going to happen," he ventured. "Anyway, isn't the world going to end in 2012?"

Jackson had intended the last statement as a joke, a touch of humor to detract from the gravity of the situation. From DiCanio's expression of absolute horror, he realized that he'd overstepped some mark. With difficulty she managed to reply, "Is that what you believe?"

He laughed. "What? Of course not! That was a joke. Melissa, if you're one of the people who can use hypnoticin, how do I know you're not using it on me?"

"To get you to help us?" She seemed flabbergasted. "Firstly, if you were susceptible to hypnoticin, you wouldn't be any good to us. Secondly, if I was using it, you'd have agreed to the mission, right away. You'd have wanted to do it, simply to please me. That's what hypnoticin does; it fills the subject with desire to assist the person who's using it on them."

"So you had to resort to money."

"Money is never enough. At best it's compensation. Think of it as danger money. Is it too much to hope for a spark of idealism from you?"

"*Idealism*," he repeated. "Isn't that what Connor gave you?"

"I'd hope your idealism is less jingoistic."

"Why the hurry?"

"Because your brother's tour of duty ends tomorrow, Jackson. He'll return to a desk job in Virginia. The opportunity to impersonate him will be gone. We'll lose our last chance to acquire the artifact, the last chance to discover the secret of our gene's ancient origins. And with it, the power to unlock our true potential. Yours as much as mine."

"I'm sorry, Melissa. Really. Without understanding a lot more, I can't do it." Suddenly, saying the words aloud released his escalating tension.

DiCanio stared at him for a second, her eyes wide with distress. She was about to answer him when the driver, whose eyes had been regularly scanning his rear view mirror, spoke.

"Professor, we have a tail."

Jackson was in the act of turning his head when DiCanio's voice stopped him.

"Don't look around, don't alert them!"

He managed to stay calm enough to say just the word, "Runig."

DiCanio asked, "Is there something you haven't told me?"

Jackson wondered briefly how far to go. He'd pushed the issue of Runig to the back of his mind. But now, surely he had to speak up? Runig had revealed one thing which simply had to be discussed.

"Chaldexx is not secure, Melissa – Runig knows about hypnoticin. You've put my life at risk, and you haven't even told me the real reason for this mission. Now you can explain or you can go fuck yourself and I'm outta here, I'll take my chances against Runig!"

DiCanio was momentarily speechless. Checking the mirror again, she instructed the driver to call ahead to the pilot, ordering that he prepare for trouble.

His outburst over, he now sat back, waiting for her response.

"OK, look. There's a second burial chamber, just like the one in Iraq. It's in Mexico. We discovered it about three months ago."

"How?" insisted Jackson.

"Jackson," DiCanio muttered, clearly irritated, "I told you we have many people in the organization. With many specialties, and we've been looking for years. Once we began to receive more specifics about the Eridu chamber from our source in the UN, we could rule out most of the leads we had. We were left with only a few.

"Like the one in Iraq, the artifacts are behind a locking mechanism. There is a space for a key-like object – about the size of a TV remote control. We call it the Adaptor. Now, we've seen the list of artifacts found in Iraq. One of them fits the description of the Adaptor. Our hope is that the Eridu Adaptor will function in Mexico."

"Where in Mexico?" he remembered suddenly Marie-Carmen's puzzled reaction to the fact that a Chaldexx employee had official business in Chetumal. The bio-reserve story had been fairly convincing, but there were a lot of ancient ruins in that part of Mexico. Was that their real reason for being in Chetumal?

"I can't answer that, Jackson. I'd have to be convinced of your loyalty. Not until we get back."

He considered for a few seconds. "So you want to get this artifact from the Eridu chamber, to use in the Mexico chamber?"

"The Iraq chamber is in the hands of the National Reconnaissance Office, Jackson. So far as we are aware, only we have discovered the chamber in Mexico."

180

"What do you think you're going to find?"

"The Adaptor is the key that will unlock an ancient technology. Each member of our society is linked to the ancients who built that chamber. We'd be unlocking the secret to our past and possibly, our future."

He stared at her. "You're serious? *Ancient* technology? How do you know you're linked to those ancients?"

"Think about it – where else did our gene come from? It doesn't appear anywhere in the DNA record of this planet until three thousand BC. We think." She hesitated, locking her eyes with his for a moment. "We believe that the ancients were survivors from a super-ancient race, possibly of extra-terrestrial origin; extra-terrestrials who mingled their DNA with ours. The buried chambers may be some relic of their civilization. And we're descended from them, Jackson, you and I."

He gaped. Ancient technology of extra-terrestrial origin? He'd heard a lot of kooky-sounding theories of ancient civilizations having contact with aliens, but surely it was all nonsense? Yet this highly credible, powerful and connected scientist seemed perfectly serious. Could it be some bizarre, hallucinogenic side-effect of the drug her company had developed?

"How powerful is hypnoticin, really? Can you use it to persuade someone to kill?"

"The stronger the inhibition, the easier it is to resist, unless the subject is seriously physically weak. Just like in the mouse experiments – the hypnoticin-treated mouse could only influence the other mice when they were all close to starvation."

"How can I believe you?"

"Hypnoticin is not a weapon of mass destruction, Jackson, or even as convincing as a gun to the head. And you'll notice that no-one is holding a gun to your head."

Jackson flopped back into the seat. He was confused, afraid. "I'd need to see a demonstration."

"Agreed; I'd hoped to show you today at the office. Your friend Runig has somewhat raised the stakes."

"I'm not agreeing to anything until I've seen this drug in action."

Gently, DiCanio said, "I can only appeal to you as a scientist, as an idealist who believes in using your talent to further the health of society on this planet. You can still go with Runig if you prefer. I won't stop you, I promise. When we get to the airport, you can either make a run for it to the jet, with me, or you can give yourself up."

He inhaled deeply. He knew what he would choose, and although he sensed no direct pressure, there was a vague feeling of powerlessness. He looked at himself in the mirror.

Jackson Bennett, secret agent for an underground society of genetically-enhanced intelligentsia?

There was a stark discrepancy between his ordinary persona and the one into which he was evolving. It was as disturbing as the growing sense of Jackson's own vulnerability.

The car was now speeding alongside the smooth, teal-colored water of Lake Thun. After a few minutes the driver turned off the road, following road signs to the small Thun airfield at Beizli. The car behind did the same.

As they approached the small terminal building, he could see a handful of private jets parked. Another one was moving, taxiing very slowly towards the runway. It was white, had two turbofans positioned near the tail and appeared to have capacity for several passengers.

Suddenly, the driver pressed his foot down hard on the accelerator. Within a second or two he'd put fifty yards between DiCanio's car and the car in pursuit.

His heart plummeted when he saw the car behind also speed up, racing to catch them. He had still hoped that they'd been wrong. Deep down however, he knew that Runig would never have simply waited for Jackson to turn up for that 8.30am meeting. He found himself joining in with DiCanio, urging the driver to speed up and pull up alongside the jet.

The jet was already moving down the runway when they reached it. Their driver slowed down to match its speed and opened the left hand rear window. The airplane's door was open and two burly-looking men leaned forward to offer a hand to lift them out of the BMW. The pursuit car was only a few yards behind them. It in turn was now being followed by two security cars, sirens blaring. He stared in disbelief at the sight of DiCanio removing her high-heeled shoes, throwing them into the jet's cabin, and then climbing out of the car window, stretching to catch hold of one of the outstretched hands.

With surprisingly little fuss, she transferred over to the jet. Now it was his turn. When Jackson kept his focus on the jet, he realized that after all, it was not so difficult. Their relative speeds matched, it was a small jump. Then, to his horror, he heard shots ring out. The car in pursuit had taken position behind the jet. The passenger had wound down the window, taking potshots at the gap into which he was preparing to launch himself.

He hesitated for just a second longer, turned to look at Priya. She seemed oblivious, gazing out of the window, knees drawn up to her chest. He said to the driver, "You gotta take her to a hosp. . ." but DiCanio's voice broke across him, yelling, "Come on, Jackson, now!"

Ahead he glimpsed, briefly, the approaching end of the runway. This was the final motivation. He heaved himself out of the car and lunged towards the jet, both hands catching the arms of the men on board. They hauled him into the jet. The plane's nose tipped into the air and all aboard clung tightly to anything in sight. The floor tilted sharply, Jackson's body hung momentarily in mid-air.

Eyes wide open, he gripped the back of a seat. He counted the seconds as the jet pulled further from the ground, hideously aware of the open door directly behind him. Less than three minutes later, the jet straightened. One of DiCanio's men manually pulled the door shut. He exhaled, long and slow. DiCanio had managed to get into a seat. He glanced in her direction.

For a second, their eyes met. Defiance? Gratitude? Circumspection? He couldn't quite fathom her expression.

Captain Connor Bennett

Once the plane was in the air, Jackson reached inside his jacket, fumbling for his cell phone. He needed to read Marie-Carmen's email properly, the one that she'd given the subject 'Worried About Iraq'. He'd barely managed to skim it before Runig – or whoever he was – had called him, but what he'd seen had been pretty crazy, full of quotations from ancient Sumerian texts. He guessed that it had something to do with what they'd seen on the website that Runig had used to trap people searching for the fifteen-letter code; the amino acid sequence of hypnoticin.

The cell phone wasn't in his pocket. He peered around, shifted his feet and checked under the seat. There was no sign. He thought back to the chaotic moment of transferring to the jet on the runway. It must have fallen then. He bit his lip. This was going to be a serious inconvenience.

During the long flight over Iraq as the plane proceeded south to Basra, Jackson was glued to the window, gazing abstractedly at the seemingly endless stretches of desert and barren land. Every now and then, he'd spot a tiny patch of green, a lush oasis of fertility, but mostly, the impression was of a harsh, almost relentlessly flat landscape.

Observing him, the pilot Hafez Kazmi, remarked, "Imagine how hard it was to make a living from this land before oil. Then remember that Iraq is the cradle of civilization; maybe the original inspiration for the Garden of Eden."

Jackson's fingers touched the plastic of the window. After a moment he turned, examining the man who was flying the jet. Kazmi was powerfully-built, probably somewhere in his fifties to judge from his face. He was trim at the waist with heavy musculature apparent under his pale blue shirt. His thick hair was about half-way to being grey, impeccably trimmed and smooth. He wore a thick beard that was even darker than his hair. Like all pilots Jackson had observed, Kazmi had that air of competence; a man commanding technology. Just the sort of hardy physical specimen that he could imagine DiCanio would admire.

He wondered fleetingly if she and Kazmi were intimate. Despite her blonde hair and detached manner, DiCanio managed somehow to avoid the 'ice queen' cliché. Maybe it was because he detected a faint air of desire in the way she gazed at him, even if the desire wasn't sexual, as Jackson now realized was probably the case. Did the same apply to Kazmi, he wondered?

"Iraq was the inspiration for Eden?" he wondered aloud, eyes taking in the vastness of a desert below. "But how?"

Kazmi chuckled, a deep, throaty sound tainted with decades of cigarette smoke. "My friend, you must gaze with historical eyes! The entire region was habitable by the good fortune of the Tigris and Euphrates rivers. The same way that Ancient Egypt grew up around the Nile. Unfortunately the Tigris and Euphrates don't flood as reliably as the Nile. When they flooded just the right amount, the soil was enriched, things were good. The country was a garden. But often, the floods were bad. The land is so flat that they'd affect an enormous area; the floods became legendary.

"The Biblical flood myth is probably based on earlier Sumerian accounts of a flood in Mesopotamia found in the Epic of Gilgamesh. In fact, some people even think that all world myths of the giant flood are actually corruptions of the Gilgamesh flood story, applied to local events. The truth is, we don't even really know when this early flood happened. Parts of the flood story have been found on clay tablets going back as far as two thousand BC. Some people think that even those are compilations of an older, much older, story."

DiCanio was staring at him, her eyes full of hopeful expectation. "This place has been central to the destiny of the world for thousands of years. *Plus ça change*. What you're going to do, Jackson, could help us unlock the secret of who we are, where we came from, the true extent of our abilities."

***

The jet landed at Basra International Airport six hours after they had left Switzerland. A car was waiting for DiCanio, Jackson and the bodyguards. The pilot, Kazmi, bade DiCanio farewell with a kiss to her hand.

"I'll have the jet fuelled and ready within three hours," he said, adding, "I've made arrangements at the house in Manama."

Jackson watched with an increasing sense of powerlessness. DiCanio's society seemed to have it all worked out. He placed a hand on her wrist. "What about the demonstration, Melissa? I said no deal until I've seen evidence that your hypnoticin works."

If DiCanio was at all slighted by the faint pressure of his hand near hers, she showed absolutely no sign of it. She remained pleasant, amicable. "I've got vials of hip33 in my suitcase. Relax, darlin', you'll get your show."

In the car, Jackson sat rigidly, brooding. He was reduced to silence by the cruel desolation of the surroundings. Despite the fact that the war had been over for years, bombed-out buildings were everywhere, the air seemed to be filled with a fine, sticky dust, there were queues for petrol. Everything seemed to be grey, tan or khaki; vivid color was in short supply. Local businesses appeared to be conducting brisk trade. Small trucks parked and sold fruit directly out of containers. Where he could catch their expressions, people looked slightly weary, but determined.

"So this is what it looks like when a country gets rescued by the United States military."

But DiCanio misunderstood his words, took them to be some kind of endorsement of his brother's actions in the war. "For now, maybe. Let's wait and see what happens when the last troops actually leave."

Changing the subject, she began to go over the plans for infiltrating the base.

Connor Bennett, they were informed, went on duty in eight hours. It would be his last shift at the underground chamber. Until then, he would not be expected to report to the base at Abu Shahrain. That was Jackson's window for infiltrating the base, hopefully with minimal fuss, leaving well before Connor returned. By the time the artifact was discovered to be missing, they planned to be long gone.

Connor's position was thought to be that of Head of Operations, Headquarters of NRO Communications, Systems Acquisition and Ops Directorate in Iraq. Why the National Reconnaissance Organization, primarily responsible for designing, building and monitoring reconnaissance satellites, should still have an operation on the ground in Iraq, had long been a mystery to Jackson.

If DiCanio was right about there being a possible link between the ancient chamber and extra-terrestrial intelligence, then it made perfect sense. Could it be that the chamber contained some kind of signaling device that might send information through space, to its place of origins? When DiCanio had asked him, Jackson hadn't listed 'alien invasion' as one of the perceived greatest threats to mankind. Secretly though, he knew that in the massively unlikely event that extra-terrestrial beings had actually reached our solar system, there wouldn't be much chance of fighting them off. Any civilization that could overcome the challenges of interplanetary travel had to be so far ahead of our own that the odds – at least in terms of technology – would be pretty bleak for humans.

Connor's position at the NRO was fairly recent. It had come as a total surprise to Jackson. He'd thought that his brother's tour of duty in Iraq had ended last year. At that time there had indeed been rumblings about his moving to Virginia. Then suddenly, he'd been sent back out. So perhaps Connor's local knowledge of Iraq had led to his being stationed out there once more? Jackson could only speculate. At least his brother was now a non-combatant.

When the car reached the more densely populated city center, there was evidence of greater post-war recovery. Fishing skips and motorboats churned through the milky-brown river. Above the second story, many buildings bore pockmarks from bullets. The area came alive in the hordes of bright, tacky shop fronts selling Turkish shawls, Lebanese sweets, fragrances, imported electronics, cell phones. As in the outlying region by the airport, the streets teemed with shoppers.

The driver dropped them outside the newly-re-opened Basra International Hotel, formerly the Sheraton. A porter took two suitcases from the trunk of the car and led them into the lobby. It was a wide-open space, overlooked by the layered arches of the hotel's many floors, clean, geometric lines of cream and brown. Subtle, concealed lighting giving the impression of lamps burning inside the windows of a hillside, Moorish village.

A few guests lounged on the generous leather sofas that were carefully positioned around the lobby, smoking whilst conducting energetic cell phone discussions in Arabic.

They checked in with minimal fuss, although DiCanio was clearly upset at the receptionist's insistence that they leave their passports.

Calculating how much time that's going to add to our getaway.

With some trepidation, Jackson realized the extent of the trail he was leaving. When it came out – as it surely would – that someone closely resembling Connor had removed something from the burial chamber, Jackson would be the first to be implicated. Now there'd be physical evidence of his intervention.

This hypnoticin stuff had better be amazing. Or I'm totally screwed.

In the hotel room, Jackson subjected himself to a buzz cut at the hands of one of DiCanio's bodyguards. Luckily for them, Connor was a stickler for his hair length, taking a weekly number three cut. It wasn't difficult to fake a 'Connor'.

DiCanio opened one of the suitcases and removed a US Air Force uniform. Jackson ran a finger over the insignia; two silver bars.

"Does it look right?" DiCanio asked him.

"I guess. . . " His brother's world was a total mystery to him. They better have done their research, or he was in dire straits.

Jackson took the uniform into the bathroom and stood in front of the mirror as he watched the transformation take place. He ran the palm of one hand over the trimmed, almost black scrub that his hair had become. With no long strands of raggedy fringe to fall into his eyes, his face seemed suddenly open. There was an air of purity, almost innocence. This wasn't how he remembered seeing his brother. The longer he stared the more he realized that his brother and he weren't all that identical, even without the differences that they had imposed on themselves. Jackson's face had retained a mischievous, boyish quality that Connor's more disciplined facial expression had somehow lost. He fastened his shirt collar and tie, slowly buttoned the jacket, arranging the lapels carefully. Jackson clenched his jaw and stared deep into his own dark brown eyes, willing them to return something of his brother to him.

"This is a heap of horseshit," he shouted through the door. "No-one's gonna buy it."

DiCanio pushed the bathroom door open. Her eyes wandered over the length of Jackson's uniformed body.

"It's perfect," she pronounced.

Irritated, he insisted, "No, it looks like Jackson Bennett dressed up in a captain's uniform. Dressed like Connor."

From behind, DiCanio took hold of Jackson's shoulders, rotating him so that they both faced the mirror.

"This is not how you see Connor. When you look at him, you see the mirror image. But to everyone on the outside, Jackson, this is Connor. So get used to it; name and rank?"

"Captain Connor Bennett, United States Air Force," said Jackson with a weary air.

One of the bodyguards, who'd been standing idly by, turned to him.

"Not like that." Then he shouted; "Airman, what is your name and rank?"

"Sir, Captain Connor Bennett, sir!" repeated Jackson in the staccato bark which he'd so often heard his brother rehearse.

The trio assessed him in silence.

DiCanio didn't appear terribly impressed, merely declaring, "OK, get your jacket and shirt off. You're halfway there."

Jackson stared. "You want me to get his *tattoo*?"

"I'm perfectly serious. You can relax; there's no time for a proper job. We're just going to ink you. A real tattoo would show signs of bleeding and inflammation; it would be rather obvious."

He began to unbutton his shirt, shaking his head.

DiCanio grinned. "The Stars and Stripes it is, then."

Medecins Sans Frontieres

Dressed once again in his everyday blue polo short and taupe-colored chinos, Jackson rode an elevator to the lobby. This time he was alone. He passed a metal ash tray and disposed of the tiny cotton wool wad, which DiCanio had jammed into the crease of his elbow to absorb the blood from where she'd injected him with hip33 – hypnoticin. The drug would now circulate in his blood and combine with the naturally expressed joust-like-factor made by his own body. The combined molecule would stimulate pathways that they didn't yet understand, to render his will difficult to resist.

"Most people naturally want to please. It seems that only a little is required to tip them over the edge. Hypnoticin supplies that extra."

The major drawback was that, in the present formulation, the drug's effects would last less than fifteen minutes. At the current cost of manufacture, it wasn't really viable as a world-changing pharmaceutical. However, Chaldexx, DiCanio assured him, was working on a new method for delivering the molecule. If it worked, a tiny amount of the drug would work for hours.

He ordered a beer at the bar and paid for it with the twenty dollar bill that DiCanio had given him. The bartender passed him a squat, sweating bottle of Efes Pilsener. As Jackson sipped from the bottle, he took a good look at the human traffic in the lobby. With his buzz-cut, a clean-shaven white face and casual dress, he stood out as a foreigner. Already some eyes strayed in his direction, wondering who he might be. An off-duty soldier? One of those technology millionaires looking for new business opportunities in Iraq?

Jackson caught sight of one man whose gaze landed on him and didn't stray. There was more than curiosity in that gaze; there was a certain, unmistakable hunger. A guy who stared directly at you for so long could only have one intention. Normally, Jackson would look away. It wasn't fair to lead another guy on. Not that he minded when girls did that; at least you'd get some flirting out of it. With a guy, flirting was out of the question. This time, however, he sensed an opportunity of an altogether different type.

DiCanio claimed that the drug could only work through use of the voice. Yet Jackson had willed that the Middle-Eastern man who was staring at him should stand up, leave his comfortable place at the sofa and join Jackson at the bar. That was precisely what happened.

The man was in his late forties, his face even more closely shaven than Jackson's except for the exceedingly trim moustache and goatee beard. His short black hair was slicked back with fragrant oil; the scent of expensive cologne reached Jackson's nostrils before the guy uttered a word. His suit was immaculate and the blue-and-yellow tie looked like a Missoni design.

He placed his drink on the counter and looked at Jackson, without a hint of a smile. Suddenly he seemed nervous. He seemed to have expected Jackson to speak first.

"What's your favorite charity?" Jackson said. The line had been suggested by DiCanio. It seemed to cause a certain amount of turmoil in the guy who'd accepted what he'd assumed was a tacit invitation to chat with Jackson.

"Charity . . .?" he said, at last. His eyes scanned Jackson's face in a way that would normally have made him deeply uncomfortable. But he stuck to DiCanio's script.

"Charity," Jackson repeated. "Your favorite one. Who'd you really like to help out? I mean, like, seriously help."

The man stared at him, baffled. A helplessness had entered his demeanor. He seemed to want to leave, but something was stopping him. Jackson could see the tension in the guy's hand as he gripped the bar rail. It was easy to imagine that Jackson's will alone held him at the bar.

"When I say *seriously*," Jackson continued, "I'm talking big money. Enough to hurt a guy, you know what I'm saying? In the wallet, I mean." He took another sip and watched the well-groomed Iraqi businessman struggle for words. "So – who'd you like? Red Cross? *Médecins Sans Frontières*? Save the Children?"

"*Médecins Sans Frontières*," stammered the Iraqi, his French pronunciation perfect. "I suppose. They helped us a great deal after the war. Good doctors, good people."

Jackson beamed. "Excellent. So why don't you call them? Donate something. Something decent. You're good for, what . . .?" Ostentatiously, he looked the man up and down. "For fifty thousand bucks at least. Am I right?"

The man blanched. Yet he didn't get angry or walk away. Rather he appeared utterly crestfallen. The amount was beyond him, Jackson could tell that much. Yet he badly wanted to be able to say yes. "Too much?" Jackson shook his head reassuringly. "How about fifteen? Is fifteen good?"

The man broke into a smile of relief. "Fifteen, yes, better! I can afford fifteen thousand, just."

"All right! We're doing this! Get out your phone," Jackson said. "Call your bank."

Then he watched as the Iraqi called his bank and demanded an immediate transfer of funds to *Médecins Sans Frontières*. When it was done, he shook the man's hand, which was now slick with sweat. He turned and headed for the elevators.

Jackson looked back only once, to see the Iraqi still standing at the bar, a glass partway to his lips. The man seemed calm. But Jackson had felt the tension in his body when he'd shaken the guy's hand. He'd obeyed Jackson, insofar as he felt himself commanded.

Part of his brain hadn't wanted to surrender; Jackson had sensed it.

Ninety minutes later, dressed in the captain's uniform that DiCanio had supplied, Jackson rolled up a sleeve. One of DiCanio's men injected him with a fresh burst of hypnoticin. He pulled the jacket back over his left shoulder and buttoned up. They dropped him just out of site of the guard station for the base, behind the temporary buildings which housed the officer's quarters. As instructed, he walked briskly, confidently through the security gates and into barracks, his head held high. Inside though, he was a hard, twisted knot. The sensation of powerlessness he'd experienced in the airplane with DiCanio was returning. The experiment with hypnoticin had given him something that was diametrically opposite; the pure rush of *control*. Where was that confidence now, he wondered? It obviously didn't come from the drug.

He had to believe, or he had not to care. But the hardness in his abdomen wouldn't let up. Infiltration, physical conflict; this was Connor's world, not his.

It was trespass.

The two young airmen on guard duty nodded at him as he passed.

"Captain Bennett."

"Afternoon, airmen," he said, imitating his brother's clipped tones. It seemed to do the trick, because they didn't give him a second glance.

The more people he passed, the less he worried. DiCanio had been right; the uniform and close resemblance to Connor were obviously enough to persuade most people that he was indeed his brother.

But I know the difference. It's all about nerve. Do I have Connor's nerve?

Jackson had memorized the map of the base whilst aboard the airplane. On the ground, however, things seemed to have changed somewhat. A new tent had been erected directly in front of where he expected to find a path leading to the lift shaft. He walked into the tent, where an enlisted airman was making and attaching labels to articles placed on large tables covered in vinyl sheeting. Each article was bagged in clear plastic.

I'm supposed to know all these people.

The enlisted man had four stripes on his arm. A sergeant of some kind, probably. Jackson outranked him, at least.

The sergeant glanced up. "Sir. Can I help you?"

Jackson went blank for just a second.

"Something wrong, sir?"

He gave a nervous laugh. This was going to be harder than he'd expected. What the heck was he supposed to say?

"I left something here . . . You didn't find my iPhone?"

"This morning? Or yesterday?"

"Let me see, when do you last remember seeing me here?"

"That would be this A.M., sir," offered the man helpfully.

"That is correct, Sergeant. Any sign of it?"

"No, sir, I'm sorry. Let me help you look."

The two men pored over the tables, Jackson taking the opportunity to examine the objects that were being accumulated. They comprised stone objects of various sizes. Could the artifact he sought be among them? From what he could see, none of them matched the description he'd been given.

Eventually, he stopped. "I must have left it in the chamber."

The sergeant seemed puzzled. "Why would you take your cell phone down there, sir? We're under strict instructions not to take wave-emitting equipment down there."

Jackson decided it was time to test the hypnoticin's power. Looking directly into the younger man's eyes, he said, "I must have forgotten to leave it up here before I went down. No big deal, it's switched off anyways. I need to go down and check for that cell. I need you to stay up here and keep an eye on things. Will you do that for me, airman?"

The sergeant nodded. He looked vaguely confused; the same look of baffled disorientation that Jackson had seen in the eyes of the Iraqi at the bar.

Pitching his voice with precision, Jackson repeated, this time louder, "Will you do that for me, airman?"

"Sir, yes, sir!" He seemed to remember, belatedly, to salute.

Jackson's eyes swept the tent. The entrance to the elevator shaft must be on the other side of this tent. A flap of canvas in the tent wall caught his eye. He pulled the flap back to reveal a sturdy metallic frame structure, the elevator shaft. The elevator consisted of a thick metal platform wide enough to accommodate up to four men. A huge pulley structure at the top of the shaft looked tough enough to take a huge weight load. The elevator appeared to be operated by a simple lever apparatus attached to the platform.

He stepped onto the platform and pulled down on the lever. It began to move, descending into the darkness. The light dimmed rapidly as the top of the shaft grew smaller.

How deep is this thing?

Full descent took two minutes. The platform came to a juddering halt at the mouth of another small tunnel walled in canvas. Artificial light streamed from behind thick plastic swinging doors, about ten yards away. There was no sound other than Jackson's own footfall. When he stopped the stillness was profound.

He arrived at the entrance to an octagonal chamber about thirty yards across and six yards high. What he saw would remain with him as long as he lived. Without recourse to any singular splendor or beauty, its captivating nature lay instead in the way his gaze became dazzled by patterns; inscriptions which followed one another, networks of the abstract, written concepts enlaced with the architectural. Each piece in the room belonged with the others, placed with precision, like the keys on a piano.

Two large arc lamps stood in the middle of the chamber. They threw harsh yellow light into the far corners of the room. The main body of the chamber was thus thrown into shadowed relief. The effect made Jackson catch his breath. It emphasized the unsettling atmosphere of the room. How many people had stood in this room, in the seven years since it had been discovered? There had to have been at least a dozen. And yet the room maintained an unsullied ambience, so much that he felt himself an intruder from the second he stepped inside. He felt as foreign as if he'd walked onto the surface of an alien planet. He felt something stir within him, transcendent; the crushing weight of history.

In the middle of the chamber stood what appeared to be a small stone platform or altar, about waist high. Around the room were stone sarcophagi, three against each wall, their lids carved with wedge-like markings.

Jackson moved slowly into the middle of the chamber. He took out the cotton gloves he'd been given, and put them on. Cautiously, he laid his palms upon the central altar. The surface was smooth, hard, calcareous, yet unlike any stone known to him, possessed of a diaphanous quality, a porcelain marble. Like the chamber, the altar was octagonal, inlaid with twenty-one stone tablets, each covered with similar markings to the lids of the sarcophagi. As he began to examine the markings more closely, he could see that each tablet's markings corresponded to one of the sarcophagus's. In the middle of the altar was a small depression, in which lay another artifact.

The Adaptor.

He picked it up, turned it over. The surface felt somewhere between smooth alabaster and a synthetic textile. There was a very slight textural give to the surface. It was somewhat larger than a TV remote control and cool to the touch. Both sides of the relic were carved with tightly packed, intricately patterned markings.

On one side, wedge-like symbols that looked vaguely familiar. He'd seen markings like this before – on various museum trips. He guessed that this place must be part of a lost ancient Sumerian city.

The reverse side completely threw him. The symbols were also glyphs, but bizarrely, they were in an entirely different language. Jackson stared at the symbols.

They looked exactly like ancient Mayan hieroglyphs.

Who Are You Working For?

Jackson slid the Adaptor into his inside jacket pocket. The temptation to look around the chamber was almost unbearable. He had only seven minutes before the effects of hypnoticin wore off. He took one last look at the chamber before he turned to leave. The elevator was as he'd left it, the platform waiting, the lever extended.

Relief began to well up inside him. Just five more minutes and he'd be out of there. He rode the elevator up, watching the square patch of light at the top of the shaft grow larger. When the lift finally stopped, Jackson froze.

Five yards away, in the passageway that connected the makeshift elevator shaft to the rest of the base, stood three soldiers in camouflage combat uniform. Jackson was staring down the barrels of their side-arms, faced by the soldiers' stony glares. From behind them came a voice that he recognized.

"Jackson Bennett, as I live and breathe."

The soldiers parted to let Captain Connor Bennett pass. Connor fixed Jackson with a look of utter disdain. "Imagine my surprise to hear that I'd been seen reporting early for duty."

"I imagine you'd be confused," Jackson's eyes flickered around the room. There was no obvious exit route. He gazed directly at his brother. "I'd prefer it if you were pleased to see me. We are brothers after all. That's what I want, Connor, I want you to be pleased to see me."

"Fuck that! Get down on the floor."

Jackson stood his ground. He threw back his shoulders, gazed past Connor and at the three soldiers. Firmly, he said "Put the guns down, fellas."

One by one, with expressions of amazement, they did.

After a moment Connor turned around, stunned. "Get your weapons up!"

"No, leave them," interrupted Jackson. At least one of the soldiers seemed to be trying to lift her handgun, but the soldier to her left placed a hand on her arm. It seemed to be enough.

Connor didn't visibly react, except to gaze thoughtfully at Jackson and then at the three soldiers.

"It's his voice." One of the two male soldiers spoke, musingly, in a lilting Tennessee accent. "He's doing something with his voice. Makes me wanna listen to him all day."

Connor's eyes blazed for a second. Then with breathtaking speed, he clasped his hand to Jackson's mouth, overpowering him, forcing him to the ground. There was a brief struggle but Jackson was no match for his brother's power and training.

Connor hissed against his ear, "Is that it, bro'? Have you learnt some kinda Eastern mind-control shit?" In the next second Connor's hands were conducting a search of Jackson's body. When he found the Adaptor he paused for a moment, incoherent with rage. When the power of speech returned, he yelled at the three soldiers.

"GET BACK!"

The men leapt backwards. They still wouldn't aim their weapons.

Connor gripped Jackson's head, pounded it against the floor. Pain enveloped him like a cloud. Jackson had an acute sense of the harnessed violence, the barely contained rage of his brother. If Connor hadn't been in uniform, anything could have happened.

As it was, Connor's fury was transient. Within a minute, the discipline of his training kicked in. Connor knelt down, one leg holding Jackson in place. A soldier pulled a roll of duct tape from his equipment belt, tossed the roll across to Connor, who pulled it tight across Jackson's jaw.

With a final shove, Connor released Jackson, who threw himself onto the ground where he sat, leaning back on his hands and watching his brother. Breathing hard, Connor shook his head in disgust. He took a plastic Ziploc bag from a pocket. With immense care, he placed the Adaptor inside the bag.

"You lousy jerk; you could have killed them. You'd better be ready to talk, or I'm gonna kick the crap outta you."

Jackson stared back at his brother, mute. This was the Connor he remembered, the arrogant, violent older brother.

***

They sat him at a desk and thrust a laptop computer in front of him. Jackson had been stripped down to his boxers and shirt. Duct tape was sealed tight across the lower half of his face.

"Here's how it works; I ask questions, you type the answers. You got that?"

Jackson nodded. Until now, he'd never been properly afraid of his brother, whose opprobrium he'd faced his whole life. If it wasn't the lack of order in his room, it was his unkempt appearance, or his lack of love for team sports. As the boys grew older, the points of disagreement had become more political. He'd always known the boundaries. He could see now that his incursion into his brother's domain was likely to be unforgiveable. Connor would never forget that he'd used their physical resemblance to compromise Connor's professional operation.

"Question One: real obvious; who are you working for?"

Jackson typed: *Hans Runig*

Connor looked unimpressed. To the sergeant sitting opposite Jackson, who was typing notes into another laptop computer, he said, "Check that out."

They waited for a few seconds.

"He's Swiss . . . listed as a stockholder for a number of companies. Biotech, nanotech."

"Arms industry?" asked Connor.

The sergeant shook his head. "No direct connection."

Jackson was puzzled. Hadn't DiCanio suggested a connection between Runig and the Department of Defense?

Connor walked around the table, looking directly into his brother's eyes.

"Question Two: why? I know you came for the artifact, but for what reason?"

Runig wants it, typed Jackson. *There's a second chamber, in Mexico.*

Connor's shock was palpable. He appeared to weigh the implications of this statement, remaining silent for quite a few minutes.

Then: "Why, Jackson? What's in this for you?"

Jackson typed his response. *Money,* he answered, adding, *for my research.*

"To think I was ready to believe that this Runig forced you into it. Or maybe the money was just to sweeten the deal? Tell me this; where'd you get that leg wound?"

He appeared contrite. Of course. He should have thought to make more of that.

"Well, for once I'm speechless. So your squishy liberal sensibilities don't matter when your science is at stake, huh?"

Jackson tried hard to look defiant.

Connor's next question threw him. "How did you know you were immune?"

Jackson blinked. He shrugged. The question was meaningless. Immune to what?

"Do you even know what this place is?"

Jackson typed: *Ancient burial chamber?*

"So that's it: the dipshit UN leaked." Connor shared a conspiratorial glance with the sergeant. "No, Jackson, 'burial chamber' is what we told the UN. It's ancient all right, a whole lot more than anyone would suspect. But it's not a burial chamber. When the UN inspection team found this place back in 2003, it was hermetically sealed. We found biological material inside some of the caskets, hairs and dust containing skin cells. We've carbon dated those remains to around three thousand BC. Here's the killer, Jackson. Turns out that those caskets aren't made of stone. We tested the material with mass spectrometry – it's artificial. Some kind of ceramic which uses organic molecules in its matrix. Those organic molecules were too old to carbon date, Jackson. Know what that means?"

Jackson was too stunned to respond. Carbon dating was a technique of limited efficacy in determining the age of any samples older than 50,000 years. How could a structure like the chamber he'd seen be older than 50,000 years? Humans had only been building even semi-permanent structures with stone or brick since around 6000BC.

Even as he typed it, he balked at the suggestion: *Extra-terrestrial origin?*

Connor shrugged. "The same thought occurred to the powers-that-be. That's why the NRO were called in to manage this op. But we've no evidence of any non-earth material here. The biological remains are human. The caskets and the central platform are made of this ceramic material. There's nothing in the atomic composition that doesn't occur naturally and pretty abundantly here on earth."

Once more, the brothers faced one another.

"How are you doing that thing with your voice?"

Jackson typed: *A drug.*

He hadn't agreed to keep DiCanio's secrets. Now that it looked as though she'd kept information from him, Jackson felt nothing but resentment. He only had DiCanio's word that hypnoticin didn't work on him. What if it did, what if she'd been playing him from the beginning, as Runig had said?

Connor didn't look too convinced by the reply. "A drug? Sure. When are you meeting Runig?"

He typed: *Twenty-five minutes.*

"You're going to lead us right to him, little brother. Don't imagine you're taking the artifact. You're gonna give Runig something else."

With this, Connor opened a drawer in the desk, from which he took something that looked exactly like the Adaptor.

"Looks pretty genuine, don't it? We made a couple of plaster cast replicas. Standard archaeological practice. What with the somewhat deadly nature of the genuine article – we can't leave it around. In fact, if we hadn't been running tests today, it wouldn't even have been in the chamber."

Jackson stared blankly.

"You don't know about the bio-toxin?"

He shook his head.

Connor's eyes widened. "Boy, did your Hans Runig get his intelligence wrong. The artifact – and the receptacle for it in the chamber – is impregnated with some kind of poison gas. I was the first person to touch it. Apart from you, bro, I'm the only person I know who can. If you'd gotten any closer to those soldiers, you'd have killed them."

For a long moment, he stared into Jackson's eyes. "Or maybe your friend Runig *did* know. This thing you're doing with you voice – it didn't seem to affect me. You and me are the only two people I know of who can touch the artifact and survive. Yeah." He paused. "It's no coincidence that they picked you, is it?" Connor stood up. "You're a piece of work, you know that? I'm almost glad that mom and dad are dead. If they knew what kind of traitor they raised."

The captain turned to leave, locked the door behind him. Then Jackson was alone. He waited for a few minutes, and then searched the room for hidden cameras. He found none.

DiCanio had evidently fallen short of telling him a few details.

Was it possible that she hadn't known that the Adaptor was impregnated with an airborne toxin? Jackson stalled for a moment. He hadn't actually seen evidence of any toxin. Yet Connor's reaction when he found the Adaptor in Jackson's pocket had been instantaneous – he'd acted to protect the three soldiers. It didn't make sense that he'd invented the toxin.

There was more; DiCanio seemed to be misinformed about the true age of the chamber. Yet her estimate had been in the right ball-park as far as the human remains went. What had Connor meant when he'd said that the chamber was not for burials?

Jackson thought about the discrepancy between the age of the structure and of the biological remains found. The most logical conclusion seemed unbelievable: the chamber had been built over 50,000 years ago and last used in 3000BC.

But 50,000 years ago there'd been no humans except Stone Age hunter-gatherers.

What was inside those caskets? Connor had mentioned traces of human remains. Were the caskets actually sarcophagi? Or something else?

The laptop computer was in front of him. He desperately wanted to talk to Marie-Carmen. Maybe she'd have some insights. Mainly though, he wanted to know that she was all right. That last email of hers had made confusing reading when he'd glanced at it at Kleine Scheidegg. She'd mentioned ancient Sumeria. Now, in the context of what he'd seen in the chamber, Jackson was eager to read it more closely.

He was about to grab the laptop, when he remembered Marie-Carmen's warning about Hans Runig's efforts to trace their Web-based activities. Surely, within a military establishment the computers would be safe from Runig's prying eyes?

Jackson opened a Web browser window and logged into his email. He checked to see if Marie-Carmen was logged into the instant messenger service. She wasn't.

The last email he'd received from Marie-Carmen was still there.

Worried About Iraq

Hey – you're too busy to think about me?

Jackson, this idea of going to Iraq worries me. You receive secrets, messages over the Internet, telephone calls, a jet to Switzerland, now it's Iraq. It's like you're a chess piece, being moved around the board.

Do you know that Abu Shahrain is the modern name for the Sumerian city of Eridu? I've been reading translations of Sumerian literature on a website owned by the Oriental Institute at the University of Oxford. There is a very famous document known as the Sumerian King List. It claims to list all the rulers since the beginning of time. Here's how it begins:

After the kingship descended from heaven, the kingship was in Eridu. In Eridu, Alulim became king; he ruled for 28800 years. Alaljar ruled for 36000 years. 2 kings; they ruled for 64800 years. Then Eridu fell and the kingship was taken to Bad-tibira.

Like the Ancient Maya, the Sumerians seem to take a much longer view of history than most cultures. If you add up all the time accounted for by the Sumerian King List, it comes to over two hundred thousand years. The first part of the Kings List ends like this:

In 5 cities 8 kings; they ruled for 241200 years. Then the flood swept over.

Ancient historians still can't agree on a date for the biblical flood, but if you take the least controversial date, that's around 2000BC.

So the Sumerian King List, if taken literally, suggests that Eridu was first founded around 244,200 years ago!

But the most interesting part is this: remember what I found in that bizarre article about the clay tablet with the strangely modified logograms? The three words which, in translation, matched part of Pedro Juan's sequence, were:

Before Lord Anunnaki

The logogram translated in the article as 'master' is lugal. Which also means 'lord', 'king' or 'owner'.

An.un.na.ki or Anunnaki was the Sumerian term for a collection of deities who are first written of in a document known as the Atrahasis.

Some people think that the Atrahasis is the original source of the flood story. The original clay tablets of the Atrahasis date back to 1700BC. But parts of the same story have been found on even older tablets. The Atrahasis is probably a retelling of an oral tradition which had existed for hundreds or even thousands of years before.

And here's where the document first mentions the Anunnaki.

When the gods instead of man
Did the work, bore the loads,
The gods' load was too great,
The work too hard, the trouble too much,
The great Anunnaki made the Igigi
Carry the workload sevenfold.

Some people have interpreted this as suggesting that the Anunnaki created human beings to work the land for them. Also, there's a definite implication of an extra-terrestrial origin for the Anunnaki; even the context of their full name, which literally means 'the people who came from Heaven and Earth'.

Well look, I see all kinds of strange conspiracy theories in my own field – for example, the idea that the Maya originated in a mysterious land to the west (some crazy people suggest Atlantis).

It's important not to over-interpret these kinds of mythologies. I mean, people in Britain don't actually think that there was a real Camelot, do they?

What worries me is that there are too many coincidences.

Why does DiCanio need you to retrieve this artifact? I think the answer to that is crucial. I don't think she's being straight with you.

How is your leg? Is my handiwork holding up?

I haven't forgotten your final comment. But I'm going to need confirmation of that in person, OK?

Marie-Carmen

Jackson read her email three times. He was struck by a line of reason extending through the enigmas of the chamber, the Adaptor and the DNA sequence. Previously tenuous connections now appeared solid.

Connor, DiCanio and Runig had almost certainly arrived at the same conclusion: the inscription on the Adaptor was a kind of instruction; part of a formula to activate the chamber.

All three parties had access to most of this same information. Except for one piece of information, something he himself had almost overlooked, something which had seemed too ludicrously improbable to be worthy of inclusion: PJ's message.

Marie-Carmen's strategy of searching the Web for fragments of PJ's DNA sequence had been a stroke of genius, Jackson now realized. Nothing else could have connected them to the extraordinary article about Sumerian knowledge of amino acids. Exactly the kind of off-the-wall connection that had put Jackson and Marie-Carmen ahead of Connor's team, DiCanio and Runig.

PJ may not have known it, but he did send me a message; a message thousands of years old.

Pressing the reply button, he wrote:

Marie-Carmen,
I'm in some trouble here; got caught trying to leave with the artifact. I can't tell what's going to happen now, but I'm going to play things as safe as possible.

I've been in the underground chamber. It is over 50,000 years old, maybe a LOT older. So maybe this famous Sumerian King List isn't so mythological after all? They also found miniscule quantities of human remains, which date from almost 3000BC. According to DiCanio, that's when the human version of PJ's gene emerges. She thinks that some of the people who carry that gene have ancestors from this area, dating back to 3000BC.

Is it possible that the ancestors were actually here, in this chamber?

Even more; there's a second chamber, in Mexico.

Maybe there's something to that website article about 'ancient Sumerian biologists'. Maybe I was right first time; PJ's DNA molecule IS a message we can read.

Can you try to decode the entire sequence? Maybe translate it into the Sumerian logograms and then back into English? See if you can find any reference to why Eridu fell. Because this ancient chamber seems to part of the ruins of Eridu.

I need to know this asap.

J x

PS Leg is doing great.

Jackson sent the reply. Then he sat, pensive for several moments. Marie-Carmen was right; DiCanio must have a compelling reason for wanting the Adaptor. She'd claimed that the counterpart in the Mexican chamber was eroded beyond use. Which implied that DiCanio knew or suspected its true function.

Could it be that the Mexican chamber was still operational?

Jackson's mind went to the stories he'd listened to as a boy, of the explorer Ponce De Leon, his search in the New World for a mythical fountain of eternal youth. Maybe the chamber in Mexico was the original source of such legends.

From outside came the sound of footsteps. Jackson closed the Web browser with a click.

Connor returned. There was a colder edge to him now. He gaze was baleful, yet coolly appraising. "Who is DiCanio?"

Jackson's eyes widened, affecting innocence.

Connor leaned forward. "We let you have access to the Web, but we were monitoring your session remotely. Look."

He indicated another icon on the right hand of the screen. Jackson rolled his eyes.

"We've seen everything you did. You really should learn more about computers. How did you get involved in something like this? You're seriously out of your depth."

Behind the duct tape, Jackson made a tiny, resigned noise. He started to pick at the edge of the tape, near the curve of his jaw. Connor just shook his head. "Not yet. Listen up. Who's DiCanio?"

Jackson pulled the laptop computer towards him. He opened a Web browser, typing 'dicanio' into Google's search box. Even on the first page of results, Melissa DiCanio was mentioned, on the website of Chaldexx Biopharmaceuticals.

He tapped the computer screen. Connor gave Jackson a withering look and then clicked on the website.

"A neuroscientist? Now I guess you're going to tell me you were telling the truth about the drug you used?"

Vigorously, he nodded.

Connor was thoughtful for a few minutes: "Boy, the Department of Defense would sure like to get a piece of that. How long does it last?"

Jackson typed rapidly: *I don't know. Tell me what the chamber does, then maybe I can guess.*

Connor seemed to consider. "We don't know what the chamber does, or did. It's a ruin, as you saw. There are several remarkable things about it: the apparent age, the incredibly well-preserved state of the structures. And of course, the bio-toxin, but since you're immune you won't have noticed that. Come on, Jackson, you're supposed to be a smart guy: work it out."

Jackson typed: *Who built the chamber?*

"That's classified."

The writing is Sumerian, right?

Connor's reply was guarded. "It's related to that, yeah. We've started a team on linguistics experts on the project back in Virginia." Then, abruptly, he said: "Why did you lie to me, Jacko? Why did you say you were working for 'Hans Runig'?"

Jackson typed: *Runig also wants the Adaptor – that's what DiCanio calls the artifact. He tried to blackmail me into it; threatened to kill me if I wouldn't, reward me if I did.*

Connor regarded him thoughtfully. "OK so – DiCanio knows about the chamber and the artifacts we found from her friends at the UN. What about Runig – how'd he get so clued in?"

Leak at Chaldexx?

"This just gets better. Any idea where we can find Runig?"

Jackson shook his head, but indicated the laptop.

Connor looked doubtful. "We've looked into it. He's listed as a stockholder for a bunch of companies, but we've found no other references to him, not anywhere. I just spoke to one of the companies he's invested in; they say they've never met him in person. Apparently he prefers to videoconference."

Then, changing the subject again, Connor asked, "This girl, Marie-Carmen. How does she fit in with all this?"

Jackson typed: *She's a friend. Hans Runig has people looking for her. He was going to use her to get to me.*

"So she's more than just a friend?"

Something about Connor's tone, quite suddenly, sent a surge of protective jealousy through Jackson. It must have shown in his eyes because Connor broke into a suggestive grin.

"Must be quite a girl. That's a very illuminating bit of research she's sent you. It's not news to us, of course. See the thing about ancient mythology is this: when there's no physical evidence for anything, it's easier to dismiss what is written as invention. After all, people have been making up stories since the beginning of time. So we're supposed to take them seriously, just because all of a sudden they're carved in stone? On the other hand, a find like this, well it sends you straight back to those ancient texts. All of a sudden they seem pretty enlightening."

Jackson thought again about the apparently bizarre decision to bring in the NRO to manage the operation. He'd glibly suggested an extra-terrestrial origin for the burial chamber, but in fact, that must now be a realistic possibility.

Really not extra-terrestrial?

Connor shook his head. "What seems more likely, but almost as controversial, is that this is the first credible evidence for a previous civilization. It's buried pretty deeply, much deeper than the earliest parts of Eridu."

As his brother spoke, Jackson found himself wondering why Connor was feeding him so much information – information which was surely classified.

Why are you telling me all this?

"I thought that'd be obvious, Jacko. We want you working with us. You don't really have another choice. The alternative would be a charge of treason or espionage. Hell, we could even send you to rot in Guantanamo."

Behind the tape, Jackson swallowed hard. Betraying DiCanio would not be easy to accomplish. He'd have to become part of a military intelligence operation. But as his brother suggested, Jackson doubted that he'd have any real choice.

Connor spoke again. "Let me tell you how this is going to work. In twenty minutes, you will leave here, dressed as me. You'll take the replica of the "Adaptor", as you call it. You'd better convince DiCanio that it's the real deal. We're going to have you followed. You can't escape us, so don't try. Tip off DiCanio and you might not survive. Do you understand?"

Jackson nodded, expressionless. Connor appeared to be satisfied. No wonder, Jackson thought. They hadn't given him much choice.

"One more thing: before you leave, I want you to write down everything you know about DiCanio. How you met, what's her plan, why she wants the artifact, how she convinced you to help. And listen up: when we catch her, which we will, your two stories had better be identical. Or else you can forget any clemency deal. If you lie to us, I'll stand by and watch them throw the book at you. Believe it, Jackson, that's quite some book."

Wonderingly, Jackson watched his brother leave. He could almost believe that his brother had never heard of DiCanio. Yet DiCanio claimed to have approached Connor first.

One of them had to be lying.

Lament For Eridu

As Jackson sweated it out in the tiny interview room in the Abu Shahrain base, Marie-Carmen was taking breakfast beside the salt-water pool of the Acapulco Princess. It being rather late in the morning, a small line had formed at the entrance to the Chula Vista restaurant. The restaurant was situated next to a turquoise lagoon with waterfalls, surrounded with coconut trees and red and white hibiscus flowers. Pink flamingos stood elegantly in ornamental ponds, grazing on dyed bird feed. Near the head of the line, Marie-Carmen recognized her companions from the previous night's dinner table.

Daniel O'Shea caught her eye. With a broad, easy grin, he waved her over.

Marie-Carmen smiled, relieved to have company and that Daniel didn't seem annoyed by the way she'd run off the night before. Jackson's predicament – and silence since yesterday afternoon's email – had her seriously concerned. Her cell phone was still switched off, but it taunted her with potential knowledge. Had Runig called her, left any message with demands, or information about Jackson? The desire to check was an unbearable itch, one she dared not scratch.

Marie-Carmen joined Daniel at a poolside table, under a large parasol.

"Good morning, beautiful," Daniel said with a beam.

"Hey," she told him. "I thought we had an understanding."

"Sure – that's what makes it possible to talk this way. You couldn't possibly think I have ulterior motives."

Marie-Carmen tapped her watch. "The Waiting List Rules? Remember?"

Daniel laughed. "I guess you left in a bit of a hurry yesterday."

"Oh, yes. I was waiting for a call. Then I stuck around and did some reading. What you told me about the Sumerians was fascinating. I ended up learning some more about Eridu. So, what happened to it, in the end?"

"To Eridu?" Daniel shrugged very slightly. "You know, the whole Sumerian culture eventually died. Not dramatically and mysteriously like the Maya cities, maybe, but still, there's a lot we don't understand about why it all just died off. As for Eridu, legend has it that it was buried in a storm."

Marie-Carmen placed her plate on the table, sat down.

"Buried?"

Daniel turned away for a second to catch the eye of a waiter.

"Right. There's a piece of literature known as the *Lament for Eridu*. It talks about a terrible storm, which swept over the city; the sky became dark even during the day, the city being covered as if by a sandstorm, destroyed forever."

They sat in silence as a waiter filled their coffee cups.

"Just how old is Eridu?" asked Marie-Carmen. "Yesterday, you told me that it was founded around four thousand five hundred BC. Well, I was reading the Sumerian King List, and according to that, Eridu is over two hundred thousand years old."

Daniel raised one eyebrow, impressed. "You found a translation of the Weld-Blundell Prism? I guess you've been reading the Electronic Text Corpus of Sumerian Literature. You know, I've actually seen the Weld-Blundell, in Oxford. It's at the Ashmolean Museum. You gotta respect the guys who transcribed and translated those markings. That's a piece of work! Yes, according to that record, the pre-flood kings had superhuman life spans, ruled for tens of thousands of years. That's one of several parallels with the Book of Genesis. After the flood, there was a 'second descent' of the Gods from heaven. The post-flood kings ruled for more normal life spans. But you know what, Marie-Carmen? It's literature! Let me ask you this; you believe everything you read that the Maya write about and refer to with Long Count calendar dates?"

Marie-Carmen shook her head. "Of course not. Among ancient peoples it was customary to weave fact and fantasy in their historical records."

"Not just ancient peoples. I think the point really is that it all happened so long ago, who knows? Think how hard it is to find the truth in the printed word, even today. There's information, misinformation, disinformation, that's even before you get to literature. In the Romances of the Middle Ages, it was the fashion to start a piece of literature with a statement that the author had found the manuscript, implying it was a historical account. Originality wasn't what people sought back then; what they loved was tradition.

"Even by the time of Cervantes, in the sixteenth century, when he wrote what's probably the first modern novel, *Don Quixote*, he begins in the style of the very Romances he's trying to emulate: 'I found this manuscript'. In the second part of *Don Quixote*, the first book has already made the hero a well-known figure. So then the author gets to refer to Don Quixote as a quasi-historical figure; 'Remember the famous Don Quixote whose story you already know?'

"The point is that, even then, everyone knew that fiction presented as truth was a game, it gave it that extra frisson. Now, just imagine if all the texts which refer to Don Quixote were destroyed and only the original book was left, and people thousands of years in the future found it. Would they believe that Don Quixote was a historical figure? The answer is that without independent verification they probably wouldn't. Think about how easy that makes it to create a historical hoax; one seemingly independent source might get any old story verified.

"With ancient history, it's hard to tell fact from fiction. You use your common sense until evidence suggests otherwise."

With that, Daniel made a start on his cooling heap of sausages, eggs and tortillas in green tomato and chili sauce.

Marie-Carmen looked beyond the crowded restaurant, past the tall coconut palms which flanked the pool, beyond the wide sands of the beach, beyond the lines of creamy surf, past the indigo of the ocean. If only it were possible to gaze into the recent past as easily as into the distant millennia of the heavens. Sometimes, studying the texts of the ancients, you could almost believe you did. At other moments, the very alien nature of those past civilizations defied understanding. It was the central tension of her field of study: how could one accurately read the past without the eyes of the ancestors?

***

After breakfast, Marie-Carmen returned to her room, anxious to check for a message from Jackson.

The door was open, with the housekeeping trolley outside the room. Marie-Carmen heard a brief rustle of activity as she wandered in to find the maid changing the pillow cases.

Both women exchanged a polite smile. Marie-Carmen took her laptop computer out to the balcony, leaving open the French window. In the far distance, she could already see the afternoon storm clouds approaching from behind the mountains.

There was a new message from Jackson. Marie-Carmen read through it quickly, disturbed by the contents. The news that he had been 'caught' struck her immediately as peculiar. Why didn't Jackson give any details about who was holding him, or the consequences of his being discovered?

So, Jackson wanted her to decode the full amino acid sequence using the key to the code she had found on www.archaeologyconspiracies.com

Decoding ancient writing had always enthralled her, even more in a new language. However, Marie-Carmen's initial assessment of the article's likely truth hadn't changed. With all the lies and hoaxes out there on the Web, how could she possibly take it seriously?

Yet for some reason, Jackson seemed to have quite radically changed his views.

Marie-Carmen had to admit that were the translated sequence to make any sense, they might be onto something.

After translating the first six logograms, she knew that Jackson was right. It made sense. Breathless with excitement and the exhilaration of discovery, she continued until the entire message was translated. She then summarized what Daniel had told her about the fall of Eridu, pasting in some quotes from the *Lament for Eridu* from the Electronic Text Corpus of Sumerian Literature.

Marie-Carmen was about to conclude the email with a message of affectionate sympathy for his situation, when from the bed she heard a sound which made her stomach lurch. Almost out of charge, her cell phone battery was bleeping.

Someone had switched her phone on.

Marie-Carmen dashed back into her room. The cell phone was partly obscured by a pillow. It had been switched on for at least thirty minutes.

She checked the last number dialed. The chamber maid must have made a long distance call before being startled by Marie-Carmen's return. Marie-Carmen's fury was superseded only by the creeping panic, the certainty that thirty minutes was enough time for her cell phone to be tracked, to reveal her location.

Marie-Carmen's hand shook as she tapped out the code for reception on the room telephone.

"I'd like the express check-out service," she said. "I'll be down in twenty minutes."

She forced herself to remain calm, to move methodically through the mechanics of escape. She went swiftly to the closet, grabbed her suitcase and began to pack. The final item into her case was the laptop. The email to Jackson remained incomplete, so she sat on the bed to finish it.

As for me, well I think it's time to move on again. Perhaps it's being so lonely here; perhaps the logogram decoding sessions have made me paranoid. But even here, I'm seeing shadows, I sense pursuit. So I'm leaving, going someplace where I'll be really alone. Why pretend to be something I'm not?

Write to me when you are safe again. Until then, let's practice a little self-preservation.
Marie-Carmen

Don't Go For Any Heroics

Connor returned to the interview room with Jackson's uniform and boots, which he tossed at his brother with a sudden burst of venom. Then he sat down to read the statement that he'd demanded. Jackson was dressed and ready by the time Connor looked up.

"Is this for real? You really expect me to take this seriously?"

Jackson remained expressionless.

"Global warming? You think DiCanio's doing this because of global warming?"

Connor's indignant disbelief was rapidly becoming something else, something more dangerous. Jackson could see the temper slowly emerge, a steady fuse smoking, exactly as when they'd been boys.

"How can I be related to you, never mind be your twin? What, now you're an eco-terrorist? Or working for one? You really believe that *this* is all she wants?" The sarcasm intensified. "So, DiCanio has, according to you, control of an international organization of brilliant, well-connected people. Who may or may not have some capacity for practicing a level of hypnosis? Somehow, this organization has found a possibly functional counterpart to this ancient technology? You think that she's out to help anyone but herself? Lookit; if she wanted to help the world, why keep the organization secret? Why not go public, at least within the intelligence community?"

Jackson looked scornful. He longed to tear off the duct tape and let rip, finally, with some of the indignation that had been building up inside him. He'd transgressed, but then so had Connor and the whole NRO. Governments pretty much by-passed any laws they felt like ignoring: that was the only way that Connor and his ilk had been allowed to remain in Iraq for so long. Now they'd been hoarding an ancient treasure that by rights belonged to the Iraqi people.

Connor was only just getting warmed up. "Bro, I had no idea you were this stupid. You actually buy into this whole idea that the governments of the free world don't actually want to protect its citizens? That people like me are so dumbass that we go fight for something that's not really worth dying for? Don't you *get* that the governments of the world are already waking up to global warming?"

Jackson merely rolled his eyes. Of course his brother would respond this way; he'd anticipated it. Connor trusted the chain of command, and was motivated in everything by a passionate love for his country and what he often referred to as 'the free world'. Jackson, on the other hand, refused to ignore the plight of the ordinary people on whom all of the world-changing ideas would inevitably tread. In the days when they'd still seen each other regularly, the brothers had invested hours in trying to persuade each other. In the end it had been pointless; consensus never reached, the validity of each other's viewpoints rarely even acknowledged.

Connor stood, arms folded, looking down at his twin who looked back with studied indifference. The two men were now indistinguishable except for the grey duct tape which still covered Jackson's mouth. Their silent stand-off was interrupted when Connor's sergeant joined them, carrying something which Jackson had to admit looked very much like the Adaptor.

Connor handed the replica of the Adaptor to Jackson. "We took the logograms from the text of the *Lament*. When your friends translate it, they'll get nothing other than part of the story of the fall of Eridu."

Jackson stared. How was he supposed to explain that?

"Your friends had better buy this story for long enough for us to get to them."

With increasing despondency, Jackson examined the replica. This was far heavier than the original that he'd grabbed less than an hour ago. The advanced ceramic material used in the chamber was lighter, more translucent. If DiCanio had the original of the Adaptor from the Mexican chamber, Jackson would have no chance. On the other hand, in the absence of any physical comparison, this replica might just buy him a few hours.

He thought gloomily about the total failure of his mission. He was still in the dark about the true purpose of the chamber. Even if DiCanio knew or suspected, he could no longer trust her reaction when she discovered his deception. Escape from DiCanio had to be his priority now.

Connor spoke again. "OK, brother, this is goodbye. You can remove the gag, but one word from you and it's over, got that?"

Jackson glared back, began peeling back the tape, careful to avoid tearing his lips. When he'd finished, Connor handed him a paper cup filled with water.

"Good luck, Jacko," Connor said, softly. "There'll be a gun on you all the way out, so don't go for any heroics. You're gonna walk free from this place, just as if you were me. Go back to your rendezvous. You'll be seeing us again real soon."

The two airmen stood aside as Jackson stepped reluctantly past. Once outside in the base, he walked by, this time keenly aware of the sullen, wary stares he drew from the staff. He walked directly to the base entrance, where two different guards from the ones he'd seen earlier saluted him.

The road back to Basra passed right in front of the base but the tiny village of Abu Shahrain was much closer, only ten minutes' walk. As they'd agreed, Jackson walked to Abu Shahrain. Hafez Kazmi was waiting in the main street, sitting next to the taxi. It had parked next to a small café, and Kazmi was smoking and drinking from a can of Pepsi.

Crumpling his can, he threw Jackson a slow, hostile glare. "What took you?"

"There were people in the chamber," said Jackson. "They were conducting some kind of experiment. I had to wait, in hiding, until they finished."

Hafez's expression instantly transformed. He dropped his cigarette, took the replica Adaptor, turning it over in his palms. Fascinated, he said, "This is incredible!"

Jackson watched in silence for a moment. Kazmi had absolutely no qualms about handling what he seemed to believe was the real Adaptor.

She'd been holding out on him. *DiCanio didn't know about the bio-toxin.* The Sect's inside informant was good, but even they hadn't infiltrated every secret of the NRO's.

"They seemed real excited about whatever it was doing," Jackson warned. "We need to go because they may be going back down there."

"You did good, man!" Kazmi slapped Jackson's back. "How did the hypnoticin go?"

"It did the job. Hardly needed it, though. Looking like this, they didn't ask any questions."

"I knew it. There's no-one we could have put in that place and gotten that result."

"Except Connor himself," said Jackson, watching Kazmi keenly.

Transfixed by the intricate inscriptions on the artifact, Kazmi was still distracted. "Yeah, sure," he answered, the sarcasm plainly obvious in his voice.

Jackson said nothing. It was looking as though DiCanio had not actually approached Connor, after all. She'd lied. Her plan had always been to recruit him. Now he thought about it, she must have begun working on a plan quite some time ago, gathering information about him. The Mexican newspapers had reported that Jackson was in Mexico and under suspicion of involvement in PJ's murder. DiCanio could easily have seen those stories, if she'd been following the news of PJ's death. She would have realized that Jackson was vulnerable as at no other time in his life. She would have guessed that if she offered him a way out of the country, he would have to take it.

It had culminated in her emailed invitation to visit her in Chaldexx. Jackson had taken it for granted that he'd been a hasty afterthought, the plan quickly executed before the artifacts were shipped out. Yet Jackson had seen little evidence that the chamber was being imminently emptied.

No; there was evidence that DiCanio may have acted opportunistically, but she'd taken advantage of some long-range planning. Given that, he wondered what else DiCanio had managed to achieve in that time.

Had she left him an escape route?

Ninhursag

At the Basra Sheraton, Jackson and Kazmi arrived to find DiCanio checking them out of the hotel. Jackson had removed his uniform jacket and tie in the car. Now he carried the jacket inside-out over one arm. When DiCanio spotted them, she broke into a grin, giving them a tiny wave. She'd changed into an outfit of white linen: loose trousers and a long over-shirt, an aquamarine silk scarf thrown lightly around her neck. Her eyes were hidden behind a pair of smoky brown sunglasses with jeweled borders, the blonde in her hair shone golden in the sharp light. Kazmi's mood too was light, confident. Jackson did his best to emulate the couple's good humor. Under the cover of his shirt, the hairs on his arm prickled, he felt rivulets of sweat beading and trickling down his back.

Kazmi lifted the suitcases and lead the way towards the waiting car, where the two bodyguards once again sat in the front. The man in the passenger seat was speaking into a small headset, nodding twice before he told Kazmi, "All set."

Once the doors closed, DiCanio touched Jackson's shoulder. "You're drenched! You should have taken a minute to change your shirt."

Jackson decided to go on the offensive. "You sent me into the field, Melissa. Don't be so surprised if I worked up a little sweat."

DiCanio seemed just a little put out, but fortunately for Jackson, Kazmi appeared to find the exchange amusing. "Leave him in peace, woman. What he did took guts. The boy's a scientist, not a soldier."

Thereafter, DiCanio said nothing more on the subject, but put a degree of space between her and Jackson. Kazmi handed DiCanio the replica of the Adaptor.

DiCanio held the object in one hand, then two, pensive. "It seems a little heavy. I think it's heavier than the one we have. It's in pretty great condition, though. Look at how crisply defined the logograms are. It looks almost as though it were made yesterday."

Jackson decided to say nothing, waiting to see where she took this line of thought.

"Describe to me exactly where you found this."

Jackson responded with an elaborate description of the chamber, emphasizing the pristine condition of all the caskets and the central altar.

"The Adaptor sat in some kind of depression, right in the middle of the altar. One end was near another depression in the horizontal plane of the altar. Like a battery, but with only one terminal. It wasn't actually slotted into the depression; I'm pretty sure that's how they activated it."

"Sounds identical to what we found in Mexico," DiCanio said when he'd finished describing the chamber. "I think that you can activate the mechanism inside each casket by pressing the appropriate altar plate. I think the Adaptor energizes or otherwise powers the altar. Maybe it really is a battery. I wish you'd tried to find out what happened if you slotted the Adaptor into position."

"I didn't like to risk it," Jackson lied. "I'd already been down there a while. I kind of wanted to get out of there as fast as possible."

DiCanio seemed, reluctantly, to agree. "We'll find out soon enough, when we get this to Mexico. It would have been good to know now." She looked at the artifact again, with some disquiet. "Maybe the heat had some effect on the molecular structure. That happens with some enamel; heat can make it disintegrate. This doesn't seem as crystalline as the one we have. Tell me, was the rest of the chamber made of exactly the same material?"

Jackson decided to limit his lies to the absolute minimum. He was quietly terrified that he'd be caught. Even to have got this far seemed faintly unlikely. Yet, DiCanio wanted so badly to believe in his success that she was, Jackson could see, making one of the worst mistakes a scientist could make; she was choosing to interpret an anomaly in her own favor.

"The altar and caskets were made of something that looked like marble, or alabaster, not so ceramic as this. Honestly, I didn't really recognize the stone either."

DiCanio was nodding again, unable to take her eyes off the replica of the Adaptor, whose inscription she now scrutinized closely. "It is ceramic," she said, her tone curt. "We did the tests. It's definitely artificial, not stone. We didn't test the Adaptor; I didn't want to risk further damage to the inscriptions. Everything else down there is made of a very strange material. Not like anything we were able to find in any patent database."

Jackson waited to see if DiCanio would make any mention of the age of the chamber, or its biological properties. But she said nothing.

So, I'm still to be kept in the dark, thought Jackson, with no small measure of anger. Clearing his throat, he came straight out with his question. "How old is the chamber in Mexico?"

DiCanio eyed him, quite suddenly, with curiosity. She seemed to be considering whether the question was fair. "Maybe seventy-four thousand years old."

He didn't have to fake his astonishment. "How could you know that? If it's an artificial ceramic? You can't carbon date back that far, so I'm assuming the method's not carbon-based."

DiCanio pursed her lips momentarily.

"You *can* date back beyond 50,000 years. There are other, newer techniques. We used electron spin resonance. Trapped energy in a sample is measured from its response to high-frequency electromagnetic radiation in the presence of a magnetic field. People have used the technique to date hominid remains back as far as one hundred thousand years. Of course we can't be too precise, but we think that we can be accurate within a couple of thousand years."

"Seventy-four thousand years," Jackson repeated thoughtfully, "the same date as the supervolcano explosion which created Lake Toba?"

DiCanio looked at him, her eyes wide, solemn. "Exactly, Jackson. Exactly."

Jackson lapsed into a silence that allowed the knot of fear deep in his belly to slowly unravel. DiCanio's car had arrived at Basra International Airport. And all through the journey, he'd glimpsed absolutely no evidence of their being followed.

Where the hell was Connor?

***

Once aboard the jet, Kazmi took the pilot's seat while the remaining four, DiCanio, Jackson and her two bodyguards strapped themselves into the comfortable passenger seats. To Jackson's bewilderment, instead of turning the jet inland to fly back over Iraq, towards Western Europe, Kazmi took the plane out into the Persian Gulf, flying south along the coastline.

"Where are we going?" he asked, openly anxious.

"Relax, my friend. We'll have you back in your lab in no time, along with the research funds we promised. First we're going to our base in Manama in Bahrain. It's been too long a day to fly back in one go. We're going to rest and transmit some data to the team in Mexico, see if they can make a start on decoding these logograms."

"I took a look at the inscriptions," remarked Kazmi. "Looks like Archaic period Sumerian. The logograms have some unusual kind of modifications."

227

"What's on the Adaptor you found in Mexico?" Jackson asked, struggling to keep his manner resolutely innocent.

"We haven't been able to read it; too much erosion."

"What are these modifications?"

Kazmi said, "Sumerian and Mayan scripts combine a number of linguistic types which are commonly seen in early writings. Both scripts employ logographic, pictographic and agglutinative aspects. They also have partial rebus elements."

Jackson interjected, "Rebus?"

"Where the pictures tell you what sounds to make, but the meaning is not literal. For example in English, you might draw an eye, a can, the sea, a sheep, and it could read 'I can sea ewe' or correctly; 'I can see you'." Kazmi continued, "Moreover, it would appear that both languages use many logograms to mean more than one word."

"You take the meaning from the context," Jackson said, without thinking. Kazmi's eyes seemed to widen just a fraction, either surprised or impressed.

"Ah, you know something of Sumerian?"

Jackson had to fight the urge to swallow nervously. It was a stupid slip, one that he couldn't afford. From now on, Jackson had to play everything as DiCanio would expect. No fancy moves, no surprises.

"Seems like a logical explanation," he said quietly, shrugging his shoulders.

"Indeed, you're quite correct. The appropriate meaning is sometimes taken from the context, but often the logogram is modified in a certain way, to denote the way it should be read. As it happens, the Adaptor we found also has strange modifications. The Mayan glyphs don't actually make any sense, so far as we can tell. Which means that we can ignore them and attempt to guess the correct context. Or we can try to find out what they mean some other way."

Jackson deduced that they must already have tried to guess the logograms' meanings, without success. They were clearly hoping that the Adaptor from Eridu had the same writing as that which was apparently effaced on the Mexican Adaptor. Sumerian writing had been initially deciphered in the nineteenth century; Mayan writing had only very recently begun to be understood. In addition, there were many more translated Sumerian texts available.

DiCanio and her organization were probably banking on the superior understanding of Sumerian writing to resurrect their project.

***

They landed thirty minutes later, in a private airstrip in Manama. As the jet came in over the harbor, Jackson could see right away why DiCanio's organization had chosen to set up a Middle Eastern base there, the city appeared bright, modern, spacious and orderly with neat grids of roads like the suburbs of a wealthy American city.

A white, 7-series BMW was waiting for them. One of the guards remained with the jet, whilst the other guard joined DiCanio, Kazmi and Jackson in the car.

They drove for about fifteen minutes, into the suburbs, stopped in front of a high metal gate. Jackson leaned over, trying to catch sight of the top of the gate. To his utter dismay he could see that the prongs of the metal gate ended in sharp points. Broken glass bottles, pressed into cement, lined the entire high peripheral wall. The only safe way out would be through the gate.

The driver activated a remote device, opening the gate. Jackson watched closely where he put the remote, winced softly when he saw the man replace it in a pocket.

The house was a modern, four-bedroomed house, stuccoed with gleaming white plaster, with grey tinted windows. Through the French windows at the back, Jackson could see a generous concrete patio, in the middle of which was a small pool of deep blue water, glacially still. Date palms lined the far end of the pool, providing welcome shade from the burning sun. Inside, the cool of the air conditioning hit them soothingly. Grey marble floors and crisp interior whites of the walls and furnishings created an atmosphere that Jackson found disturbingly clinical. It didn't look as though anyone spent much time here. Some of the sofas still wore their plastic coverings.

"I'd like to shower, if I could," Jackson said. "Then I really need to email the lab."

DiCanio seemed almost to have forgotten about him.

"Of course," she said, removing four sodas from the kitchen refrigerator. "Hafez will show you to a room you can use. Then he'll show you the office. We have broadband Internet access. I'll need to use the main computer, and the scanner. But there's another machine. Feel free to use it."

Jackson paused. "Maybe I'll send the emails first. Then I can relax."

DiCanio merely gazed at him expectantly as she pulled the tab on a can of lemon Perrier.

"When should I tell them to expect me back?" Jackson asked, facing her down.

"If everything works out, we'll get back to Interlaken tomorrow. My driver can take you to Zurich and you can fly out to San Francisco. Unless you'd like to come back to Chaldexx, talk some more about the hypnoticin experiments."

Even in the stupefying haze of tension, Jackson could still just about recall what it felt to be a scientist, genuinely and purely fascinated with science for its own sake.

She'd expect me to want to know more about hypnoticin.

"Absolutely. I'd really love to discuss that some more, Melissa, if you have the time."

Jackson went into the office. He breathed a sigh of relief that the screen of the computer he'd been assigned wasn't overlooked by the operator of the larger computer. Nevertheless, he remembered the remote monitoring icon which Connor had pointed out to him in the NRO base at Abu Shahrain. Was DiCanio paranoid enough to spy on people in her own, inner sanctum? He glanced around but couldn't see any kind of camera pointing at the screen.

It was a risk. But he had to find out what was happening with Marie-Carmen. DiCanio's body language did not suggest that he was under suspicion – yet.

There were many messages in his inbox. Jackson forced himself first to change the password, using ten alphanumeric characters in his new password. His email account was beginning to accumulate a wealth of evidence. He had to keep it secure at all costs.

He opened a new browser window and began composing an email addressed to his lab boss. In a separate window he simultaneously read the only email in which he was actually interested.

Jackson,

The DNA code; you were right, as hard as that seems to believe! The message makes sense when read in Sumerian!

The amino acid sequence translates literally as:

Dubsag lugal anunnaki. Melim idim. Igilul na til dubsag melim.

(I have no idea how correctly to interpret the grammar, so I've guessed at the punctuation.)

In English:

Before Lord(s)Anunnaki (those who came from Heaven and Earth), frightening splendor makes men weak. Awakened Man is long-lived owner (of) frightening splendor.

The bracketed suggestions are my own attempt to make some grammatical sense of the phrasing. I've ignored one of the repeated amino acids. Words are rarely repeated that way in a linguistic sense so it would make sense that, occasionally; the linguistic meaning would bow to the biological!

Could 'frightening splendor' refer to this new-found ability which you claim to have? Or could it be something else?

I found the names of the main deities: they were An (god of heaven), Ki (goddess of Earth) their son Enlil (God of wind), and Enki (God of the watery abyss).

Ki is also known as Ninhursag.

As well as denoting deities, 'An' and 'ki' also refer to heaven and earth as places.

An.un.na.ki is used in this context as 'those who came from Heaven and Earth'.

You asked me to find out how what happened to Eridu: the city was destroyed by a tremendous storm. The sky darkened during the day. But read for yourself: this is from the 'Lament For Eridu':

The evil-bearing storm went out from the city. It swept across the Land – a storm which possesses neither kindness nor malice, does not distinguish between good and evil. Subir came down like rain. It struck hard. In the city where bright daylight used to shine forth, the day darkened. In Eridu where bright daylight used to shine forth, the day darkened. As if the sun had set below the horizon, it turned into twilight. As if An had cursed the city, alone he destroyed it.

When did this happen? I don't know. Maybe this was the flood? The King List certainly finishes listing the Eridu kings after the flood. Or maybe it was an earlier event."

As Jackson read, blood thundered in his ears; revelation flooded through him.

Ki is also known as Ninhursag

He memorized the translation as rapidly as possible, lips moving slightly as he mumbled it to himself. Finally, he read the epilogue to Marie-Carmen's email, in which she described her flight from the hotel. For a few seconds, he could barely move with fear. He read the email again hurriedly, almost unable to believe what she'd written. What he saw chilled his bones.

His predicament was far worse than he'd imagined. Jackson's hand trembled as he closed all the windows and emptied the record of the pages from the Web browser's history and the temporary Internet files. He placed his hands in his lap, trying to hold them still. His breath came in short, irregular gasps, which he struggled to control. Fear was invading him now, filling out his body like a balloon

DiCanio approached the room, carrying a small tray on which she'd placed two drinks and a plate of snacks. When she looked at him, she was visibly surprised.

"You're shaking."

"It must be the air conditioning," he managed to say, "against the wet shirt."

"Hit that shower, right away!" Her tone was both maternal and domineering.

Jackson stood, watching as she took her seat. She had a digital camera, and the replica of the Adaptor. Once she'd sent off the scanned image of that text and her people had translated it, he knew it would be over for him. If only they'd thought to use something other than a well-known text! Discovery of a quote from an existing text would surely be too suspicious for DiCanio to remain taken in much longer.

Like a dead man walking, Jackson stumbled towards the shower room.

Rescue was nowhere in sight. Jackson understood finally who he was dealing with, exactly who he had been dealing with all along.

Frightening Splendor

Jackson leaned his forehead against the cool tiles of the shower cubicle as the water sprayed over his head. He was exhausted. The staples in his wound tugged uncomfortably against the skin. He was still reeling from the implications of what he'd read in Marie-Carmen's email.

There was little doubt. His life was in danger, more than at any point until now. As he showered, he began to galvanize himself against the imminent threat. He knew that his own resourcefulness, which may have made the difference up to this point, could not save him. Knowing that his fate lay almost entirely in someone else's hands was terrifying.

Once again, Jackson found himself thinking about his friend, PJ. How much had PJ really known that day in the airport? He thought back over PJ's somewhat tenebrous words to him that day.

Something is coming.

The DNA had encoded for a molecule which bound not only to PJ's *phoenix* maize protein, but also to the human version of that protein. In Chaldexx's hands this molecule, 'hypnoticin', had been found to confer in the carrier an eerie ability to plant suggestions in other people's minds. Jackson couldn't deny that he'd sensed something preternatural when he'd looked into the eyes of Connor and his men. They'd struggled to hang onto their orders. Under the influence of Jackson's voice, they had appeared perturbed, perplexed, yet unafraid.

But Connor was able to resist. If DiCanio had been truthful about anything, it was this: hypnoticin wouldn't work on Jackson or his brother. Given that DiCanio appeared to have no knowledge of the bio-toxin that was exuded by the Adaptor, his resistance to hypnoticin was likely central to her decision to recruit Jackson.

Marie-Carmen's translation of the Adaptor sequence threw up possibilities which seemed incredible, unthinkable. Yet as much as Jackson struggled to avoid their implications, he couldn't.

Was it possible that extra-terrestrial visitors had long ago introduced foreign DNA into the human genome?

He had to admit that there was no evidence to prove that some external tampering had never occurred within the human genome. In Jackson's own mind, if this had taken place it had done so without any intelligent direction – accidental contamination of a species' DNA from biological material imported on a comet. Such a theory still hovered on the periphery of respectable scientific debate. Some quite influential members of the scientific community had voiced a similar opinion, including Francis Crick the Nobel-prize winning co-discoverer of the DNA structure.

Once DNA found its way into the terrestrial canon, there were a number of mechanisms by which DNA could move from one species into another. The most likely was within the infectious cycle of a virus. The fact that *joust*, *phoenix* and now Chaldexx's human homolog – the hypnoticin response factor – were all retrotransposons, the evolutionary result of ancient retroviral infection, only confirmed in Jackson's own mind the likelihood of their relatedness.

Seeing that underground chamber with his own eyes, touching the strangely alien surfaces of the caskets, the Adaptor and altar, had introduced within Jackson the beginnings of a new belief.

Connor and DiCanio had independently alleged that the material from which those structures were made was artificial. Both agreed that the construction was ancient beyond any other building previously found on the planet. DiCanio claimed to know that the structures which her organization had found in Mexico might even predate the notorious caldera explosion of 74,000 years ago. Which could be linked to the recent discovery that, at the same time, the human race had been reduced to a population of 10,000 individuals.

Could this mean that whoever had built the structure had belonged to some even more ancient civilization, previously unknown to current society, the very memory of which had been extinguished by the holocaust caused by the Sumatran caldera explosion that had formed Lake Toba?

As Jackson thought about what he'd read in Marie-Carmen's emails, the translations of the ancient clay tablets of the Sumerian civilization, he wondered whether in fact some memory of a pre-holocaust civilization had in fact persisted.

Before Lord Anunnaki frightening splendor makes men weak. Awakened man is long-lived owner of frightening splendor.

Whether PJ had been aware of it or not, this was the real, the biologically-encrypted message which he'd sent Jackson.

'Frightening splendor' had to refer to some aspect of the mental power unleashed by hypnoticin, at least in human beings who carried the gene for the hypnoticin response factor.

Why encode the message of power, the description of the effects of the protein within the very molecule's code? To Jackson, this seemed far-fetched, even for a supposedly impenetrable ancient race. The properties of proteins were derived from their three-dimensional shapes and other chemical factors which led ineluctably from their amino acid composition. Attaching a linguistic interpretation to those amino acids should not be able to influence the resulting molecule.

He wondered if it were not after all possible that it had been the other way around. Possessing the amino acid sequence of a 'molecule of power', the ancient scientists may have taken the names of each component of the molecule from a sentence or phrase which described its activity. In this way, the amino acids were named from one or more original, significant protein. Their use in other contexts might be irrelevant, as randomly meaningless as our own names for amino acids. Hence the supplementary signs – or 'determinatives' – found in both the Sumerian script and Maya scripts used on the Adaptor: this was the ancient scientists' way of saying, "But when you see the logogram differentiated like this, it refers to the amino acid named after this word."

The conclusion Jackson drew from this was so thrilling that even under the needles of hot water, he felt his skin turn to goose flesh.

Had he stumbled across the genetic secrets of an ancient race?

The Adaptor that he'd held in the chamber had been inscribed with fifteen symbols; in Mayan on one side, in Sumerian on the other.

PJ's DNA molecule was fifteen amino acids long – the sequence of hypnoticin.

Was it possible that the Adaptor was inscribed with an encoded version of the same sequence? Jackson felt his skin turn to goose flesh. That amino acid sequence wasn't merely the key to 'frightening splendor' – the weakening of wills in the people around. It was the formula for something else – something involved in the function of the Adaptor. And it was possible that at this moment, Jackson was the only person alive who knew.

Jackson's had only agreed to go to Iraq out of fear of Hans Runig, following the deadly attack at Kleine Scheidegg. Hans Runig wanted his help to stop Melissa DiCanio. Yet fundamentally, Hans Runig and DiCanio wanted the same thing – the Adaptor, the secret of PJ's molecule.

Marie-Carmen was right. There were now too many coincidences.

You receive secrets, messages over the Internet,
telephone calls, a jet to Switzerland, now it's Iraq. It's like you're a
chess piece, being moved around the board.

The truth had been within reach almost from the
beginning. But Jackson had only seen it when he read Marie-
Carmen's last email.

Ki, the ancient Sumerian deity, the Earth Goddess,
also known as *Ninhursag.*

Ninhursag. Hans Runig.

It was an anagram; the sly jest of an adversary who
couldn't resist a sardonic jab at her prey. *Hans Runig* was
nothing more than a virtual being; the alter-ego of Melissa
DiCanio.

What this implied about DiCanio's own vision of
herself and the members of her organization was troubling
enough. Moreover, it hinted at a strategic process; detailed
planning whereby DiCanio had created her own apparent
nemesis. An alternate identity that she could use to
investigate, secretly, anyone on the track of hypnoticin.

Whether he'd allied himself with DiCanio, or with
Hans Runig, DiCanio had ensured that whichever team
Jackson chose, he was working for her.

How many other members of her organization had
been taken in like this? How widespread was knowledge of
DiCanio's double existence as Hans Runig? Or had that
particular identity been created for the sole purpose of
trapping the any scientist who stumbled across the fifteen-
letter sequence of hypnoticin?

PJ was one such person. Once he'd fallen into the
trap, the jaws of this particular Venus had begun to close.
He'd become inexorably ensnared, crushed in a relentless
grip.

Somehow, PJ had caught a faint whiff of the danger
he faced, in time to set up the message for Jackson. Yet . . . it
was still too much of a coincidence. Jackson's recruitment had
been crucial to DiCanio's organization, on the basis of his
resemblance to Connor. Connor had only been assigned to the
NRO within the past six months, by which time Jackson's
involvement with PJ had been long established.

The more he thought about it, the more the reach of DiCanio's power alarmed him. He had only begun working on *joust* as a result of a suggestion from DiCanio. The same might well be true of PJ Beltran. Connor's own move to the NRO had been surprising, and sudden. Could it be that Connor too had been subject to her Machiavellian manipulations?

Over dinner in Grindelwald DiCanio had told him, "The society includes several individuals placed quite highly within the United Nations." So far as Jackson knew, they were all hand-picked on the basis of their occupation and the fact that they could use hypnoticin.

Jackson was shivering as he dressed. Slowly, he pulled on his jacket, almost absent-mindedly checking the pockets. It was beginning to look as though his arrival at this house in Manama was an appointment that had been made for him some years ago.

***

As he stepped out of the bedroom, he knew instantly that the ordeal had begun. Standing guard outside his door, Kazmi stood impassively, distant; anger visible only in the grim set of his mouth as he brandished a pistol. Without saying a single word, Kazmi cracked the gun across Jackson's jaw. The force of the blow knocked him to the floor. For an instant, his vision blurred. When he opened his eyes he saw drops of blood trickling across his cheek.

DiCanio's voice was now as cold, as brutally aloof as he remembered she'd been when they first met in Houston. "It would seem you haven't been altogether honest with us, Jackson."

There was no way that DiCanio could yet be absolutely certain of the truth. Jackson realized that prevarication was the only way to buy more time. His mouth filled with the warm, rusty taste of blood. He spat on the floor.

"What the fuck is wrong with you?" he yelled.

"Pick him up," ordered DiCanio. Kazmi complied, dragging Jackson to his feet.

DiCanio leaned forward, opened her mouth slightly. She lowered her eyes, seemed about to lift her right hand, perhaps to strike him, but at the last minute stayed the impulse. When she spoke her words were forced, hard and brittle as icicles.

"Jackson. Sweetheart. Don't waste any more of my time."

For the second time that day, Jackson had felt himself on the receiving end of the aggression of a professional warrior. The reality was unprecedented in his experience. The shock of his own nerves jarring, the crunch of his own bones and the letting of his own blood under the force of another adult man's fury; no filmic version of such an event could have prepared him.

Connor had last wrestled Jackson when they were fourteen, not yet fully grown. Since then, he'd successfully avoided most contact sports, had never been in a fight. Even the few kick-boxing classes he had taken had been solely concerned with the practice of balletic movements. No substitute for real, hand-to-hand fighting.

"Jackson: I think that this Adaptor is a fake."

He wiped blood from his mouth and said nothing. DiCanio shook her head. "Better speak up now, darlin' or things gonna get a whole lot worse."

"Melissa." He could hardly keep the tremor out of his voice. "I don't know if it's a fake. I didn't see what they were doing in the chamber, I only heard. When I went down there, this was the only object which matched your description."

DiCanio frowned. "Hafez tells me that you took much longer than we'd anticipated. Now your story is that they were conducting some experiments down there, which you had to wait out. But this Adaptor you brought us, it looks brand new, Jackson. It feels heavier than the one we found in Mexico. All of that, I could just about believe. This Adaptor is inscribed with text from the *Lament of Eridu*, written thousands of years after we know the chamber was last touched by human beings. Now, that just don't seem right."

"Melissa, please, I just did what you said to do, I brought the thing that you said was the Adaptor, from the chamber . . ."

"You want me to believe that your brother planted a fake before you got there? I'm not saying it isn't a good story, sugar. It's just that for Connor to have anticipated any kind of infiltration, someone must have got to him first. I'm guessing that someone was you."

Jackson hesitated, and the hesitation was deadly. With little more than a slight inclination of her head, DiCanio signaled to Kazmi. He grabbed Jackson with his left hand, pulled back his right fist and slammed it into his face. Jackson managed to turn away just enough to avoid having his nose broken, but Kazmi's solid fist connected with his cheek bone. His eye juddered in its socket. A sunburst of pain exploded in his face. The energy of Kazmi's punch threw him backwards; he toppled towards the sofa.

"Now maybe you warned your brother, Jackson, and maybe you didn't. But when in doubt, I find it's safest to assume I've been betrayed."

A kick followed, to Jackson's ribs. Sharp, intense pain radiated throughout his torso. His hands moved to shield his own face, only to find them being grabbed and pulled behind him.

She was telling Kazmi to tie him up. Shock was setting in. Jackson could barely think straight. Where the hell was Connor? He was supposed to have followed, to prevent exactly this. In another minute his hands were bound together, above his head. He was being strung out between the two leather sofas. He heard DiCanio saying something about getting no blood on the floor. Jackson's shirt was being ripped open.

Silence fell on the trio. Jackson strained to focus. DiCanio came into view, then Kazmi. She was speaking, but her words were falling around him like shards of glass. He couldn't see where they fell or concentrate on their meaning.

This knife, she said. *This knife.*

A blade came into view. It was small, no longer than a finger, about as broad as a thumb. It was in Kazmi's hand. He'd grown up in a small mountain village in Iran, she was saying. His father was a goat herd. A boy might learn a useful skill in such a place; how to slaughter a goat, how to bleed the animal and retain all the flavor of the flesh. How to remove the skin in one piece.

A terrible clarity exploded in Jackson's mind. The shards of glass assembled into one solid form now, something recognizable.

A skinning could be made to last hours, Kazmi said. Intense, prolonged pain was involved. The suffering was quite beyond imagination. Blood loss could be kept to a minimum, making the death slow. In the hills where he'd grown up, a goat's throat would be cut before it was skinned. That was mercy. Sometimes though, because boys will be boys, they'd catch a goat and stake it out. They wouldn't bother with the slaughter, but proceed directly to the skinning.

"I've never seen the whole operation performed on a man," Kazmi said. He ran the blade across his own thumb and winced as a line of blood appeared. "In the Persian War, we captured an Iraqi, a Ba'athist from Saddam's own village; one of the *Fedayeen Saddam*. We wished to send a message to Saddam, so we removed a piece of this man's flesh, the skin of one arm. The man had a tattoo, very characteristic. All of Tikrit knew him by that tattoo. We sent the skin to Saddam, as a message. It was a very neat job. The hand too: just like a bloody glove."

The blade hovered over the tattoo they'd inked onto Jackson's chest earlier that day. The red-and-blue of the Stars and Stripes.

"If we send this to Captain Bennett, do you think he'll get the picture? You think he'll be a good brother and send us the Adaptor?"

Jackson found his voice. "No. Please." He began to struggle against the hard plastic handcuffs they'd fastened onto him. It was no use. Within seconds they bit into his skin and he felt his own blood lubricate the bindings.

243

DiCanio leaned over him. "I think you know where the real Adaptor is. I really hoped that you'd help us, Jackson. Of course, I had to have something up my sleeve."

The blade cut into Jackson, just level with his sternum. The stroke was firm and steady. The entire line was scored before even one drop of blood appeared. Then, as though the blood had been sprayed on him with a fine hose, a line of it suddenly appeared on his chest. The pain followed about a second later, sharp and tight. Kazmi pulled back, examined his handiwork. He grinned, broadly. "Perfect! Just under the dermis. The muscle wall should be perfectly intact!"

Kazmi leaned over him, peering closely at the next edge of the inked flag. He brought the knife forward and scored Jackson's skin again. Blood trickled out immediately this time and ran towards his belly. Kazmi seemed disappointed with himself. "My apologies," he murmured, as though he were a barber who'd just used the wrong razor comb. "That time wasn't as good. Clearly, I'm out of practice."

He brought the blade back against Jackson's skin. With meticulous care, he sliced alongside the third edge of the flag. Terror flooded his every pore. He felt a scream of sheer panic rising in his throat. It took all his self-control not to let it go.

Then he heard something which gave him a tiny shred of hope. Far away, but unmistakable, was the thrumming sound of a helicopter. It was growing closer.

Jackson dared not show even remote interest in the sound. Within seconds, however, the noise had roused the suspicions of DiCanio and her associates. Kazmi glanced up, moved the knife to Jackson's throat, pressed the blade against his jugular vein.

"Were you followed?"

In wordless terror Jackson gazed at him. DiCanio raised the Adaptor above her head. Her features were suddenly and unnervingly distorted by a twisted grimace. She hurled the artifact down onto the marble floor. It shattered into three pieces. She picked up one piece, examined it with an immediate, accusatory glare at Jackson.

Baked clay encased within a thin glaze. The counterfeit nature of the article was obvious.

DiCanio's countenance grew incandescent, furious. "We might as well just kill him now."

Jackson exploded. "You think the NRO will care? They made me do this, forced me to come back to you, as bait! They threatened to send me to Guantanamo as a terrorist if I refused! But you still need me, remember? I've seen the *real* Adaptor; I know what it can do. Don't you want to know?"

DiCanio stalled. "What are you talking about?" she asked incredulously.

Jackson was desperate now. His chest was covered in the crisscross patterns of tiny rivulets of blood, deep red stains were appearing on his open, white shirt. He was about to reveal the NRO's greatest secret about the Adaptor – the fact that it was protected by a deadly bio-toxin to which few were immune.

DiCanio crouched low until she was level with Jackson. "Come on, Jackson. What have you seen the Adaptor do?"

The helicopter was in the neighborhood; its low droning was unmistakable. Jackson hesitated. If he told, it might jeopardize Connor even further, literally to save his skin. But what could he do? There was no good reason to let himself die. Maybe DiCanio was some kind of eco-extremist, as his brother claimed. So what? He was broadly sympathetic to the 'Green' cause. He certainly wouldn't side against them at the cost of his own life.

"The Adaptor – can't be handled by just anyone. There's some kind of poison gas released when you touch it. Connor isn't affected, neither am I."

Uneasily, DiCanio shot Kazmi a conciliatory glance. "That might actually be true. We've come across that kind of use of a poison gas, with this ancient technology. Didn't know the Adaptor had it, though."

Kazmi lowered his gun. Like DiCanio, he didn't seem too taken aback by Jackson's news.

"Guess ours was too badly damaged," DiCanio said, thoughtfully. She didn't seem totally convinced, yet Jackson could tell that she knew enough to know that he could well be telling the truth.

Interjecting, Jackson said, "If I'm lying then you'll soon know, when you use me to get the real Adaptor back for you. But my price for that is my safety . . . and Marie-Carmen's."

His eyes met DiCanio's, watching revelation sweep across her features.

"You're Hans Runig, Melissa. I know."

DiCanio continued to stare at him in stunned silence. "Well, darlin'," she murmured. "Ain't you all kinds of smart . . . ?"

"We don't need him to get the Adaptor," Kazmi urged. "We can use Madison or one of the others. Let's just kill him and go!"

"No." Her tone was measured. "You can't be sure who is resistant to those poisons. If Jackson is telling the truth we'd better start with him. We'll take him with us."

Kazmi sliced through the sticky, blood-coated plastic handcuffs that bound Jackson's wrists and ankles. He strode up the stairs, taking them two at a time, into the office. He pushed back a panel in the ceiling, pulled down a ladder and ascended. He followed with his shirt still open to the waist and spotted with blood. DiCanio was last onto the ladder.

When Jackson reached the top of the ladder, he stood, looking around the large extension to the house. A white helicopter was parked there, standing on a circle that had been painted onto the concrete floor. Kazmi was already inside the helicopter, preparing. About a yard above the helicopter, a slatted metallic ceiling began to roll back, exposing the darkening sky. It was now dusk. He could clearly see the lights of the other helicopter which had been flying low around the district.

Jackson suspected that Connor would be just as surprised as he to find their tracer rising into the sky, rather than disappearing down a fast road. Fleetingly, he wondered where they'd placed it. He'd seen such things in films, knew that they could be practically undetectable, tiny microdots embedded in a scrap of adhesive plastic.

Kazmi assumed the pilot's seat. He passed a chunky-looking pistol to DiCanio, who turned it on Jackson. She pressed him towards the two passenger seats behind the pilot and co-pilot's positions. Jackson took a final glance around, hunting for escape routes. There was no choice but to join them in the helicopter.

The second helicopter began to approach, its occupants clearly intrigued by the sudden activity on this roof. Kazmi started up the motor. The blades leapt into action. The second helicopter now hovered thunderously above the house, its dark, matte surface practically invisible against the evening sky.

Then the shooting began, bullets burst glass and ricocheted off the body of the helicopter. Sitting nearest to the flank under attack, DiCanio ducked low, doubled up, briefly ignoring Jackson.

For a precious few seconds, Jackson noticed that he was unguarded. The gun in DiCanio's hand was pointed at the ground, somewhere between her knees. Before he'd even properly registered any conscious plan, Jackson lunged at the door handle. He opened it and flung himself out.

He'd guessed that they could only be a several feet or so off the ground but when at the last instant he saw the lights of the house, Jackson managed to grab hold of the helicopter's leg before he fell. Deafened by the twin roars of the two helicopters, he clung on for his life. DiCanio's helicopter was already twenty yards above the roof.

Jackson couldn't make himself let go.

Kazmi swung the helicopter over the yard Jackson spotted his chance. The pool lights were on. They illuminated the water just enough for Jackson to realize that they were probably directly above it, albeit three stories off the ground.

Shaking, he screwed up his eyes. Jackson let go. He plunged downwards.

He landed feet first, with a resounding splash. By the time he hit the bottom of the pool Jackson had lost enough momentum to break the fall without smashing any bones. As he surfaced, he saw DiCanio's white helicopter disappear behind the house. The lights of the second, bulkier craft, beamed down onto the pool, picking him out. Jackson heard his brother's voice from a megaphone.

"Jacko? That you?"

Jackson bellowed back, as loud as he could, although his breathlessness made it impossible to make much noise. To his amazed relief, Connor's helicopter began to approach. One of the men aboard tossed a rope ladder overboard. Jackson grabbed hold of it and started to climb. Then he spotted another chilling sight.

The bodyguard who'd remained in the house was opening the French windows. A sudden bolt of energy flung Jackson backward. The bodyguard was firing at him. Jackson felt a heavy punch on his left side. A wave of heat burst inside his shoulder and he screamed. His left hand lost its grip on the ladder.

From somewhere above him, Jackson heard the noise of a submachine gun rip into the air. He turned to watch as the bodyguard tumbled head-first into the pool.

The helicopter pulled away sharply, rising vertically. Jackson clung on. His right arm was wrapped tightly around the rope ladder that was now being raised by the men above. In his other shoulder, there was steady throb of agony. He began to tremble with shock. The last thing Jackson saw before he passed out was the man who'd shot at him, splayed out in the dimly lit pool. Blood swirled red in the blue water, a steady flow from the body.

Friends in High Places

The night air of Manama was warm and faintly dusty. Jackson breathed heavy and slow, forcing deep inhalation, trying to emulate what he'd seen practiced on TV by women supposedly in labor. Connor's injection of lidocaine had frozen part of his shoulder. It took the edge off the pain. The bullet had snagged the collar bone, but not broken it. Connor had used tweezers to pull out the bullet, while Jackson lay rigid, his entire upper body a symphony of agony. Then shock had begun to take a hold. He thought fleetingly of Priya and the shoulder injury he'd seen her take. The young woman had skied like a champion after that injury and yet here Jackson was, incoherent.

The more he thought about it, the more likely it seemed that even Priya's injury had been faked. What if she'd merely been hit with a rubber bullet, and then herself aggravated the injury with a concealed weapon? The entire subterfuge had been designed to convince Jackson that Hans Runig was a threat to DiCanio as much as to him.

It had worked.

When he'd injected Jackson, Connor had made a point of telling him how impressed he was. The partial skinning of the fake tattoo on his chest had drawn attention, too. One more cut and his torturer would have started to peel the flesh away. After some initial surprise, Connor's reaction had seemed mainly one of amusement; brutality measured for its novelty value. Jackson was still trembling. He didn't want Connor and his colleagues to see just how badly shaken he was.

Thankfully, Connor's attention was now focused elsewhere. He sat up in the front of the craft, talking to the pilot. From his position on the floor, Jackson couldn't see what was happening directly in front of the helicopter, but he could hear from Connor and the pilot's discussion that they were gaining on the smaller helicopter, which they referred to as "the R44".

The pilot was saying something about them flying back to Iraq. Connor seemed to disagree. "No – they're planning something; trying to confuse us. If they go back to Iraq, they're target practice. Here in Bahrain, we'd be in a difficult position. In Qatar, who knows? It all depends on whether DiCanio has contacts in the Royal Family."

He tried to sit up. His voice sounded faint, even to himself. "Don't take too many risks. She's well-connected. Friends in high places." Absently, he added, "and she's probably going to use the hypnoticin."

Connor said, "Hypnoticin?"

Jackson paused. "The 'Eastern mind-control shit'."

"Oh that," Connor muttered, dismissively. "The neuroscience thing. What does it do?"

"It's something to do with inducing suggestibility."

"Sounds interesting, this Professor DiCanio. What's she doing getting mixed up with the race to get into these ancient chambers?"

He shrugged. This wasn't the right time to get into his own theories for how ancient survivors of an advanced civilization might have used retroviruses to introduce their own DNA into plants and animals. There was an edge to Connor's interest in DiCanio that felt somehow suspicious. Maybe Connor's determination to pursue DiCanio was because of the attempt she'd made to steal the Adaptor. Yet Jackson sensed that there was something else going on. Connor and his team seemed altogether too prepared, the operation too smooth.

It was as though DiCanio was the answer to a question that Connor had been asking for quite some time.

Connor peered through binoculars. "My guess is they're headed for Qatar. It's not far away; the coastline begins just over the horizon."

The Air Force Blackhawk flew behind the R44, remaining just out of shooting range. Approaching the coast of Qatar, the blinking lights of the oil refineries and the lights from cars streaming along the coastal highway became visible. Kazmi led the way, flying the R44 over land, proceeding due East across the peninsula. Then, without warning, Kazmi swerved northwards.

Connor remarked, "Change of plan. I'm guessing they're headed for Madinat Al-Shamal. Small town at the northern tip of the peninsula."

In the distance, Jackson could see lights on the ground. Roads were laid out in a characteristically modern grid, and a few larger buildings were lit up. The two helicopters flew right towards the inky black Persian Gulf, keeping the town to their right. Seconds later they were, once again, flying over water. Not far away, gas burned at the top of stacks on the oil rigs in the Gulf.

The R44 made a sharp turn towards the right, the Blackhawk followed. Connor removed a small pair of night goggles from his jacket and fastened them over his face. As he adjusted them, he moved his head, scanning the sea below and ahead. He pointed towards the southwest.

"That's it! They've got some kind of boat waiting."

Jackson peered into the pitch black below. He couldn't see anything where Connor pointed.

Connor released his safety belt and hurried into the back of the helicopter. He opened a panel, removed a large mound of wrapped, khaki plastic.

"They're gonna land on a boat. I see a helipad, but the boat isn't slowing up too much. It's gonna take some pretty smooth flying. Her pilot must be good."

"Hafez Kazmi," Jackson offered, "he's ex-Iranian Air Force."

Connor didn't look up from his work. "Figures," he said, almost to himself. "They'll be hard to catch. What are they armed with?"

"At least one gun. Automatic I think."

"They'll have more," Connor said shortly, "If this guy is ex-military, he's stashed weapons all the way on his escape route." He turned to Jackson, another smirk forming on his features. "Got some bad news for you, bro'. You'll have to come with. See, I have no idea what these guys look like. If I lose them in a crowd, I'm counting on you to I.D. them for me."

Jackson's mouth was still opening to ask where Connor was planning to go, when Connor flung open the door of the helicopter. Jackson could hear the throbbing pulse of blades on the smaller craft, sight of which could now be plainly had through the front window.

The R44 dropped suddenly. The Blackhawk followed, plummeting like a stone. He felt his stomach sloop up within his abdomen, and almost gagged.

Connor worked quickly, strapping on a backpack. "How long?" he yelled at the pilot, the noise of their own blades almost drowning his question.

The pilot answered, "Thirty seconds?"

Jackson watched, bewildered, as his brother thrust a large flashlight into his hand.

Then Connor spoke, firing instructions like a machine gun. "When we get lower, you're going to jump out in the dinghy. It will inflate the second you hit the water. Like an airbag. Then I'm going to 'chute in. Shine your flashlight, so I can find you. It won't be a long drop, so be sure to keep that light shining up, straight into the sky. You got that?"

But Jackson could only mumble, "I'm jumping out?"

Connor unfastened Jackson's seat belt, pulling him to his feet. "You don't think about these things, Jacko, you just *do*. Got that? Don't think, just do."

He pushed him away. "I can take care of myself. Give me the boat."

Connor stood back, evidently pleased. He unrolled the plastic package until it was open far enough to envelop Jackson, and passed it to him.

He pulled the plastic around his body, then made for the open door.

Connor looked down at the sea below. They were now close enough to see the waves by the lights of the Blackhawk. Shouting the count, he pushed Jackson over the edge.

For the second time that evening, he felt himself fall into the void. Tons of emptiness weighed abruptly on his stomach. He hit the water with crash, felt the dinghy suddenly simultaneously explode and inflate, cushioning the impact of landing. He was now lying in a small inflated boat. The black waves of the Persian Gulf lapping gently around him.

About a hundred yards away, he could just make out the lights of a large speedboat, over which the helicopter had been hovering. The dark obscured the movements of the passengers. Seeing the boat suddenly speeding away from his own position, he guessed that DiCanio had escaped. Kazmi must have remained aboard because the helicopter now took off. It flew ahead, continuing east, the coast to his right.

Jackson shone the flashlight directly upwards, as his brother had instructed. After dropping him and the dinghy onto the water, the Blackhawk had ascended quickly. Just seconds later, he saw a small parachute open. It lifted Connor higher into the sky.

Connor dropped slowly, swinging from side to side, directing his parachute carefully toward Jackson's light. With a triumphant yell, Connor landed squarely in the middle of the dinghy. He pulled in his parachute, and stuffed it into his backpack. Then he cracked open the Velcro strips which held a small motor against his chest. He began to work on fastening the motor to the rear of the boat. Jackson responded swiftly by shining his flashlight on the area.

"Keep your eyes on that boat!" ordered Connor.

It took Connor less than two minutes to get the motor started. Overhead, the Blackhawk had turned around and flew out to sea, following Kazmi in the R44.

Jackson beamed the flashlight ahead of the boat, into the black depths of the sea. DiCanio's yacht was now too far ahead to be caught by the beam. Connor, wearing his night goggles, was tracking their positions.

Their inflated dinghy slapped the water rhythmically as they followed the larger, faster boat which carried DiCanio. Within minutes it was obvious: they were unlikely to catch up. Yet Connor remained determined, focused. They couldn't gain much speed, but the faster boat remained steadily just in sight.

Jackson rubbed his shoulder. The cold prickling of the anesthetic was uncomfortable, irksome. The bright lights of the shore were now clearly visible. There were a few large, blocky buildings. A small pier stretched into the sea and a small number of yachts were moored alongside.

DiCanio's yacht reached the pier and spun violently, creating a wave in its wake. DiCanio could just be seen dashing towards the shore, accompanied by the boat's skipper. As the dinghy neared the pier, the brothers were almost thrown clear of their craft when the heavy swell from DiCanio's boat hit them. Jackson and Connor's dinghy reached the pier just in time for them to glimpse DiCanio and her companion being picked up by an orange-and-white taxi at the end.

The brothers bolted down the almost deserted pier. The added weight of Jackson's soaked clothes slowed him considerably, and the heavy, wet denim chafed. A couple of yacht owners, men dressed in long, crisp white *thobes* worn over white cotton trousers and enjoying drinks whilst seated on their decks, watched in amazement as for the second time that night, the stillness of their small town was shattered by newly arrived foreigners.

Parked along the coastal road were several cars. Connor examined the line swiftly and rejected them all. At the end he found a sierra-red Harley Davidson DynaGlide motorcycle. The immobilizer was not engaged, theft being unheard of in that town. He watched as Connor worked for a couple of minutes, using tools he'd extracted from his equipment belt, fiddling with the ignition mechanism.

As far as Jackson was concerned, Connor had the motorcycle's engine purring in lightning speed. The problem was there was neither sight nor sound of the taxi that had retrieved DiCanio and her escort.

Other yacht owners had now emerged, disturbed by the commotion. Seeing Jackson and Connor on the Harley, one of them yelled loudly. The sounds brought even more men onto the pier, shouting admonishments. By the time the observers realized what was happening, the brothers had disappeared westwards along the coastal road.

Jackson wrapped arms tightly around his twin's waist. Despite himself, Connor's actions so far that night had begun to inspire in Jackson the faintest twinges of a hero worship that he hadn't experienced in two decades. Connor's determination to catch their prey was infectious. Even though Jackson couldn't help feeling that it was destined to fail, he admired Connor's derring-do. Not for one second did Connor seem to accept the possibility of failure.

They tore past the last few buildings of the town, following the highway into the barren rockiness of the country's interior. There were a few cars on the road. Nevertheless, Connor rode the motorbike at over ninety miles per hour, overtaking every vehicle they encountered.

Jackson was about to shout a question, but realized that at this speed, his brother would hear nothing. Instead, he concentrated on holding on tightly as the bike continued to gain speed. After about ten minutes, they saw a car with taxi markings, about eighty yards ahead. Connor accelerated once more. Riding that Harley, Jackson was finally racing along the desert road faster than he'd ever moved on land before.

The taxi, an E-series Mercedes, lunged ahead as soon as the Harley ventured within fifty yards. The two vehicles remained approximately the same distance apart as they careered dangerously along the road, swerving as they passed every obstacle. Shortly after they passed a sign to 'Al Zubara' the Mercedes, without any prior indication, pulled off the main road and into the slip road.

Connor was only just far enough behind to make the turn-off without crashing into the side of the road. Hitting the cats-eyes at the edge of the carriageway, the Harley launched into the air, landing with a crashing jolt. The Mercedes, now almost a hundred yards ahead, made another sharp turn. It disappeared to the left.

As Connor and Jackson skidded around the same corner, they could just see the Mercedes disappear behind the heavy doors of a large stone-built fortress. Connor slowed down. He stopped the motorcycle in front of the solid-looking gate, which sat in a small opening cut into the thick stone wall.

"Friends in high places? Yeah, that looks about right."

Civilian Geek-Boy

The tires of the motorcycle crunched against the sandy pathway. Connor began slowly to circumnavigate the structure, looking for a way in. The fort itself was square-shaped with circular towers in three of its corners and a rectangular tower in the fourth. The walls were high, thick, substantial. There was no sign of anyone around. There were no other buildings within immediate view. No cars were parked outside; no sounds could be heard emanating from within.

Night had fallen completely but the sky glowed faintly, iridescent with the light of nearby cities. For as far as they could see, the sands around them shimmered with a ghostly luminescence. The shadows cast by the fortress loomed ominous and stark. To Jackson, they struck a chord; a metaphor for the end of their road. DiCanio's disappearance inside that towering keep seemed almost inevitable. Everywhere they went, he feared, they would find doors closing before them, voices silenced as DiCanio vanished within the protectorate of her recondite society.

Before Jackson could share these impressions with Connor, his brother drove the Harley back down the entrance road, stopping further along. He turned off the engine and signaled for Jackson to dismount before he slid off the bike. Connor turned to gaze back at the fortress. Its hard lines framed against the luminous night sky, the keep seemed impenetrable.

Connor sighed. "Well, there's only one way out of that place."

"What is it?" asked Jackson. "It looks real old."

"Some kind of military fort. I'd guess it's a museum these days: most of these historic buildings are. It'll be closed at this hour. She has to leave sometime. It's worth waiting, at least until tomorrow."

"Are you kidding?" said Jackson. "The people on that pier will have reported us for taking the Harley! The police will be along any minute."

Behind the night goggles, Connor's eyes scanned the surrounding landscape.

"Maybe, maybe not. I'm gonna see if there's someplace we can hide. They won't look very hard. I doubt they'll look for us here. Most likely they'll think we've gone across the interior, to Doha. But this place? It's closed. There's nothing around."

Jackson recognized the logic of Connor's reasoning. He could hear the noise of cars zooming by on the highway from which they'd come. Unless they'd actually left a rubber burn on the road, Connor was probably right to believe they'd be undisturbed, at least for a few hours.

Then Jackson thought of a flaw.

"What if DiCanio's people tip off the police?"

Connor thought for a few seconds. "Good point. Maybe we'd better make a show of driving away. We'll come back real quiet, with the lights off."

Connor started up the Harley again and they both climbed aboard. They rode back towards the highway, until the fortress was out of sight. He then turned around, extinguished the lights and engine. They rolled the machine back quietly to the just within sight of the entrance to the fortress. Connor pointed out a small rise, about one hundred yards away.

"We can hide behind that, camp out, keep watch and look out for any car leaving the place."

The brothers rolled the bike to the small hill, dropping low enough behind it so that the fortress was completely out of sight. Connor approached the crest of the rise, lying flat on his belly. He examined the building with the binoculars, then he removed his equipment belt and stripped out of his desert camouflage flight jumpsuit. Underneath, Connor wore a plain white T-shirt and shorts. He tossed the flight suit towards Jackson, saying, "Here. You should get out of those wet clothes. Lay them out on the sand."

Jackson looked down at his clothes. Connor had a point; they were sodden and blood-stained. He undressed to his boxers and then climbed into the flight jumpsuit. It even had his name on it: a label with the word 'Bennett' was embroidered on the right breast pocket. He left the jumpsuit open, letting air get to his wounds. They were throbbing badly now, fresh and impossible to ignore. Exhaustion was beginning to swamp him. He longed to give in to it, but Connor wouldn't stop whispering. Anxiety chewed away at him. If DiCanio was the power behind 'Hans Runig', then what of Marie-Carmen? Her last email to him had ended with a hurried, slightly mysterious farewell. She'd left the hotel in Acapulco. Why? Where had she gone next? Marie-Carmen had no idea what she might be up against.

Somehow, he had to warn her.

Jackson focused back on what his brother was saying to him; planning their water consumption, how they'd organize the sleep shifts. The guy had to be joking. Jackson was in no fit state to fight anyone now. He stretched out a hand, touched his brother's arm.

"Is your phone working?"

Connor peeled away the wrapper from a stick of Big Red chewing gum and popped it into his mouth. "Sure thing bro, you want to call your girlfriend?"

"I wish. She's keeping her phone switched off. I need to email."

Connor took out his phone, which was encased in a thick, black rubber case. He tapped the screen a few times and handed it to Jackson. Jackson typed a quick email to Marie-Carmen.

Hans Runig is Melissa DiCanio. Ninhursag – I guess it's her idea of a joke. I've stopped helping her. There will probably be consequences. Please stay out of sight. I'll find you, we'll be together soon. That's a promise.

When Jackson returned the phone, Connor read the email, chewing his gum. A sweet, spicy smell of cinnamon wafted from his mouth. He glanced down at his brother, one eyebrow raised. "You like this girl a lot?"

259

Jackson closed his eyes and exhaled slowly, through pursed lips. The pain was building to levels that were getting hard to control. "I think I love her," he said. What the hell – it didn't matter now. Might as well be truthful.

"You think you love her," Connor repeated, pensively.

Jackson rolled over slightly so that he could see his brother's eyes. They were gazing back with a quizzical, amused look. Connor chewed the gum, thoughtful for a few seconds. "Good. I'm glad you found a girl to get serious about. It's time you cared about something apart from science."

"This from the guy who signed up to the air force before college."

"Yeah well, it's just me, Jacko. There are good, practical reasons for someone like me to remain unattached."

Jackson didn't reply. There was no point in rerunning their old argument about whose job was more significant.

"You got something for pain?"

Jackson took the two tablets that his brother held out. He gulped them down with a mouthful of water. Connor spread out the parachute silk and rolled up one end to use as a pillow. Jackson lay down and closed his eyes for a moment. He could feel the blood pumping along the wound on his chest.

"You did OK today, Jacko. For a flabby, civilian geek-boy. I'm almost proud of you. Aside from the fact that you got caught stealing from your own government."

Jackson sighed. "DiCanio totally manipulated me. She had a gun to my head as Hans Runig, and a fistful of dollars as herself."

"There's always a choice Jacko. You could've just said 'no' to both."

Almost inaudibly, Jackson replied, "I tried."

"So now you'd better try help us catch her. You have no idea how much we want to talk to this bitch." Rather abruptly, he stopped talking.

There it was again. Jackson was certain that Connor hadn't meant to let that last part slip.

"You've been wanting to talk to her? For how long?" Jackson tried to sit up. "Are you saying that you know about DiCanio and her society?"

There was a long silence. Finally, Connor spoke. "We knew there was someone else out there who knows about these chambers, who built them and everything."

"Okay – *who* built them?"

His brother faced him with eyes that were two sharp, white points glinting in the reflected starlight. "There's something pretty big going on here. We're only just fitting together the pieces. These underground chambers are not the only evidence of some kind of ancient technology."

"What else is there?"

"We've found aircraft."

"Ancient aircraft . . . ?"

"Not ancient; new. Working. People flying them and shit."

"People – not aliens?"

"Correct. Not aliens. People. With access to technology that's fifty, a hundred years ahead of anything we know how to do. DiCanio and her society, they're connected to it all, somehow. We need to know what they know. We need to find their chamber."

"Why?"

The question appeared to derail Connor. "Why? You think we can just let clandestine groups fly around the world controlling weird ancient technology, injecting people with mind-control drugs? You really believe that DiCanio just wants to solve the planet's climate problems? Exactly how is that gonna happen? A few quiet words in the ears of some billionaire, Chinese factory owner? Or they planning something a little more substantial, a little more disruptive?"

Jackson said nothing. Now that he'd connected DiCanio with Hans Runig, he doubted that her ambition was anything quite as altruistic as reversing climate change. He had to admit, it had been a persuasive argument, at the time. Many scientists he knew felt extremely passionate about climate change; but not enough to resort to kidnap and murder. As far as DiCanio went, he'd assumed her interest in hypnoticin was more likely to be academic – a crucial step on the way to that elusive prize of prizes; the Nobel.

Even that didn't make sense, in the context of what Jackson now understood.

"Those two chambers, Connor. What are they for?"

Above him on the ridge, Connor glanced around. "Get some sleep," he ordered, ignoring Jackson's question. "I'll wake you in three hours."

"What are they for?"

Still facing away, Connor shook his head. Outlined against the stars, he could see the rhythmic movement of Connor's jaw working the cinnamon-flavored gum. "I can't tell you that, little brother. Because I don't know. Now get some sleep."

Jackson could only comply as far as closing his eyes. Unlike Connor, he lacked the discipline to snatch sleep when he saw any opportunity. Overwhelmed with the day's experiences and the multiplicity of possibilities for his future, Jackson's mind raced. There was no chance to rest.

Why was he prostrate on the floor under a roof of desert stars, standing guard over a fortress with his twin brother? As far as Jackson was concerned, choice hadn't yet really come into it; the only option he was ever given was to opt out, not in.

Now, he had some time to think about it. With good reason, he feared DiCanio and her organization. What he had seen could well represent just the tip of an iceberg. She'd been putting the group together for years. Jackson had a piece of information which DiCanio and her group had yet to elucidate. There was little doubt that she would stop at nothing to get that information.

Connor and the NRO were trying to uncover some greater mystery than the simple existence of ancient technology. It was pretty clear that Connor wasn't going to divulge any more than he'd already told Jackson. Well, fine. Jackson could also play that game. Connor hadn't promised Jackson anything yet; not safety for Marie-Carmen, nor immunity to prosecution.

Jackson had only one card left to play – the solution to the puzzle of the Adaptor inscription.

If he was right, it could be the answer to the mystery of the ancient chambers. Connor had referred to the chamber as 'technology'. Maybe that amino acid sequence was a formula – a biochemical required to activate the chamber.

Uneasily, Jackson realized that the entire body of evidence relating to this theory was held on his webmail account. Should DiCanio or Connor's people crack his password, he would have nothing.

Was that what DiCanio was doing inside that quasi-medieval structure? Jackson couldn't help wondering. While he and Connor waited under the sky, was DiCanio unraveling his final secret?

The Good Soldier

There was still no moon. Jackson was staring into one of the darkest skies he could remember. The stars were impossibly bright, oppressive in their density. He hadn't camped out in the desert since he'd been a small boy. Then as now, Connor had been the one to insist on tending the watch – in that case, over the small fire which they'd made themselves. Or more accurately, which Connor had built and lit; he'd barely trusted Jackson to gather firewood and tinder. Jackson remembered finding the experience difficult, uncomfortable and totally lacking in the magic he'd anticipated. Until the sky blackened completely, revealing the stars. That night too, there'd been no moon; the stars had leapt out of the sky, as tangible as a thick frosting of diamonds sprinkled over crushed black velvet. Jackson had been breathless with the clarity of that moment. He couldn't decide which rich seam of heaven to stare at first.

After that experience and for many years afterwards, Jackson had dreamed of being an astronomer. Eventually he'd been betrayed by his lack of ability in mathematics. By then however, he'd already begun a life-long love affair with the puzzles of the genetic code. From the moment when as a teenager he'd read James Watson's account of the cracking of the structure and code of DNA, he'd begun to forget about the planets and wonder what secrets were stored within that remarkable molecule.

Now, eighteen years later, he found himself once more asking the question he'd pondered all those years ago as a boy in Yellowstone National Park. Could it be that our world was alone, that amongst all those countless points of light, only ours could support intelligent life?

Aged ten, Jackson had felt certain that there was life elsewhere. What he'd seen today made him start seriously to doubt the conventional scientific wisdom that we were, in fact, entirely alone.

Connor had spoken of aircraft; he'd alluded to the technology of the underground chamber. The sarcophagi-like nature of those caskets, the involvement of molecules composed of amino acids; both pointed to some kind of advanced medical function. How could such technologies have existed 74,000 years ago, without external assistance? And how could a complex, technologically advanced society have vanished with almost no trace? Jackson couldn't help recalling DiCanio's portentous words reminding him that in the end, all of earth's prior civilizations had been extinguished, defeated. Or like the Ancient Maya, apparently of their own volition, they had simply given up the ghost.

One day, he mused, doom might rain down from the sky, obliterating humanity as it once had obliterated the dinosaurs. That idea was terrifying enough, but it could hardly be prevented. The idea that humanity itself might bring about its own demise was more disturbing.

Jackson knew that his brother was at heart the good soldier; obedient and patriotic. Connor didn't have any problem in following orders, had no inner conflict about the goals he served. The USA's entire military strategy was predicated on their own armed forces retaining their position as the world's supreme fighting force. The mere suggestion of anything superior had to be dealt with, ruthlessly.

How easy it must be to live your life that way, Jackson thought, with a touch of envy. He couldn't curb his own curiosity. He would always rather know the truth than obey orders. Fundamentally, he mistrusted everything that came out of the mouth of any elected official. Even if he had helped to elect them. That was the one, irreconcilable difference between Connor and him.

A faint breeze picked up to the west of their position. It rustled through the fronds of a small palm grove nearby. Over the course of the next hour, Jackson stirred uncomfortably on the hard ground. The pains in his shoulder and chest had returned with a fiery vengeance, and his leg wound still occasionally stung. He was exhausted, yet unable to sleep, unable to find answers to his questions and, most worryingly, unable to decide to which side of this argument he truly belonged.

Just as finally he began to drift off, Jackson was awakened by Connor hissing at him. He was pulling on the damp jeans that Jackson had discarded earlier that night.

"Wake up, get everything ready to go!"

Jackson checked his watch. It showed the time as 4:04am. Connor's body was tense as he peered through the night-vision goggles. "A truck," he murmured. "Refrigerated. Looks like a food delivery. My guess is she'll use this as a way out."

Jackson picked up Connor's equipment belt, noting that it held no weapons. Clearly, his brother still didn't trust him.

"Why the subterfuge?" he whispered. "If she reported us for following her, the police would have found us by now."

"No; if she bought that little ruse last night, then the police think we've gone ahead to Doha. She'll be afraid to use that Mercedes again in case we're waiting to ambush her on the way. My money's on this delivery truck."

Connor slid backwards down the ridge. He stood dusting himself off, and gave Jackson a triumphant wink. "Hop aboard. You're gonna come along and help me catch this fish. Let's get started down the road before they work out that they've been seen."

They headed back onto the main road and took the highway to Doha. At this time of night, the roads were almost entirely empty. Connor sped ahead until any headlights behind them were just dimly visible. They rode across the barren landscape until they reached an even broader road, the main Eastern highway connecting most of the country's main towns with the capital, Doha. Connor took them off the road, concealing the Harley behind a row of desert palms which lined part of the major highway.

After a few minutes delivery truck approached. As it passed under a street lamp, Jackson could see that it was covered with writing in Arabic and illustrations of cows, milk cartons and yoghurts.

"That it?"

Connor nodded. "You see her?"

Jackson hadn't seen anyone in the driver's cabin, except a single driver. "She must be in the cold storage section."

Just as they were about to start the engine once again, they heard another car approach, its lights on full beam. It passed them seconds later, about two hundred yards behind the dairy truck.

It was a taxi – an E-series Mercedes.

Dumbstruck, the brothers stared impotently at the car. Hurriedly, Connor started up the engine, waiting for the taxi's tail-lights to recede into the distance.

"I say she's in the milk truck," Jackson said.

Connor peered into the mirror. "I wonder."

They took the coastal highway, staying barely in sight of the Mercedes's lights. The sun had just begun to set fire to the eastern horizon. As Connor and Jackson rode closer to Doha with the Persian Gulf on their left, the sun rose directly above the water's horizon, a blazing distraction in their peripheral vision. In front of them, the light on the road grew hazy, a vaporous chiffon which made it almost impossible to keep sight of the two cars in front.

By the time they rode into the outskirts of the main city, the entire sky in the east had turned a delicious shade of mauve. Apart from an occasional market truck or taxi, there was no traffic. The taxi they were following slowed as it drove onto the Doha Corniche, a four mile-long stretch of waterfront gardens and coastal paths. The dairy truck, they could just see, was still ahead of the Mercedes.

As the dairy truck approached the end of the bay, it turned down the road into the harbor. The taxi followed. On the short spur of highway within the harbor complex, the dairy truck continued directly towards the end, where a collection of elegant club houses occupied the wharf. The taxi, in contrast, took the first right turn towards the yacht marina.

Arriving at the turning, Connor stopped the bike.

"Follow the Mercedes. I'm gonna see where that truck goes." He removed a sidearm from a weapon holster, and handed it to Jackson, who answered him with a questioning look.

"For security," said Connor, placating him. "If she's not in the truck I'll be back real quick to save your ass."

Jackson took off at a trot. The taxi had already vanished from sight, but as he turned the corner he could just make out a man and woman in traditional Arab attire getting out of the taxi and walking down the third and final pier, about a hundred yards away. By the time Jackson reached that pier, however, there was no sign of activity. The moored yachts rocked in a gentle tide. Aside from the occasional slap of water against a boat's hull, there was almost no sound.

Twenty boats were moored along the pier, ten on each side. Jackson began walking up the pier, peering into the window of each yacht's cabin. He reached the end, without spotting any sign of the couple he'd seen disembark from the taxi. Jackson was turning back when he thought he saw a movement through one of the windows. For a split second he had clear sight of the woman. She was dressed in a black flowing dress, covered with a black *abayah*. Jackson leaned forward, balancing on the guard rail of the closest yacht, trying to take a closer look.

A voice sounded, close behind him; a sharp, tenor voice, carefully-enunciated, American English with a distinct Arabic accent.

"Hey, American! In my country it's considered most impertinent to look at another man's wife in such a way!"

Jackson spun around. Less than two yards away, a gun was pointing at his head. The weapon was firmly gripped in two hands, by a man dressed in white robes with a red-and-white, check-patterned *ghutra* on his head. He looked to be in his late twenties, handsome, pale and with high cheekbones, clean-shaven. His aim was rock-steady as he waited for an answer from Jackson.

"She's your wife?"

"Even if she weren't, you'd need a lesson in manners. Put your gun on the floor."

"I don't have a . . ."

Jackson heard the click of the safety catch being removed. "Gun on the ground, friend. Now."

Jackson withdrew the pistol he'd been given by Connor. He placed it beside his right foot.

"Kick it over here."

Jackson did as he was ordered. The guy leaned down, without taking his eyes or the gun from Jackson. He picked up the gun, tossed it into the bay.

"This is private property. Tell me, American, do you happen to own one of these boats?"

Jackson stared. There was something wrong with the man's voice. Some words were pronounced without a trace of a foreign accent. Was it possible that the guy was faking it? In the distance, Jackson could hear the Harley. Connor was on his way.

"I'm sorry if I offended . . ." Jackson began. "I was looking for someone. I thought she might be here."

He began to move.

"Who told you to move?"

This time, there could be no doubt. The young guy had fired the words rapidly, fluently. The 'Arabic' accent had disappeared.

From the end of the pier, a third man's voice rang out. "Better drop that gun, pal."

Jackson didn't dare to budge. His brother had arrived.

The guy in the Arab costume glanced briefly over his shoulder at Connor, who had stalled the Harley about forty yards away from their position. Connor was taking careful aim at Jackson's assailant.

"At this distance?" The young man forced a laugh. He'd thrown out all pretense of being a local. He indicated Jackson, with the gun. "I think *this* guy is in more danger than me."

"I don't," Connor said, drily. "But then, I've shot down Iraqi MiGs as they buzzed around my jet like angry little bees. A stationary target at forty yards, that's kid stuff."

There was the briefest of pauses. Then a shot rang out. The Arab-costumed man gave a short, sharp exclamation. The pure white sleeve of his *thobe* bloomed suddenly with his own blood. The man's pistol fell to the ground with a heavy clunk.

Connor sounded irritated. "Jacko, what are you waiting for; slam the bastard!"

Jackson lunged forward. He landed a well-aimed kick to the guy's torso, knocking him backwards into the water.

"So you *can* move." Connor peered over the edge of the jetty, watching the man in the water wriggle out of his *thobe*. In another minute he dived beneath the surface and disappeared under the jetty.

"That's all I got," Jackson said. "That's my one move. Nice shooting, by the way!"

"Not really. I was aiming for his head."

At that moment, a yacht started up its engines. It was the boat on which Jackson had observed the woman in black Arab dress.

Connor raised his voice above the engines. "Is that her boat?"

Jackson paused. "Yeah. I'm pretty sure."

In fact, he had nothing but a hunch. He'd seen the woman's face for less than a second and her veil had obscured most of that. But Jackson had noticed an anomalous lack of eye make-up. Most of the women he'd seen in Iraq, Bahrain and even Qatar had eyes made-up dramatically enough that even the briefest glimpse – which was all he'd ever caught – was memorable. The woman on board had paid no such attention to her eyes.

Abruptly, the yacht pulled away from its moorings. It began to maneuver out of its position. Connor sprang into action. He hurled himself and the bike forward. Jackson darted aside, balked as he watched Connor climb up the bike, standing on the seat as the bike took off from the end of the pier. In mid arc, Connor launched himself further into the air, using the seat as a platform. He flew gracelessly through the air, thudded to a crashing halt against the hull of the yacht, now about thirty yards away. One arm was outstretched and grabbed at the mooring rope.

Connor was hanging on with his left hand. In his right hand he still clutched a gun. Scrabbling at the guard rail with his two smallest fingers, Connor had just managed to grab hold of the rail with his left hand when the woman arrived on the deck.

She aimed an automatic pistol directly at Connor's head. He dropped below the line of the deck, hanging by his fingers, still clinging to the boat. A second later, the woman leaned over the guard rail. The head-dress of her chador was lopsided, revealing a glimpse of the blonde hair beneath. Connor was confronted with the owl-like gaze of her dark glasses. He shifted, breathing hard. He couldn't both hold on and point his gun at her, so he merely held on.

"You've gotten a little greedy," the woman told him. "Always a mistake." She spoke with a faintly Texan drawl, her disguise summarily betrayed. "Now, from the heroics we've just witnessed, I'm guessing you're Connor, not his nerdly twin brother. You're gonna have to decide: do you want to climb aboard?" She paused. "So, do you want to shoot me, Captain Bennett? Can't have it both ways."

Connor exhaled, eyeing her closely.

"Let go," DiCanio said firmly, "Or I'll shoot."

"Don't shoot me, Melissa," Connor said suddenly, mimicking the tone of Jackson's which most annoyed him. "Please. I know what's written on the Adaptor. Not the *Lament for Eridu* – the real inscription. I've seen it, deciphered it."

A beat passed. Connor saw confusion cross her face, uncertainty. Her eyes went to his clothes, the plain white T-shirt and blue jeans of Jackson's into which Connor had changed as they rested outside the desert fort.

Hesitantly DiCanio said, "Are you telling me you're *Jackson* . . . ?"

Pushing out from the yacht with all the force in his legs, Connor launched himself backwards into the water. He shot at DiCanio, twice in rapid succession.

At the edge of the pier, Jackson staggered in disbelief. He'd heard shots ring out, seen both DiCanio and his brother fall. It was far from obvious which way the gunfire had gone.

As he watched, to Jackson's relief Connor began to move. He floated up to the surface, rolled onto his front and began to swim the thirty yards that separated him from the jetty. DiCanio's yacht continued to navigate out of the harbor.

There was no sign of the young man in Arab costume who'd accompanied DiCanio to the moorings. Whatever DiCanio's fate, someone else was steering that craft. Even now with the yacht around eighty yards away, Jackson could still just about see that she lay where she'd fallen, on the deck. Meanwhile Connor's slow crawl brought him closer, the sidearm still clutched in his right hand.

By the time Connor reached the jetty and began to haul himself out of the sea, the yacht was fading into the distance, silhouetted in the sunrise in which finally, the faint sliver of a new moon had appeared.

Just another yacht making sail into the wide expanse of Doha's bay.

Agent Fletcher

The same sweltering morning that had begun with the dusty taste of a desert mist, Jackson found himself transported back to the top secret NRO base near Eridu. He was under escort, guarded by Connor and two aides.

Connor had scarcely waited to watch DiCanio's boat disappear. Dispassionately, he'd donned a pair of Air-Force-issue sunglasses taken from the flight suit that Jackson was wearing and then cut away the name label on the suit.

His knife had sliced through the fabric, the blade just millimeters from Jackson's skin "Well, Jacko. Time to face the music."

"*You* shoot at a couple of civilians; that's nothing. But I try to take a hunk of ancient stone and you're threatening me with Gitmo." Jackson had said, angrily rubbing his injured shoulder. He'd checked the dressing; it was now soaked through with blood.

Connor had pushed Jackson's fingers aside, examining the wound. He'd run his finger over the neat rectangle that Hafez Kazmi had begun to carve into Jackson's skin. The inked drawing of the Stars and Stripes had mostly faded now, washed away by the sea and Jackson's own blood and sweat.

"These marks are going to last," he'd remarked. His eyes had met Jackson's. "Don't worry about it. Girls like scars."

"Maybe the kind of girls you go out with."

"Trust me. This Marie-Carmen chick? She's gonna flip. Now, don't be a jerk. I've seen guys make less fuss when they've lost a limb on the battlefield."

Even so, he'd taken a fresh dressing from his first aid kit and applied it to Jackson's shoulder. Then he'd taken up his position on the Harley again.

"If I ever see her again," Jackson had said, his voice suddenly hollow.

"Play ball, little brother, and we'll help you find Marie-Carmen. You've got my word on that."

Jackson hadn't been able to react. The constant alternation of threat and promise was becoming unbearable,

"We're going back to Iraq, to Eridu. This time you're not going to bullshit us; you're going to spill. For example, that weird shit your girlfriend wrote about in her email. You're going to explain that. Then I want to know everything DiCanio told you."

"What makes you think she said anything?"

Connor had merely laughed. "It wasn't finished between you and her was it? You know how come I know? Because she thought I was you, bro'. For just a second on that boat, I persuaded her that I was good ol' Jackson come home to the team. That's when I took the bitch out. So you tell me, what did DiCanio think you still had to offer?" He nodded, once. "Yeah. I told her you knew what was written on that Adaptor. She believed it, she stalled. It was a shot in the dark, but I was right, wasn't I? You do know."

***

Later that morning Jackson's USAF Blackhawk had returned. It had picked them up from the US airbase in Al Udeid, some thirty-five miles south of Doha and flown the brothers back to Basra.

Back in Eridu, Jackson was shown back into the tiny room where he'd first been interrogated. Connor was joined by a female colleague dressed in civilian clothes: a white linen blouse and sand-colored cargo pants. "Mr. Bennett, it's good to meet you. I'm Dr. Harper Fletcher. I work here with the Captain."

She was a slim, petite African-American woman with short, sculpted dark brown hair, delicate hands and eyes, aged somewhere in her thirties. Even though she'd made no mention of the Agency, from her civilian clothing Jackson guessed at once that she was from the CIA branch of the National Reconnaissance Office. As she took a seat opposite Jackson, he found himself wondering which one of the two was planning to be 'bad cop'. Probably Connor, he figured, with a measure of exhaustion. His brother seemed to enjoy an excuse to pound him.

"We understand that you have some more information for us," said Harper, her tone even, reasonable. "Would you agree?"

"What she means, Jackson, is that you can tell us now if you're planning on playing this straight, or you can save us all a lot of time and we can ship you to Guantanamo."

Jackson didn't know whether to laugh with scorn or hurl abuse at his brother. His threats – empty or otherwise – were becoming tediously repetitive. For a few hours in Qatar, Jackson had actually found himself beginning to admire those qualities in his brother that doubtless made him the effective fighter that he was. As boys, it had been difficult not to envy Connor the favor he'd inspired in their father – a man who'd seen Connor that way from the very beginning.

Yet how easily Connor, the bully, could emerge. Was it perhaps the presence of a milder, more considered and thoughtful expression of his own genes that goaded Connor into this machismo? Or did he simply lack the subtlety to behave any other way?

"Don't waste your breath with threats, Connor. Unless that's part of your strategy to impress Dr. Fletcher here. If it is, hey, don't mind me; whatever gets you through the night."

Connor and his colleague exchanged wry glances. "Asshole. I'm leaving you with Agent Fletcher. If I have to listen to more of your whining, I think I'll be sick."

He left the room without looking back.

Harper said gravely, "That was out of line, Jackson. The Captain's doing his best to keep you out of serious trouble."

Jackson rubbed his temples. "I guess we have some sibling issues." What made this almost worse was knowing that, in some measure, he'd have to be grateful to Connor for whatever crumbs he now received. Jackson sighed, resigned. "We haven't really communicated for the past few years. I didn't even know he'd become part of the NRO."

"Captain Bennett has been involved with this project from the very beginning. Like me, he was with the team that discovered the chamber when he was assisting the weapons inspectors."

"Right. Next you'll be telling me that this chamber was the real reason for the Iraq War."

"Not the reason – but it made taking charge of this find an absolute priority. We couldn't afford for it to fall into the wrong hands."

"The wrong hands being?"

"Your friend Professor DiCanio. For example."

"But the US is going to be out of Iraq by the end of next year, isn't that what the President promised?"

"Now you understand our urgency to solve, finally, the riddle of the Adaptor."

"So the NRO can control this 'ancient' technology. Sure, why not. You're the good guys, right?"

She smiled for a second then with a graceful movement, drew up a hand to conceal it. "Captain Bennett is of the opinion that you are afflicted with something that's common in intellectuals; the ability to see all sides of an argument."

There was a baffled silence. "Connor said those actual words?"

Very slightly, Harper shook her head. "Not exactly those."

"His approach is so superior," Jackson said, adding sardonically, "Hoo-ya!"

Harper continued to smile behind the folder that she now held before her face. She had the air of a highly-educated woman, used to interacting on the same level as someone like Jackson. He wondered whether she could be drawn into telling him more about the NRO's operation in Eridu.

"What's your story, Agent Fletcher? You seem to be hitting somewhat below your weight-class here with Connor."

"Is that your roundabout way of asking me about my educational background? I consider myself honored to be part of this project. I think you know that, Mr. Bennett; I think you have some idea of what this is all about."

"Look," Jackson told her, folding his hands together. "What I know is total conjecture. I have no evidence for what I *think* I know. Everything was told to me by Melissa DiCanio – someone whom I have every reason to believe could be lying."

"Why don't you tell me anyway," Harper conceded, "and let us be the judge? If in doubt, remember that actions speak louder than words. Whatever DiCanio told you, we've still got the evidence of the lengths she went to get hold of the Adaptor, and to escape."

There was a momentary silence. Then, her eyes twinkling with more of the same self-satisfaction, Harper removed a single sheet of paper from the folder.

"Captain Bennett suggested I reacquaint you with the contents of your last email to your friend Marie-Carmen. You may have failed to recall quite the extent of your revelations therein, Mr. Bennett. Might I politely request that you take an opportunity to make a full and frank disclosure at this time? It would go well in your record, would enable the NRO to extend to you a relationship which I'm convinced would be mutually beneficial."

"You want me to work for you?"

Harper demurred. "This is not a civilian organization, Mr. Bennett, and I'm not convinced that you are Agency material. However, there is scope for certain collaborative projects, with civilians of sufficiently high security clearance."

"I'd qualify for that kind of clearance?"

"Not to put too fine a point on it, Jackson, I think you'll find it the only way to return to your normal life. People with this kind of knowledge simply can't be allowed to roam free, talking to heaven-knows-who."

Harper placed the single sheet of paper in front of Jackson, waiting quietly as he read.

Jackson scanned the very brief email he'd sent to Marie-Carmen. There was almost nothing to it.

Hans Runig is Melissa DiCanio. Ninhursag – I guess it's her idea of a joke. I've stopped helping her. There will probably be consequences. If you haven't already heard from your niece, find out where she is. Please stay out of sight. I'll find you, we'll be together soon. That's a promise.

Had Marie-Carmen's email to him on the subject been equally inscrutable? He'd read and replied to that email the first time he'd been left alone in this very interview room, whilst unknown to him, his every action on the computer was being observed. Without the exact text of the email in front of him, Jackson found it impossible to remember what they'd stated explicitly, and what they'd omitted.

"Do you have the text of her email to me?" he ventured hopefully. Either they knew everything now, in which case this was just a test. Or else they still needed Jackson to crack open the final mystery of the Adaptor.

A slow, knowing grin spread across Harper's features. "The Captain mentioned that you might ask me that. I hope you see now that in this case most certainly, honesty is the best policy. Jackson, we're on the same side. Trust your own people; we're the only ones who can protect you now, and Marie-Carmen and her family."

Jackson felt his resolve crumble. Harper was right; he couldn't fight his brother any longer.

Over the next two hours, Jackson divulged almost everything that DiCanio had told him about the ancient chamber and her theory about the genetic link between members of her society and the civilization that built the chambers.

Agent Fletcher was mostly guarded in her response, but Jackson doubted that it all came as a surprise to the NRO. Jackson reminded himself that Connor may well have withheld a good deal of information about the underground chamber; in fact, he was sure to have done so.

"She made no indication as to the location of the chamber?"

"No. But I believe that Chaldexx – or DiCanio's society – has some kind of base in Chetumal."

"That's in Mexico; in the state of Quintana Roo."

"Right. There are a lot of Mayan remains there. One side of the Adaptor has Mayan inscriptions, doesn't it?"

Harper nodded. "I think we may have some idea where to look. Did she mention any of the other chambers?"

"There are more?"

She gazed levelly at Jackson. "In total, there are five."

"I see. Well," he considered, "I'm really not sure that DiCanio knows that."

"If her people have found one chamber, they know. The inscriptions inside the chamber near here make it quite clear that there are five."

"Where are the other chambers?"

Harper was silent.

"I get it. You're not going to tell."

"I'd consider it, Jackson. But we need more from you. For example, what is the nature of this code, which you and Marie-Carmen discussed in your correspondence?"

"Marie-Carmen thinks that some cuneiform symbols – in modified form – might signify amino acids."

"Then we can work out the code," Harper told him. She removed a second sheet of paper from her folder. "This is a transcript of the cuneiform inscription on the Adaptor. We also noticed the strange supplementary signs; we didn't know what they meant. I've seen nothing like it, especially not in the Archaic period signs, which is what is used on the Adaptor."

"What's the difference in the Archaic script?" asked Jackson.

"Well, one difference is the degree of pictography in the symbols. Compared with later versions of the script, the Archaic period symbols look more like drawings of something, less like abstract markings. The number of basic components from which all the language symbols are derived, is smaller. Nearly sixty per cent of the symbol repertoire is made up of modifications of other symbols. You see a lot of different kinds of modifications, including the kinds which are designed to help disambiguation of a symbol which can mean more than one thing. That's what we think the supplementary signs on the Adaptor script are about."

Jackson regarded Harper with appreciation. "This is your thing, isn't it? This is why you're on this case."

She replied frankly but with modesty, "I'm a graduate of the London School of Oriental and African Studies. I specialized in Akkadian literature, so I'm very familiar with the Sumerian scripts. Although Sumerian and Akkadian languages are different, the Akkadians appropriated the Sumerian cuneiform script.

"So, Agent Fletcher, have you worked out what the Adaptor says?"

The question seemed to surprise her. "Naturally; I've known for a while. It says: *Dubsag lugal anunnaki. Melim idim. Igilul na til dubsag melim.*"

Her sudden transition into the exotic-sounding, barely comprehensibly ancient tongue was astonishing, not what Jackson had expected. Harper smiled again, widely and showing perfect teeth. "You already know that too, isn't that correct? I'd translate it as *Before the masters who came from Heaven and Earth, a frightening splendor makes men weak. The long-lived, awakened one is possessed of such frightening splendor.*"

"If you already know what it means . . ."

"Oh, but it has another meaning too. This second meaning is what has eluded us for so very long."

"That's where you think I can help."

Calmly, Harper blinked. "Indeed."

"It's an amino acid sequence," Jackson said, his eyes fixed upon hers. "The formula for a molecule that might unlock the function of the chamber."

Who We Serve

Two hours later, Harper emerged from another room, clutching the transcript of the Adaptor inscription. Her face, for the first time since Jackson had met her, displayed something akin to wonder, her cheeks were flushed, her eyes shone with the light of revelation.

"The inscription makes sense," she said breathlessly. "As an amino acid sequence: I found a version of every one of the logograms found on the Adaptor."

Jackson pushed back his chair. He looked at the single-letter sequence which Harper had scribbled underneath the copied inscription. It was fifteen amino acids long; a peptide.

He recognized it immediately: the sequence he and Marie-Carmen had derived from PJ's DNA molecule; the amino acid sequence of hip33; hypnoticin.

Harper continued. "The rest of the inscriptions are instructions for where to apply the peptide molecule."

"Where to apply it?"

"On the Adaptor. This molecule must act like a sort of conductor, interacting with part of the control panel of the chamber."

"How soon can we get a sample of this made up?"

"There's a pharmaceutical plant in Basra, which has a peptide synthesizer. They're going to send it by courier. We should have it by the evening."

Hours later as dusk was setting in, a plastic test-tube of the freshly-made peptide tucked into Jackson's pocket, Jackson and Connor descended into the chamber. The elevator sank them into the abysmal darkness, a faint glow of light at the base of the shaft growing brighter by the second. In utter silence they walked into the chamber. This time, at leisure to look around properly, with no fear of imminent discovery and capture, Jackson stared, transfixed by his surroundings.

His first brief experience of that ancient gallery had left a profound impression upon him; since that day whenever he'd closed his eyes for anything more than a few moments he'd been unable to quell the images which at once flooded his consciousness, his memory unable to contain anything but the most fleeting semblance of what seemed by the day more like a vision, an insubstantial phantasm.

But as he stood once more within the octagonal space, the endless symmetry of the symbolism and architecture imposed itself. Under closer observation, Jackson could see now that not only were the lids of the sarcophagi – or caskets – engraved with long cuneiform inscriptions, but so was the base of the altar. In the top of the altar were seven very narrow slots, hardly three millimeters thick. The Adaptor sat in the same position as before.

"There's something I want to show you," Connor told him. He picked up the Adaptor with a gloved hand, held it lengthways in his palm, then appeared to squeeze gently, rubbing his thumb gently along the side of the artifact. He seemed to be concentrating, as though threading a needle. After a second or so there was a tiny sound, like a small pop of pressurized gas escaping. At one end of the Adaptor, a square leaf of material appeared to slide out, emerging from the apparently seamless structure of the article. It was about one inch square and about two millimeters thick.

"We think that this little pop-out fits into a tiny groove here, buried within the larger groove into which the Adaptor slots when it is in position."

"The question is," Jackson murmured, thinking aloud, "How can an amino acid sequence be used to activate the Adaptor?"

"Any ideas?" asked Connor.

Jackson thought a few moments longer. "Just one," he said. "And I can test it right now."

"Good," Connor said. "Because we need to activate this chamber."

"Why?"

"I told you we'd found traces of human remains in the chamber. Well, in three of the caskets, there are more than traces. Three of those caskets are occupied, Jackson. And whoever is inside has been there for thousands of years."

Jackson stared in amazement. Connor's implication was utterly clear. "But the chambers are over seventy thousand years old. It's not possible for someone to survive that long in suspended animation, surely!"

"Maybe so. But I think there might be survivors." Jackson's reaction to this seemed to trigger something in Connor. "That's what DiCanio wants, isn't it? That's why she wanted the Adaptor, that's why she's been after you. She wants to activate the chamber in Mexico. Maybe there are survivors of this ancient civilization there, too."

"The 'long-lived awakened man.'"

"Right – the 'masters who came from heaven and earth.' Fairly portentous, when you think about it. What do you think 'frightening splendor' means?"

"Something that I don't think will work on you and me."

Connor turned to him, stalling. Jackson just grinned. Finally, he had his brother hanging onto his every word. "The 'Eastern mind-control shit', remember? The same molecule, when you inject it, gives you the power to influence people."

"The 'frightening splendor makes men weak'."

"Right. It's too much for it to be a coincidence."

"So they're spelling out some kind of prophecy – in chemicals?"

Jackson shook his head. "I think it's more like they named those glyphs after their words for the amino acids in that molecule."

"The molecule came first?"

"It's like, the basis for their genetic superiority. If they really were the 'masters' then they were accustomed to being in power. Their words of power came from this molecule."

"But the power won't work on us . . ."

"If I'm a descendant, then so are you."

"Weird. We're going to try to wake up our super-great grandparents."

284

"Let's hope they're pleased to see us."

"Let's hope we're not too late."

This time it was Jackson who paused, holding back his brother. "Too late? For what?"

"Those ancients had to have a pretty important reason; all this trouble to keep their people alive for all that time."

"Such as what?"

"Global catastrophe, brother. Don't tell anyone, but it might just be that the ancient Mayans were right."

Jackson stared. "The . . . Mayans?"

"DiCanio's guy on the pier at Doha Corniche, the American towelhead? His image was captured by nearby CCTV. His name is Simon Martineau. He's wanted by the FBI, amongst others, usually travels under an alias – Simon Madison. Earlier this year, Madison interfered with an operation we had to recover an ancient Mayan document, a codex. It was once owned by the pilot who crashed the incredibly advanced aircraft that we captured."

"Hafez Kazmi mentioned a 'Madison'," mused Jackson. "He seemed to think he might be immune to the Adaptor bio-toxin, too."

"Makes sense that they'd know about the bio-toxin," Connor said. "They seem to know quite a bit about this ancient technology."

"The ancients that are still around, even now?"

"If not them, then some folk who know how to build their technology."

"What's in the codex?"

Connor shook his head and shrugged. "I'm not sure we'll ever know. Someone beat us to it."

"Madison? DiCanio?"

"Maybe, maybe not."

"What – there's someone else looking for the codex?"

Connor became hesitant. "We're aware of another group, based in Mexico. That's the limit of what I can tell you without putting you under non-disclosure."

"Does this codex have something to do with the ancient chambers?"

"We don't know how, but it's all connected. 2012, Jacko. That's what this is about. Those ancients knew something about the Mayan calendar end-date."

Jackson was silent, thinking of what DiCanio had told him about the origin-date of the gene they shared: roughly 3000BC. The Mayan calendar start date was in 3114BC. Had that been when the last survivors had been revived? Was the Mayan calendar end-date the marker for another landmark event?

Connor rubbed his hands, stuck them into his trouser pockets. The desert air cooled sharply as night fell. "Those ancients left survivors and technology to help us," he said. "You can't even touch their technology unless you have some sort of inherited, protective factor. Yeah – we've learned a lot about this whole 2012 situation from the inscriptions in the chamber, but not enough. Without that codex, without at least a chance to talk to these ancient survivors, we're helpless."

"DiCanio wants to revive the ancients in the chamber in Mexico. Maybe she's trying to help?"

"There you go, seeing all sides of the argument. You've met the woman. You really think she's in this to save the world?"

Jackson thought for a minute. DiCanio and her associates had come across as brilliant, fiercely intelligent and determined idealists. At the dinner in Switzerland, he'd felt a degree of sympathy with them, if truth were told. Idealists wanted to change the world. Hypnoticin might give DiCanio the means to achieve this. Jackson recalled, with discomfort, the exhilaration of those moments when he'd used hypnoticin. Was it possible that such power could ever be used in a benign fashion?

"I think she wants to save the world, yeah. But she may also want to change it."

Connor grasped Jackson's arm near the bicep. He pointed at the insignia on his own jacket. "Then you'd better remember: this is who we serve today, Jacko; the US of A. That's how we save the world."

The Original Parents

The chamber must have been buried at least thirty yards below the ground. There was no sign of a natural cave system: the rock walls were clean, showed signs of having been cut. Jackson found himself wondering how the location had been chosen. There were five chambers, according to Agent Fletcher. Were the others close by? What was their purpose?

Connor told him, "The other chambers are scattered across the planet. We figure it's a redundancy system."

"In case some chambers were destroyed?"

"There would be a lot of possible outcomes, over seventy thousand years. You'd need several types of redundancy: more than one chamber, enough survivors in case some didn't make it."

"Seventy thousand years, though. It's hard to imagine how you could resuscitate any kind of brain activity after that long."

"That's what our science guys figured," agreed Connor. "But if the chamber was used as a hibernation complex, there's no reason why the caskets have to be used for the entire period of time. Maybe they only last for a few thousand years at a time."

"That could work," Jackson said. "Someone would have to be revived every so often and then re-hibernated. You could appear to be practically immortal, skipping through the millennia, living just a few days in every thousand."

"You're saying they'd *have* to be revived every few thousand years?"

"I'm guessing some kind of suspended animation could last a few thousand years. However much you slow down the metabolism, there's always going to be a finite amount of aging. A system where you revived a few people every few thousand years might be safer."

"Like a kind of daisy chain."

"Five chambers. Each one with twenty-one caskets. That's quite a bit of redundancy in the system."

"Jackson – only three of the caskets in this chamber are occupied."

"Three?" He considered for a moment. "If all you need to pass on is genes and knowledge, two should be enough."

"Two?"

"The original parents. Adam and Eve. Or like in Noah's Ark. Male and female."

Connor gave a soft laugh. "The Ark?"

"Why not? We're in the right place for it. The Sumerian legend says that Eridu was destroyed by a giant storm."

Picking a spot that was well-lit by the arc lamp; Jackson knelt on the ground, took a folded sheet of vinyl from his pocket, spread it and smoothed out the wrinkles and creases. The rectangular plastic was about the size of a tea-tray. He began to empty the contents of his pockets onto the sheet; a mechanical pipette, some small plastic test-tubes with lids in a blue polyvinyl rack about three inches square and a screw cap polypropylene tube of a biochemical solution. He proceeded to set up a series of dilutions of the peptide solution that had been shipped in earlier that day.

Connor crouched down. "What are you doing?"

"There's a technique known as Surface Plasmon Resonance," replied Jackson, eyes on his work. "It uses the binding event between two proteins to generate a tiny electrical current. The amount of current is determined by the strength of the binding. You bind one protein to a hard matrix, usually on some kind of silicon chip. Then you flow a solution of the second protein over it. When you get binding, you get a change in the current. Now, in theory, you could use such a system to introduce an exquisitely sensitive lock-and-key mechanism. It would use very little energy and be extremely precise. So, to answer your question, what I'm doing is getting ready to test whether this peptide, whose amino acid sequence code is written on the surface of the Adaptor, is in fact the key which unlocks some activation mechanism.

"I'm starting with some really low dilutions. If the process is real sensitive, then too much of the peptide will overload it, it could sorta blow a circuit. The peptide might bind so tight that we'd never get it off, we'd never be able to try again."

Connor interrupted, "Whoa, whoa, you say you're gonna do something potentially irreversible?"

"Hey, find me the precise instructions for how much of the peptide to use, and we'll be fine!" Jackson said angrily. "What's that? You don't have them? OK. Let's do it my way. Trust me Connor; this is what I do."

Jackson dropped a small amount of the lowest dilution of the peptide solution onto the extended leaf. He then carefully inserted the Adaptor, fitting it into position. They waited for a second or two; nothing.

"OK, let's try ten times that much," Jackson said, and repeated the process using the next dilution of peptide. Again, nothing.

This happened repeatedly until Jackson had only one dilution left to try.

"We'd better hope this is the one."

When he inserted the Adaptor, again nothing happened. With a sigh, Jackson was just about to remove it, when Connor stopped him.

He pointed to the central altar. "Look."

Later, Jackson would attempt in vain to recall exactly the spectacle which he witnessed. Possessed of an ineffable quality, the next moments seemed scarcely transmittable by mere language. It began with a faint garnet-colored shimmering, which emanated from the inscriptions. The writing seemed literally to become projected in front of them. One of them – Jackson wasn't sure who – had the presence of mind to switch off the arc lamp, plunging the brothers momentarily into darkness. The holographic writing glowed, sharp and defined in the pitch black, suspended in mid-air.

From above the central altar rose a small sphere; dazzlingly bright; Jackson couldn't look directly at it and noticed that Connor too was shielding their eyes. It rose about one yard above the altar and then began to rotate. The speed increased with every rotation, until discrete pulses of energy broke free from its surface, like solar flares being pinched from the surface of the sun. Bright streams of pure energy were hurled free, every time closer to where Jackson and Connor stood.

They backed away, watching as the flares of light extended to the caskets. When they did, a hazy, particulate suspension began to emanate from the edges of the sarcophagi. After another minute or so, the doors began, slowly, to slide upwards, drawn back into hidden gaps in the ceiling.

The two brothers were still, reverently so. The air immediately around them crackled with static; there was a smell of scorching, bone-dry cotton, wafts of hot air. As the ceramic doors pulled away, three bodies were revealed in the sarcophagi. They were perched on stands, titled slightly backwards. All three were dressed in one-piece, pale-colored robes, the fitting snug against the contours of their bodies and covering them from neck to toe. Their arms hung loosely down by their sides, their hair was long, straggly and white. Two of the survivors were men; their thin, grey beards touching their chests. The third was a woman, barely more than five-feet tall, her skin dark, her frame delicate and slim. For several long moments, the three were as still as corpses. Then finally, the woman's right hand twitched. It rose, painfully slowly, to touch her cheek. When she did so, her eyes opened. She blinked.

In the glow of the inscriptions which still hovered in mid-air, Jackson thought he saw his brother's eyes glisten. A vertiginous feeling swept through him. He opened his mouth, tried to say something to Connor. But he couldn't. Knowing that they had witnessed the secret, hypothetical rite which might lie at the center of every civilization known to the planet, Jackson felt an infinite sense of yearning, an infinite sense of awe.

End of the Line?

To: Marie-Carmen Valencia
From: Jackson Bennett
Subject: End of the line?

Well, I'm back in the dustbowl called 'Iraq'. You have to see this place to believe the mess that twenty-five years of history have made of this part of the world. Just a short flight over in Bahrain and Qatar, they've got it all together. This was once the cradle of civilization. There's been a whole lot of 'decline and fall'. By the end of next year, all the troops are supposed to be moved out. Will things improve? It's anyone's guess.

I write and write, yet still; nothing from you. Where are you? I have to know.

When they brought me back here, I thought I was about to face some pretty serious accusations. But Connor and I made a deal: if I agree to be recruited as a special operative for the National Reconnaissance Office, he'll file paperwork to show that he recruited me from the beginning, as a double agent.

The rest, I'll tell you in person, when I find you. Which I'm going to do. If I have to search the world, I'll track you down: we have unfinished business.

J x

Connor watched Jackson finish the email. He handed him a cup of coffee.

"Take out the part about me filing paperwork to show you were a double agent." There was a momentary pause after which he added, "And the part about working for the NRO."

Jackson didn't argue: there was no point. His brother was better informed than he of the lengths that the government would go to spy on its own people. Instead, he directed his attention to the progress of the recently revived survivors.

Connor sighed. "Two of them are not doing so good. The third, the female, is awake and talking. Agent Fletcher has been going in to debrief."

"Amazing. Talking to a human being from a civilization so lost that we didn't even know it existed. That's got to be pretty bizarre."

"Fletcher's in her element. No-one knew how Akkadian or Sumerian would sound when spoken aloud; no-one's spoken them for thousands of years. Turns out Fletcher's accent is a little off, but she's learning fast."

"What do they speak? Akkadian? Sumerian?"

"Something even older. It seems to have been the progenitor language of both."

"Does this survivor have a name?"

"She's called 'Ninbanda'. Fletcher likes her, I think, although the old lady is kind of alarmed at what's happening to her pals."

"Why?"

"Seems that if they don't make it, we're in big trouble."

"We . . . ?"

"All of civilization. The 2012 thing."

Jackson was silent. His thoughts were now almost entirely preoccupied with finding Marie-Carmen. It seemed grossly unfair that a shadow of catastrophe should fall at this particular moment of his life.

"Let's hope they make it, the other two. What do they call themselves?"

"*Erin-si*. Fletcher says it means 'People of Memory'."

"What do they remember?"

Connor shrugged. "Let's hope they remember how to save the planet from whatever they think is headed our way in 2012."

Jackson finished rewriting his email to Marie-Carmen and leaned back so that Connor could inspect what he'd written. Then he encrypted the message and pressed 'Send'. He took a long sip of the hot, watery coffee. "So, are you going to follow up DiCanio's death?"

"We're actually thinking of sending you to the funeral to find out who shows up," Connor replied, sneaking a grin.

"Not a great idea. I suspect our next meeting wouldn't go very well."

"It might never happen. Chaldexx still hasn't reported that she's missing."

"Would you? Their investors are going to get pretty mad."

"Let's see," Connor said. "Maybe give one of your contacts at Chaldexx a call, when you get to London."

Jackson thought back to the moment he'd seen DiCanio fall. Was it possible that she'd survived? No-one had rushed on deck to help her; the boat hadn't turned around to allow anyone to exact their revenge. It had appeared as though the boat, losing its captain, had simply sailed out to sea, where it might remain for days or even weeks before DiCanio's body would be found.

Yet that other guy, Simon Madison, had simply disappeared from the pier. Had he found his way onto the boat, after all?

With some reluctance, Connor told him, "Your plane's waiting on the tarmac." He gazed at Jackson for a few seconds, seeming to search for the right words. "When you find your girl, bring her in. We can protect you both."

"*When* I find her? She could be anywhere."

"The second I hear anything, bro', you'll know."

Jackson gave a weary nod. Three days growth of beard and the slightly different nap of his hair already emphasized the differences between them. The wounds in his torso were bandaged now, his chest felt lopsided. Compared to Connor who was tanned, fit and smooth-shaven, dressed in his uniform slacks, blue shirt and tie, Jackson looked spent and exhausted. The brothers embraced for several seconds. Then without another word, Jackson strode away from Connor and towards the military transport plane.

Arriving at the RAF airbase in Fairford, England, Jackson took a taxi to London Heathrow where he checked in on a British Airways flight to San Francisco. As soon as he'd passed through security, he went straight to the electronics store and bought a new cell phone. By the time his flight was ready to leave, Jackson had configured the device to receive email from his account as well as news articles from a collection of RSS feeds. He strolled through the corridor to the waiting airplane, and periodically checked for a message from Marie-Carmen. From that moment until the moment when the in-flight announcer asked passengers to turn off their phones, Jackson hardly took his eyes off his cell phone, waiting for the tell-tale, blinking red light that might bring news of Marie-Carmen.

Twelve hours later as Jackson was climbing into a taxi at San Francisco International Airport, an article hit his cell phone's RSS news feed.

Scientist reported missing in Middle East yacht mystery

DOHA, QATAR: A Cambridge University neuroscientist, Professor Melissa DiCanio was declared missing late yesterday by Qatar officials after fishermen discovered her empty yacht and raised the alarm.

The motorized boat had been abandoned and had floated into the Persian Gulf. The cause is uncertain. While divers are currently out searching for bodies, the international scientific community is wondering what she was doing in the Middle East.

Professor DiCanio was born in San Antonio, Texas. She began her career at Baylor College of Medicine, Houston. She has been a Visiting Professor at the University of Oxford.

In 2006 she was awarded the Cambridge University Chaldexx Chair of Neuroscience. Since then DiCanio divides her time between her research group and her post as Chief Scientific Officer.

Colleagues have expressed anxiety. Chaldexx CEO Michael Carter commented: "Melissa is part of a family here at Chaldexx. We're obviously concerned for her safety. But our work will continue, in dedication to her vision and insight. We hope she will return to us soon."

Chaldexx BioPharmaceuticals is a privately-held company based in Interlaken, Switzerland. The investors must now hold their nerve during an uncertain time as the company faces speculation about the possible impact of DiCanio's loss.

It was beginning to look as though Connor was right: one way or another, DiCanio had decided that the time had come to exit from public life. Jackson's pulse sped as he checked his new messages. Apart from another flurry of emails from the lab, there was one new message. It wasn't from Marie-Carmen.

The subject of the message was 'Message from Ninhursag'. The sender, once again, had routed the email through an anonymous mail server.

Jackson,

I regret that you have turned your back on your true family. We would have treated you well.

Our organization exists. It is a commemoration of the event by which the ancestors achieved the resurrection of their ancient civilization. The future is our dominion, Jackson. No-one else has foreseen with such vision. All others strive for continuation. Only we accept and embrace the fundamental truth: civilization as it is organized on this planet is a moribund concept. It doesn't even require a cosmic event to deliver the death blow.

Yet such an event is coming in 2012 – the hurricane that will cleanse – something about which those in power are perfectly well aware. Don't expect them to save the planet – all they care about is the continuity of their own hegemony. We alone have accepted that this is a chance for a renewal of humanity.

The end is coming. Our time is now.

If you ever change your mind, we will welcome you. Remember Jackson, your powers, your potential make you valuable, irreplaceable. Your duty to your planet, to the human species should be clear. You know how to reach me.

Your sister in the Sect of Huracán.

The timestamp on the email showed that it had been sent at 23:42 on December 7th – the night before the shooting at the harbor in Doha. The somewhat cryptic nature of the message was puzzling. Surely the time for clarity had arrived, yet DiCanio chose this time to descend into obfuscation. Was she really the author of the message? Or had she simply been replaced with another member of this 'Sect of Huracán'?

There was only one thing he could think to try now: the 'Hans Runig' website. Grimly, he typed the fifteen-letter sequence of hypnoticin into his cell phone's web browser.

This time no text box opened; the site appeared to be dead.

Those Who Waited

All the way home from San Francisco Airport Jackson rode the taxi, distracted; the damp fog that swirled was as tangible in his head as in the streets of his home city.

There was no comfort in going home, only the return of his solitude and the promise of the daily grind of work. Maybe it was the pale grey light after the dazzling sun of Iraq, maybe it was the fact that he'd come home empty-handed. He couldn't even muster the usual excitement for his research.

PJ Beltran was dead. There would be no collaboration with Chaldexx BioPharmaceuticals, whose staff now behaved almost as though he had never existed.

As agreed with Connor, he'd called Andrew Browning at Chaldexx whilst in London, waiting for his flight to the USA. Browning had been 'unavailable'. All email Jackson sent to Browning was automatically, if politely deflected. Although he had the impression that DiCanio's apparent disappearance had induced a shockwave within Chaldexx, Jackson couldn't help but find it odd that no questions were being asked of him. Andrew Browning, at least, was aware of Jackson's meeting with DiCanio, just two days before she disappeared. Wasn't Browning even a little curious about the events following their flight from Switzerland?

There was something unnatural about the whole affair.

Or maybe what troubled Jackson was the continued silence from Marie-Carmen. Her final email had been sent during her exit from the Acapulco Princess. Where had she been since then? Hovering around the confines of his subconscious was the grim possibility that she'd been captured by DiCanio's organization.

Jackson kept reminding himself that without his old cell phone, he and Marie-Carmen couldn't call each other. Even if he'd dared to try, even if he believed that the danger from DiCanio had abated, Jackson had no record of her phone number, or address; only her email, which he had memorized. All other contact details had been stored in his old Blackberry, which he had to assume, since he'd dropped it into DiCanio's chauffeur-driven car, was now in the possession of DiCanio's people. Marie-Carmen couldn't go home, couldn't switch on her phone. It simply wasn't safe.

Logically, rationally, the ominous silence from Marie-Carmen could be explained. The trouble was that for days now, Jackson had been incapable of much rational thought when it came to Marie-Carmen.

Apart from the single question he'd asked Jackson during the night they spent outside the fort in Qatar, Connor hadn't wanted to discuss Marie-Carmen.

"If they got to her, they got to her. Or maybe she went home? Go home, get some rest, then try to get in touch with her. Who knows, bro'? Maybe she went cold on you."

The prospect of returning to work wasn't enough of a distraction, in fact he found himself actively avoiding the idea. Professionally, Jackson knew he'd made a Faustian bargain with regards to his research. The NRO would guarantee his funding, but the work would never be published. He would help the NRO in their continuing investigation into the secrets of the Sect of Huracán, as Jackson supposed he should now refer to DiCanio's organization.

Jackson would have to start from the remaining sample of PJ's DNA sequence, which he'd posted from Mexico City to his friends, Adam and Rosalie. This would allow him to study PJ's version of the hypnoticin gene in its original context. PJ had discovered a natural source of hypnoticin – but where? Chaldexx had, according to DiCanio, searched for and failed to find such a gene. DiCanio had wanted that gene badly. She'd gone to murderous lengths to try to steal it from PJ and Jackson.

Jackson's findings about hypnoticin would remain a state secret. Fame and fortune might elude him, but what did it matter? He had unknowingly stumbled across one of the world's most astonishing secrets.

If somehow, an ancient civilization had found a way to introduce one gene into the human genome, who was to say it stopped there? Their descendants, others like Jackson and Connor, might have untapped abilities of which they were not aware.

The Sect of Huracán would have come to the same conclusion. They would doubtless continue with their own plans – whatever they were. Connor seemed certain that some crisis would threaten the planet at the end of 2012. But his – and the NRO's – idea of saving the world was probably quite different from that of the Sect.

From what Jackson had seen of them, the Sect of Huracán was not to be trusted.

The taxi drew up in front of the three-story wood-fronted house in which his apartment was located. Jackson stared out of the taxi window. The fog had almost dissipated; he could see his apartment through a thin veil of mist.

He walked to the door, heard the taxi drive away behind him. A cyclist flew past; there was the sound of a car door opening, a group of students towards the end of the road, mere outlines in the mist. They were laughing. As he faced the porch, Jackson groaned, remembering his lost keys, which he hadn't seen since his slide down the forested hillside in Tepoztlan. Exhausted, despondent and aching, he leaned his head against the door.

Behind him, he heard keys jingle, and a voice; her voice.

"Looking for these?"

Jackson turned around. Marie-Carmen was standing just feet away. Her hair was loose and fell in waves over the collar of her thigh-length brown leather jacket. She smiled at him, quizzically. He glimpsed the beginning of a warm smile. Against her chest, Marie-Carmen clutched was a brown paper bag of groceries. Dangling from the fingers of her right hand, a small bunch of keys rattled.

"You dropped them in the car that first night."

Jackson could barely move; he couldn't take his eyes off her.

Marie-Carmen took a step towards him. "When you left Switzerland, I knew they'd got you; Hans Runig, Ninhursag: we should have thought about Sumerian mythology, right from the beginning. It was DiCanio, all along. I figured the safest place for me was the one place you couldn't be; your place. I still had the addresses of those people you asked me to mail your DNA to; I met Adam and Rosalie. They told me where you live."

The one important address he had never entered into his old cell phone, Jackson realized, was his own.

Finally, he found his voice. "How could you stop contacting me, just like that? Didn't you know what that would be like for me?"

Marie-Carmen put down the groceries. When she spoke, her tone was careful, her voice gentle. "Jackson, I couldn't risk that you'd joined them. I had to know, before we met again, which side you were on."

Jackson said, "You know, don't you? That I'm one of them, I've got the gene."

Marie-Carmen nodded. "It was the only reason for them to be so determined to get hold of you. It was always you they wanted, not just the DNA."

"I could never join them, Marie-Carmen. They killed PJ, they killed Simon Reyes."

"They threatened PJ's family, too. They're in hiding now"

Jackson hesitated for a second. "I can help them to stay hidden. My brother made me an offer . . ."

"Better than what DiCanio offered you?"

"It was less millennial secret society of illuminati, more run-of-the-mill clandestine government agency." He shrugged. "I don't have a lot of choice, to be honest."

"I see; so this isn't all due to eleventh-hour patriotism?"

"Marie-Carmen," he said softly, "*they killed PJ*."

"I know. I don't think DiCanio and her people will easily give you up."

"They have some serious competition; you, my brother Connor."

As they talked, they drew closer, Marie-Carmen reached up, tentatively fingering the lapel of his jacket. With a teasing murmur, she said, "Look at your haircut . . ."

"You should have seen me in his uniform," was Jackson's laconic reply.

Marie-Carmen moved her hands up to his shoulders. "But Connor, he's this all-American, action-man, fighter pilot guy – isn't that right?"

"Yes, that's right. You'd hate him."

She squeezed him, gently. "I've missed you."

He leaned in, his lips close enough just to brush against hers, and whispered, "I hope you kept my place all nice."

"Aren't you going to take me inside?"

He let himself be drawn against her, wincing slightly as she pressed against the wounds on his chest. The cold, wet air felt like home then, and the pale lights of the building seemed finally to welcome him.

But when Jackson closed his eyes he saw the unending sands of the desert; forgotten mounds in the wilderness, thousands of years of buried memories waiting, and no-one there to witness them. Somehow, through all the terrors of history, those memories had survived.

Until he felt the warmth of Marie-Carmen's breath against his cheek, his thoughts were of those who waited.

Acknowledgements

The Descendant was my first novel, written almost a year before the first *Joshua Files* book launched my career as a published author. Heartfelt thanks to my dear friend Dr. Magda Plebanski, who read and loved an early version of this story. Also to my agent Peter Cox for encouraging me to bring my 'techno-thriller manuscript' out of the drawer, also to former *Joshua Files* editor Polly Nolan, who helped me to craft a quality manuscript from that first draft. It was wonderful once again to work with talented young designer, Gareth Stranks who created the jacket art. Huge and special thanks to Richard Howse for his excellent creative and technical genius in bringing *The Descendant* Alternate Reality Game to life on the Internets! Most of all, thanks to my husband David for his patience and support as well financial, marketing, and technical advice and assistance.

Finally, thanks to all the readers of *The Joshua Files* who supported me through that series. I hope that you'll enjoy this extra tale from my little fictional world.

Sumerian translations were provided by the Electronic Text Corpus of Sumerian Literature

Black, J.A., Cunningham, G., Ebeling, J., Flückiger-Hawker, E., Robson, E., Taylor, J., and Zólyomi, G., The Electronic Text Corpus of Sumerian Literature (http://etcsl.orinst.ox.ac.uk/), Oxford 1998–2006.

Copyright © J.A. Black, G. Cunningham, E. Robson, and G. Zólyomi 1998, 1999, 2000; J.A. Black, G. Cunningham, E. Flückiger-Hawker, E. Robson, J. Taylor, and G. Zólyomi 2001; J.A. Black, G. Cunningham, J. Ebeling, E. Robson, J. Taylor, and G. Zólyomi 2002, 2003, 2004, 2005; G. Cunningham, J. Ebeling, E. Robson, and G. Zólyomi 2006.

M.G. HARRIS

M.G. (Maria Guadalupe) Harris was born in Mexico City but moved to England as a young child. Before becoming a writer, M.G. worked as a scientist and ran an Internet business.

On regular visits back to Mexico, M.G. became fascinated by Mayan archaeology and made several trips to Mayan ruins in Yucatan and Chiapas. One such trip planted the seed of the idea for *The Descendant* and *The Joshua Files*. While recovering from a skiing accident that resulted in a broken leg, M.G. began writing *Invisible City*, the first book in the Joshua Files series, on a laptop next to the bed.

M.G. is also the author of GERRY ANDERSON'S GEMINI FORCE ONE. She writes for young adults as M.G. Reyes.

When not wandering around the exotic settings for her novels, like Mexico, Brazil and the Swiss mountains, M.G. and family live on a quiet street in Oxford

INVISIBLE CITY

M.G.HARRIS

First book in the five-part series, THE JOSHUA FILES

When his archaeologist father goes missing after an air crash in Mexico, UFO-obsessed Josh Garcia suspects alien abduction. He starts a blog to voice his fears and finds like-minded friends. But after he discovers his dad was murdered, Josh is caught up in a race to find the legendary Ix Codex - a lost book of the ancient Maya containing a prophecy about the end of the world.

"As thrilling as a rollercoaster ride, this fantastical world of spies, spirits, ancient prophecies and hidden cities tests Josh to his limits and he comes to understand the conflicting demands of friendship, family, loyalty and duty." *The BookTrust*

The Joshua Files vs The Descendant

A (brief) interview with M.G Harris

Which came first?
I wrote *The Descendant* before starting *The Joshua Files* but decided to keep in a drawer and crack on with writing for young adults, since my own daughter was the ideal age for *The Joshua Files*.

How are the timelines of the two stories connected?
The Descendant takes place in December 2010 and ends about a week before the action described in *Ice Shock*, the second book of *The Joshua Files*.

Did any other members of Team Joshua work on The Descendant?
Yes, *The Descendant* was edited by Polly Nolan, who also edited *Zero Moment* and *Dark Parallel*, books three and four of *The Joshua Files*.

Are any parts of the story of The Descendant picked up in The Joshua Files?

The fifth and final instalment of *The Joshua Files*, *Apocalypse Moon* brings in Captain Connor Bennett and another character from The Descendant. Professor Melissa DiCanio makes crucial appearances in *Ice Shock* and *Zero Moment*. The whole mystery of the '2012 prophecy' is finally unraveled in *Apocalypse Moon*.

The Descendant - An Alternate Reality Game

The mystery continues online.

Fourteen-year old Josh Garcia (of *The Joshua Files*) is troubled enough by his own adventures. But when his godfather PJ Beltran is murdered in Mexico City, Josh helps PJ's 13-year old daughter to solve the mystery of his murder.

If you've enjoyed *The Joshua Files* or *The Descendant* then the Alternate Reality Game (ARG) will give you a whole new insight on the story, the chance to eavesdrop on the characters online.

Your first clue?

Google *where is Gabi Beltran*

For more information, videos and clues, see

fb.com/thedescendant